Center Fire

Chris Mason

Published by Quaternary Publishing Ltd., 2012.

Center Fire

Chris Mason

Published by Quaternary Publishing Ltd.
quaternarypub@gmail.com

Chapter 1

Derazhnya, Ukraine
Sunday, February 5, 1:53 a.m.

A bitter wind slashed down from the mountains looming over the missile site. Philippe Sottile shivered and turned his back to the snow that stung like sand. Once again he pulled up the collar of his fur coat, but it wasn't enough; he was freezing. He felt an overwhelming yearning for his villa on the Côte d'Azur—drenched in warm sunshine, looking out over the calm blue waters of the Gulf de St. Tropez with a willing girl leaning on his arm—but he fought it down.

Glare from the security lights flooded the compound, banishing the night even though half of the lamps were burnt out, perhaps never to be replaced. The Ukrainians were even poorer now than when they had been part of the Soviet Union. There were only four miserable structures in the complex, all built of rusted, corrugated steel: a small control shack, a barracks, a garage and tool shed, and an outhouse-sized hut for the electrical generator.

Eight squat concrete pillboxes were spaced evenly in a ring around the buildings, surrounded by an electrified fence topped with razor wire. The launch tubes rose only a meter or so above the snow-covered ground; the missiles stood vertically well below the surface. Each launcher carried six MIRVs, each of which was powerful enough to destroy a small city, and that thought was enough to warm Philippe's heart so that he momentarily forgot the bitter cold.

The doors of one of the launch tubes were drawn back, exposing a shaft leading down into the earth. Philippe tried to lean over to see what was happening, but he could see only the smooth wall of the tube. He sighed and pulled himself up to kneel on the gently sloping concrete rim. It was rough and intensely cold under his knees.

Five meters below him, Jensen and the Ukrainian sergeant were standing on a retractable steel grid, suspended above a void, their heads

1

close together as they worked to remove a third warhead from the launcher. Two others had already been loaded into their crates and replaced with dummies. Below the men, the tube extended down perhaps fifty meters, most of its volume filled by the rocket. The launcher's nose cone had been removed, exposing four real MIRVs and the two identical dummies, standing vertically like lethal pencil-tips.

"Jensen," Philippe called.

Jensen looked up. Sweat shone on his black face and ran down into his beard. *How could they possibly be hot down there when it's thirty below up here?*

"What?" Jensen yelled back. He wiped his face with the back of his hand.

"How is it going?"

Jensen gestured rudely without speaking and went back to his work. Perhaps it was not heat that made Jensen sweat; perhaps it was the fact that he was dismantling a nuclear weapon. Interesting: Philippe had never seen Jensen nervous before.

A few minutes later the sergeant bellowed something incomprehensible. A private ran up and leaned over the edge of the tube. The sergeant yelled again, and the soldier ran off to the small crane, drove it forward and lowered a cradle down toward the missile. Within the cradle—a web of steel tubes and nylon straps—was an exact replica of one of the warheads, an orange-tipped gray cone about two meters in length. It looked just like the originals, but it was almost entirely hollow. Instead of propellant, control circuits, and a nuclear bomb, it contained only a few circuit boards cannibalized from a video game, whose sole function was to report that the warhead was operational.

Philippe leaned over the opening again and watched as Jensen and the sergeant, both large men, struggled to lift the real warhead into the cradle. They grunted and cursed, one in English and the other in Ukrainian. The sergeant shouted again, and the winch slowly lifted the bomb up out of the launch tube. It rose past Philippe, trailing behind as the crane turned, then it swung like a pendulum when the crane stopped, buffeted by the wind. When the warhead had settled, the winch lowered it down until it rested inside a wooden crate sitting among others just like it on a flatbed lorry.

Another Ukrainian private and Philippe's friend Jacques Lanotte climbed up onto the flatbed and released the cradle. Beside Lanotte's giant frame, the emaciated soldier looked like a child.

Jensen and the sergeant were almost done connecting the third dummy warhead. Philippe hopped down off the concrete rim and went to help Lanotte and the soldier move the other boxes into place, hiding the warheads. Three crates, carefully situated in an inconvenient location but not in the exact center of the stack, held his MIRVs. The rest contained tractor parts made in Ukraine to be exported to Poland.

As Lanotte began tying down a canvas tarp, Jensen and the sergeant climbed up the access ladder and out of the launch tube. Philippe walked back to talk to Jensen, rubbing his mittened hands, which were starting to go numb. He pulled at the collar of his coat again; the damned thing wouldn't stay up.

Jensen was just pulling on his parka. He flipped up the hood and zipped the coat.

"All is well?" Philippe said.

"No problem." David Jensen was a big man in his mid-thirties, ten centimeters taller than Philippe, with a husky, muscular build. He was black and American, both of which Philippe was willing to forgive since Jensen was so useful to him. Over the years he had actually grown fond of the man, until his dark skin and short-cropped wiry hair and beard no longer looked strange.

"Lanotte will be done shortly," Philippe said, putting his hand on Jensen's elbow. He nodded toward the stolen Mercedes parked on the other side of the lorry. "Meet me inside in a few moments, and tell *her* to come in a few minutes after that."

Jensen nodded and strode off toward the car. Philippe, watching him open the door and lean inside, thought of the woman waiting there. *So far everything is going according to plan. Soon we will both have our reward. I'll be rich again, and you—*

He clapped his hands to warm them and started toward the control shack. *Well, if I'm lucky, Carla, you'll be dead.*

* * *

Someone turned out the lights when Philippe was halfway across the yard. Now the job was done they were no longer needed, but the imbeciles could have waited until he got inside. He stopped for a moment in the nearly utter blackness, waiting for his eyes to adjust. The Big Dipper was almost straight overhead. The moon had set hours ago, and the single naked bulb shining above the building's entrance seemed hardly brighter than the stars that winked at him from the black sky. Philippe started forward again through the blowing snow.

Just inside the building was a small foyer for hanging coats and boots. Philippe opened the inner door to the main room and stepped inside.

The ancient squalor must have preceded the fall of the U.S.S.R. In one corner a small coal stove threw out no discernible heat, only a thin wisp of smoke. The other corners were full of trash. Near the doorway was a battered gunmetal office desk covered in papers, overflowing ashtrays, and thick books of regulations and procedures. A pair of fiberglass and metal chairs sat before the desk, bent and cracked as though someone had been beating them against the walls. Farther back in the room, an electronics console was littered with food wrappers and more full ashtrays. The floor was so dirty that it might actually have been packed earth. Bare light bulbs shone dimly from cords hanging from the low, scuffed ceiling.

At the very next inspection all of these men would be shot. But, of course, there would be no more inspections. This installation was scheduled to be decommissioned within the month.

He was alone for only a moment. Captain Gosanko, the officer in charge of the missile emplacement, emerged from a door in the back of the hut, nodded brusquely at Philippe, and turned his back to rub his hands together at the stove.

Philippe removed his hat and coat, setting them on one of the abused chairs. The room was chilly, and he immediately considered putting the coat back on, but decided to ignore the cold. After testing whether the other chair would hold his weight, he sat down.

Philippe Sottile was forty-seven, but looked a decade younger. His leanness, partially obscured by loose-fitting black pants and a military-style ribbed sweater, was visible in his face, with its hawkish nose, strong chin, and brown, wide-set eyes. With thin fingers he combed his light brown, thinning hair back off his forehead, took a Gauloises from a gold case, and lit it with a matching gold lighter. He smoked patiently, watching the Ukrainian captain and flicking ashes onto the dirty floor.

He could hear the other three soldiers open the outer door and begin taking off their overcoats in the anteroom. The two privates entered and stood at attention against the wall across from him. Their uniforms were standard U.S.S.R. khakis, worn and threadbare, with the Soviet insignia ripped off. The sergeant, no better dressed, went straight to the electronics console at the back of the room and sat down in a squeaky swivel chair. With an oath and a swipe of his hand he brushed the panel clean of rubbish, then unbuttoned his shirt pocket and removed a key, which he inserted into the panel and twisted.

Captain Gosanko turned to watch the sergeant. The captain was dressed in a new Ukrainian army uniform that strained to cover his gross belly. He was middle-aged, with an ugly, puffy face that bore a huge red nose like a bull's-eye. The two privates seemed to be starving to death. Gosanko was evidently not one of those officers who looked to the welfare of his men before his own.

The sergeant worked intently at the console. Philippe had no idea what the man was doing; he left the technical details to Jensen. After a few minutes the door opened again and his own men came in, still wearing their parkas. Jensen handed Philippe an aluminum briefcase, then he and Lanotte took up positions flanking the doorway. They unzipped their coats and stood alertly with their arms at their sides.

As the sergeant continued his inscrutable twiddling, the privates watched the two big men nervously, moving nothing but their eyes. *Yes, boys, as you'll see in a moment, they're quite dangerous.*

Jensen was large, but Lanotte was a giant, towering over his black partner. A massive build, barrel chest, and huge hands and feet made him look like a professional wrestler. His face was thick, with pronounced brows, a fleshy nose, and deep brown eyes partially obscured by the blond hair that fell to his shoulders.

Philippe had finished his second cigarette before the sergeant shut down his console and sat back. He swiveled to face the captain and barked out several short sentences in Ukrainian, a language that Philippe did not understand. Philippe inclined his head at the captain.

"Comrade Sottile," Gosanko said in Russian, "the system is operating perfectly. The dummy warheads respond correctly to our tests. The system was down longer than expected, but still within acceptable limits. The sergeant is certain that no one noticed the swap."

Philippe looked at Lanotte, who nodded agreement with the translation. Philippe and Lanotte had been friends since childhood, and while Philippe loved him as a brother, the basis for their long relationship was pragmatism. Lanotte was not only a strong man, he was also a polyglot, speaking more than twenty languages like a native. He had learned Ukrainian just for this job. Now confident that everything was in order, Philippe stood up and placed the aluminum case on the desk. He opened the catches and flipped up the lid.

It pleased Philippe to see shock and greed instantly overwhelm the soldiers' faces. In the briefcase before them was more wealth than any of them could earn in a lifetime—in American dollars. As the privates leaned in to ogle the money and the captain took a hesitant step forward, Philippe stepped back against the side wall and nodded to his men. Jensen and Lanotte shrugged their shoulders and reached inside their coats—and were suddenly holding Uzis in their hands.

Gosanko froze and the privates leaned back with unabashed fear on their faces; their sidearms were snapped uselessly in their holsters. But the sergeant rose slowly from his seat, with his hands in plain view, eyes darting around the room, judging angles and strategies. Philippe held out a hand.

"Comrades," he said in Russian, "before we conclude our transaction, there is one more detail to discuss." He saw the captain wince at his French accent and smiled. *Every barbarian thinks the world is full of barbarians.*

He took another cigarette out of his case and lit it. Philippe saw that the sergeant was still trying to figure out how to survive the coming blood bath. Lanotte had his Uzi trained directly on the sergeant's chest.

"Now," he continued, "I admit that I did consider killing you all at this point." The private on the left went pale under his dark, unruly hair, but the sergeant seemed to relax a trifle. "That would have been the safest, the simplest and, of course, the cheapest, thing to do." Philippe drew deeply on his cigarette. His hands were still cold. "Nevertheless, I hate doing business in that manner. It's really not my style at all. In any case, we have a better chance of leaving the country if you are alive and dutifully reporting that all is well. No, you may think me naïve, but I would rather pay you than kill you. After all, we may work together again someday, *n'est-ca pas?*"

Carefully staying out of the line of fire, Philippe closed the briefcase and shoved it across the desk toward the captain.

"That does leave me with a problem, however," he said. "How can I trust you? I mean, comrades, no offense intended, that you have already proved yourselves to be traitors and whores. Perhaps once the money is squandered or squirreled away your conscience will start bothering you. Or perhaps Captain Gosanko will be greedy. He doesn't look like the sort of man who would split this fortune evenly, does he?" Philippe clucked in disapproval. "Perhaps he will cheat you, and you will become justly upset and decide to take steps. This is a serious problem for me, wouldn't you agree?"

No one agreed. No one even moved. Philippe dropped the cigarette onto the floor and stubbed it out with his toe.

"I have a solution. Two solutions, actually." Philippe picked up his coat and started putting it on. "First, there is a bonus in that briefcase. Ten percent more than we agreed." The captain looked startled. The sergeant's eyes narrowed as he tried to guess what game Philippe was playing. The privates were still in shock. "That is part one of my solution."

Suddenly the door flew open and a hooded figure swept in. The door was shut again so rapidly that no one had a chance to move. Larotte, standing behind the door, had lost cover for less than a second.

"This," Philippe said, "is part two."

The newcomer was dressed in a long, black cloak with a deep hood that shrouded his face. Flakes of snow hung suspended on the thick material, giving off diamond glints as small hands emerged from the sleeves of the cloak and threw back the hood.

All four soldiers gasped as the face of a young woman was revealed. It was a pretty but not a beautiful face: her nose was a trifle too large, her mouth just a bit too wide. Her hair was black and curly, cut short. Green eyes twinkled in the weak light thrown by the bare bulbs. She took a step forward and the Ukrainians, to a man, stepped back.

Philippe laughed.

"I am so happy to see that you remember Carla," he said. "She is the one who got you into this mess, isn't she?" He picked up his mittens and his hat.

"I trust, comrades, that what is left of your honor, and this money, will ensure your silence. But if not..." Philippe's voice grew as hard as steel. "If you ever breathe a word of what happened here tonight, to anyone, even to your drinking companions, even to your wives, Carla will know. She will hunt you down, and for every moment of the days that it will take you to die, you will wish you had never been born." He looked at each of the soldiers in turn. Even the sergeant's face had gone pale. Satisfied, Philippe clapped his hat back on his head.

"So, comrades, it was a pleasure doing business with you. Good night." He stepped around Carla and went outside.

Jensen and Lanotte followed him, one at a time, alert for trouble. Philippe looked back and saw Carla standing casually, staring at the little men frozen in their squalid little hut. She suddenly turned and swept out, a grin still on her lips. She didn't bother to close the door.

* * *

"They remembered you," Philippe said to Carla as they walked to the Mercedes together. She smiled ferally. "I admit, you are rather... unforgettable."

Carla stopped to face him as they reached the car. She reached into the pocket of her cloak and Philippe tensed. Her hand came out holding the car keys, and he relaxed, feeling foolish.

"You drive," she said, and got into the car.

Philippe looked up at the mountains surrounding them, majestic but still only foothills of the Carpathians. There were no trees visible, just the snow-drifted concrete leading up to the fences and snow-covered scrub beyond. He opened the door and got into the car, hoping he would never see this desolate place again.

Despite the cold, the Mercedes started up with a purr. Lanotte and Jensen climbed into the lorry and the flatbed drove off slowly toward the entrance gate. Philippe followed it out of the compound, glancing into his rear mirror in time to see one of the scrawny privates running after them to close the gate.

After half an hour on narrow, rutted roads, they reached the village of Derazhnya. The squat stone houses were dark. It took only moments to pass through the town, to the one-lane road leading north. They drove through a broad valley between high ridges, occasionally passing an isolated, unlit farmhouse. For a time the road wound through a thick stand of evergreen trees, but otherwise the land was mostly barren, rolling hills under half a meter of snow.

Philippe was relieved when they finally reached a paved two-lane road. The lorry paused briefly before turning left; no traffic was visible in either direction. The car bucked as Philippe pulled off the dirt road up onto the pavement, and then they were traveling smoothly on a highway with only occasional potholes and a few small snowdrifts.

Now that driving did not require his full attention, Philippe glanced over at Carla, who seemed to be asleep. Just as well, for he had nothing to say to her. They had been lovers once, when she first came to work for him over a year ago, but that had not lasted long and now he could not say just how or why their affair had ended. She had traveled widely for him—that must have been the reason. He knew he would not have broken it off, at least not so quickly, for he had never known a lover quite so... interesting as Carla.

Dawn was still an hour away when they reached the outskirts of L'vov, in the far west of Ukraine. Philippe followed the lorry off the highway onto a side road, and eventually up a gravel drive to an abandoned farm. As he parked the Mercedes near a ramshackle barn, Jensen and Lanotte climbed down from the cab and headed toward the farmhouse.

In the moonless night Philippe watched Carla remove her cloak and toss it onto the seat of the Mercedes. He felt a pang of lust as she opened the rear door to retrieve a more practical woolen coat. Carla was thin and athletic, and her tight rump was on display when she bent over. She put on the coat and buttoned it, then reached in again to retrieve a small purple duffel bag.

"Now," Philippe said, "you will begin in Seattle?"

"Yes, Philippe." She sounded bored.

"You know Chen's e-mail address, correct?"

"Yes," she said with a sigh. "I still think you're being unnecessarily paranoid."

Philippe snorted and shook his head. "You should know better than anyone that we have to be careful. What would the Mossad give to know where we are and what we're doing? Or Interpol, or the RVS, or the CIA?"

Carla held up her hands. "Okay, okay," she said. "You're right. Any spook would give his left arm to catch you and take away your new toys. But it's silly for me not to be able to call you. What if I can't get access to an e-mail system?"

Philippe shrugged. "You'll manage. You always do."

She glared at him for a moment, then gave in. "Traveling expenses," she reminded him.

Philippe reached into his coat and brought out a thick envelope of cash. "That's all I can spare for now. Our funds are running low." Carla put the envelope into her coat pocket. "You'll get your cut as soon as we make the sale. You know the rendezvous locations and dates?"

Carla nodded.

"All right," Philippe said. "Anything else?"

She shook her head. Philippe touched her arm.

"Work quickly," he said. "The longer we keep the warheads, the more likely it is that some spook, as you say, will try to steal them."

Philippe pulled up the collar of his coat and walked away. Halfway to the farmhouse he turned back, but Carla was already gone.

He looked up. Despite the distant city lights washing out the sky, thousands of stars twinkled down at him. He decided that they winked in laughter, merciless laughter. He was on his own, they seemed to say.

Yes, I may be on my own, but yesterday I was just a retired arms dealer. Today I am a nuclear power.

He was tired. He decided to tell Jensen to set alarms on the truck.

* * *

That afternoon, after getting some sleep and eating a cold meal, they left the farmhouse as they'd arrived, with Philippe following the others. They drove west toward Poland. An hour later they reached the customs guardhouse at the border. Philippe pulled up close behind the lorry and powered down his window. He reached inside his coat and made sure that his pistol was loose in its holster.

The Polish customs guard climbed slowly down the stairs from his warm shack. He was short and fat, and his face was already red from the cold. Lanotte rolled down his window and handed the guard a clipboard with their manifest. The man gave the back of the lorry a cursory glance: tractor parts in crates, covered with a tarp. He squinted up at Lanotte.

"Where's Mikhail?" he said in Polish.

"Ah, poor Mikhail," Lanotte said, in Polish with a Ukrainian accent. He shook his head. "He has the flu, a bad one, and Veronya is sick with worry. But he is strong, he may be back next week."

The guard looked back up at him and then at the crates, but didn't even bother to walk around the flatbed. He checked the manifest one more time before handing it back and waving them on through.

Philippe pulled up to the checkpoint. The guard asked him something in Polish. He answered in Russian, and the guard asked him in the same language if he had anything to declare. Philippe said no, and the man gratefully waved him across the border and started the climb back up to his warmth and his tea.

Freedom. Poland, land of opportunity: shipping, rail lines, good roads, airplanes, and feeble border security. In a few days he would have his new merchandise safely hidden away and ready for sale.

They would make a fortune. Ever since the Soviet Union had crumbled, everyone said how easy it would be to steal nuclear weapons. But he, Philippe Sottile, had been the first to actually do it. The pent-up market demand was enormous. When he sold them—to an honorable customer, if possible, but to the richest customer if not—he would be able to retire again, this time forever. Then he and his three lovely wives would live for the rest of their long lives in the comfort and luxury that they deserved.

But not yet. They had to hide the warheads, and Jensen had to make them work. Carla—or Olivier—must find a buyer. Then the trickiest part, the delivery. They had to do all that and not get killed in the process. Then he could deal with Carla, his lovely, dangerous Carla. He wondered what the Mossad would give him if he handed her back to them, trussed like a pig.

Philippe followed the lorry, daydreaming. He could enjoy this pleasant drive through the Polish countryside, but then the work would begin.

The easy part was over.

Chapter 2

It began drizzling again. Derek Narr backed up a step so he was standing under the bakery's awning. *Seattle in February.*

Downtown rush hour was almost over. It started about two o'clock these days, after ebbing briefly from the morning crush, and the traffic never really stopped, it just thinned out a bit. It had been dark for almost two hours, and now the only pedestrians were a few stragglers rushing past—heads hunched down as if that would protect them from the rain—and a knot of people waiting outside the Federal Building for a bus.

Derek shivered. The field jacket he wore came to mid-thigh and was not quite warm enough. He walked into the Starbucks next to the bakery, where the bright lights and the sensual smell of roast coffee were almost enough to warm him up. He ordered coffee, black, surprising the young barista. No one in Seattle drank plain coffee anymore. Her albino white hair hung down in thin bangs past thick black eyebrows. She had two nose rings, a short black skirt, and a black, skin-tight turtleneck with nothing underneath. Very cool.

Derek hated cool. He thought there might be something provocative in the way her eyes twinkled when she handed him his change, but he just dropped the coins in the tip jar and walked back outside. He stood under the bakery awning again, sipping the scalding coffee.

He was a large man in his early forties, with short, dark brown hair. Hazel eyes brooded in a strong, square face that was dominated by a startling, very thick mustache.

A gust of wind blowing off the Sound reminded Derek of his ex-wife. He shivered again and took a gulp of coffee. Marjorie had loved Seattle, loved its gloomy weather; loved prowling the Market, dodging the bums on the waterfront, window shopping in Pioneer Square. Derek thought the city was too hilly, too breezy, too crowded. It was hard to drive in.

He preferred the Eastside, where he'd grown up, where there were fewer one-way streets and no street people.

He finished the coffee and threw the paper cup in a trash bin near the bakery door. There was no point in thinking about Marjorie. He forced himself to concentrate on tonight's business. The plaza here was elevated above the street. Below him, a Metro bus pulled up at the stop in front of the Federal Building. When it pulled away again, only one person was left, an obese woman bundled up under her umbrella, clutching a Nordstrom shopping bag and looking miserable.

The traffic had died down and the seventh floor of the Federal Building was dark. He had been watching it since dusk and was now certain it was deserted. It was time to move.

Riding the covered escalator down from the café level to the street, Derek imagined he was a gerbil: the tube above him looked just like a giant Habitrail.

A middle-aged couple strode past him, arm in arm, the woman holding her umbrella high, the man walking outside its protection and getting wet. There were no other pedestrians, except for the fat woman still waiting for her bus. Down the street the lights of the Daily Planet newsstand winked out. The brick courtyard in front of the Fed, with its stone arch and standing stones, was empty. The Federal Building itself was mostly dark—even workaholics went home on Friday night.

He walked around the block, down the hill past the Exchange building, from which someone was surely watching him, to stand beside the brass brazier outside the Post Office's Federal Station, a handsome stone and brick building totally unlike the stained concrete and arrow-slit windows of the Fed.

The hill he'd just come down was steep: ground floor here was three stories below Starbucks. Derek counted up to the seventh floor. Only one window was lit in the FBI office. He didn't expect it to be entirely empty; someone would be working in the message and computer centers, but they were on another floor. There might even be a few agents working late, but Derek wasn't worried about that.

He smiled to himself, enjoying the irony of spying on the FBI.

Derek walked back up along the south side of the Federal Building, staying on the edge of the cascade of brick plazas that stepped its way downhill. The steep grade barely registered on his mind. Almost halfway up the block, he turned into a brick driveway that led to an underground parking garage that was closed up tight. Beside that was an impregnable steel door, which he ignored; the keypad on the wall beside it was the only way of opening it. Instead, he walked over to the fire door in the adjoining wall.

He didn't know why a fire exit needed a deadbolt lock and a handle on the outside—perhaps this was how firemen would get into the building—but it was the perfect entry for him. He could be seen only by someone who had followed him up the drive, or who was watching from high up in the Exchange building.

Derek took a pair of latex gloves from a pocket of his jacket, pulled them on, and got a small case with his lock picks from another pocket. He pushed the tension tool into the lock, inserted a pick, and after a few moments of effort the lock turned. He pulled the door open and stepped inside.

It was dark and utterly quiet. The only illumination was the faint ready indicator on an emergency light high up against the ceiling. Derek took a small flashlight out of his jacket and by its light replaced his lock picks. He followed a hallway of bare cinder block walls to a tee intersection with a wider passage that led off to the left and right. A short distance away he found the freight elevator he'd been told to use.

Nothing happened when Derek pushed the call button. There was a small key plate below it. He got out his tools again and swiftly picked the lock. When he pushed the button again, the door opened immediately. He pressed 7, but nothing happened. Derek sighed, used his picks on the key slot in the panel, and pressed 7 again. The doors closed and the elevator started rising.

The noise was startling. The cables pinged and rang, the doors rattled, and he could hear a groan from the winch far above him. When the elevator opened at the seventh floor, he was amazed not to find someone waiting for him with a gun. He stepped out into a dark hallway and the elevator clunked shut behind him.

On the wall directly before him a large wooden sign bore the seal. He smiled and rubbed the raised stars and badge with a gloved hand, then set off to explore the Seattle field office of the FBI.

* * *

His instructions were unclear. Derek spent five minutes roaming the maze of individual offices and cubicles before he figured out where Chapa's office was. The FBI occupied about half of the floor, a space large enough to be confusing, especially since it was dark and he could never see very far in any direction. Clusters of cubicles short enough to look over were interspersed among conference rooms and real offices with tall glass walls that blocked his view. He kept running into dead-end corridors. Eventually he came to a long hallway with offices that had windows to the outside. Derek ducked into one and recognized the view—the low building just below him was Warshal's Sporting Goods, so he was on the north side. He followed the hallway to the west side. After walking almost halfway around the building, just as he was starting to curse under his breath, he found it.

An engraved plastic nameplate on the door read, "Kevin J. Chapa, Special Agent."

He had neither seen nor heard anyone as he blundered around, but Derek paused for a moment and listened intently. A soft whoosh of air was blowing through the heating system, accompanied by the fans of several computers that had been left on. Just at the edge of his hearing he could detect a high-pitched sound that might be from emergency lights or the perimeter security system—which he had side-stepped.

Feeling reasonably safe, Derek stepped into Chapa's office and half-closed the door. The blinds were open, giving enough light for him to see without his flashlight. He would have bet his house that someone was watching from behind one of the darkened windows in the Post Office just across the street. He considered waving to his audience but stifled the impulse. *Just get the job done.*

Chapa's desk was L-shaped, with the short leg under the window and a bookshelf built in above the long leg. Derek sat in the desk chair and swiveled around to look over the room. It was fairly tidy: papers littered the desk, and the stacked-up In basket was about ready to topple over, but the floor was clear, the bookshelves full of binders looked organized, and both file cabinets were closed and locked. The only other furniture was three guest chairs.

Derek turned back to face the computer in the corner of the desk. He picked up a photograph in a lucite frame standing beside the monitor. Three dark-haired children, ranging from perhaps four to nine years old, posed on a swing set, smiling stiffly and squinting in the sun. He hadn't known that Chapa had kids.

It was convenient that the computer monitor was in the corner. The observers would see him working, and perhaps see the glow of the tube, but they wouldn't be able to tell exactly what he was doing. Derek turned the computer on. While he waited for the system to boot, he looked over the papers lying on the desk. The one he wanted was right on top. It was a laser-printed sheet with the FBI seal at the top and a "Confidential" stamp printed near the bottom. The text was a brief for applying RICO against the Gugliemo family, the controversial owners of a string of nude dance clubs around Seattle. There was also a short description of the evidence the FBI had collected so far. Derek slid the paper into his lap, folded it, and slipped it into his jacket pocket.

His mission was now completed, except for the annoying task of convincing the observers that he had ferreted the information out of the FBI computers himself—which was probably impossible—and then getting out of the building safely.

The computer screen showed the FBI seal against a sky blue background. A black line at the bottom of the screen asked for his logon ID. *Right, as if Chapa would actually give me one.* He cracked his knuckles and was just composing in his head the first line of garbage he would type when he felt something cold and hard press against his neck, just below his right ear.

"Be quiet," a voice hissed. "If you move, you're dead."

Derek's chest went hollow and his back tingled. He started to raise his hands but the metal thing in his neck jabbed him.

"*Don't* raise your hands," the voice said.

Derek put them back on the keyboard and waited nervously. *Calm down, it's just an agent working late. I can talk my way out of this. Worst case, we can just call Chapa.* But if it really were an agent, the man would be standing in the doorway, covering him, while he shouted, "Freeze!" FBI agents didn't sneak up behind you and whisper in your ear. *Well, if it's not an agent, who the hell is it?* A cold trickle of sweat ran down Derek's temple. *I am in big fucking trouble.*

The voice spoke again in a husky whisper. "Don't turn around. Leave your hands on the keyboard. If you move one muscle, I'll kill you." The gun barrel left his neck, and Derek felt a powerful urge to turn and see who was behind him, but he fought it down. The gun was probably pointing right at his head. He heard someone sit down by the door.

"What are you doing here?" the voice said, but this time it was merely quiet, not a whisper, and Derek realized with a jolt that the gunman was a woman. Once again, he fought down the urge to turn around. She might only be a woman, but she had a gun.

"What the hell are you doing here?" she said again. The irritation in her voice jerked Derek out of his surprise.

What am *I doing here? This was a stupid idea.* "Uh, working late," he said hopefully.

"Bullshit," the woman said. "You're not Bureau."

Neither are you. He heard her move and imagined her raising the gun. He closed his eyes and took a deep breath, expecting a bullet. What he got instead was almost worse.

"Log on," the woman said.

Jesus, I don't have a login. "I don't have a login."

"Then what were you about to type?"

Derek's brain was blank. How could he explain what he was doing? He wasn't sure he understood it himself any more. He said the first thing that came into his head.

"I was going to hack into the system."

"Then do it."

He wanted to kick himself. So much for trying to talk his way out of this. "I don't know if I can," he said.

"If you want to live," the woman said, "you'd better try."

"Uh... all right. But give me some time, okay? I've never used this system before."

"You've got two minutes," she said.

Two minutes! Impossible. Derek felt himself slip into overdrive. In the old days, when he'd written software for a living, he had occasionally run into horrible bugs the day before a deadline. Sometimes it took the whole day just to find and understand the things. Sometimes it was easy to find them, but in order to fix them a whole section of code had to be rewritten. Then he would find himself working like a madman, focused like a laser, oblivious to distractions, without the need to eat or sleep.

He felt his mind racing. The best way to break into a secure system is to get access to an unrestricted terminal—a master console. Could he find one? They would probably all be in the computer center, which wasn't even on this floor. He didn't know exactly where it was, and there was no chance she would let him go looking for it. Even if she did, and they found it, he would need a card key to get in. That wouldn't have been a problem if he'd brought the right equipment, but how could he have known he would need it? This was supposed to be a sham break-in.

Forget about the computer room. Could he find a login? And a password, too, damn it! In lots of the places he'd broken into, lazy employees kept their current password written down somewhere in the office. He glanced around the desk but decided it wasn't worth searching for one. This was a new system, the FBI agents would have been well trained, and there hadn't been time yet for them to get lazy. He'd bet his life that Chapa kept his password safely in his head.

Okay, forget about finding a password. Could he just type in random strings? He gave that up instantly. How long would she wait before she realized that he was stalling and just shot him?

What about a back door? Wait a minute... Derek struggled to remember something floating at the edges of his memory. He wiped the sweat off his forehead and closed his eyes.

"Well?" the woman said.

"I'm thinking."

"You have one minute left."

Damn it! What was it... Then he remembered.

At Comdex last year in Vegas, he'd been sitting at a bar, getting drunk on margaritas and checking out the waitresses in their skin-tight sequins. Kurt Hopstetter had shown up at his elbow and they'd switched to tequila, straight. He hadn't seen Kurt in a few years, but surprisingly, Kurt hadn't been his usual big-mouthed self. He'd hunched over the bar, tossing back shots and sucking on lime wedges, and acting coy about what he was working on.

"It's big," Kurt had said.

"So? Who's the client?"

"Can't s-say. It's a s-secret. But it's big, old buddy, big." He'd grinned that big, lame, drunk grin that meant, "You can guess if you try hard." Derek had been too ripped to figure it out, or even to care very much, so they'd headed off to the blackjack tables instead. Later he'd heard that the FBI was on the verge of automating, years after the CIA and most of the other government agencies, and that they'd hired a small firm to do the work.

Kurt's company was pretty small, and they were very good. The timing was right. If it *had* been Kurt that installed the FBI's new system, he *must* have left himself a back door. Even though Kurt would never get a chance to use it, just knowing that he had access to the FBI's computers would give him a permanent hard-on.

Derek thought hard. What was the name of that cat Kurt always bragged about, the one that could open the refrigerator door? It liked to drink beer. The cat had weighed twenty-three pounds and died happy and old. Whenever Kurt got drunk he would drag out stories about the genius cat, smarter than any dog he'd ever known.

Derek typed in "Shadowfax" and hit the return key. The system replied, INVALID LOGIN ID, and asked for it again. Derek slumped back in his chair. He'd been sure that would be it.

"Time's up," the woman said. "Are you done?"

"Give me a minute," Derek pleaded. "I think I can get it."

She snorted but didn't shoot him. *Think!* What else was Kurt obsessed with? His stupid cat and...

His ex-wife. She'd slept around almost from the day after their honeymoon. Maybe that was Kurt's fault—honeymooning in Shreveport,

Louisiana had probably not been a brilliant idea, and he drank too much and worked too hard. A beautiful, stacked, rather dim blonde was not going to stay home knitting while Kurt worked all hours to build his business.

After they'd divorced, Kurt came up with a pet name for her. What was it? Her name had been Goldie, of course. Kurt laughed his head off every time he called her by that nickname. The proof of how stupid the bitch was, he'd always said, was that she'd taken him to the cleaners *before* he got rich.

Derek sat up straight and typed "Goldenbitch." The screen cleared and gave him a menu of options. He leaned back in his chair and sighed with relief. He could imagine Kurt laughing like a jackass at the joke: what he would do with Goldie's back door if he ever got the chance. It was too bad he couldn't call Kurt and tell him that he'd found his stupid hack—if he even lived through the night.

"Good work," the woman said from behind him. "Bring up the Witness Protection Program."

* * *

She came up close behind him. Derek's first glimpse of her out of the corner of his eye didn't reveal much. She had short, dark hair and was wearing some kind of patterned shirt worn over dark pants. Then the gun was back in his ear. He selected the WPP option. A new menu popped up and he waited for further instructions.

Derek's fear was starting to ebb now that he had cracked the system. If she were going to shoot him for no reason, she would have done it by now. He was cooperating, and he'd actually been of some use to her—he doubted that she, or anyone who didn't know Kurt well, could have found the back door. He didn't have a lot of options as long as she had a gun on him, and he still had no clue who she was or what she wanted—

"Bring up the Query command," she said, and Derek did. A form popped up asking for details. "Look for John Hildreth."

Derek typed 'Hilldred.' The gun tapped his ear, startling him, and he retyped it correctly after she gave him the spelling. He hit Return and waited while the sand ran out of a little hourglass on the screen. *Cute,*

Kurt. Before the woman had a chance to get impatient, Hildreth's dossier appeared. There was a picture: pockmarked face, broken nose, buzzed hair, and a vicious, exultant smile that showed stained teeth. His new name was John Roscoe, with an address in Montana. The text listed charges—all of them dropped—case numbers, agent names, cross references; it more than filled the screen.

"Can you print it?" she said.

Derek found a print command on the file menu. "I don't know where the printer is."

She tapped him on the ear with her gun again. Derek was getting really tired of that. She knocked on the desk, and he looked down and felt like an idiot. There was a laser printer at his knee, under the short section of the desk.

"Pay attention," she said. Derek sighed and printed the file. It took several minutes for the single sheet to come out. As he handed it back to her, it occurred to him that, if she didn't kill him, what she was making him do was a perfect smoke screen for his employers. This was exactly what they'd paid him to do: break in, find something, and print it out.

The woman looked over the sheet, then folded it up and stuck it in a pocket of her jeans. "Turn it off," she said.

Derek flirted with the idea of leaving a clue for Chapa in the way he shut the system down. If Chapa found his computer on and his monitor off, he would see the Hildreth file, and it might lead him to the woman. But she was probably smart enough to know he'd just turned off the monitor, and she might shoot him if she turned it back on and saw Hildreth's face still there. What if he just switched off the computer without logging off—would the system stay logged on? Probably not; the network would time out and cut the connection. With a sinking feeling, he went back to the main menu and logged off, then turned off the power.

"Turn around," the woman said, and Derek panicked. As long as he hadn't seen her face, he was safe. Now he'd be able to identify her and she'd have to kill him for sure.

"Wait," he said, "I haven't seen your face yet. You got what you came for, so why not just let me go? I did what you wanted, right? I can't—"

"Shut up and turn around."

He bit his lip and swiveled the chair slowly. She was sitting just inside the doorway with her legs drawn up and a huge gun balanced on her knee, pointing right at his head. *Oh shit.* He closed his eyes.

What? She was laughing? He opened his eyes. The gun was still aimed at his forehead, but she was laughing quietly.

"I won't kill you unless you do something stupid," she said. "What's your name?"

"Derek. Narr."

"Okay, Derek, I'm glad to see you're not a complete imbecile. When did you put on the gloves?"

Derek looked down at his gloved hands and back at her, and was finally calm enough to really see her. She was young, late twenties, with curly, short black hair. Her face was beautiful; no, it wasn't really beautiful, but there was something... The way she was sitting hid her figure and her height, but he could see she was slim.

"Before I entered the building," he said.

"Good. No fingerprints. Now what were you doing breaking into the FBI? No bullshit, now." She waved the gun at him, as if he needed a reminder, and he noticed that she *wasn't* wearing gloves. What did that mean, that she didn't care if she left fingerprints?

Derek decided to keep it simple. There was no point telling her all of it.

"I was hired by a local wiseguy to sneak in and see what the FBI has on him. He thinks they're going to arrest him for racketeering and he wants advance warning."

She thought for a second and shook her head. "Doesn't make sense. It's got to be easier just to bribe someone. Or threaten them."

"He tried that. Every messenger he sent is in jail. And he can't threaten them, he's a small-time thug."

"So you work for this sleazebag?"

Derek shuddered. "No, I hate the guy. I'm just a contractor. My line is industrial espionage, but the money on this job was too good to pass up. And I'm small-time, too. This guy can't muscle the FBI, but he did a pretty good job on me."

She cocked her head to one side and looked him up and down. Derek decided to try again.

"Look, you've got what you need, you can just let me go now, right? I can forget your face in two seconds, and who'm I going to tell, anyway? The FBI?"

The woman shook her head and smiled the most horrible smile that Derek had ever seen. It was feral and hungry, beautiful and dangerous. Derek felt like a rabbit in the jaws of a wolf. He shivered and knew she was going to kill him.

"Ordinarily," she said, "I'd just kill you now. It might be fun to leave the Bureau a little mystery, right here in their inner sanctum. You're obviously not supposed to be here. But you saved my ass—I was expecting paper files. I thought I'd just have to break into a filing cabinet. When did they automate?"

Derek was too shaken to reply. His heart was racing and his skin felt cold. He just shrugged.

"Doesn't matter," she said. "You obviously know computers, so you might come in handy again. And you're kind of good-looking, in a way. So I have a better idea. Get up."

As Derek stood, she vanished into the hallway; he wasn't quite sure how. She hadn't stood up, she'd just sort of unfolded and swung around the doorjamb. She must be assuming, as he was, that they were being watched from outside, but he wanted to be seen and she didn't. When he stepped out into the hallway she was already on her feet, her gun pointed at him. Now that they were both standing, he could see that she was about six inches shorter than he was, and slender. He probably had a hundred pounds on her. He shouldn't have any trouble getting away from her if he could just deal with the gun.

"Come on," she said softly. She led him down the hallway to a conference room near the center of the building. "We're leaving a bit more quietly than you arrived," she said as she shut the door behind them. The room contained nothing but a large wooden table and high-backed chairs. "There are two agents on this floor right now. I can't believe they didn't hear you, rattling up in that lift."

"I didn't see anyone."

"I know. I followed you from the moment you got off the lift."

Under her direction, he put one of the chairs up on the table and climbed onto it, trying to maintain his balance as it rolled slightly on the slick table top. Then he pushed aside one of the acoustic tiles in the ceiling.

"Listen," she said, and he looked down at her. "We're going to crawl through the ceiling. I'll tell you where to go, and I promise you, if you try anything heroic, I'll shoot you."

"What about those two agents? They'll hear the gunshots."

"I'll deal with them after you're dead," she replied, and his skin crawled. "Do you understand me?"

He nodded and she waved him up. He pulled himself up into the space above the ceiling.

Steel beams stuck out from the true ceiling about two feet overhead. Wires hung down from bolts embedded in the concrete, supporting the tiles. The concrete and steel had been sprayed with something foamy. Derek moved out of her way, keeping his weight off the center of the tiles; he didn't want to crash through and get shot before he had a chance to stand up.

His kidnapper hoisted herself easily up into the cramped space. She pulled her legs up and replaced the tile.

"Go straight ahead," she said, and they started crawling—Derek leading the way, following her directions. There was enough light filtering up from the fluorescents to see where they were going. He concentrated on where he put his hands and knees. They skirted several support struts, vertical I-beams, and a wall made of cinder blocks that might have been an elevator shaft.

Finally, she told him to stop. She lifted aside an acoustic tile and abruptly dropped through the opening, head first. Derek peered down to see her standing below him, looking up. She should have landed on her head. *Too bad, that would have solved my problem.* She waved him down, and he carefully lowered his feet into the opening, then let himself drop, landing in a crouch.

They were standing in a short hallway that ended in a door to the stairway. The woman opened the door and grabbed a broom from the stairwell. Using its butt end, she maneuvered the tile back into place.

Derek followed her down the stairs, wondering how there could be such a whopping big hole in the FBI's security. The hallway leading from the public elevator to the FBI offices was covered by security cameras. The waiting room was also monitored, and the door into the office could only be unlocked by a receptionist sitting behind bulletproof glass. But, if you were only willing to crawl through the ceiling, you could bypass all that just by picking the locks on the doors of the east stairwell. It was so simple that he didn't believe it; something strange was going on.

They went down to the end of the stairway in the basement. The woman stopped to pick up a purple gym bag and a heavy woolen coat. A sign over the door announced that an alarm would sound, but she shoved it open and there was no siren. They emerged onto a loading dock on the south side of the building, below the brick terraces, like the drive from which Derek had entered but farther up the hill.

The rain had stopped. The loading dock was dark and the woman was distracted putting on her coat. Derek hadn't actually seen her gun since he crawled up into the ceiling; she must have stuck it in the small of her back or something. This would be his best chance.

She stood slightly ahead of him and to his left. As she raised her right arm to slide it into the sleeve of her coat, he made a fist and swung it at her back, intending to knock the wind out of her—but he missed! As he recovered from his swing, he realized that she wasn't there. Before he could turn to look for her, her foot jabbed him hard in the belly, driving the breath out of him, and he doubled up and fell to his knees.

She was standing right in front of him, smiling. Derek was overwhelmed by rage. He launched himself at her—and she wasn't there. He yelped as he flew over the edge of the loading dock, and managed to tuck in before he hit the wet bricks. He rolled, recovered, and scrambled to his feet.

Suddenly she was in front of him again. Derek swung a fist. She ducked under it and hit him three times, each blow like the strike of a sledgehammer. He realized that he was sitting on his ass on the driveway, and he couldn't breathe.

"Relax," she said. She was crouching beside him with one hand on his shoulder. "Try to breathe deeply."

Jesus! He'd never seen anyone move that fast. After a moment he caught his breath.

"Football, right?" she said.

Derek grunted. "High school. Hurt my knee in college, though, so I had to quit. How did you know?"

"That was a classic tackle. But you're used to hitting big, slow, beefy targets. Listen to me, Derek." He looked up at her. "I don't need a gun to kill you. If I'd been serious, you'd have been dead after the first swing. Now, this little practice bout has been fun, but I think we should get going."

Derek took another deep breath. He still felt a little dizzy. "You have a name?"

She smiled and offered a hand, effortlessly hauling him up off the ground. "You can call me Carla." She walked back to the loading dock and grabbed her bag. "Where's your car?"

Derek peeled off his rubber gloves and stuffed them into a coat pocket. He found his keys and led her toward the parking lot two blocks away. The drizzle started again as they reached the nearly empty lot, making halos of angel hair around the street lights. Derek beeped his Explorer and they climbed in.

"Where do you want to go?" he said wearily.

Carla smiled and settled back into her seat. "Let's go to your place."

Chapter 3

Special Agent George Frieder put the binoculars down on the window ledge, took off his glasses, and rubbed his eyes.

"Got a smoke?" he said.

His partner, Watson Holbrook, patted his pockets and cursed, then grabbed his trench coat off a chair and searched it. He found a rumpled pack and squeezed it gently.

"One left," he said, and handed the pack over.

Frieder shook the last one out, absent-mindedly crushing the empty pack and tossing it onto the floor. He lit the cigarette with a Bic lighter and held the first drag as if it were dope.

"This is bullshit," Frieder said as he blew smoke.

Frieder was tall—six foot three—and built like a cinder block wall. His deep black skin made him difficult to see in the dim light, although his shaved skull picked up highlights from the lamps in the street below. Frieder put his steel frame glasses back on and picked up the binoculars again. Smoke from the cigarette dangling from his lips swirled past the branching scar on his right cheek. He didn't give a shit if anyone saw the glowing coals or not.

He scanned the seventh floor again. No lights were showing, and no movement. They'd spent four hours staked out in this small office on the corner of the ninth floor of the Post Office. They could see straight into Chapa's office from here, and most of the way up Marion Street toward First Avenue.

It was almost two hours since he'd seen Narr walk around the Federal Building, go up Marion to the parking lot entrance, and after a while enter Chapa's office. Narr had worked at the computer for somewhat longer than Frieder had expected him to, and then left. Frieder had watched carefully for half an hour, expecting Narr to leave the same way he'd gone in, but the son of a bitch never came out. Something was wrong.

"Call Shaffer," he told Holbrook, still watching the street.

"Okay," Holbrook said. He took out his phone and punched in the number. "Holbrook," he said. "He still hasn't come out." He listened for a moment, then covered the phone with his hand. "She wants to know if he might have slipped past us."

Frieder took the binoculars away from his face and turned to look at his partner. They had worked together for so many years that the other agents called them the Friedbrook Twins. Frieder had no idea what they were talking about. He was six inches taller than Holbrook, forty pounds heavier, and, at forty-eight, three years younger. He was black, Holbrook was white. Okay, they wore the same kind of glasses and they both smoked. Big fucking deal.

Holbrook's shirt sleeves were rolled up, showing the tiger tattooed on his thick right forearm. His brown hair was buzzed short. Green eyes looked back at Frieder expectantly from beneath drooping eyelids. Frieder turned back to the window.

"Tell that bitch she can come over here and blow me."

Holbrook lifted the phone. "Frieder says no way." He listened for a moment. "She says we should call Chapa."

"Not yet," Frieder said. "Tell her to get—who else is over there, Cadwaller?—get Cadwaller to help her search the office. If she can't find anything, *then* I'll call Chapa."

Holbrook relayed the message and hung up.

"She wants to know if he slipped past us?" Frieder said. "What does she think we're doing over here, napping? Jerking off?"

"Aw, she's okay," Holbrook said. "She's just trying to be thorough."

"Well, she pisses me off. Chapa thinks she's some kind of genius, but all that proves is that he needs to get laid more often."

"I'd fuck her," Holbrook offered.

"Big surprise." Frieder lifted the binoculars again. "Where the hell are you, Narr?"

* * *

Sheldon Varnes sighed and picked up his Thermos of coffee. He poured himself a cup and looked over the street again. Narr should have come out over an hour ago. He took a sip of the still-hot coffee and nearly spilled it as he saw a tiny light flare briefly in one of the dark windows in the Post Office building, diagonally across from his position. He watched closely and could see a dim red glow. Someone was having a smoke. Stupid Fed. Hadn't the man heard about lung cancer, emphysema—giving away your position?

Varnes took out his phone and tapped in a number.

"Hey, Johnnie," he said merrily. "You know you got company?"

"Huh?" Johnnie sounded half-asleep.

"Yeah, there's a Fed one floor up from you and about three windows over. They must be staking out Narr, too. What the fuck do you make of that?"

"How you know it's a Fed?"

"Because I don't think any postal workers are going to be smoking in a dark room at ten o'clock on Friday night, you dummy. You seen anything?"

"Nah," Johnnie said. "He left about an hour ago. I could see him real good, playing with that computer. Then he picked up a piece of paper, then he just sat there for a while, then he left. That's it."

"Okay, I'm giving up. You go on down and meet me at the car. I'm going to call the boss and see what he says."

"Okay," Johnnie said, and they hung up.

Varnes punched in another number and took another sip of coffee. *God, I love Seattle. Best damned coffee in the world.* The phone rang five times before somebody answered.

"Uh huh," Gugliemo said.

"Hey, boss, Shellie here. We lost Narr."

There was a long pause. Finally, Gugliemo said, "Tell me you're joking, Shellie. And then I'm still going to rip your tongue out, because you interrupted me in the middle of some very important business to tell me this stupid joke."

The "very important business" was probably some dancer with fake tits who'd had to lift her head so Gugliemo could pick up the phone.

"Sorry, boss, no joke. We saw him go in, we saw him do the job, but he never came out. I'm thinking he either got out some other way, or the Feds nabbed him." Now was probably not the best time to mention that the Feds were watching Narr, too. "What do you want us to do?"

Gugliemo was silent for so long that Varnes wondered if he'd dropped the phone. He knew how distracting "very important business" could be. Varnes decided to show some initiative.

"How about if Johnnie and me go watch Narr's house? If the Feds got him, there's not much we can do. But if he got away clean, we can keep an eye on him."

"Okay," Gugliemo said, and hung up.

The boss and his women. Varnes finished his coffee and screwed the cap back on the Thermos. Too bad Gugliemo was practically impotent. If he'd been a real man, he wouldn't have to spend so many hours with some broad's face in his lap, and maybe then he could pay more attention to *real* business. Maybe then they wouldn't have to hire this chump Narr to find out what the Feds knew.

Varnes grabbed his camel hair coat, his binoculars, and his Thermos and looked around to be sure he'd got everything. As he walked toward the elevators, he thought about getting a new job. Gugliemo was a screw-up and everyone knew it, and sooner or later the Feds were going to take him down. Better to be somewhere else when that happened.

He pushed the elevator button and wondered what the coffee was like in Arizona.

* * *

The sublime strings of a Mozart quartet played in the background, but Kevin Chapa barely heard it. He lay stretched out on his couch with his eyes closed, thinking. The living room was dimly lit by a floor lamp in the corner. He looked asleep, but Chapa didn't sleep much, and never on the couch. This was his thinking place.

Chapa was thinking about his oldest son, Peter, who had started high school this year. His mother found some marijuana in his bedroom while she was gathering dirty clothes. Five minutes later she was on the phone with Chapa, screaming and crying. He'd listened without really paying attention, remembering that he'd once thought that the only good thing about being divorced from Jeanne was that he'd never have to listen to her ranting again.

After six years of divorce he still had to endure her crying jags at least once a month. They might as well still be married. She'd screamed even louder when he suggested that she simply replace the joint and stop going into Peter's room. He'd promised to have a serious father-to-son chat the next time he talked to Peter. Seeing him in person would have been better, but Chapa could rarely get away from work long enough to fly to Miami.

Chapa was forty-one, and his wiry black hair was going to silver faster than he could believe. He'd been with the Bureau for almost twenty years, but only the last few had really aged him. Until they separated, Jeanne had listened to everything he vented at her, put up with the danger, the long hours, and calls in the middle of the night—and he never realized how much that meant to him until she was gone. He rubbed his face with his hands and tried to think how to get Peter to lay off the pot. Maybe he could get some of his old buddies at the Miami Bureau to stage a mock arrest. That might scare him enough to go straight.

The phone rang, shattering his peace, but not really startling him. He was used to being interrupted by the phone. He picked up the cordless off the coffee table.

"Chapa," he said.

"Frieder here."

Chapa sat up and reached for the stereo remote, clicking it off. "Go ahead." His brown eyes were wide open now. His naturally olive skin, the gift of his Mexican grandparents, looked unnaturally pale. He slouched forward on the couch and rubbed his face again with his left hand.

"The break-in went as planned, but there's been a slight complication." Frieder's resonant voice was wound tight.

"What kind of complication?"

"He's vanished," Frieder said. "We saw him go in, we watched him fake hacking into the computer, and no one's seen him since he left your office. He didn't come back out the way he went in, and Shaffer says he's definitely left the seventh floor. She searched with, uh, Cadwaller."

Chapa considered the possibilities for a moment.

"The entry security system is still on, right?" Frieder said yes; so he didn't go out the front door. "And Shaffer didn't hear him go down the elevator again?" Frieder said no. "Well, someone missed him. She was in the can, or you were having a smoke, or something."

"No, sir," Frieder said, but his tone said, "Fuck you, sir." Chapa smiled.

"Well, I don't see the problem. As long as you're sure Gugliemo's goons didn't grab him when he walked out the door—"

"No way."

"—we'll just wait for his call as planned."

"Yes, sir," Frieder said.

"Okay, tell Shaffer to turn the full security suite back on and go on home."

"Yes, sir."

Chapa set the phone down and lay back on the couch. He went over the plan again in his mind. Derek had insisted that they let him break in himself, but if Chapa hadn't had most of the security system shut down, starting the freight elevator would have rung an alarm. And, of course, then they would have known how and when Derek left the building. *If* he had. Chapa didn't dismiss the possibility that Derek, for whatever reason, was still in there somewhere. But if he was, they would find out when he tried to leave.

There was no point worrying about it. Tomorrow morning they would just go over to his house and ask him what happened.

Chapter 4

Carla Citrullo gazed out the window of the Explorer as downtown Seattle swept by. The city was beautiful under low clouds, alive with sparkling lights in the clean air now that the rain had stopped.

Derek had driven without speaking since they reached the freeway, which was just fine with Carla. She hated getting-to-know-you chitchat, especially with someone she might have to shoot sooner or later. He changed lanes—after signaling, checking both mirrors, *and* looking over his shoulder. Carla made a mental note not to let him drive if they were ever in a hurry. She could imagine him politely pulling over and slowing down to allow someone who'd been shooting at them to pass.

They passed marinas, houseboats, and a football stadium. At the crest of a hill she looked down on a floating bridge ahead. To the right the lights of another floating bridge, miles away, looked like a miniature string of pearls lit against the dark, seething water. Soon they were driving a few feet above the surface of Lake Washington. A gust of wind blew spray off the lake into a sheet of water that seemed to hover over the bridge—then it crashed down, blinding them. Derek flipped on the wipers.

It had taken Carla weeks to work her way out of Ukraine and across Europe, to Canada and finally into the States. Ever since she'd arrived in Seattle a few days ago, she'd felt like an alien studying a new world full of weird organisms. She'd spent the last nineteen months scuttling in the filth of Europe with vermin that made cockroaches look like the kings of evolution, so this was a rather severe culture shock. It seemed long ago that she had been born and raised in Canada, in a city somewhat like this one, but she was no longer used to the casual wealth and the extravagance on display everywhere she looked.

All these people driving, for instance: the taillights made a solid red line ahead of them. There was no other practical way to get across the lake: no train, no ferries. You could take a bus, but hardly anyone did: in American cities, buses were for the poor and the crackpots. No one with any money at all thought twice about hopping into their car and driving, in exactly the same direction and at exactly the same time as a thousand other people. It was insane.

At the end of the floating bridge they climbed up away from the lake, and Derek left the highway. Apartment complexes and residential streets alternated with strip malls and an occasional lonely stand of evergreen trees. Carla watched it go by, brooding. Everywhere she'd been on the Eastside was like this: no one had to drive more than a few blocks to get to a video store.

They ended up in a sprawling, affluent development in which every one of the large houses had yard lights of some sort: spotlights on pine trees or fountains, low-voltage lights marching up the driveways. The garage was the focus of each house, dominating every façade, and there was no path from the street to the house other than the driveway. Many of the houses had parking lots or circular drives. Like the roads, the architecture was dictated by the tyranny of cars.

The night was dark, but the many street lamps showed that the lawns were well-tended and bordered with tidy shrubs. The houses themselves all looked alike: large windows, cedar siding, and monstrous brick porticoes, arched or crenelated, near the garage.

Every owner tried to make his cookie-cutter house unique, but the result was only stultifying sameness. Carla found it all disquieting. This was not like the consistency she had seen in Jerusalem, Edinburgh, and other old-world cities, where strict building codes, a sense of style, limited building materials, and poverty had often combined to give entire cities a consistent look and similar construction. This was something sadder and somehow disturbing.

She could fix the problem with a grenade launcher—and a hundred grenades.

Derek drove the Explorer into a cul-de-sac. After a straight stretch, the street curved back on itself around a curbed planting area, bare except for a short leafless tree in its center. He pulled around the planter and into the driveway of a house like all the others. Two garage doors faced the street, one larger than the other, flanked by an arched two-story brick portico. Derek pushed a button on his visor and the larger door began opening. They drove inside and sat waiting: Derek for instructions, Carla for her sixth sense to spot any trouble.

There was another car parked to her right, a sleek black sports car of a type she'd never seen before.

"Who's inside?" Carla said.

"No one. I live alone."

"No wife? No girlfriend? No one?"

"I'm divorced. I don't even have a dog."

"There are two cars."

"Yeah. I have two cars."

She drew her pistol from the midriff holster under her shirt and Derek jerked back a little. "You'd better be right."

She opened her door, grabbed her bag, and stepped down. Sacks of steer manure and fertilizer were piled between the Explorer and the sports car. To avoid tripping, she had to lean on the Explorer with her left hand. This lent some credence to Derek's claim that he lived alone. If someone routinely got out the passenger side of the Explorer, this stuff would have been moved long ago.

Derek pushed a button to close the garage door, then unlocked the door into the house. As they stepped inside, he tapped out a code on a security panel and Carla raised her gun to point in his general direction. He held up his hands.

"Calm down," he said. "I'm just turning off the alarm. It's not even wired to the police station."

They were standing in a small hallway: laundry room to the right, bathroom to the left. Next to the bathroom was a closed door. She gestured at it and Derek opened it, revealing a den with dark wainscoting and a lot of visual clutter, but unoccupied. She nodded and Derek led her into the main part of the house.

The family room contained a brick fireplace, a big-screen TV, black leather couches, and a thick glass coffee table. A pair of Japanese watercolors hung in the wet bar alcove.

She set her bag down by the door. "Show me the rest."

Derek dropped his keys on the wet bar counter and walked out of the room. Next was a casual eating area off the kitchen, which was outrageously large: the cooker and a small sink were on a big island in the center of the room, the refrigerator was enormous, and there were two ovens.

"Do you cook?" Carla said.

He said he did, but she doubted it. The kitchen was spotless.

The dining room was furnished with table and chairs of dark cherry wood and two matching hutches filled with old china. The formal living room was completely empty. In the main entry hall, a remarkably ugly chandelier shaped from tiers of glass shards hung suspended from the ceiling over two stories above. They went up a broad, curving staircase that ended in a little sitting area above the foyer, with a crammed bookshelf and a small couch. A short hallway to the left led to three bedrooms, two of which were empty and shared a bathroom. The third had its own bath and a queen-sized bed.

The other way led to the master suite. The bedroom was nearly filled by a massive sleigh bed, two tall dressers, and an armoire. The sybaritic bathroom had a Jacuzzi tub and a shower big enough for two, and a separate little room for the commode. The walk-in closet, almost the size of the smallest bedroom, was nearly empty: half a dozen pairs of pants, a few dozen casual shirts, and three pairs of shoes.

As they started back downstairs, Carla realized that a woman must once have lived here. There were little details she had noticed without registering at first. The dresser in the guest bedroom had a runner that matched the duvet cover, the master bedroom draperies were a floral pattern, and the love seat in the reading nook at the head of the stairs was too feminine, completely at odds with the leather furniture in the family room. Apparently Derek hadn't fully exorcised his ex-wife's ghost. Interesting.

"Let's go back to your den," she said.

She hadn't got a good look at the room before, just an impression of clutter, which she now saw was caused by scattered equipment and piles of books. Each end of a built-in desk held a computer, both turned off. There was another large desk, carved cherry, with a wooden chair on casters standing before it and a closed notebook computer on top. Components of yet another computer lay on the floor. A long leather couch stood against the far wall.

She motioned to the couch with her gun. Derek took off his coat, draped it over a chair, and sat down heavily. Carla shrugged off her own coat and sat in the wooden chair. It moved beneath her, and she rocked in it experimentally. It was surprisingly comfortable.

They glared at each other for a moment, then Carla holstered her weapon. Derek's eyes tried to follow it but she could tell he hadn't figured it out yet.

"It's a midriff holster," she said, and drew her gun again, slowly, by pulling up her flannel shirt and reaching underneath. The gun lodged just below her breasts. "It's a relatively fast draw and it's hard to spot. But it makes it difficult to give hugs."

Derek watched her put the gun away. "I don't really picture you as the hugging type."

"You're right. Tell me again why you broke into the FBI."

Derek sighed and crossed his legs. "I already told you everything. The Gugliemos run most of the strip joints around Seattle. They're also into prostitution and drugs, but the family is small potatoes, I'm not sure you could even call them a mob. There's a protest group complaining about a new strip club opening in their neighborhood. They went to the FBI with the idea of using the RICO law to shut Gugliemo down. The FBI liked the idea—"

"Okay, I get the picture." She looked around the room. "So you don't usually work for the scumbags, and burgling the FBI doesn't strike me as your primary business. What is?"

Derek shrugged. "Hardware companies hire me to sneak into a competitor's labs and get an early idea of what they're doing. I've ripped off software, too. Sometimes a PI will ask me to break into an office and copy disks or steal papers."

"So you're a B&E contractor." Carla watched him struggle with the unpleasant truth before nodding reluctantly. She was continually amazed by people's need—and capacity—for rationalization. "Okay, what's the next step? You're supposed to hand over the goods to these scuzzbos?"

"Yeah. I have a meeting with them at nine tomorrow morning."

"You're going to miss your meeting," she said. Derek tensed and uncrossed his feet; he looked ready to jump. "Relax, I'm not planning to kill you. But you can forget about your scuzzy friends, because we're leaving here before nine."

"Leaving?" Derek's voice rose. "To where?"

"Montana."

"Montana? I can't go to Montana! This is about that, what's his name, Hildreth, isn't it?"

"Yes," Carla said.

Derek jumped off the couch. His voice got even louder.

"Look, lady, I don't know who you are, and I don't really want to know. I can't go to *Montana.* If I don't show up at that meeting tomorrow, I'm fucked. The Gugliemos may just be punks, but they'll kill me if I don't hand over that data."

Carla swiveled in the chair as he started pacing, rocking it forward and back. She thought this might be the most comfortable chair she'd ever sat in. She considered taking it with them.

"I've been cooperating," Derek said. "What did you tell me, you were expecting *paper* files? There's no way you could have broken into that system yourself. I did you a favor, so how about doing me one? Go to Montana by yourself, see this stupid Hildreth, and kidnap *him* if you want company so bad. I'll tell you what, you can even take my car. Please?"

"You're right," Carla said, "you've been very helpful. That's why you're still alive. And you might be helpful to me again someday. Now, if I were you, I'd get some sleep, because we're going to be getting up early."

"Oh, come on," Derek shouted. "This is bullshit. I can't—"

Carla stood up. Derek put up his hands to ward her off.

"Wait a minute," he said. "I know you're a kung fu goddess, you can probably cut my head off with your little finger, but I think I'm entitled to know what's going on. Who the fuck are you? Why are you going to Montana? And what the hell do you need *me* for?"

Carla stepped in closer and Derek took a half-hearted swing at her. She dodged the punch easily, slapped him briskly on each cheek, and kicked his legs out from under him. As he started to fall, she used his weight to swing him up and throw him onto the couch. He landed heavily, rocking it back against the wall, and lay there stunned, staring at her.

"First," she said, "it's aikido, not kung fu. Second, I need you, so you're coming. And third, I'll tell you what you need to know and nothing more, and you're just going to have to live with it, because the alternative," she let her voice go cold, "is that I shoot you right now and head out without you. Those are your only options. Come with me quietly or die. Which will it be?"

Derek said nothing for a long moment. Then he gathered himself and sat with his legs up on the couch.

"Are you going to let me sleep in my own bed?" he said.

"Sleep right there. It looks comfortable."

He closed his eyes briefly and shook his head, but then he reached for an afghan lying draped over the back of the couch and spread it out over himself. She heard him grumbling under his breath as he turned his back to her and settled in, lying on his side.

Carla sat back down in the wooden chair, watching him and thinking. She'd thought he was asleep when he spoke again.

"My ex always said I should get out more." She laughed quietly and pulled Hildreth's dossier out of her pocket.

* * *

Carla studied the paper by the light of the green-shaded desk lamp, trying to decipher the Bureau's acronyms and memorizing Hildreth's repugnant face and the sordid facts of his life. When she was sure Derek was asleep, she searched the den, finding nothing illuminating about him, settling for a road map of the U.S. and a street map of Seattle. She worked out several routes from Derek's house to the tiny town where Hildreth lived in his new identity, trying to think of everything that could go wrong—on their way and once they arrived—and devise a strategy to handle each case. She pondered how to deal with Hildreth.

Eventually her thoughts drifted back to Philippe. He would be dug in by now, waiting for her or Olivier to find a buyer for his nukes. She was certain that Olivier would fail; the old man had been continuously drunk since the '70s. Philippe hired him only because they worked together before Philippe retired. *That doesn't say much for Philippe's judgment. Maybe he's getting careless.*

Everything would have been so much easier had Philippe been just a tiny bit more stupid. Her mission would be over by now and she'd be back home. But his paranoid security procedures made it impossible for her to find out where he'd taken the warheads. The only way she could contact him was through e-mail, which unlike phones or the post could not easily be traced to a physical location.

She was going to have to do what he wanted. Hildreth would give her a name, she would send it on to Philippe, and hope that things worked out.

Derek was a complication. She put down the maps and watched him sleep. Ordinarily she liked to keep things simple. Most men would have forced her to kill them by now, but he demonstrated an intriguing mixture of rebellion and compliance. He'd saved her mission in the Bureau's office, and he knew computers, which might be useful. And he *was* rather handsome. She'd been alone for a long time. She leaned back in the chair. *This could get interesting.*

* * *

Someone knocked on the front door. Carla was on her feet with her gun in her hand before she knew she was awake. Morning light seeped in around the edges of the blinds covering the den's only window. Derek slept soundly on the couch, lying on his back with one arm over his eyes. Carla checked her watch. It was almost seven, time to get up anyway. As the knock came again, her ears rang with the surge of adrenaline. *Why don't they just ring the bell?*

She shook Derek and called his name, but he didn't wake up, so she pulled his arm out of the way and slapped his face, hard. He jerked up abruptly, mad but awake. "We have company."

"What?"

"Someone's at the door."

"Oh, shit," he said. "Just ignore it. Maybe they'll go away."

"Get up. Maybe it's just the paper boy, but it could be your mob pals. If they won't go away, get them to come inside—and shut the door behind them."

Whoever it was knocked again, a lot louder this time. Carla followed Derek to the front door and stood just inside the empty living room—out of sight from the foyer, but if someone looked in the front window they'd see her. Too bad; she didn't have time to come up with anything better.

Derek looked at her pleadingly one more time, and she lifted her gun in argument. He looked exactly as if he'd spent the night on the couch in his clothes. His clothes were rumpled, his hair stuck straight up in places, and his face was puffy. He peered through the peep hole in the door, said, "Oh, shit," and opened it.

"Jesus, Derek," a man's voice said, "you look like crap." That wasn't the paper boy or a salesman, and the voice sounded too cultured to be mob; it was authoritative, brisk. Carla took a deep breath to steady herself.

"Come on in, Chapa," Derek said. *Chapa?* The name sounded familiar. Carla heard Derek open the door wider and two people walked in. The visitor spoke again.

"This is Special Agent Shaffer. I think you two spoke on the phone last week."

Bureau! What the hell were they doing here? And they knew Derek and seemed friendly—they weren't here to arrest him. Had the whole break-in at the field office been some kind of trap? No; more likely a sting. What had she stumbled into?

So many things were clicking into place that she missed the next few exchanges between Derek and the agents. She'd thought the security at the field office was unbelievably primitive. They must have disabled part of the system to let Derek do his thing. That had been good luck for her. And the paper she'd seen him stuff in his pocket: it was a plant, because they didn't think he could break into their computers. They'd probably be astonished to know that he *had* hacked in—or had he?

"—didn't see you leave. When you didn't check in last night, we got worried. What time did you leave the building?"

"Come on in," Derek said, "we can talk in the kitchen."

Carla heard him shut the door and they started walking toward the kitchen. She whipped around the wall with her gun held firmly in both hands. One of the agents was a woman. The man was closer, less than three feet away. She pointed her gun right at his head and moved farther out into the foyer.

"Would you like some coffee, Agent Chapa?" she said pleasantly.

The agents slowly raised their hands. Chapa started turning his head to look at Derek, but Carla clucked at him and he turned back.

"What the hell is this?" he said calmly. "We're federal agents. Put the weapon down, ma'am, and step back."

"Derek," Carla said without taking her eyes off the agents, "frisk them." She saw something change in Chapa's eyes. *That's right, this is no mistake.*

"What?" Derek said.

She frowned without looking at him. "Goddamn it, Derek, don't you watch TV? *Frisk* them!"

"Derek," Chapa said, "don't be an ass. We're federal agents, for Christ's sake. Step aside and let me talk to this—who are you, anyway?"

Carla ignored him, keeping him covered. She stepped back and to the side to keep a clean line of fire while Derek patted him down. Chapa was a few inches shorter than Derek. He could stand to lose ten or twenty pounds. His wiry black hair was going gray and his eyes looked tired.

Derek pulled a pistol out of a holster under Chapa's coat, a Colt nine millimeter. He held it firmly, with the muzzle pointed down. "That's it," he said. Carla wondered if he'd thought for a second about turning the gun on her, but he was playing it smart.

"Step over to your left," Carla told Chapa. "Keep your hands up."

Chapa backed out of the way. Derek gingerly patted down the woman. Shaffer kept her blue eyes on Carla the entire time. She was in her mid-thirties, average height, athletically slender. Her blonde hair was tied back from a pretty, round face. Something about the way she blinked seemed strange. *Contacts.* Derek took Shaffer's gun, a Glock compact nine millimeter. *Good taste.* Carla had always preferred Glocks.

Derek stepped back with the weapons.

"No backup pieces?" Carla said. "I'm surprised." She gestured with her gun. "Into the kitchen." When the agents had passed her, she took the guns from Derek, who looked relieved to give them up.

"You are in deep, deep trouble, Derek," Chapa said. "You've just committed a felony."

"Oh, shut up," Carla said to keep Derek from whining. "He's under duress. I beat the shit out of him last night—twice." She instructed the two agents to sit at adjacent chairs in the eating nook. Now they couldn't be seen from the front of the house; there would be another pair of agents waiting out there. "Derek, go get some duct tape or something to tie them up with."

"Don't do it, Derek," Chapa said.

"I told you to shut up," Carla said, tapping him lightly on the head with the barrel of her pistol. "Go on, Derek."

"Sorry, Chapa," Derek said. "You have no idea." He went out to the garage.

With the gun muzzle against Chapa's head, Carla reached under his coat and plucked handcuffs from his belt. "Hands," she said. He put his hands behind his back and she cuffed him, then did the same with Shaffer. She walked around the table, took the phone on the counter off the hook, and leaned against the bay window, studying them.

"Would you mind not pointing that at me?" Chapa said. She was still covering him. "It would ruin my day if it went off accidentally."

"Don't worry," Carla said, but he didn't seem reassured.

"What is it you want? Do you work for the Gugliemos? How do you think you're going to get away with kidnapping federal agents?"

Carla just kept looking at him. They stared back, probably memorizing her face, but Carla didn't care. In a moment, Derek came back with a roll of strapping tape, the thin kind with threads running through it.

"No duct tape?"

"This is stronger," he said, and she snorted.

"Tape their legs to the chair." Derek pulled out a small pocket knife to cut the tape. When he was done, she told him to do the same with their arms. "Does your notebook computer have a modem?"

"Sure."

"Good. Pack it up, and grab some clothes, too. Hurry." He rushed off. "Your timing is lousy, Chapa," she said. "If you'd come a few minutes later, we'd have already been gone, and you'd have been spared all the ribbing you're going to get at the office for the next year."

"You can still get out of this alive," Chapa said. "Put down your weapon, untie us, and no one will hurt you."

Carla laughed. "You've got balls, Chapa, but Derek was right. You really have no idea what's going on." Derek hustled past on his way upstairs. "If you weren't Bureau," she told Chapa, "you'd be dead right now. So just be thankful, and shut up."

Derek was taking too long. She didn't want to call to him—she didn't want the agents to think she was getting nervous. As she was starting to consider what to do if he didn't come back soon, she heard a toilet flush. A moment later he clumped down the stairs carrying a small suitcase.

"I've got to pee," she said.

"Okay."

"Come with me." She holstered her gun, picked up the agents' pistols, and went into the bathroom near the garage. "Sit down right there." She pointed to the wall across from the bathroom door, then, without shutting the door, dropped her pants and sat on the toilet, watching him. He turned his face away in embarrassment and she smiled to herself. *Delicate sensibilities.* When she was done, they went back to the kitchen. The agents stopped struggling and looked up as the two of them walked through the door.

"You might as well take it easy," Carla said. She could see anger and repressed fear on their faces. "Your friends are going to walk through that door in two minutes to free you, so don't bruise yourselves trying to get loose. Derek! Grab your things. We're leaving."

Carla walked into the family room and dropped the agents' guns into her bag. Derek grabbed his keys, wallet, and the computer. They retrieved their coats from the den and went out into the garage.

She pointed to the car. "What is this thing?"

"SVX."

"What?"

"Subaru. Sports car. It's fast."

"Good. Get in."

Carla opened the driver's door, threw her bag into the back, and swung easily into the low seat. It was a two-door vehicle; Derek had some trouble flipping the seat forward so he could get his gear into the back. As he sat down, she held out her hand for the keys, and he dropped them into her palm, frowning. She started it up and the engine hummed. Derek reached up to the visor for the garage door opener, but Carla caught his wrist and smiled at him.

"Let's make it a surprise," she said.

Derek blanched. "Oh, no." He scrabbled for his seat belt.

"Good idea." When they were both fastened in, she revved the engine up to a screaming 5,000 RPMs, released the parking brake, and popped the transmission into reverse.

The little black car exploded through the garage door. Aluminum struts were flung into the air like javelins and plywood shards strafed the air. Carla managed to keep the car under control for just under one second, until they reached the street, but she lost it when she hit the bump at forty miles an hour. The front of the car fishtailed and the rear end slammed into the left front corner of a gray sedan parked alongside the planting bed in the center of the cul-de-sac.

Carla laughed out loud as she shifted the car to drive. She looked behind her: the other two agents she'd been expecting, one black and bald, the other white with a buzz cut, both beefy and wearing glasses, stared at her incredulously from the front seat of their steaming car. In the rear-view mirror as she peeled away, she saw the agents scramble out of their car and run after her. As she brought her eyes forward, she saw two more men with mouths agape in another car, a white Lincoln parked at the mouth of the cul-de-sac. The driver was swarthy, with slicked-back hair, the passenger had a pockmarked face. Then she squealed out of the cul-de-sac and they were gone.

"Goddamn, Derek," she said, "you were right. This fucker *is* fast!"

She glanced over at him and laughed again. His face was white and he looked as if his heart had stopped. She screeched around two more corners, slowed down to the legal speed limit, and headed toward I-90, still laughing.

Chapter 5

"Holy shit!" Johnnie said. "Did you see that?"

Varnes glanced in the rearview mirror. The two Feds had quit chasing after Narr and were trudging back to his house. What did the morons think, they were going to catch a car on foot? Now that they weren't watching, he pulled a careful U-turn away from the curb and out of the cul-de-sac, driving normally until he turned the corner, then he floored it.

That was definitely Narr in the passenger seat, but Varnes hadn't seen the driver. He hadn't even been positive that the geek was back home until Narr blasted out of his own garage. Interesting exit. Varnes wondered if the two Feds inside were dead. Then he wondered what kind of moronic double-cross Narr thought he was pulling.

"Holy shit!" Johnnie said. "That was—"

"Do something useful," Varnes said. "Call the boss." Johnnie took the phone out of his coat pocket and started pushing buttons, moving his lips silently. Varnes hated it when he did that.

He was only guessing which way Narr had gone. The son of a bitch had a good head start, because the would-be track stars were only thirty feet away from Varnes's car when they gave up and turned back. If he'd peeled out after Narr, they'd have got his license plate number and come looking for him later, and the boss would've killed him for sure. But if it were him rocketing out of here, he'd head for I-90. You could drive that baby all the way to Boston.

Thank God the traffic wasn't bad on these side streets. Eastside traffic could be a bitch.

"Mr. Gugliemo," Johnnie said into the phone. "Shellie wants to talk to you. Hang on."

Varnes took the phone. "We found him, but he's on the move again."

"Where to?" Gugliemo said crossly. He sounded like he'd been asleep. *Shit.*

"I think he's heading toward I-90. We're shooting on over there right now."

They were stuck behind a red minivan going below the speed limit in a no-passing zone on a two-lane road. Varnes edged over to the left—there was no oncoming traffic—and veered into the left lane, roaring past the minivan. The fat-faced mommy driving it jerked away in surprise and almost creamed her little kiddies on a telephone pole. *Learn to drive, bitch.*

"You *think?*" Gugliemo said. "What the fuck is wrong with you guys?"

"We're doing our best, boss," Varnes said. He roared through a stop sign without even slowing down. They were only a block from the freeway, then they were passing directly under it. "It got a little complicated. I don't think I should explain over the phone."

Varnes dropped the phone into his lap and used both hands to take the turn onto the entrance ramp at fifty miles an hour. The tires squealed, the big Lincoln wanted to tip up onto two wheels. Varnes wrestled with it and got the car back under control. He was betting his life that Narr was headed east—it would be too dangerous for him to go downtown. Every cop in the state was going to be looking for him in five minutes. He picked the phone up again as he stomped the gas. The boss was shouting.

"—that crazy fucker and bring him here. I want to know what the hell is going on. If he's two-timing us, I'm gonna grind up his ass and use it for bait all summer."

Gugliemo thought he was a hot-shot fisherman, but he never caught anything but sunburn. It would help if he'd spend even a little bit of the time he wasted on his boat holding a rod instead of having some babe hold *his* rod.

Varnes was passing cars like they were fence posts. The heavy traffic was going the other way, and the few cars driving east were dawdling along. Gugliemo was still ranting in his ear, but Varnes ignored it. He'd be able to tell by a change in pitch when the boss ran out of steam and started saying something worth listening to.

Then he saw the black sports car just ahead of them.

"We got him, boss," he interrupted.

"About fucking time," Gugliemo said. "Stay on his ass, and you bring him back here." He hung up.

"I hate this job." He passed one more car, pulled into the center lane, and slowed down to pace Narr. If things went well he'd be able to stretch this bullshit chase out all day. He wasn't in the mood to deal with Gugliemo in person today.

* * *

"Did you get the license?" Chapa asked Frieder as he sawed away at the tape binding Shaffer's feet. The chef's knife Frieder had found was dull. "Almost done," he told Shaffer, who was waiting patiently.

"No, sir," Frieder said. "They peeled out pretty fast." He'd been standing pretty much at attention ever since he'd freed Chapa; Chapa had insisted on cutting Shaffer loose himself. *He's probably embarrassed as hell.* Well, they all had something to be embarrassed about.

"It had to be Narr's car," Frieder said. "Holbrook's talking to the state patrol right now. We'll have the plate number in a minute."

Chapa finally broke through the strapping tape. It hissed as he peeled it off Shaffer's pant legs.

"She's got our weapons, sir," Shaffer said.

"Yeah, I know."

He looked around the kitchen, walked over to glance into the family room. Shaffer rubbed her wrists. They had been bound for less than five minutes.

"I want a forensics team out here right now," Chapa said. "She must have left prints."

"It might be a good idea," Shaffer said, "to have them go over your office, too." Chapa glanced at her sharply. Shaffer nodded at Frieder. "They didn't see Narr leave the building last night. This morning he shows up with a mysterious woman—"

"She's a pro," Chapa said. "A hitter. I'd bet heavy money."

Shaffer's ponytail bobbed up and down as she nodded agreement. Chapa allowed himself a small smile. It was cute.

"You're right about my office," he said. "Maybe they rendezvoused after Narr left the building, but maybe *she* got in some other way and they left together the same way." He nodded at Frieder. "Okay, get two teams, one here and one in my office." Frieder took out his phone and called the office.

Chapa turned to Shaffer. "Did you notice she had a slight accent?"

"Hard to place," she agreed. "Canadian English, but there was something else. French, maybe, or Russian."

"Check the passport watch list. And I want an artist ready as soon as we get back to the office. Maybe we can get a hit from IIS." The Intelligence Information System was used to ID unidentified subjects. If you had a good sketch or photograph, the system could pop out a name—*if* the suspect was in the system.

Holbrook barged in the front door. "We got the license," he said. "The car matches one registered to Narr. I ordered a state-wide APB."

"Good," Chapa said. He looked around again. There was nothing else he could learn here, and he didn't want to make forensic's job any harder. He gestured to Shaffer and they went outside.

It looked as if a bomb had gone off in the garage. Metal struts and chips of plywood littered the driveway and hung from the surprisingly small, ragged hole. Skid marks led down the entire length of the driveway to Frieder's car, which was still smoking. Chapa shook his head: if he had parked *his* car in front of the big door, instead of over to the left by the smaller one, Narr and the woman would have crashed into it and they'd be in custody right now. Stupid mistake.

"Let's go back downtown," he said to Shaffer. "Our tame snitch has become a hitter's lap dog. I want to know why. But mostly I want to know who she is."

Chapter 6

Carla pointed at an exit sign. "I just love the names out here," she said. "*Issaquah.*" She glanced at Derek. He'd got his color back, but he wasn't in a very good mood. That was understandable. "Sorry about your garage."

"My garage? How about my *life?* How am I going to straighten this out? Gugliemo will shoot me on sight and ask questions later—then he'll shoot my corpse because I don't answer him. We're probably on the FBI's Ten Most Wanted list by now. My life is over, and it's *your* fault!"

"You should have told me you were working for the Bureau. If you hadn't lied to me, you wouldn't be in this mess."

"Go to hell. You kidnapped *me,* remember? I had everything under control."

"Bullshit," she said. "You were working a sting for the Bureau, right?" Derek nodded sullenly. "What kind of protection did they offer after they nailed the scuzzbos?"

He turned to face her. "What are you talking about?"

"Did you think Gugliemo was going to sit meekly in jail when he knew who put him there? Did you get any kind of guarantee from the Bureau? Witness relocation—anything?" He just looked at her bleakly. "Listen to me, Derek," she said. "One hour after Gugliemo was behind bars, you've got a contract on your head. One day later, you're dead and the FBI would have another piece of evidence in their case."

"Well, this isn't a whole hell of a lot better."

Carla gave him a few minutes to calm down. She drove carefully just over the speed limit. They had entered the freeway in a light industrial zone, but the buildings petered out into low wooded hills until they reached Lake Sammamish, where the houses crowded together at the waterfront and thinned out the farther they climbed up the surrounding slopes. As she drove toward Issaquah, they entered the foothills of the Cascade mountains.

Most of the hillsides, some of whose crests were white with snow, were covered in dark green firs that from a distance made them look fuzzy. The evergreens were interrupted occasionally by small towns, ugly clear-cuts, and stands of bare-branched deciduous trees. One hill was denuded and half gone, in the process of being chewed away by heavy quarrying equipment.

The car was quick, very comfortable, and it hugged the road like a snake. Half of the traffic heading east was commercial trucks, many of them pulling two or three trailers, and even on the hills she passed them easily. She looked at Derek again. He was staring out the side window, apparently calm.

"Tell me about the sting," she said. "The scuzzbos muscled you..."

"I didn't want to do it. I tried to turn them down, but they insisted. There were some clumsy threats. I told them I didn't think it could be done. They said they had confidence in me."

"So you went straight to the Bureau."

"Yeah. I figured, if these guys were too stupid to take no for an answer, fuck 'em." He shifted in his seat. "Chapa arranged to have some of the security systems disabled, and he had the information I needed printed out and waiting for me. All I had to do was put on a show for the idiots watching from across the street."

"Then you hand over the goods and the Bureau gets it on tape and nails them for conspiracy, racketeering, B&E, and about twenty other federal crimes."

Derek nodded glumly. He hadn't really given a lot of thought to what would happen after.

"Well," she said, "so maybe I saved your life by pulling you out of there. Now we're even, because I owed you one. If they hadn't gutted their security to let you in, I might not have been able to get in, either."

"What's this about? Who's this guy in Montana?"

"The less you know," she said, "the better off you are." He grunted in disgust. "I know you think that's bullshit, but it's true. In a few days this will be over, and despite what you think now, you'll go back to your life.

The Bureau will grill you like a salmon steak, but if you really have no idea what's going on, they'll let you go." He just stared out the side window.

"Why didn't you try to get away when Chapa showed up at your house?" she said.

Derek looked at her briefly before turning back to the window. "Because it was only three to one."

"There were two more guys outside."

"I didn't know that. I figured you'd kill me, and then you'd probably shoot the agents, too."

Carla nodded. It would help that he wasn't stupid or macho.

The speed limit increased to sixty-five as they started up a long hill. Carla sped up to seventy and turned on the cruise control. Almost immediately, she had to move into the left lane to pass a double-trailer truck that was slowing down on the hill. As she pulled back into the right lane, she caught a movement out of the corner of her eye. In the left-hand mirror she saw a large white car pull abruptly into the passing lane, cutting off a small, red convertible. The white car surged forward. Carla eased off the gas a little, shrinking the space between her and the truck she'd just passed. By the time the white car had reached the front of the truck, there wasn't enough room for it to pull in behind her, so it speeded up again to pass her. Carla glanced over as it passed. The windows were tinted, but she recognized the pockmarked face. It was the same car that had been parked on Derek's street.

The Lincoln pulled into the right lane just ahead of them and slowed down. In a few seconds they were crowding it, and Carla moved into the left lane to pass it.

"Moron," Derek said. "He must be from Idaho. They all do that."

"Do you recognize those guys?"

Derek glanced at the driver as they passed. "You mean these idiots in the Lincoln?"

"They were parked on your street when we blew out of your garage."

"You mean they're following us?"

"Do they look familiar?" Derek started to turn around to look back but Carla stopped him. "Don't," she said. "They must work for Gugliemo."

"What should we do?"

"Nothing for now." She kept an eye on the Lincoln. It continued to drop back slowly until a car with skis on the roof pulled in between them. After a few minutes, the distance between them had stabilized at about five car lengths. They must have panicked when they lost sight of her around that big truck. *Amateurs.*

The road was getting steeper as they climbed toward Snoqualmie Pass. The hills had grown into mountains, most of the sheer slopes still covered in snow, and the trees near the peaks were dusted with fresh snowfall like confectioner's sugar. The road was wet and the sky was dark and overcast, but there was no precipitation. The highway widened into three lanes and Carla found herself passing more trucks and small cars on the grade. Many of the cars were loaded with skis on the roof. A sign announced that they were seven miles from the pass.

The highway had been divided since they got on, but now the opposing lanes were drawing farther away as a ravine widened and deepened between the two sides. The mountains rose up abruptly on their right, forbidding and close. Opaque, laminated sheets of ice covered boulders and walls of rock where small streams had repeatedly frozen as they ran down the nearly vertical faces. The opposing lanes continued to draw away from them, until the gap between them was over a kilometer wide, and the tops of fully-grown firs swayed gently thirty meters below the roadbed.

The surface of the highway was starting to get slushy. Carla pulled into the left lane to give a wide berth to a snowplow blasting slush off to the right. The runny mess clung to the rock faces, adding to the ice already encrusting the wall. She glanced in her rear view mirror. The Lincoln had followed her into the passing lane.

On her left, the guard rails had become banked up with snow. The snow plows must pile it up when they worked to the left, and then it slowly melted. What was left behind looked like a jump ramp leading off into the chasm...

Carla turned off the cruise control and sped up to eighty. Derek shouted in alarm as they hit a patch of slush and skidded. The car's wide tires gave them feeble purchase on the icy road. The road banked left and right in wide curves, following the edge of the mountain from which it had been carved.

"What the hell are you doing?" Derek said. "Slow down!"

The Lincoln had accelerated to keep up with them. When they hit a straight stretch of road, Carla pushed the button to roll down the window and got a shock. The side windows had a black line running from front to back about halfway up, which she had thought was some demented attempt at styling. It was actually the dividing line between the fixed part of the window, above, and the part that opened, below.

"What the hell is this?" she shouted over the frigid air blasting in. Derek seemed to be struggling to come up with an explanation for the window. "Forget it! Take the wheel."

"What?"

"Take the fucking wheel!"

He leaned over and grabbed the wheel with both hands, swerving a little until he got used to steering from the passenger side. He kept his eyes glued to the road, his knuckles white from gripping too hard.

Carla drew her pistol and looked out the side mirror. The Lincoln was pacing them, hanging back about three or four car lengths. They were still climbing toward the pass, now just a few miles away.

"Hold it steady," Carla shouted. She took her foot off the gas, and their car immediately began to slow down. Before the Lincoln's driver could react, he had closed the distance to less than ten meters.

Carla turned in her seat and stuck her right forearm out the window, pointing her gun back at the Lincoln and sighting in the side mirror. She took a deep breath, let half of it out, and aimed at the Lincoln's left front tire. Time slowed down. Their car hit a slippery spot and skidded slightly, but Derek corrected immediately. The Lincoln's driver must have finally touched his brakes, because he was starting to pull back just a bit. It felt to Carla as if she had five full minutes to gauge the cars' relative speeds and deceleration, wind deflection, Derek's slight movements on the wheel. At exactly the right moment, she squeezed the pistol's trigger once, twice. The shots sounded like party poppers in the wind.

The Lincoln's left front tire blew out with a visible explosion, as if the tire had been filled with talcum powder. The car jerked sharply to the left, to the right, and then swerved drastically left. The flat tire hit the snow banked up on the guard rails and the car lofted into the air, corkscrewing in a leisurely clockwise spin. The Lincoln seemed to sink slowly, spinning like a maple seed, until it vanished from sight in the ravine.

Carla grabbed the wheel back just as Derek reflexively let go.

"Jesus Christ!" he said.

She hit the gas and pulled back into the center lane, then closed the window and holstered her weapon. In a moment they were cruising once more just above the speed limit, as if nothing had happened. The rear view mirror showed a column of black, oily smoke rising up out of the canyon. She looked at Derek and grinned.

"Holy shit," Derek said. He looked behind them at the roiling smoke receding in the distance. Then he turned back and settled into his seat. "Holy shit."

Carla glanced at him and smiled again. "Two less scuzzbos."

Chapter 7

The setting sun touched the sere hills of the Massif des Maures to the west. Overhead, sparse tendrils of cloud glowed orange and rosy pink, standing out brilliantly against the deepening blue of the sky. Philippe Sottile pulled on a gray wool cardigan and stepped out onto the balcony outside his living room. The pink granite tiles seemed to glow in the reddish light. He looked out at the cobalt, slightly choppy water of the Gulf de St. Tropez, drew a deep breath of the chilly air, and leaned on the wrought-iron railing. This was his favorite time of day, the lull just before sunset, when the day's worries were behind him and the evening's pleasures hovered just out of reach, enhanced by anticipation.

Somehow, these days, those pleasures rarely lived up to his expectations. *Perhaps I'm getting old.* He pondered without alarm the prospect, not at all imminent, of settling down someday. Should he ever resolve to simplify his life, it would take him years just to decide which one of his three wives to keep.

He thought of calling Camilla, but that happy idea reminded him of an unpleasant duty: he had meant to call Chen this evening. He took his phone out of his pocket and punched in Chen's number. There was no immediate answer, but Philippe let it ring: he knew Chen was home.

"Oui," Chen said at last, yawning audibly.

"Ah, Chen, asleep already?" Philippe said. "Wake up, it's nearly evening. Time to work."

"Philippe, you pestilent dog, leave me alone. I've worked hard all day. Now is the time to sleep."

Philippe could hear Chen sitting up in bed. After a rustling sound came the unmistakable zing-snap of a cigarette lighter opening. Chen exhaled noisily.

"Now that you've ruined my rest, what do you want?"

"You promised you would be ready today. I'm calling to see if you're going to disappoint me again."

"When have I ever disappointed you?" Chen said.

"Too many times to count. Now, tell me you're ready."

"I'm ready."

Philippe waited for him to go on, then sighed. Chen was going to punish him for waking him up.

Augustus Chen was one of Philippe's oldest business partners; only Lanotte had been with him longer. Although he wasn't reliable enough to trust with delicate matters, Philippe used him now and then as a contractor. He was full-blooded Chinese, but Philippe had never been able to determine when or where the man had been born, or what nationality he claimed. Perhaps he didn't know himself.

Once they had got drunk together at Philippe's favorite bar in Ste. Maxime, just around the Gulf from St. Tropez. After half a bottle of Kentucky bourbon, Chen had finally explained his preposterous first name.

His mother had been a whore somewhere in China in the '60s. Somehow she managed to escape the anarchy of the Cultural Revolution and ended up in Hong Kong, convinced that all of China's troubles were caused by the West. She studied history to understand how her god, Mao, had been corrupted. Eventually she traced the West's decrepitude back to the first Roman emperor, Augustus, whom she mistakenly claimed had perverted a healthy republic, and in a fit of contrariness, she named her infant after him.

She never expected anything but pain and disappointment from her son. Even before her death from tuberculosis, Chen had been trying hard to live up to her low esteem, apparently more determined each year to kill himself with substance abuse, bad diet, and imprudent business deals. Philippe didn't like him especially, but he found him useful, if somewhat hard to work with—like right now.

"Details, please," Philippe said. He looked out over the water. The sun was gone and stars were beginning to twinkle, seeming to grow in number as he watched.

"Jensen finished the video this afternoon," Chen said. "I'll have copies made tomorrow."

"Good." Jensen had been working for days on a video to prove to potential buyers that they really had the weapons and knew how to detonate them. "What about the arming boxes?"

"The last one will be ready tomorrow."

"And the delivery van?"

"Monsieur Le Merde, how the hell should I know? Talk to your gorilla."

"Careful," Philippe said. "Lanotte is no ape, he is my best friend." He could hear Chen smoking as he sulked. "Are you checking for messages from Carla and Olivier?"

"Every fucking hour," Chen snapped. "Except when I'm asleep, which isn't very often these days."

"I want to be certain you know the delivery procedures. You've memorized the numbers, the drop points, and so on?"

"How could I forget them? Lanotte makes me go over it again and again. I tell you, I'm ready, I'm just waiting for e-mail from that filthy slut."

Where did that come from? "Ah, that's no way to talk about our comrade," Philippe said. "She's just as important to this operation as you are, my friend." That was a sop to Chen's vanity: he could have been replaced by a reliable answering service.

Chen muttered something that Philippe couldn't quite make out. No one liked Carla, but Philippe's instincts told him that this was something else.

"What did you say?" Philippe said.

"Nothing. Let me go back to sleep, for pity's sake."

"I didn't think you and Carla had spent much time together, Chen. You've only met her once, isn't that so? Or did you two have a... relationship before we left to procure the merchandise?"

Chen was silent for a long time. Finally, he snorted softly.

"No, we never had a *relationship*. I'm just tired, and now I'll need another hit to get back to sleep, thanks to you." He paused again. "You know how she is, Philippe. You never know when she's going to throw you to the floor and decide on the spot whether to fuck you or slit your throat."

Philippe knew this very well. But why did *Chen* know this about a woman he had met exactly once, for half an hour?

"Go back to sleep," Philippe said. Chen grunted and hung up.

So Carla had suborned Chen; but for what purpose? What could Chen possibly give her? Or had she just been playing with him, a little diversion during the anxious days leading up to their Ukraine trip? He would have to talk to Lanotte about this in the morning.

Philippe felt tense. He needed to go out, but first he should call Camilla. He punched in her number in Niterói and checked his watch. It was almost four p.m. there. As he lit a cigarette, he imagined her taking a siesta on her balcony, looking across the Baía de Guanabara to Rio. She would be wearing one of the crisp white shifts that she preferred, with nothing beneath it, and white sandals that complimented her dainty feet. Her long, dark hair would be flying loose in a slight breeze, her skin would be brown from the sun. She was a perfect wife, and his first: so beautiful, so patient. She waited chastely for him to come home from his long business trips, and when he did, that white gown fell gracefully from her smooth shoulders and she was transformed from a chaste, expectant wife into a creature of ravenous fire.

She picked up the phone, and her delicious voice murmured, "Alô?"

"Ma cher Camilla, c'est moi," Philippe said. They spoke for half an hour, pointedly not discussing his business, and talk of the weather soon descended to explicit sexual fantasies. He promised to come home as soon as he could; she promised him unending ecstasy when he did; he pledged his undying faithfulness and said goodbye.

Later that evening, Philippe found a pretty little French girl down in town, with short brown hair, petite breasts, and a small bottom. Although she was as different from his voluptuous, brown Camilla as the sea was from the sky, he bought her a fine dinner and several bottles of wine. After she had seen the Gulf de St. Tropez from his balcony, they played out all the fantasies that he and Camilla had shared over the phone, and he fell asleep curled up contentedly against her firm, boyish rump.

* * *

The warehouse was just one whitewashed stucco building among many. Philippe passed the front entrance and glanced at the house across the street, where the half-mad woman who owned the warehouse lived. At his only meeting with her, before they'd gone to get the missiles, she had cackled like an old woman, though she was in her mid-forties and had been lovely once. Her husband and daughter had died within days of each other a few years back, and grief had curdled her wits.

The woman had urged him to sit down at her filthy kitchen table. She settled across from him, with her smudged face and wild hair. When she offered to read the Tarot for his business and he reluctantly agreed, she swept her arm across the dirty checked tablecloth, knocking encrusted dishes to the stone floor, where they shattered. Slowly she dealt the cards, mumbling constantly, and Philippe forced himself to sit patiently through the tedious process.

She promised him success in his business, declared him to be an honest and steadfast man, and asked for two months' rent. Philippe paid in cash and declined when she wanted to give him a personal reading. It wasn't that he disbelieved—he simply mistrusted readings from the insane.

Philippe walked down the alley that ran alongside the warehouse. The tall building blocked the weak morning sunlight, making the cool morning colder. Halfway down the block he came to a door recessed into the rough stucco wall. He knocked on the metal surface, causing several flakes of green paint to drift to the ground.

The door opened slowly. As Philippe stepped inside, one of Lanotte's hired guards, a thin dark-haired man with a cowlick, nodded to him and closed the door behind him. A dozen or so mercenaries had been hired to patrol the warehouse. The night shift was the largest, but three of them typically manned the doors during the day, with a fourth walking the inside perimeter. Philippe had not bothered to learn their names; they were deferential, but they never spoke to anyone but Lanotte.

The cavernous space was unnecessarily large, but the location was perfect. Port-Grimaud was just a few kilometers down the road, if their buyers should wish to move the merchandise by sea, and access to the highways was easy, with Nice and its airport only seventy-five kilometers away. The mad landlady charged a fair price, and, best of all, the warehouse was within walking distance of Philippe's house.

The building was empty except for the crates piled in its very center, the warheads mixed in with the tractor parts. The air smelled of diesel fuel. As Philippe walked across the bare concrete floor toward the stack of crates, he could hear Jensen and Lanotte talking indistinctly from the opposite side of the pile. He glanced up toward the ceiling hidden in darkness far above. Only the supporting trusses were visible, looking like some giant spider's elaborate web. It was ridiculous to have such a huge space: he could have used a small garage, if it could be defended and if he could pull the van inside. But Jensen had found the place for him, and Jensen had a taste for large, empty buildings.

Philippe found Lanotte sitting on a bar stool, watching Jensen work at a tall bench improvised from empty metal drums, cinder blocks, and thick plywood. Jensen liked to work standing up. He was soldering a circuit board, looking through a large magnifying lamp that hung from a jointed arm. A ring of reflected light shone on the dark brown skin of his face. *Ah, merde, they're talking physics again.*

"I don't understand," Lanotte said in his gravely voice. "Why are there three families? Why not one, or two? Why not an infinite number?" His fleshy face was wrinkled up in confusion or possibly disgust.

"That's just how it is," Jensen said without looking up from his work. He carefully touched the soldering iron to the circuit board, sending up a thin wisp of smoke, and nudged his glasses back up his nose. "No one knows why. The world we see is composed of particles from the first family. The other two families only show up in high-energy accelerators now, but they were very common right after the big bang."

Philippe leaned against a crate and folded his arms. Jensen was constantly trying to teach particle physics to Lanotte, and the giant seemed interested but skeptical. The theories seemed to have nothing whatever to do with the real world.

Lanotte shook his massive head, sending his long blond hair bouncing. "This standard model of yours is bullshit. Every fundamental constant is empirical—the theory can't predict *any* of them." *That's my Jacques.* Lanotte looked stupid and clumsy, but he was neither.

"But it works," Jensen said. "It's one of the most successful theories in history." He unplugged the soldering iron. Turning, he caught sight of Philippe and nodded hello.

"I hate to interrupt the lesson," Philippe said, "but how are we doing? Chen said you're done."

"One minute," Jensen said. He swung the magnifying lamp away and grabbed an aluminum lunch pail that was sitting nearby. With deft fingers he inserted into it the circuit board he'd just finished, snapped on several connectors, swung the lid closed, and handed it to Philippe. "This is the last one." He took off his glasses and rubbed the bridge of his nose.

Philippe turned it in his hands. It looked like a normal lunch box, the sort that a construction worker might take to the job. The outside was shiny, corrugated metal, marred only by two holes that Jensen had drilled in it. Behind one of these was an earphone jack. From the other a small bunch of long wires trailed out, terminating in Y-shaped connectors.

Philippe released the catch and swung up the domed lid. Inside the box were some simple controls, a battery about the size of a pack of cigarettes, and the circuit board Jensen had just finished. Jensen showed him how to operate the controls—knobs and dials with LED displays.

"This turns on the power," he said, pointing to a small toggle. "This dial sets the current time, this one here sets the detonation time. This is the arming switch. This toggle controls the detonation mode: timer or external signal." He indicated the earphone jack. "You can wire this to a cell phone or a radio, or if you're insane you could even use a manual trigger. These wires connect to the warhead."

Philippe closed the lid and hefted the box. He was impressed by its simplicity and small size. "Russian arming boxes are the size of a suitcase," he said.

"Yeah." Jensen grinned with pride. "The American ones aren't much smaller. Primitive stuff, but of course those are supposed to survive battlefield conditions. I used some off-the-shelf components, but there are three EPROMs in there that I programmed myself."

"And we don't need arming codes?"

"Not any more. I bypassed those circuits."

Philippe set the lunch pail back on the workbench and beamed at Jensen. "Excellent work!"

"I have a few final tests to run," Jensen said, "then I'll be done. It should take an hour or so."

"Magnificent!" Philippe turned to Lanotte. "Is the van ready?"

Lanotte nodded and got up from the stool. Philippe followed him to the white van parked just inside the big garage doors.

The vehicle was a full-sized, used Chevrolet van that they had bought from a package delivery service. Philippe opened the passenger door and looked around the inside. Wire mesh separated the front compartment from the rear, which had no windows. Lanotte led him to the back and opened the twin doors. He had installed new carpeting and four bucket seats in the back. A wine cooler was bolted to the floor, and a heavy black cloth, rolled and tied up for now, could be dropped across the mesh to prevent the passengers from seeing outside.

"Perfect," Philippe said.

"I tuned it up," Lanotte said. "It was idling pretty rough."

Philippe closed the doors and leaned back against them, folding his arms. He looked up at Lanotte. "How are the guards working out?"

"Perfectly. They're cautious, they're professional, and they have no curiosity at all."

"Good." Philippe paused a moment. "Something came up when I was talking with Chen last night."

Lanotte grimaced. Philippe knew that he didn't trust Chen. It was true that Chen over-indulged in alcohol and drugs; the man had more vices than a Mexican dog had fleas. But Philippe had thought he knew how to work around them, until now.

"I think Carla may have compromised Chen," Philippe said, and Lanotte's expression shifted from contempt to delight. Lanotte had been looking for an excuse to eliminate Carla ever since he'd met her. "Chen was quite agitated when I mentioned her name, yet they shouldn't have had any contact beyond our first meeting. It doesn't make sense unless she had further contact with him, but I can't imagine what she hoped to gain. See what you can find out, and start working on a plan to cover him during deliveries."

Lanotte nodded, looking happy: at last, a chance to remove the two biggest thorns in his heel.

"You have some contacts in the States, don't you?" Philippe said. Lanotte said he did. "Activate them. I want to know where she is and what she's doing. We'll have to be especially careful of any buyers she sends us."

"We can't let her ruin this deal," Lanotte said.

"Indeed. This is our chance to get seriously, stinking rich, old friend. And when it's done, and we're retired and safe, I have a bonus for you."

Lanotte smiled. "Carla," he said, and the hunger in his voice chilled Philippe's blood.

Chapter 8

Seattle, Washington
  Saturday, February 25, 9:17 p.m.

William Gugliemo closed his eyes in pain and leaned back in his leather chair. It squeaked, and for the third time that day he remembered that he wanted to get someone to fix the damned thing. He felt as if the entire world, including for Christ's sake his office furniture, was out to get him.

The pain in his head wasn't going away, and neither was the bad news, so he opened his eyes. His security chief, Marty Alonso, stood uncomfortably on the other side of the desk, trying to appear both efficient and innocent. Gugliemo didn't want to look at him; he was getting so fat his clothes didn't fit right any more. His belly strained the buttons of his shirt and his doughy face was twisted up into a pleading smirk.

Gugliemo wanted to shoot him, just on principle. The Greeks—or was it the Romans, he could never keep them straight—had the right idea. Someone brings you bad news, you kill the fucker. Not out of blame, but just because it made you feel better. But he couldn't shoot Marty. He needed the fat slob, and he didn't kill people himself any more; that's why he *had* Marty. But it sure would make him feel better.

He looked around the shoddy office. His tastes had become more refined as his fortunes grew, and the simple metal desk and cabinets that he once had thought businesslike now seemed merely cheap. He considered torching the place, but redecorating was probably a better idea.

Just deal with the problem.

"You're telling me," he said, "that no one heard from Shellie after he called me this morning?"

"Right, boss," Marty said.

"And that we found out he was dead because the *cops* came to tell Joyce that they found her husband fricasseed at the bottom of a ravine out by Snoqualmie Pass?"

"Uh huh."

"What time did Joyce find out?"

"About six o'clock."

"Why didn't she call us right away?"

"I think she tried, boss. You were out to dinner, Tony took the call, and he didn't want to disturb you."

"And then Tony went home and left a note on your desk. Which you just found twenty minutes ago?"

"Right, boss."

That does it. I'm going to shoot every one of these goddamned morons and start over. Marty looked even more scared than usual.

"I guess Johnnie was in the car with Shellie," Gugliemo said.

"Uh huh."

"So his mom's probably having a heart attack right now. Did you check on her?"

"Not yet, boss. I can go right now—"

"No, forget it, I never liked the old hag anyway. Let her croak." Gugliemo rubbed his eyes and smoothed down his hair. He was thin in an unhealthy-looking way. Sallow skin was drawn tightly over the bones of his face, with dark smudges beneath his eyes. He hadn't been sleeping well since he'd discovered that the FBI was after him. *What's their problem, anyway? I'm just a small businessman, why can't they go after the big money and leave me alone?*

Gugliemo tapped his upper teeth with the nail of his right index finger.

"So Shellie and Johnnie are dead, we don't know why, and Narr is gone. Right?"

Marty nodded. "The cops told Joyce they think Shellie was driving too fast. He hit a patch of ice and flew off the road."

"Well, we'll take care of Joyce." He didn't really like Joyce; she was scrawny and she thought she was better than everyone because she had a Master's degree. Big fucking deal. But Gugliemo took care of his people, even dumpy widows of smart-asses like Varnes. "I want to know what the fuck is going on with Narr."

"I went by this afternoon to check his house," Marty said. "The garage was busted open, like a bomb went off. There were Feds all over the place, though, so I couldn't get a close look. I don't think Narr was home."

"Of course he's not home, you dope. Shellie said he was heading toward I-90. Then he was *on* I-90 and he told me he had him." Gugliemo thought for a moment, then realized that he'd missed something. "Wait a minute. Why are the *Feds* at Narr's house? Did the dumb shit mess up and leave prints?"

"I don't know, boss."

"Well, you don't know much, do you?" Marty cringed.

Gugliemo was confused. Could Narr have taken out Shellie? No, that was impossible, Narr was just a computer nerd and a cheap B&E man. Shellie's accident must have been... an accident. He was headed east on I-90, so Narr might be out of Washington by now. There wasn't much east of Seattle until you got to Spokane, and who would stop there? What the hell was Narr doing?

Now I'm in a fucking pickle. He still didn't know what the FBI was up to, and the guy that was supposed to tell him was on the run. If the Feds got to him, Gugliemo would be in worse shape than ever. Narr would spill his guts and the Feds would put Gugliemo away.

Marty was fidgeting. Gugliemo sighed in exasperation.

"We've got to find Narr and take him out," Gugliemo said. "Call Maroni's people in Vegas. We're going to need some help."

"Okay, boss," Marty said, and, pathetically relieved, he scuttled out of the room.

Gugliemo tried to think it through. Narr had either found something really juicy and was running to hide it, or he'd screwed up the break-in and was simply running away. Either way, if the Feds were at his house, they had to be after him, too. Gugliemo had to get to him first. Well, with help from Maroni's guys, that shouldn't be too hard. And Gugliemo wanted him alive. He wanted to find out what Narr had learned, and why he was running. That could be fun; that might take a few days. By the time he got done, Narr would be begging for a bullet.

Then Gugliemo would break his own rule about not shooting people and give him one—personally.

Chapter 9

Seattle, Washington
Saturday, February 25, 11:12 p.m.

Kevin Chapa relaxed on his thinking couch, staring at the ceiling. They weren't getting anywhere. Derek and the woman were long gone. They had an APB out on Derek's car, but it had apparently vanished. They had two sets of prints from Derek's house, one of which was Derek's and the other wasn't in the computer. The forensic team hadn't found anything in Chapa's office but his own prints.

Chapa turned his head and looked at Shaffer, who was sitting in a big easy chair by the schefflera tree. *Oops.* He got up and went into the kitchen for the watering can. He watered the five-foot tree liberally, then looked it over. The thin, lobed leaves were dark green and shiny. They appeared to be healthy, although he couldn't remember the last time he'd watered the thing. Shaffer watched this ritual tolerantly. Chapa sat down on the couch, facing her.

"Any ideas?" he said.

"I was thinking about calling Myron."

Chapa, surprised, examined her face carefully. Her blue eyes sparkled even in the low light of the single-bulb lamp in the corner. She had one of those round faces; not fat, just... round. Her blonde hair was tied back, and now that he thought of it, he'd never seen it *not* tied back. She was quite pretty, actually. She looked back at him serenely. *Maybe she's over him.*

"Why?" he said.

"We're not getting anywhere on the woman. I thought he might be able to help."

He considered her again. "Are you okay with that?"

"Kevin," she said, with exasperation he was pretty sure was feigned. He loved it when she called him by his first name, which was never on duty, which meant almost never at all.

"Emily," he said.

"Myron and I broke up two years ago. I'm over him."

"Sure," Chapa said. "Whatever you say. You want to go through channels?"

"Takes too long. I lived with the guy for three years, I think I'm entitled to ask him for a favor now and then."

"I don't think the CIA would agree with you."

"Okay," she said, "you're the boss. You want me to go through channels?" Her voice grew chilly. "Sir, I know someone in the CIA who may be able to help us in our current investigation. Would you like me to file a request through the proper channels for his assistance?"

Chapa couldn't hold back a grin. "Nah. Takes too damned long."

They glared at each other for moment in mock contest. Finally, he lay back down on the couch.

"You got anything else?"

"I have a few ideas," Shaffer said. "I want to go back to the office for a while to check them out."

Chapa felt a disappointment he couldn't name. "Anything you want to talk about?"

"Not yet. I'll give you a report at our morning meeting. I still need to think them through."

"This is a pretty good thinking couch," he said. "You could think here."

"No," Shaffer said, "I couldn't." She stood up.

"Okay." Chapa waved his hand at her. "Eight o'clock sharp."

"Good night, sir." She headed for the door.

"Hey, Emily." She turned with her hand on the doorknob. "Don't call me 'sir' when we're off duty, okay?"

"Yes, sir," she said, grinning.

"And it's Saturday night, for Christ's sake. Relax for a few hours, huh? Working too hard is bad for your complexion."

"I'll try to remember that." She gave him a look. He knew that look, and he knew that they both wanted to find this woman so badly it made their trigger fingers itch. She'd tied them up and stolen their weapons. Even ignoring the humiliation, the paperwork on *that* would keep them busy for weeks.

After he heard her car drive off, Chapa closed his eyes and tried to sort out just what it was that he wanted. Shaffer was very smart and an efficient agent. She had degrees in chemistry and political science, and had worked on two congressional election campaigns, both successful, before joining the Bureau. He hated the idea of trying to do without her. She'd played a critical role in nearly every major case he'd worked on since he'd moved to Seattle from Miami six years ago.

On the other hand, he was starting to feel that old tug in his chest, that familiar hollow sensation that he remembered so clearly, even though the last time he'd felt it was twenty years ago when he met his ex-wife. What do you do when you're falling in love with someone that works for you?

I guess you just ignore it. He turned his thoughts back to Derek and the mystery woman.

* * *

Chapa drummed his fingers on his desk. Shaffer was fifteen minutes late. Weak, gray light filtered through the low clouds outside, and then through the half-closed blinds of his office. Frieder and Holbrook sat beside each other in identical postures: left leg crossed over right knee, right hand holding papers or folders, left arm cocked with fist on hip, wearing nearly identical eyeglasses. They looked like photographic negatives of each other, Frieder black and bald and Holbrook white and bristly. *These guys have been working together too long.*

Shaffer rushed in and closed the door behind her.

"Sorry I'm late, sir," she said, and sat in the last empty chair. She brushed back a strand of hair that had worked loose from her ponytail and started sorting through the papers she was holding.

Frieder gave her a disgusted look and spoke first. "Okay, still no results from the APB, but something interesting turned up on I-90 yesterday morning. There was a fatality accident around eight o'clock, two guys driving a white Lincoln Continental went off into a ravine and got cooked."

"So?" Chapa said.

"The driver was Sheldon Varnes, a known associate of William Gugliemo."

Chapa nodded. "Yeah, I know Shellie. He's the only smart guy in Gugliemo's entire organization."

"It took the State Patrol a while to bring the car up out of the ravine and ID the stiffs."

"Too bad," Chapa said. "What's the point?"

Frieder smiled. He had perfect, white teeth, which Chapa found odd since the man smoked like a volcano.

"Two witnesses to Varnes's accident reported that a black Subaru SVX had been driving erratically just ahead of the Lincoln immediately before it took its dive. One of the witnesses was a truck driver. He said the Subaru passed him going at least eighty-five."

"The trucker was probably doing eighty," Holbrook said.

"Not on that hill," Frieder said. "They were about two miles west of Snoqualmie Pass when Varnes bought it." Frieder looked down at the paper in his hand. "The Patrol interviewed three other witnesses. None of them noticed the Subaru." He sat back, pleased with himself.

Chapa said, "Are you saying that was Derek's car and Shellie was chasing him?"

"Yes, sir," Frieder said. "That's what I think. The timing works out perfectly."

"I agree. So, we have Derek and the woman heading east on I-90 from the pass. What have you got, Shaffer?"

Shaffer rearranged a few more pages in her pile before looking up. "Sir, I think I know the woman's identity and their destination."

The three men sat in stunned silence for a moment.

"What?" Chapa said.

Shaffer smiled at them and brushed the hair out of her face again.

"We got nothing from IIS on the artist's sketch of the woman. We can't match her face with any mug shots in the system. But I gave the picture to the CIA and they found her. It's an 89%-confidence match."

"Hold it," Frieder said. "You gave a picture to the CIA and they *found* her? Overnight? It takes a week to get that kind of shit through channels." He looked in appeal to Chapa, who just shrugged.

"I know someone," Shaffer said. "He owed me a favor."

Frieder stared at her for a moment, then leaned back in his chair. "Walkenshaw," he said. Chapa was impressed; he'd thought he was the only person in the Seattle office who knew about Shaffer's thing with the spook. But she ignored Frieder and looked down at the top sheet in her stack.

"Her name is Carla Citrullo," she said. "She's a Mossad agent."

"What!" Chapa rose halfway up out of his chair.

"Yes, sir," Shaffer said. "She works for Israel's secret service." Chapa dropped back into his chair. "That's why she's in the CIA computers. The agency has known about her for five years, but there's no record of any previous activity in the U.S. They don't know much about her, and they don't have prints, but they do have rumors from several informants that the Mossad has been looking for her for a couple of years."

Chapa frowned. "What do you mean, looking for her? You said she worked for them."

"My, uh, contact thinks that she may have gone freelance. AWOL."

"Jesus Christ," Chapa said. "A renegade Mossad agent. How did she hook up with Narr? And why?" *And no wonder she could handle us like sheep.*

No one said anything. Frieder looked positively sour; he wasn't going to be much help for a while until he got over being upstaged by Shaffer.

"What else have you got in there?" Chapa asked her.

"We got two clear sets of prints from Derek's house. One set is his. We assumed the other prints were from this woman, Citrullo."

"Right," Chapa said. "But the second set isn't in the computer, and you just said the CIA doesn't have her prints, either."

"No, sir, but I found those same unidentified prints here."

"Nope," Frieder said, wagging his head. "Forensics said this office was clean."

"Not in your office, sir," she said to Chapa, ignoring Frieder. "In the east stairwell."

Chapa smiled. He felt proud of her, and a resurgence of his affection from last night that he sternly fought down. Beneath that, he felt the thrill of the hunt. He knew Shaffer: she was just getting started.

"Special Agent Shaffer," he said, "why were you looking in the east stairwell? That's outside of our office—it's even outside our security."

"Yes, sir. But they had to get out somehow. Frieder and Holbrook didn't see Derek leave. We checked the tapes on the security cameras, so we're sure he didn't go out the front door. And yet we know he left that night. So last night I walked around the floor, trying to figure another way out. I ended up in the east stairwell. Her prints were all over the doorknob on this floor, and on a broomstick in the stairway."

"A broomstick?" Holbrook said. "Did she fly in?" No one laughed.

"She must have used it to jigger the acoustic tiles. I think they crawled through the ceiling."

"Where does that stairwell come out?" Chapa said.

"At the loading dock off Marion Street," Shaffer said. "It's half a block up from the entrance Derek used. That's how they missed him." She very carefully didn't turn her head to look at Frieder, but no one could have missed the derision in her voice. "Derek goes in alone by one door, but he comes out with a woman by another. We were looking for a solitary man. He walked right past us."

Chapa glanced at Frieder, whose eyes were closed in pain. Holbrook looked confused.

"So we know she was in the building," Chapa said, "and they must have left together." He looked at the papers in her hands. "What else?"

"She didn't leave any prints in your office," Shaffer said. "Maybe she got Derek to do all the work, and he would have been wearing gloves, or maybe she wiped her prints. But she's Mossad, so I decided to assume that she'd been in this room with Derek."

"Okay," Chapa said tentatively.

"Well, she must have had a reason to be here, and we know they entered separately. Derek implied that he was being coerced, and she said so herself. So I wondered if they actually logged on to your computer."

"Hold it right fucking there," Frieder said. "That's impossible."

"He's right," Chapa said. "I never gave Derek a login."

"It's not supposed to be possible," Shaffer agreed. "But what if it is? Remember that Derek does this for a living: he breaks into offices and computer systems. *I* wouldn't know how to break into our system, but that doesn't mean it's impossible."

Chapa snorted. "Go on."

Shaffer glanced at the papers in her hands. "I had the sysop check the log. Someone logged onto your computer at 8:07 p.m. two days ago. There was no login ID—the sysop said that's impossible. When I pushed he said *maybe* they could have used a back door."

"What's that?" Holbrook said.

"It's a loophole," Frieder told him. "A programmer can leave a secret password in a system to let himself back in after it's finished."

"Let's remember when this is over," Chapa said, "to go after the guy who installed the computers." He suppressed a laugh when Shaffer made a note. "So, what did our hacker do after he used the back door?"

"He got into WPP," Shaffer said: the Witness Protection Program. "He printed out the short file on a John Hildreth." She held up a duplicate of the file Derek had printed. "His new name is Roscoe and he lives in Montana."

"So that's why they're headed east on I-90. Who is this guy Hildreth?"

"He was an arms dealer," Shaffer said. "He gave himself up for immunity and relocation, and he sold out a bunch of suppliers, including some very big names in Europe."

She handed over all her papers. Chapa looked them over: fingerprint matches, the CIA file on Citrullo, blueprints of the seventh floor, sysop log for the night Derek broke in, and the dossier on Hildreth. He picked up his phone and ordered a Bureau jet to take them to Montana.

"Frieder," he said, "I want you to copy all this stuff and contact the CIA—Shaffer can give you Myron's number." Frieder smirked at her. "See if they're willing to talk to the Mossad and get Citrullo's file." He handed the papers to Frieder, who nudged Holbrook. The two of them left together.

Chapa got up and walked out from behind his desk. "You don't like them much, do you?" he asked Shaffer.

"I don't have anything against them personally. But they're fuck-ups."

"They've had some successful cases."

"You're the boss. But run their stats some time. They're fuck-ups."

He shook his head and gestured her out the door.

"We're leaving from Boeing field in an hour," he said as they walked down the hall. "Get hold of the resident agencies in Kalispell, Missoula, and Helena. Tell them we think Citrullo is going after Hildreth and we want a full-scale intervention. I want air photos—new ones. I want at least a dozen agents, and a helicopter."

Chapter 10

Derek awoke to the sound of the shower running and didn't know where he was. Then he remembered and rolled onto his back, stuffed both pillows behind his head, and gazed up drowsily at the grimy plaster ceiling.

After shooting out their pursuers' tire, Carla had driven on as if nothing unusual had happened. The smoke from the burning car was visible for only a moment before the twisting road put half a mountain between them and the scene of the murder. Stunned, Derek watched silently as they reached the pass with its ski resorts and hotels. The highway nearly doubled in width to allow vehicles room to maneuver and pull off. Buses and cars with ski racks jammed the parking lots, and the ski lifts were full. Then they passed the hubbub and started down the long slope out of the Cascades.

As they left the mountains behind and entered the rain shadow of the Cascades, the lush growth of trees thinned out. Just outside Ellensburg, the last pine disappeared behind them. Steep hillsides of lush grasses faded into rolling hills covered with gray and dusty sagebrush. When they crossed the Columbia River, flowing placid and wide through the arid hills, Derek finally came up with something to say, but before he could say two words, Carla told him to shut up.

They stopped in Spokane to get gas. Derek asked if she wanted to change drivers, but Carla only laughed. After they left I-90 for Route 2, he tried again.

"How long are you planning to hold me hostage?" he said.

"You're not my hostage. Who would ransom you?"

"Okay, your prisoner."

"You're not a prisoner, either. Let's just say you're a... reluctant volunteer."

"You have a gift for euphemism," Derek said. "Let me be more clear. When the *fuck* are you going to let me go?"

Carla looked at him briefly before turning her eyes back to the road. She seemed to be enjoying driving *his* car.

"I'll make a deal with you, Derek," she said. "I need your help with one more thing. If you do it, and don't try to escape or get me arrested in the meantime, I promise I'll let you go tomorrow."

"You're just going to let me go."

"Sure."

Yeah, right. "What's this thing you want me to do?"

"I want you to send an e-mail message for me."

"*What?*" She didn't respond. "We could have done that from my house last night! Why did you have to tie up those FBI agents, kill a carload of innocent people, and drive to Montana just to send an e-mail?"

"Because the information I need is in Montana."

"With this Hildreth guy?"

"Right."

Derek looked out the window, trying to fight back rage and frustration. As the desert gave way to the foothills of the Rockies, the landscape was growing greener again. Evergreen trees were scattered thinly on the hills. *How did I get into this mess?* Unfortunately, the answer was infuriatingly clear, and she was driving his car. He turned back to face her.

"Are you going to tell me what this is all about?"

"If I tell you, I can't let you go," Carla said. "Your choice."

"You mean, you'll kill me." She didn't respond, which was answer enough. "Why should I trust you? How do I know you'll really let me go?"

"I have no reason to lie to you, and anyway you don't have a lot of options. You can try to escape, or try to contact the Bureau, or you can cooperate for one more day and then you'll be free. There's only one choice where you wind up still breathing."

Derek couldn't see any way out. How bad could it be to just go along? He'd seen enough to be sure she could kill him if she wanted to—quickly and easily, with no regrets. If he trusted her and played along, he'd be no worse off. One more day...

"Do we have a deal?" she said.

"Okay. I'll help you send your e-mail. And tomorrow you let me go."

They pulled into Kalispell around five in the evening. Carla went into a motel office to register and didn't seem concerned whether Derek would stay put—but she did take the car keys. She had him call out for a pizza, and while they waited she studied a local map that she'd bought in the motel office. Derek tuned the TV to an old black and white movie and watched it without understanding what he was seeing.

After they ate, Derek brushed his teeth and took a shower. When he came out of the bathroom, wearing only his UW running shorts, Carla was still reading the map. He started to get into the bed by the door, but she wordlessly pointed to the other one. Shrugging, he slid between the musty-smelling sheets and instantly fell asleep.

* * *

Now he watched for Carla to come out of the bathroom. He had no idea what to expect: she might stride out nude, or wearing slinky lingerie or a long cotton nightgown. After a few minutes she did come out—in black jeans and a blue flannel shirt hanging outside her pants, but barefoot. Her short, curly hair was still wet, uncombed. She carried a small, floral-patterned grip.

"Get going," she said, and he rolled out of bed and walked stiffly to the bathroom. This was not like any motel experience he'd ever had before. During the years he'd compulsively cheated on Marjorie, he'd seen more than his share of cheap motels with women he barely knew. He wasn't normally shy, but now he found himself acutely aware that he was wearing nothing but shorts. He was grateful that his morning erection had subsided, but Carla was ignoring him, searching for something in her duffel bag. *Probably looking for more bullets.*

After using the toilet, Derek shaved the two-day stubble from around his mustache with an electric razor, got dressed, and they went outside. The windshield was covered in frost. Derek found an ice scraper behind the passenger seat and started clearing the windows as Carla started the car.

The morning was clear and sunny, but bitterly cold. The wind blew right through the field jacket that had always been perfectly adequate for Seattle's mild winters. He hadn't thought to bring a heavier coat, or a hat and gloves. By the time he was done scraping, Derek's hands were stiff and blue.

At the gas station down the road from the motel, Carla got out to work the pump, so Derek went into the Quik-Mart. He found a Montana highway map that was easier to read than Carla's smudgy county map, then spotted a big coffee urn in the corner. He poured two large cups—knowing somehow that she would sneer at cream and sugar—and picked out a box of cinnamon doughnuts. Carla came inside and paid for everything without a word. The clerk was a stout young woman with chapped cheeks and cracked lips, wearing a frayed green apron the same color as the sign outside. She glanced from Carla to Derek and back, as if expecting *him* to pay, but she took the money without comment.

They headed north up Route 93. Only a foot of snow lay on the ground and the road was dry. Cinders skittered under the tires. Very shortly they had left the small town of Kalispell behind.

Derek nearly spilled his coffee in the struggle to fold the new map so that it showed only the northwest corner of the state. Between sips, he studied the area. Cinnamon and sugar from his doughnut fell like tiny hailstones onto the Rocky Mountains.

"What's this guy's address?" he asked Carla. She lifted her butt off the seat so she could pull Hildreth's dossier out of her back pocket and hand it to him. Derek unfolded the paper gingerly—it was still warm from her body heat. The address was near the bottom of the sheet: Route 37, Rexford. He looked at his road map, using his thumbnail and the map's scale to measure the distance. "It looks like we drive sixty miles north on 93, then just past Eureka we turn left onto 37." He folded up the dossier and tossed it onto the dashboard. "This guy lives in the middle of nowhere."

"No, he doesn't. Tactically, it's not a bad location. He's isolated, but not far from a major highway and a reasonably large town. And he's only ten miles from the Canadian border, so he could hop across if anybody official came looking for him." She glanced at him. "Our Mr. Hildreth is a rabbit."

"Well, I hope he's not a killer rabbit."

"You leave Hildreth to me," Carla said, taking a sip of coffee. "If he has big, nasty teeth, I'll pull them."

Just outside the small town of Whitefish they passed a large resort hotel and a golf course. Derek expected to see at least one or two groups of fanatic duffers playing in the snow, but the links were abandoned.

They plunged into the forest. Dense Douglas fir and lodgepole pine crowded up almost to the roadway on both sides. Derek was surprised that so many of the trees were dead, until he realized they must be western larch, a deciduous pine. He checked his map again. The Whitefish Range was supposed to be off to their right, but all he could see were the trees. Without warning, the forest vanished as they came to a clear-cut. Mountains loomed in the distance like gigantic shark's teeth, blazing white with snow above metallic gray granite. In the foreground, a devastation of trunks and piles of slash spread for hundreds of acres. The ground itself looked corrugated, and the thin blanket of snow did nothing to hide the ugly scars of heavy machinery, but soon the trees closed back in around them.

As the woods slowly grew thinner on their right, Derek spied a tiny town in the distance, off the path of the highway. Over the next few miles, he saw other bypassed hamlets that the road had missed, and thereby doomed. The beauty of the scenery lulled him almost to sleep. He remembered early-morning drives with Marjorie to go hiking in the North Cascades. Whenever she drove on those trips, he invariably fell asleep long before they reached the mountains. But when Derek drove, the rhythm of forest and mountains, punctuated by small, seedy towns, hypnotized him without making him sleepy and left him wondering why he didn't leave the city more often. Would he ever get the chance to go hiking again?

* * *

A wooden sign declared, "Population 1102." Derek didn't think that Eureka—Greek for "I have found it"—was a good name for a town whose only major road was the federal highway: he doubted whether anyone had ever found what they were looking for here. Carla drove into an empty parking lot, cracked asphalt surrounded by misshapen piles of snow and cinders. Since they'd arrived in town, they'd seen only two other cars. Everyone must be at church.

"Come on," Carla said. She led him to a phone booth outside a small, closed grocery store and paged impatiently through the thin phone book, which covered a dozen communities in the Whitefish area. Derek peered between large white posters advertising the weekly specials into the darkened store, seeing nothing but tall, deserted aisles.

"Stupid," she said. Derek looked at her, but she wasn't talking to him. "Now I've got you."

"What?"

"He's in the book," Carla said as she punched in the number.

The FBI dossier gave Hildreth's phone number—why was she looking him up?

"Hello, Mr. Roscoe?" Carla spoke in a breathy, unctuous voice that made Derek bark out a laugh. She frowned at him and he shrugged apologetically. "This is Mary at Allstate Insurance here in Kalispell? How are you this morning? I'm calling today to tell you about our new, low rates on homeowner's insurance..." Grinning, Carla held the receiver away from her ear. Derek could hear Hildreth screaming into the phone, then silence. Carla hung up and grabbed his arm. "Let's go."

"What was that about?" he said as they got into the car.

Carla turned back onto 93. "Now we know he's home."

"Well, you knew he wouldn't be at church. But we already had his phone number; why look in the book?"

"If he's listed," Carla said, "he's used to getting telemarketing calls. Even people out in the toolies have to put up with that shit. If I'd just hung up or apologized for dialing the wrong number, he'd be suspicious—now he's just mad."

A mile or so out of town they came to the intersection with Route 37. A big, green sign announced that Lake Koocanusa was six miles ahead.

"Help me look for Hildreth's place," she said. "Remember, he's called Roscoe."

There'd been no address on the FBI sheet. "No house number in the phone book?"

"No. Just look for his name."

The pines came up right to the road, two lanes of asphalt with narrow gravel shoulders and dikes of dirty snow piled up on each side. They passed one paved side street, which vanished into the trees, and occasional gravel driveways, each of which had a rural mailbox out at the road. Some of these hung from chains or pivoted on long arms as defense against the snow plows.

After a few miles Derek spotted the name Roscoe painted crudely on the side of a galvanized mailbox that hung from a gallows-like frame. Carla drove past it, turning right into the next gravel drive, a quarter mile farther on. She pulled the car under overhanging pine boughs at a wide spot in the driveway, about fifty feet in from the road. No house was visible from here, and the trees would hide the car from the road. Carla got out and popped the driver's seat forward. She rummaged in her bag for a moment, dropped something heavy behind the seat, then another something, and straightened up with her bag in her hand.

"Bring your stuff," she said.

"We're walking?"

"This visit is a surprise, Derek. If we just drove up, he'd have plenty of time to run away or hole up in his cellar. Or get his guns. Do you want to get shot?"

"Well, I don't want to freeze," he complained. "You didn't tell me we'd be *hiking*. I didn't bring any warm clothes."

Carla unzipped her duffel and took out a heavy woolen jacket, woven with large red and gray geometric designs. She looked him in the eye as she put it on and zipped it up.

"Think ahead next time," she said.

Right. Think ahead. Don't sneak into the FBI's office when there's a murderous kidnapper lurking there. Don't help her tie up the FBI agents that could have rescued you. Always wear layers and bring a hat and gloves. Well, at least he'd remembered the clean underwear.

She was waiting impatiently. He got his bags from the back seat, shut the door, and started following her toward the road, when he realized that he'd never checked to see how much damage she'd done to his car. He turned and looked back: it was amazingly little considering that she'd driven through a garage door. The paint was deeply scratched and the rear had a few dents, but that was it. He hustled to catch up.

"Why are we carrying our bags?" he said. "Why don't we just leave them in the car? This is the country—no one's going to try to steal anything, and anyway it has an alarm system."

"We're not coming back."

"What do you mean? You're not just going to leave my car here, are you?"

"Yes," she said.

He stopped walking, and she stopped, too. They were a few yards away from the road. On either side of the gravel drive, snow was piled hip-high.

"We're abandoning my car?" he said.

"No. *You're* abandoning your car." She reached into her pocket, fished out his keys, and tossed them over.

Derek caught them absent-mindedly and dropped them into a jacket pocket. They couldn't just leave his car. He loved that car.

"I love that car," he said.

"It's a great car, but it's time for a new one. We're lucky we weren't pulled over by state troopers. And since we're headed north, we're going to need something that can handle snow."

"We're going north?"

"Canada."

"Canada," he said. "I thought you were letting me go today."

"I am. In Canada."

"Am I supposed to walk back? And where are we going to get a new car?"

She started walking toward the road. Derek sighed in exasperation and ran a few steps to catch up.

"Hildreth is going to lend us his car," Carla said.

"People just naturally give you things, don't they?"

She smiled and they headed toward Hildreth's driveway. The asphalt road was clear and wet, with snow piles several feet high at each shoulder. Brownish-red cinders crunched under their feet. Derek's computer bag was slung over his left shoulder, with his left hand in his pocket, but he was holding his small suitcase in his right hand and it was getting numb. A stiff breeze blew from behind them, and he shivered. Carla also had no hat or gloves, but she didn't seem to notice the cold at all.

When they had almost reached Roscoe's mailbox, Carla grabbed Derek's elbow and guided him off the road. They climbed carefully over the snow pile, but when they reached the undisturbed snow on the other side of it, Derek immediately sank in above his ankles. He cursed and tried to walk lightly as he followed Carla into the woods.

She led him to a tall Douglas fir well away from the road. He stood beneath the lowest branches in the bare circle around its trunk, snowless and littered with pine needles. The surrounding trees blocked most of the wind, so despite his wet feet and pant legs, he felt warmer. The woods were less dense than Derek had expected from the road: thirty feet separated many of the trees, though some were so close together that their branches intertwined. In the larger gaps, spindly, bare branches of undergrowth stuck up above the snow. They dropped their bags.

"I want you to wait for me right here," Carla said.

"What?" He was out of patience with this pointless maneuvering. "I could've waited in the damned car!"

"I won't be long," she said. "I'm going to scout around, then I'll come back to get you."

"Why don't I just come with you?"

"Because you're already wet and cold, and I don't want you lumbering around in the snow when I'm trying to be stealthy."

"I don't lumber," Derek said.

"Yes, you do. Rest here under this tree and I'll be back in half an hour or less."

"Oh, great, half an hour. I'm freezing *now*."

Carla shook her head and squatted down to unzip her bag. She took out an oversized black wool sweater and tossed it to Derek.

"Put this on," she said, "and stop whining. I'll be back soon." She pointed a finger at him threateningly. "Don't move."

She ran off into the snow, gliding as gracefully as an ice skater. In a moment she had vanished into the trees.

"I never whine," Derek said. He took off his jacket, pulled on the sweater, and then shrugged into the jacket again. He felt a bit warmer, but his hands were still cold, and his feet were wet and freezing. He pulled up the collar of his jacket and stuffed his hands in the pockets. He stomped his feet a few times, but that didn't really help. *I'm going to get the flu—or pneumonia.*

He caught sight of Carla's purple nylon sports bag lying in the pine needles beside his own bags. He looked around, but Carla was long gone. He was tempted to search it—maybe he could find a clue to who she was and what she was after. *But if I touch her bag, she'll pop out from behind this tree and break my arm.* No: she was fast and strong, but she wasn't a comic book super-villain. She was off in the woods somewhere, spying on Hildreth. If she came back and found him searching her bag, he would just say that he'd been looking for a pair of gloves.

He squatted down and unzipped it, sorting through the clothing: a flannel shirt, white socks, a few pairs of panties, a white T-shirt, a gray jog bra. A couple of granola bars. Derek unzipped an inner pocket and discovered two spare magazines for her gun. He picked one up and thumbed the cartridges on top: jacketed nine-millimeter. The clip held seventeen rounds. *Very dainty.* He put it back and closed the zipper.

The only other item was the grip he'd seen her carry out of the bathroom that morning. It was the size of a small purse, made of heavy, floral-patterned cloth. Derek opened it. Toothbrush and toothpaste, shampoo, soap box, hairbrush, tampons, tweezers and tiny scissors, a sewing kit, safety pins, and a big hunting knife.

Derek lifted the knife and unbuckled the black leather sheath. The handle and blade were made of the same dark gray material, too light to be steel. The blade was about five inches long, serrated on the upper edge. His fingers fit inside the grip, so the back of the handle could be used as brass knuckles. He sheathed it and, as he returned it to the grip, noticed a small tool kit.

It held a pair of pliers, wire cutters, a magnifying glass, screwdriver, a small hammer, spools of wire. He put everything back as it had been and stood up. What had he learned? A knife but no pajamas; tools but no makeup; bullets but no personal items at all. No one packed this way. He leaned back against the tree and jammed his hands into his pockets. He could see his breath; the sky had gone cloudy, and he thought it was getting colder.

A few moments later, Carla stepped out from behind a tree twenty feet away. Derek was startled so badly that he lost his balance and almost fell down. He managed to pull his hands out of his pockets and catch himself before he landed on his face. Carla laughed at him and picked up her bag.

"Christ!" he said. "Don't do that!" This was so close to the scenario he'd imagined that he felt his face flushing and was glad he hadn't taken any longer looking through her bag.

She said, "Come on." Derek grabbed his bags and followed her. She led him through the snow, up a gentle rise leading away from the road.

"So," he said, "how did it go?"

"Fine. Hildreth has dogs, so we need to be quiet and stay downwind until we get to the house."

"Downwind."

"The wind is from the northwest," she said, pointing. "His house is southwest of here, so if we're careful, the dogs won't smell us coming. Okay?" Derek nodded and they started walking again. "There's a nice new Blazer parked by the house. And he's still home, and alone." She glanced at him as they stepped over a fallen tree. "What have you been up to?"

Derek almost panicked, thinking that maybe she'd seen him pawing through her things, but she couldn't have scoped out Hildreth's place *and* spied on him. She hadn't even been gone fifteen minutes.

"Nothing," he said. "Just trying to stay warm."

They continued up the hill and came to Hildreth's driveway. She held a finger to her lips. They walked up the shallow grade, trying to go quietly on the gravel. Coming around a bend in the drive, Derek saw an A-frame log cabin not far ahead, with a dark green Blazer parked under an attached carport. A tall woodpile nearby was covered with corrugated metal held down with rocks. Smoke drifted up from the stone chimney and blew away from them.

When they neared the cabin, a German shepherd that had been sleeping on the front porch jumped up and began to bark fiercely. A second, almost identical dog came skidding around from the back of the house and stood between them and the house, barking out of phase with its twin. Carla walked forward slowly. Derek followed reluctantly, until they were about ten feet from the nearer dog, which continued to bark.

"Nice doggies," Derek said. "Eat her first, okay?"

"Shut up," Carla said. "Don't say one word."

The door of the cabin banged open and a man carrying a shotgun stepped out. Derek recognized Hildreth from the FBI photo, but he'd grown uglier since the picture was taken. Black, unwashed hair hung down to his shoulders, he looked heavier, and he'd lost his exultant smile—but the broken nose and pitted face were the same, and he looked just as mean. Hildreth stared at the two of them, scowling, with the shotgun held in both hands. It was pointed at the ground, but his finger was on the trigger. He shouted at the dogs, who stopped barking but held their ground.

"Who are you—what do you want?" he growled in a raspy, nasty voice that Derek instantly hated.

"Our car broke down," Carla said. Derek was impressed that there was a slight shake in her voice, as if she were really afraid of the dogs—and the gun. *If these dogs had any sense, they'd run for their lives.* "Down at... I mean, a ways down on 37. We were wondering if we could use your phone to call a tow truck?"

Hildreth squinted at Carla with a gleam in his eye and stuck the tip of his tongue out between his teeth. He looked her up and down, then glanced at Derek briefly. Derek tried to look dim-witted. *I'm just the gutless, dickless husband who lets his lusty wife do all the talking.*

"Ain't got no phone," Hildreth lied.

"Oh." Carla looked at Derek helplessly, then turned back to Hildreth, frowning charmingly. "Could you tell us where we can find one, then? Maybe my husband could go call someone while I wait here? It's pretty cold out."

Hildreth looked as if he might start drooling. The shotgun drooped further. *He's going to go for it.*

"Sure, that would be fine," Hildreth said. "Wickerson's down the road a ways, he's got a phone. Your husband could hike over there, can't be more than a mile."

"Wickerson's," Carla said, and took a few steps closer to Hildreth. She was just a few paces away from the porch, standing right next to the closer of the dogs, which growled at her.

"Shut up, Rax," Hildreth commanded the dog. "Yeah, Wickerson." He turned his attention to Derek for the first time. "You want to go down 37 about half a mile and take the first drive on the right." *That's where she left my car.* "Old Wickerson's always at home, never goes nowhere, don't know nobody. He'll let you use the phone." He turned back to Carla. "And you come on inside and get warm by the stove, pretty lady."

If Carla were anyone else, their lives would be in danger. Hildreth might shoot Derek in the back as soon as he turned away, or maybe he would wait until Derek returned, after he'd had a chance to subdue the pretty wife. Old Wickerson was half a mile away and possibly deaf, so who would ever know? As it was, Derek almost felt sorry for Hildreth. The man was standing on the brink of hell and didn't even know it.

Carla smiled sweetly at Derek. "Could you go, honey? It's not that far."

Derek shrugged. "Sure, hon, no problem." He started walking back down the driveway. If she wanted him to go, he was gone. He touched the car keys in his jacket pocket. He was perfectly happy to be turned loose here, still in America and with his car within walking distance. *Thank God, the nightmare's over...*

"Derek," Carla said.

He turned back. Carla was standing on the porch, holding Hildreth's left arm twisted up behind his back, her gun pushing up under his jaw. Hildreth, twisting his head away to escape the pistol, still held the shotgun in his right hand, pointed at the ground.

"Get inside the house," Carla said, with the chilling voice that Derek knew too well. "If you even twitch, I'll kill you *and* your dogs. Derek, come on. No, leave the bags."

Derek walked uneasily past the nearer dog, who looked confused but let him pass. On the porch he sidled past the second dog, watching it carefully, and gratefully closed the door behind him.

Just inside, coats hung on pegs above scattered boots and shoes. One look at the kitchen off to the right was more than enough: dirty dishes were jumbled in the sink, trays and boxes from microwave dinners were piled up on a small table, and trash formed unstable slopes against the walls. The sweet smell of rotting food made Derek gag.

A half-closed door on the left was probably the bathroom. Then the dark, narrow hallway ended in the main room of the cabin, paneled with rough wood. A basketball game was playing on the grimy screen of a large TV in the corner. *Wait a minute—no one plays basketball on Sunday morning.* It must be a tape.

In another corner, a black wood stove radiated welcome heat. Derek felt light-headed after standing in the cold for too long, but he shook it off. The floor around the stove was littered with wood chips and small pieces of bark, and the firewood was piled too close for safety.

A relatively new couch faced the TV, but the striped pattern was smeared with what looked like axle grease. More kitchen refuse, engine parts, newspapers, and unidentifiable junk were scattered over a battered wooden coffee table and much of the floor. Most of the outside wall was a sliding glass door that led out onto a small, snow-covered deck. A stairway led to a loft. Based on what he'd seen so far, Derek definitely did *not* want to go up there.

"Take the shotgun, Derek," Carla said. She still held Hildreth's arm up behind his back.

Derek snatched the gun out of Hildreth's hand. He didn't know what to do with it; he'd never held a gun in his life. Finally he grabbed the stock in his hand and rested the muzzle against the floor.

Carla walked Hildreth toward the couch and pushed. He fell onto it face-first, and it took him a few seconds to clumsily turn himself over and settle into the cushions. He glared up at her. She stood at ease between him and the TV with her gun pointed at his head.

"You're dead, bitch," Hildreth said.

Carla turned from the waist and shot the TV in the exact center of the tube. Derek flinched as the imploding tube showered glass shards all over the floor: the shot was deafening. She turned back and was instantly covering Hildreth again. Derek examined the smoking, sputtering TV curiously. He'd always wanted to do that.

"I hate basketball, don't you?" Carla asked Derek.

"No, not really," he said, more calmly than he felt. His nerves were jangling and his ears were ringing. "I watch the Sonics all the time."

Hildreth was staring at the dying TV as if Carla had just shot his daughter.

"Your name is John Hildreth," Carla said. "The FBI gave you the name Roscoe. You were formerly a business associate of Jean Pequinot."

Hildreth tore his eyes away from his dead TV.

"Who are you?" he said. Carla didn't reply. After a moment of silence, Hildreth squirmed. "What the hell do you want?"

Carla stared at him for a moment longer. Without taking her eyes off Hildreth, she said, "Derek, I think you need to use the bathroom."

"What?" he said.

"Go lock yourself in the bathroom for a few minutes."

"I don't understand."

"I want to have a private conversation with Mr. Rabbit." She glanced at him briefly and nodded toward the front door. "Just set the gun down."

Derek shrugged and carefully placed the shotgun on the floor. He went back to the hallway, opened the bathroom door, and stepped inside. He almost gagged again as he shut the door. This would rank near the top of all the filthy gas station restrooms that he'd ever seen. A few clean streaks stood out through the filth in the sink. There was mildew around the bathtub, trash overflowing the wastebasket, and the toilet seat was up over a bowl that had probably never been cleaned. It smelled like an outhouse. He would rather find a tree outside, in the freezing cold and despite the dogs, rather than use that toilet.

The door popped open an inch, startling him. He peeked out into the hallway, but it was empty. The latch must have let go. Derek grabbed the handle, intending to close the door silently, but realized that he could hear them talking in the other room. He carefully opened it a bit further and could just make out what Carla was saying.

"—Philippe Sottile? He was Pequinot's second in command, retired a few years ago."

Hildreth mumbled something.

"I guess he left before you retired Pequinot permanently. You shipped some really big arms dealers, didn't you? Pretty impressive. A week after you squealed to the FBI, the CIA, Interpol, MI6, and the Mossad hit them all at the exact same moment."

"What do you want, lady?" Hildreth said. "I don't know what the hell you're talking about. And I never heard of these frogs—what's their name, Peckerno and Softique."

"Well, Philippe's heard of you. He says you're the only man left alive who knows where we can pick up the loose ends of Pequinot's contacts."

Hildreth mumbled again.

"Sorry to hear that," Carla said. "If you don't know anything, I'll just have to kill you."

"Wait, wait," Hildreth squealed.

Derek was leaning his forehead against the door. It creaked and he jerked back in alarm, but nothing happened, so they must not have heard the noise. He pulled the door open another inch.

"—know something," Hildreth was saying. "What's in it for me?"

"You get to live," Carla said. "Not that I would call this living."

Hildreth mumbled again.

"Okay, I can give you some money, too. Five thousand, if you give me names, phone numbers, addresses, whatever I need to contact them."

Mumble.

"I'd take it if I were you," Carla said. "Take it and run. If *I* can find you, maybe some of your old friends could find you, too. I don't think they'll be as forgiving as I am."

"Okay, okay," Hildreth said. "What kind of buyer are you looking for?"

"Major players. Somebody who can afford the serious stuff."

"What do you mean, serious?"

"Nukes," Carla said.

Derek felt a chill run up his spine. *What does she mean by that?* There was a long pause.

"Shit," Hildreth said at last. "There aren't many. You'd probably better start with—"

"No," Carla said. "Write it down."

Nothing but silence for over a minute. Derek's neck was getting stiff from trying to listen through the crack in the doorway. As he straightened up and stretched, he heard something outside. He tried to see out the window over the toilet, but it was streaked and filthy, and he didn't want to try to open it. He listened carefully and could hear an airplane—props, not a jet. He opened the bathroom door and walked out into the living room.

Carla stood near the ruined TV, glancing at a small sheet of paper while she kept one eye on Hildreth, who sat hunched and miserable on the edge of the couch. Carla looked up as Derek walked in.

"Derek, why don't you wait out—"

"Did you hear that plane?" he interrupted.

"What plane?"

"Just a minute ago, a plane flew right over us. It sounded kind of low."

Carla folded the paper she was reading and tucked it into her shirt pocket.

"Keep an eye on him," she said. Derek picked up the shotgun. Hildreth looked at him wearily, all the malevolence he'd shown earlier drained away. Carla went to the sliding glass door and scanned the sky, frowning.

Hildreth seemed about to speak when Carla said, "Oh, shit." She turned from the window and without hesitation shot Hildreth twice right between the eyes. Derek dropped the shotgun, clapping his hands to his ears against the noise. Brains and blood spattered the back half of the room. Drops of blood landed on the wood stove and sizzled. Hildreth's body twitched once and slid down onto the floor.

"Jesus Christ!" Derek said. He could barely breathe. The sharp smell of gunpowder gave way to the stench of Hildreth's blood and feces. As the echoes of the thundering shots faded, a pool of blood began spreading on the floor around the dead man's head. "Jesus Christ." He leaned over and retched, but nothing came up.

"Derek!" Carla said.

He looked up at her and saw the gore dripping down the far wall, and doubled over again. He realized finally that he wasn't actually going to vomit. *What the hell is going on? Why did she do that? Oh Christ, maybe I'm next...*

"Derek!" Involuntarily, he straightened up and his eyes locked onto hers. "Snap out of it," she said. "I have to go. That was an FBI spy plane. There'll be fifty agents here in half an hour."

He stared at her stupidly.

"Derek!"

"Okay, uh, okay," he said. He glanced at the corpse again and shuddered.

"Derek," she said, "I'm *not* going to shoot you. Listen to me! Calm down."

Derek took a deep breath and stretched his neck, rotating his head in a circle. He threw his shoulders back and let the air out slowly.

"Why did you do that?" he said. "The guy gave you what you wanted."

"Because the FBI's going to be here soon, and he would have told them everything. Don't worry about him, Derek, he was an evil man and he got what he deserved. You need to worry about yourself."

Another chill ran up his spine. "What do you mean?"

"You were in the bathroom the whole time we were talking, right?"

Derek knew what would happen to him if he admitted having heard their conversation, so he just nodded. His eyes wanted to drift back to the bloody corpse, but he forced himself to focus on Carla.

"Then you're free to go," Carla said.

"What?" He shook his head; he must not have heard her right.

"I was going to send the message from here, but now we don't have time. You can walk back to your car if you want to, or just wait here—the Bureau will arrive in a few minutes and you can explain what happened."

"You're letting me go now—here?"

"Yes. You don't know anything, and it'll be easier for me to get away without you. So run, or stay, it's up to you." She turned away and headed toward the door.

Oh, that's perfect. Lovely choices. Stay here and maybe get shot by a nervous agent. If they don't kill me they'll just question me for a week. Or I could get in my car and drive back to Seattle, and *then* be interrogated. Or Gugliemo could grab me, torture me, and then shoot me.

Well, those were the worst cases. What was the best he could hope for? If he testified against Gugliemo, maybe the FBI would relocate *him*. Or Gugliemo could resist arrest and get killed. Then Derek could get back to his life.

His pointless, absurd life: breaking into stupid companies in order to help some other idiotic company make more money. Every now and then he could look forward to working with a hairball like Gugliemo. He lived alone, dated women that he picked up in bars or coffee shops, slept with them two or three times, and then got bored. He had found the perfect woman once, but he couldn't keep his dick in his pocket, not even to keep her.

Suddenly, Derek loathed himself and his life. He was consumed with the desire to know what Carla was doing, and why. What was so important that she had to shoot that car following them? And now she'd killed Hildreth right in front of him. Who was she? Who was she working for? Did she really say "nukes?"

He looked up and was surprised to see that Carla hadn't reached the front door yet.

"Carla," he said. She turned around. "If I wanted to come with you, you wouldn't shoot me, would you?" She looked at him thoughtfully for a moment, then walked back to face him.

Standing before the dripping wall of blood that she'd decorated with the contents of Hildreth's skull, with her gun held firmly in her hand, she said, "Derek, I will never shoot you."

He didn't know whether to believe her or not. He didn't really care. Of all the paths he could take from this moment in time, the only one that remotely interested him was following Carla. He was probably in shock, and not competent to make a decision right now, but fuck it.

"Okay," he said. "I'm coming."

She smiled, not the fierce predatory rictus he'd seen before, but a real smile.

"Come on," she said, "we have to get out of here fast." They started toward the front door, but Carla stopped so suddenly that he bumped into her. "Shit. I forgot about the dogs."

"You're not going to shoot the dogs, are you?"

"Not unless I have to."

Carla opened the front door. Before it had swung even halfway, one of the shepherds flew through the opening, slamming her into the wall, and launched itself straight at Derek. He had enough time to lift his left arm to his chest before the dog hit him and knocked him off his feet. It clamped onto his forearm, sending a searing pain up to his shoulder. Derek screamed, but as the dog started to shake its head, he remembered playing halfback in college. He'd been hit plenty of times by monsters bigger than this one, and it sure as hell hurt a lot more.

Derek rolled to his left a little. As soon as his right arm was free, he punched the dog in the gut as hard as he could. The shepherd *woofed* and let go of Derek's arm. He was just starting to push it away when Carla suddenly appeared behind the dog, grabbed its head, and twisted. Something snapped and the dog went limp.

She hauled him to his feet. He looked down at his arm. The dog had torn through his coat and into the flesh. It was bleeding, and there was blood on the floor, but the wound didn't seem to be gushing. Carla picked her gun up off the floor and they stepped outside. The second shepherd immediately leaped from their left and Carla shot it once in the chest. It yelped and tumbled into the snow beside the porch, writhing and whining. She shot it again in the head and it lay still.

"Nice dogs," Derek said.

"Let's go. You can bleed later."

The Blazer was unlocked, so they threw their bags into the back. Carla found the keys in a tray between the front seats. As Derek fastened his seat belt, Carla started the car and pulled down the driveway. When she reached Route 37, she turned right and floored it.

"Look for a first aid kit," she said. "We'll be in Canada in fifteen minutes."

Chapter 11

Rexford, Montana
Sunday, February 26, 11:51 a.m.

Some of the agents were leaving now that the site was secured. Three resident agencies, small local offices of the FBI, had managed to gather almost twenty special agents by the time Chapa and Shaffer landed at the small airport in Kalispell. Less than an hour later, Hildreth's house was surrounded by agents and Chapa was hovering over the cabin in a Bureau chopper, looking down through binoculars from the co-pilot's seat while a sharpshooter hung from a harness out of the open door and Shaffer clung on in the back. Then the agents on the ground radioed that they were too late.

They couldn't be certain how late until the medical examiner arrived, but Chapa had enough experience with murder scenes to guess. Hildreth's body was still warm and the blood was in the early stages of congealing. If they had arrived just one hour earlier, Derek and Citrullo would still be still inside the cabin, Hildreth would still be alive—not that his death was any great loss—and all of Chapa's questions would have answers.

He stood on Hildreth's front porch with his hands in the pockets of his overcoat, looking off into the tall, dark trees. Although the day was gloomy and it was cold enough that he could see his breath, this was a pretty setting, ruined by the dead dog lying in the snow to his right. The other one was inside. Chapa was trying to visualize what had happened here, so far without success.

Another carful of agents left. The remaining dozen or so were searching the area around the house. When they were closing in on the cabin earlier, several agents had noticed fresh footprints in the snow, and now they were trying to sort out their own tracks from the ones that had been there before. So far all of the suspicious footprints appeared to be from the same small pair of running shoes.

Shaffer was sitting in the passenger seat of one of the Bureau cars, talking to someone in Kalispell over the radio. Their cell phones wouldn't work out here. She finished and walked back to join him.

"Let's have another look," he said. They went back into the house.

Chapa stopped at the dead German shepherd lying just inside the door and squatted down to examine the animal's body, being careful not to disturb it or the drops of blood on the floor nearby. The forensics team was expected in half an hour or so, and until then he had ordered the rest of the agents to stay outside. They had disturbed things enough when they broke into the house, not knowing that it was already over.

"Broken neck," he observed. "Why didn't she just shoot it like the one outside?"

Shaffer said nothing, but she walked carefully around the dog to a vantage point where she could look out the front door. Chapa looked up at her, back down at the dog, and then outside.

"It charged when they opened the door?" he said. "Still doesn't tell me why she didn't shoot it." She shrugged. "Make sure forensics checks out this blood here. I'll bet it's not Hildreth's."

Shaffer would do no such thing. The forensics guys would dice her up if she insulted their competence with such an obvious suggestion. He was just talking. Shaffer knew that, and he knew that she knew: they'd worked together for six years.

The cabin was small, dark, and filthy. The wood paneling was too dark, sucking up the dim light coming through the sliding glass doors. From the looks of the disgusting kitchen, Hildreth had the hygiene of a cave bear. Chapa wrinkled his nose at the smell, but he'd seen a lot worse in Miami.

The living room was a gory mess. Hildreth lay in a pool of his own blood in front of the couch. Most of his brains were splattered on the wall behind it. Chapa was intrigued by the TV. A jagged hole in the middle of the cracked screen was perfectly centered. *Nice shot.* The TV was directly across the room from Hildreth's body, so it couldn't have been hit by a stray shot meant for him. A shotgun lay on the floor near the stairway, but a shotgun blast would have blown out the whole screen. Citrullo must have shot the TV, but he couldn't imagine why.

"Special Agent Chapa?" someone called from outside.

There was nothing else he could learn from this mess until the M.E. and forensics were finished. He led Shaffer back outside. One of the local agents, Kopecky, was standing on the porch. He was short and broad, wearing a dark coat and furry, peaked hat that made him look like a black bear.

"What's up, Kopecky?" Chapa said.

"Three things, sir. We've found Narr's vehicle. It was parked down the road a ways, in a driveway owned by a Mister..." Kopecky checked his notebook. "Wickerson. We have someone talking to him now." Chapa doubted they would learn much from the car. "And, uh, the forensics team is here." That was fast; were they efficient or just eager? They probably didn't get to investigate many serious crimes out here.

"Okay," Chapa said, "have them get started right away. What's the third thing?"

"Sir, would you mind talking to the Lincoln County sheriff for a moment? We try to maintain good relations with the locals, and he's getting a bit, uh, agitated."

Chapa sighed. "Go take a look at the car," he said to Shaffer. "I'll go talk to Sheriff..."

"Pierce, sir," Kopecky said.

"Pierce. Where is he?"

Kopecky led him down the driveway to the sheriff, who was standing beside his patrol car, impatiently watching the agents hustling around. Sheriff Pierce was not the obese, tobacco-chewing hick that Chapa had half expected. He looked more like a successful lawyer than the sheriff of a rural county on the border with Canada: tall and thin, well-dressed in a heavy overcoat, with eyebrows so light they were almost invisible.

"Sheriff Pierce," Chapa said. "I'm Special Agent Chapa, in charge of this investigation." They shook hands.

"Mr. Chapa," Pierce said, "I'm a little concerned about getting full access to the information your people are collecting here."

Chapa listened patiently. The man was used to dealing with the resident agency in Kalispell, but the Seattle agents seemed to make him nervous. Chapa reassured him that everything they learned would be shared with him, praised his past cooperation with the Kalispell RA (of which he knew nothing), and excused himself as soon as possible. The Bureau always made an effort to cooperate closely with the local police, who often ended up essentially working for the FBI, helping solve cases that otherwise could have taken twice as long to crack. But Chapa had little patience with the mechanics of the process, especially when he had to do it standing in the freezing cold.

He looked around for Shaffer, but she hadn't come back yet. He did find a large Thermos of coffee and a stack of paper cups in the back seat of one of the cars, and the coffee wasn't bad. Chapa had nearly finished his cup when he spotted Shaffer walking up the driveway, her ponytail swinging charmingly from side to side.

He poured another cup of coffee and handed it to her as she came up. She thanked him and took a sip.

"So?" he said.

"We broke into the car easily enough, but it took a while to kill the alarm."

"Really? I didn't hear it. How far away is the car?"

"About half a mile. You really didn't hear it?" She took a larger gulp of the coffee; it wouldn't stay hot for long in this cold air.

"Find anything interesting?"

"Our sidearms," she said. Chapa stiffened. Having to surrender his weapon had been like being stripped naked in public—no, worse. "They're bagged for evidence, but I checked them out. Neither had been fired."

Chapa grunted. That was some consolation. At least their stolen weapons hadn't been used in a crime. He was conscious of the weight of his replacement piece in the shoulder holster.

"Anything else?"

"They left Hildreth's dossier behind. Some maps, a couple of coffee cups, and they didn't eat all their cinnamon doughnuts."

"I'll be sure to mention that in my report," Chapa said. Shaffer grinned. They turned to watch the activity. The agents tracking the footsteps in the snow were nearly done. *They have to be Citrullo's. What was she up to out here?* He leaned back against the car.

"Maybe we should have set up a roadblock on I-90," Shaffer said.

Chapa shook his head. "Couldn't justify it. She just tied us up for a few minutes. Now if she'd killed us, that would be different."

"So, why didn't she?"

"Kill us? Good question. Maybe she's smart. She probably guessed we'd have backup outside. She'd have to take them out, too, and that could have been difficult. And then, of course, every agent in the country would have been looking for her."

In sixty years, only thirty agents had been killed by perps in the line of duty. The Bureau was proud of that, and they took the death of an agent very seriously. If Citrullo was Mossad, she would know that. But Shaffer didn't look satisfied.

"You have any theories about what happened here?" he asked her.

"He was an arms dealer."

"Right."

"She used to be Mossad."

"Uh huh," Chapa said. "It smells like something big, doesn't it?"

"It smells, that's for sure."

They were quiet for a moment, thinking. Chapa said, "Let's go back to the Kalispell office and see if Frieder got anything out of your friend, Myron. If not, maybe you can call him yourself." Chapa watched several agents walk out of the woods and stamp the snow off their boots. He pushed himself off the car they were leaning on. "All we can learn here is *what* happened; not *why*." They started walking toward the cabin, where the head of the Kalispell RA was directing his men. He would be able to tell them what car they could take; the helicopter had left long ago.

"They may be headed into Canada," Shaffer said.

"Good point," Chapa said. "We can get in touch with the RCMP from Kalispell. Maybe the Mounties will..."

"Get our man?" Shaffer said with a smile.

"I'm more interested in the woman. My gut tells me Derek is a pawn. I want the queen."

Chapter 12

The sunny morning had become an overcast afternoon, perfectly matching Derek's mood. They reached the Canadian border in less than Carla's fifteen minutes. The elderly border guard, thin and graying, waved them through with barely a glance into the car. Carla gave the man a big, beaming smile, and he grinned ruefully back as he opened the gate. The moment they were through, Carla's smile snuffed out like a candle thrown into the ocean.

Derek struggled out of his jacket and peeled back his shirt sleeve. The dog had bitten him in the middle of his left forearm. The skin was punctured, but the wounds weren't deep and the bone was intact. The jacket had prevented it from getting a good grip, but the bites looked bad enough—two pairs of raised, purple spots caked with blood—and they hurt with a deep ache. The bleeding had stopped, but his shirt was ruined. He cleaned the punctures with alcohol swabs from the first aid kit he'd found, then put antibiotic ointment onto each puncture and wrapped his arm in gauze.

"I think you'll live," Carla said when he finished, and that was the last word she spoke on the five-hour drive to Calgary.

Derek didn't have much to say, either. He was amazed and disgusted to find that the shooting had left him sexually excited, and the road vibrations made it worse. He watched the scenery go by, trying to take his mind off his raging erection, hoping that Carla wouldn't notice it.

He didn't know much about Canada. He'd only visited once before, with Marjorie, shortly after they were married. They'd caught the ferry from Seattle to Victoria, a very British town on Vancouver Island, just across the border. After high tea at the Empress Hotel they'd stayed there overnight and taken the bus the next morning to Butchart Gardens. The Sunken Garden had been their favorite, an explosion of meticulously tended flowers, shrubs, and trees down in an old quarry. At the garden's edge they stood on the rim of a deep gorge. Below, a river flowed placidly and a fountain sprayed water high up into the wind, in a constantly-changing pattern that would not repeat itself for five hundred years.

His marriage to Marjorie had been all downhill from there.

Most of Canada was north of Seattle, where in the dead of winter darkness fell at four-thirty, and at the height of summer the sky could still be blue at ten. The growing season would be short up here—perhaps that was why Canada had only one-tenth the population of the U.S.

They followed Route 3 through the Rocky Mountains and came out onto the prairie before heading north. When Carla stopped for gas and a bathroom break, Derek didn't even bother to suggest that he could drive for a while. They maintained their silence during the rest of the drive.

What was she thinking? Was she replaying Hildreth's murder over and over in her head, or was she even thinking about it at all? She didn't seem particularly upset, but she'd been quiet like this after she took out the Lincoln too, so maybe this was how she dealt with murdering someone.

Or maybe she was just daydreaming and the killing meant nothing to her. He knew zilch about Carla, other than that she was lethal. He was beginning to reconsider his decision to go with her. His life was a mess, certainly, but Chapa might have helped him, once he'd convinced the agent that Carla had coerced him. But Derek couldn't see a way to back out now.

He watched the frozen farms go by—the stubble in the fields sticking up from the snow like a three-day beard, the barns in need of paint, the isolated farmhouses—and brooded until they reached Calgary in mid-afternoon.

Derek waited in the car while Carla checked them into a motel, struggling to stay awake although it was just three-thirty. He brought his things and the first aid kit and followed her up a wooden stairway that needed fresh paint and new treads—some of them looked rotten. The room was somewhat nicer than last night's, with two big beds and walls that were not constructed of cinder blocks. They dropped their bags on the beds and looked at each other for a moment.

"I need a shower," Derek said. Carla nodded.

He unwrapped his bandage and stood under the hot water long after he was clean, until the muscles in his back and neck started to relax. When he was dry, he put more antibiotic on the punctures and rewrapped his arm. He tossed his bloody shirt in the trash, put his pants back on, and went out into the room. Carla grabbed her kit and took her turn in the shower. Derek sat on the bed, listening to the water run and staring at the bad watercolor hanging on the wall. A country path meandered through fields of high grass under a blue sky, finally disappearing into thick woods. *Just like me.*

Carla stepped out of the bathroom naked.

Derek felt a shock run through his body. It seemed to start in his gut, reverberate from his head to his feet, and finally settle on his groin. She leaned against the door jamb, watching him. The room lights were off and the curtains were drawn, but there was enough light to see by. Her short, curly hair was still damp, her breasts were full, not too large, with dark brown nipples. The triangle of pubic hair was black. Derek had guessed she had a good body, but this was extreme: she was slender, and the muscles in her arms, legs, and stomach were well-defined, like a marathon runner's.

I don't know if this is such a good idea. But his body had other plans. The erection he'd endured for hours was back, stiffer than ever.

Carla walked over to his bed with the graceful, lissome, dangerous stride of a panther. She sat on the edge of the bed and put a hand flat on his bare chest. He cupped one breast in his palm; the skin was warm and soft. She slid her hand down to his groin, stroking him.

In a while, she pushed him back gently and unzipped his pants. He lifted his butt to let her pull them off, and then she took his shorts. She pushed his legs apart, knelt between them, and kissed his belly. He felt her take him into her mouth.

Derek had been with a lot of women, but he'd never experienced anything like this. Waves of intense pleasure surged up from the base of his penis, but somehow he managed to keep control. He looked down, wondering what she was doing to him that could possibly feel so good, but the light was dim and her head, moving, blocked his view. He closed his eyes and sank back against the pillows.

"Jesus," he moaned, "that is so good."

Carla stopped, licked the tip of his penis lightly, and said, "They taught us how to do this in the Mossad."

Frantic with lust, it took Derek a moment to understand what she'd said. Someone had taught her to do that? Then his brain reengaged and he remembered what "Mossad" meant. He jerked upright and shouted, "*What?*"

Carla gripped him lightly in her left hand and pulled up her legs so she was sitting on them. She brushed her damp hair, which had been falling forward, off her forehead.

"It was part of advanced training," she said.

Derek was in shock, and found himself almost laughing. "Wait, wait a minute. You're in the Mossad? The Israeli CIA? You're a *spy?*" A lot of things made sense all of a sudden, but perhaps ignorance had been better. He glanced down and was astonished to see that his erection hadn't subsided.

"I *was* a spy. I'm retired now, I work for myself." She put her other hand on his chest and pushed him back against the sticky headboard. "Relax, Derek, I told you I'm not going to shoot you." She looked down at him. "Anyway, you're the one with the loaded gun."

He was having trouble breathing. "Are you telling me they taught you to do... *that*... in spy school?"

"Sure. It's a useful interrogation technique. For... softening up the enemy."

He was still hard. "Well, it's not working. When did you—"

Carla put her other hand over his mouth and slid back down. "We can talk later."

She went back to work on him, and after a moment Derek couldn't think anymore. It was too easy to let his questions and fears drift away while she was doing... that. Somewhere in the back of his mind, a tiny voice insisted that there had better be some answers soon, but waves of sensation drowned it out. When he was sure he was about to explode, she suddenly stopped and slid up his body so they were face to face.

"My turn," she said with their lips practically touching. "I like it gentle at first."

Derek gave it his best, licking her until she bucked and groaned. She tasted sweet and clean. When he stopped and looked her in the face, she grinned at him and pulled him up.

"Don't you want to be on top?" he said.

"Later."

It was much later, when the daylight was gone, after she had been on top and underneath and a few places that Derek had never had a woman before, that his eyes opened suddenly. He hadn't realized he was falling asleep. Carla was sitting naked on the other bed with her back to him, and in the dim light he thought he saw bullet scars on her right shoulder.

* * *

Derek awoke screaming in the middle of the night. By the light of the nightstand lamp he could see Carla, still nude, sitting cross-legged on the other bed, facing him. She looked up at him from the map she was studying, and while still half-asleep himself he wondered if she *ever* slept.

He couldn't remember the nightmare that had startled him awake. Something vicious and deadly had been chasing him, but the details were gone, leaving nothing but his pounding heart and the memory of sharp teeth. He rolled onto his side and looked at Carla. She returned his stare for a moment before going back to her map. She was resting her head on the back of her fist, like Rodin's Thinker. Though one breast was flattened against her upraised arm, he could trace the contours of the other with his eyes, and the thatch of hair between her legs was just visible.

What the hell am I doing? He fell back to sleep.

Chapter 13

Carla snapped awake abruptly, as usual, scanning the room quickly for dangers. Derek was lying on his back on the other bed, asleep, his mouth open slightly. She rolled quietly onto the floor, did ten minutes of stretches and limbering exercises, and went to use the toilet.

After pulling on her underwear, she slipped on the midriff holster. It fit over her ribs, just under the bra, like an oversized Ace bandage. She popped out the pistol's magazine—nine rounds in the clip, one in the chamber—then replaced it and holstered the gun. While putting on the same jeans and shirt she'd worn yesterday, she glanced at Derek. He looked so much younger when he was asleep: the wrinkles and worries smoothed out and made him appear to be in his early thirties, her own age.

She wasn't quite sure yet what she was going to do with Derek. She barely knew him. He had some computer skills, which she wouldn't need after today, he could pick locks, and he might know something useful about electronics. Otherwise he had no training that would be of any help to her. He was worthless at hand-to-hand fighting and he flipped out every time she fired her weapon. Having him tripping after her like a puppy could get her killed. Still, while she hadn't intended to keep him, she hadn't been unhappy when he volunteered to come with her.

Yesterday had not gone according to plan. She would have killed Hildreth whether he knew anything or not, because sooner or later the Bureau would discover her interest in him, and Hildreth would fold for the feds even faster than he had for her. She couldn't afford to have the Bureau interfering in her plans. Their role was to chase her, like hounds after the stag, and to eventually lose the scent.

Derek shouldn't have been in the room when she shot Hildreth—he was supposed to stay in the bathroom or wait outside. But once she saw the plane circling overhead, there was no more time for delicacy.

Unfortunately, it had taken longer to calm Derek down after she shot Hildreth than it would have taken to get him out of the room beforehand. She had planned to e-mail Philippe from Hildreth's house, then drop Derek off in some tiny Canadian town. With the Bureau right on their tail, she'd had to scrap that plan, and then Derek had confused things even more by deciding to come along.

It wasn't a disaster that Derek had seen her execute Hildreth. For one thing, it reinforced her control of him: he would think of her as that much more dangerous and ruthless. And then he'd displayed a common male reaction to unexpected violence, sexual arousal, and that was useful, too.

Sex was often a valuable tool. It could be a potent weapon, a way to lower a man's guard, an easy technique for getting him alone and in the most vulnerable state possible. She had convinced men to do the most amazing things by making forceful suggestions at just the right moment in bed—those dimwits in the Ukraine, for example. And sometimes, like last night, she enjoyed it, too. She had initiated sex with Derek partially because she needed the release herself, but more importantly to bind him to her. If he was going to be on her flank, she had to be able to trust him, and sex was the best way she knew of to give him a stake in her survival.

She pulled out the newspaper she'd stuffed inside her shoes. They were dry, thank goodness. Despite years of rigorous training and field work under harsh conditions, she still hated wet shoes. The Mossad hadn't managed to turn her into a machine, though God knows they'd tried.

Derek was still sleeping. She'd given him an extra half hour, but now it was time to go.

"Derek," she said softly. When he didn't stir, she barked, "Derek!" He sat up abruptly and looked around wildly. "Get up," she said, "it's time to get going."

He grunted and rubbed his eyes, lurched out of bed, and walked stiffly to the bathroom, apparently unaware that he was still naked. Carla waited patiently while he used the toilet and shaved, thinking through her plans for the day.

* * *

It took three cups of coffee before Derek was fully awake. He looked awful, despite almost twelve hours of sleep. There were bags under his eyes, and the wrinkles on his forehead were more pronounced. Frowning, he finished his last bite of strawberry waffle.

The cheerful orange Formica tables in the pancake shop did nothing to improve Carla's mood. She picked at her omelet and finally gave up, setting her fork down. She wasn't very hungry, and the food here was tasteless. She sipped at her coffee and grimaced; it was weak and bitter. During her years in the service in Israel, she'd got used to the thick, strong coffee preferred in the Middle East.

The waitress, in a hideous orange-and-white striped apron, came by to refill Derek's cup. She'd been ignoring Carla since they sat down, flirting constantly with Derek, who was too groggy to notice. The woman was very young, pretty in a malnourished, washed-out way. A better diet and some exercise would have pushed her over the edge into attractive, but Carla could see this girl's future in the other waitresses who were standing behind the counter—overweight and flaccid, dyed hair, squinty-eyed from cigarette smoke.

Derek watched the girl walk away. It was the first time he'd noticed her, so the coffee must be working.

"You're not a morning person, are you?" Carla said.

"Ordinarily, yes. But the last few days haven't exactly been ordinary." He set his cup down and pushed his plate away. "What's on the agenda for today?" He lowered his voice. "You're two for two on shooting people. Gonna go for three?"

She leaned in as if to tell him a secret, and he did the same.

"Don't tempt me," she said. "I could use some target practice."

He pulled back. So did she. "You said you wouldn't shoot me."

"Not unless you ask for it."

The waitress returned to ask Derek if he wanted anything else. Carla imagined something useful to do with the girl's apron strings, but that was just a fantasy; she didn't kill innocent civilians. But when the waitress hesitated too long after dropping the check, Carla growled deep in her throat. The ninny jumped and scuttled away, looking back nervously, and suddenly Carla felt cheerful again.

"Why did you do that?" Derek said. Carla just smiled and left some money on the table. They walked back to the car and headed north into town.

It was a little after seven-thirty, and traffic was light. Most of the businesses along this stretch of road related to automobiles: used car lots, RV sales, oil and lube fast service, foreign car repair. Few were open yet. Carla drove slowly and finally found what she was looking for. She turned into the parking lot of a body shop that was still closed and drove all the way to the back of the prefabricated building.

She got the tool kit from her bag. Derek followed her over to a powder blue Volkswagen Golf that had evidently lost an argument with a tree. The left front quarter panel was crushed and the tire was flat, the driver's door was scraped and dented in, and the front bumper was touching the ground.

"Don't tell me," Derek said, "we're trading cars again." He frowned dubiously at the smashed VW.

"Just the plates," she said, and used a screwdriver to remove the Golf's Alberta license plates. In a moment she had swapped them with the Blazer's Montana plates and they were back on the road.

* * *

The houses were small, each a single story, with one-car garages, some attached to the houses and some not. Most were painted white, with varying trim colors. All but one of the driveways had been shoveled. The yards were covered by about a quarter meter of snow.

Carla drove past the one she was interested in. There was nothing unusual to distinguish it from its neighbors. It had white siding with green trim and a matching green front door, false black shutters at the windows, and a gray shingle roof from which most of the snow had fallen. A detached garage stood back from the house. A shoveled walkway ran from the front porch to the driveway.

She pulled into a driveway at random, turned the car around, and parked two doors away; from this position she could see about half of the driveway. The house cut off her view of the garage. Derek looked around for a moment, but there really wasn't anything to see, so he settled into his seat and closed his eyes. A few minutes later he was snoring softly.

Carla waited patiently. In the yard a tall, thin maple drooped naked branches. The entire front of the house was edged with evergreen shrubs still covered with snow. A black, wrought-iron railing surrounded the small front porch and ran down the left side of the steps.

She was trying very hard, but she could not remember playing in this yard.

Just after eight-thirty, a middle-aged woman, bundled up in a long coat and gloves, stepped out of the front door. Her hair was black streaked with a generous amount of gray. She locked the door and walked briskly to the driveway and back to the garage. A moment later a blue Chrysler sedan backed carefully down the drive and stopped at the street. This made Carla smile: she hadn't seen another car in the half hour she'd been watching the house. The woman carefully looked both ways before backing out toward Carla, then she drove slowly away.

Carla waited ten minutes to be sure her mother hadn't forgotten anything.

"Derek," she said softly, and predictably he didn't respond. "*Derek!*" He bolted upright in his seat.

"Huh?" He looked around frantically until he saw her smiling at him. "Will you please stop doing that?"

"Wake up. Time to go to work." She started the car and pulled it all the way into her mother's driveway, stopping right in front of the garage. "Bring everything," she said, and got her own bag out of the back seat.

Carla had never had a key to this house, although she'd grown up here: they hadn't locked the doors back then. She led Derek to the snow-covered back porch. Her mother had rarely used this door, preferring the front entrance, and it somehow bothered Carla that this inconsequential thing, forgotten until this moment, had remained unchanged. She took the small case with her picks out of her back pocket, and a moment later had the door open.

"That was a little slow," Derek said as he sidled past her. She glared at him, picked up her bag, and followed him inside.

The mud room was spotless. Several coats hung on hooks by the door, with boots and shoes arrayed neatly beneath. Mops and brooms stood next to a deep stainless steel sink in the corner. Had there *ever* been any mud in her mother's mud room? She couldn't remember.

In the small, tidy kitchen, Carla set her bag on the floor and looked around. This room she remembered. The aged refrigerator and stove were avocado green. The floor was worn linoleum in a geometric design that didn't really go with the yellow birds and blue flowers of the wallpaper. Breakfast dishes were drying in a rack on the floral tile counter by the sink. Everything was sparkling clean.

Carla recalled baking cookies with her mother and sister in this room, but the memory carried no emotion, as if she had not been that flour-dusted, skinny little girl but merely watched her in a movie.

"Can you set up your computer here?" she asked Derek. He looked around the kitchen. There was a small table by the bay window, and the phone had a long cord.

"Sure," he said. He took the notebook computer and several cables from his case and connected them. Carla sat down beside him as he hit the power switch and the machine started up. "Let's see, I'll need an access number. Uh... maybe I'll just use the 800 number."

Carla was very well trained on PCs, but this was a Macintosh—it didn't look too different. She watched Derek slide his finger across a flat little pad where she'd expected a trackball. After a minute or two he sat back. She hadn't followed exactly what he'd done—he'd worked too quickly and she wasn't familiar with the system—but she recognized the purpose of the e-mail composition window on the screen.

"The address goes here," he said, pointing with his finger. "Then type your message here. When you're done, click on the 'Send Now' icon, and that's it." He pushed the computer over to her. She looked at him expectantly, and he sighed and got up. "I'll wait in the living room."

She entered Chen's name and e-mail address. Philippe was paranoid about receiving the e-mail himself, so he was using Chen as a mail stop.

Hildreth's list of contacts was in the breast pocket of her shirt. She read the dead man's angular, tilted scrawl, typed it in carefully, and double-checked it. Before sending the message, she copied the text. *Here it comes, Philippe, you worthless son of a bitch. I hope you're ready.* She moved the cursor up to the 'Send Now' button and clicked it.

She found the command to create a new message and put in another memorized address, then pasted in the same text she'd sent to Philippe. At the end she typed the one-use code phrase that would identify her message as genuine. It was too bad that security on the 'Net was so poor—the code phrase wasn't tamper-proof, but this was still faster and safer than phones or physical messages. Carla sent the second message. She poked around for a moment until she found the outgoing message folder. She deleted the two messages she'd sent, checked the deleted messages folder and deleted them again, then shut down the program and the machine. She debated whether to destroy the computer and decided against it; she might need it again.

Then she sat back and put her hands in her lap. Phase two, identifying potential customers for Philippe's warheads, was complete. In theory, her part of the scheme was now over. She should be able to relax at the rendezvous in France until Philippe showed up with her share of the money.

That was a fairy tale, of course. Chen had told her that Philippe had no intention of paying her, nor of letting her go. If she knew Philippe, he already had a plan for giving her back to the Mossad—dead, most likely, so she couldn't talk. She had served her purpose—making him rich—and she was too dangerous to keep around. He knew the Mossad was after her, and sooner or later, inevitably, they would catch her. If they took the time to make her talk before putting a bullet in her head, she could put a rather abrupt end to his retirement plans.

No, Philippe had to kill her. Her only consolation was that, twenty-four hours from now, he would have a *real* reason to want her dead. Then he would hunt her down, wanting blood, and if she wasn't very careful and very smart, he would get it.

* * *

Derek waited several minutes before poking his head into the kitchen. She looked at him tiredly, stood up, and brushed past him. The living room was faded: beige wall-to-wall carpet almost worn through in places, walls covered with tired floral wallpaper and family photographs. A pearly-gray sofa beneath the picture window, a low, dark coffee table, a floor lamp, an easy chair, and a padded wooden armchair crowded the small room. None of it looked familiar.

Carla sat in the armchair. Derek slouched down on the couch.

"Do you know whose house this is," he said, "or did you borrow it like Hildreth's car?" He thought he was being funny, but she wasn't in the mood.

"It's my mother's house," she said.

He blinked, then frowned. "I thought you said you were Jewish?"

"I think you mean Israeli," she corrected. "But yes, I'm *half* Jewish, on my mother's side. I was born here, but I emigrated to Israel when I was eighteen."

"Really?" He thought for a moment. "Why?"

How much should she tell him? She had no long-term strategy for Derek, so she wasn't sure what spin she wanted to give her story. Before she could decide, he changed the subject.

"What was in the e-mail you sent?" he said.

"You're better off not knowing."

"I knew you'd say that. Well, tell me this: what're we going to do now?"

"We'll stay here for a few days." She shifted in the uncomfortable chair. "The FBI doesn't know where we are, and your scuzzbo friends lost us when I wiped their tail. We'll be safe here, for a while, at least."

"What's your mom going to say when she comes home and finds us here?"

"She'll ask us what we want for dinner," Carla said. "Look, I don't want to talk about my mother." The chair was giving her a backache. She stood and grabbed Derek's arm. He came up off the couch like half-cooked noodles. "Want to see my room?"

*　　*　　*

She lay face-down on the bed, Derek still collapsed on top of her. Their sweat mingled and ran down her ribs in cool little rivulets that tickled. She felt much better.

After he got off of her, she rolled off the bed and walked down the hall to the bathroom. When she returned, Derek was sitting cross-legged at the foot of the bed, watching her. She sat against the headboard and pulled her legs up under her. She had never had sex in this room before—she never took high school boys seriously—but to her surprise she felt not even an echo of guilt about misusing her childhood bedroom.

Carla remembered this room quite well: it was almost exactly the same, except the movie posters were gone. The wallpaper was orange and yellow stripes with hovering bluebirds—she had picked it out herself at age twelve when her parents remodeled the house. Her father had been patient when she helped him hang it, laughing gently at her mistakes. It took her years to realize that the cheerful stripes were the bars of a cage that held the bluebirds prisoner.

The bent-wood bed frame, the pine dresser with its doilies and her collection of tiny horse statues, the white wooden chest where she'd stored her dolls—these things were part of her somehow, or at least part of her past, but she had no idea where that innocence had gone; or if it still existed, where it might be hiding under the hard polished carapace of her training.

"How old are you?" Derek said.

He sat naked, at ease, his large hands resting on his thighs. Droplets of moisture glistened on his thick mustache.

"I'll be thirty-one tomorrow," she said.

"Tomorrow? Really?" He pursed his lips. "Well, happy birthday. Maybe your mom will bake you a cake."

"Sure," she said. "I'll invite all my childhood friends over for a party."

"Ice cream. Balloons. Presents."

"Party favors. Pin the tail on the donkey."

"Why did you emigrate to Israel?"

She smiled and looked at the walls where her movie posters had hung. Why not?

"Sean Connery was so cool," she said. "Roger Moore—I don't know, he just didn't have as much style, but I saw all his movies anyway. I had to watch Sean on TV, I was too young to see him in the theater."

"What are you talking about?"

"For as long as I can remember, I've wanted to be a spy. I was a teenager before I realized that all the spies were men—except for Mrs. Peale, of course. By then I was ready to actually do something about it, but I wasn't even sure if Canada *had* spies." She stuffed a pillow behind her back.

"Canada's armed forces didn't interest me—it's all search-and-rescue, anti-sub drills, and U.N. peacekeeping missions. I thought about moving to the States, but I hated the CIA—all they're good for is overthrowing democracies and giving misinformation on Russia. And even if I could have stomached that, they probably wouldn't have taken me—female agents still have a tough time *now*."

"Geez," Derek said. "It's like deciding what college to go to."

"Yeah, but the decision wasn't very hard. My mother was—I mean, *is* Jewish, and no one in the world is better at espionage than the Israelis. And being female wasn't a problem: in Israel, women are *required* to serve in the military." She smiled. "I'd been saving my baby-sitting money. The day after I graduated from high school, I bought a one-way ticket. My parents were furious, but I was an adult, there was nothing they could do."

"So what happened?"

"By the Law of Return, I was legally a citizen the moment I stepped off the plane in Tel Aviv. I'll never forget that day, the sky was such a deep blue. It was hot as an oven, but there was a breeze that smelled like a spice shop. They sent me to the ulpan to learn Hebrew, then I joined the IDF—the army. After my two years, I transferred to Aman—military intelligence."

"Wait a minute," Derek said. "You were a soldier?"

"Yeah, I joined just too late to help invade Lebanon. I was stationed there for a while, though."

"Jesus."

"After two years in Aman, I heard the Mossad was starting a new class. The tests were torture... but they took me. There still weren't many female katsas back in '86; I was the only woman in the course. Training took three years that seemed like a decade, but I had a knack for it—I graduated second in my class. After a few years in the field, they sent me back for kidon training: assassins." She smiled for a moment, remembering the classes on strategy, operational security, mortal combat with and without weapons, communications, computer training. "God, that was fun."

"Fun?"

She took her eyes off the ceiling and looked at him. He was frowning.

"Yeah, fun" she said. "For a while, anyway; then things got complicated. There's a lot of politics in the Mossad, and it can get pretty nasty. I started running into roadblocks because I wouldn't sleep with my boss. I had ideas about how things should be done, I wasn't afraid to say what I thought, and they didn't want to hear it. I made some powerful enemies. They were just about to bust me, so I walked."

"You quit?" he said.

"Yeah, I vanished right in the middle of a mission. You could say I resigned without official leave and went freelance. That was almost two years ago. So here I am."

"Right. Here you are: kidnapping me, tying up the FBI, and shooting people. It's nice work if you can get it."

She crossed her arms over her chest and just looked at him.

"Well?" he said. "What's the point of it all? What are you doing?"

"I'm not ready to tell you about the op yet."

"Op? You just said you were retired."

"I am retired. I told you, I'm working freelance. Now what's your story?"

"Don't change the subject. Why won't you tell me what's going on?"

"Because you don't need to know," she said. He glared at her. "Come on, I want to know how you ended up sneaking the Bureau. How did you get into that line of work?"

It was interesting to watch Derek struggle with his impatience; it had been a long time since Carla had known anyone so guileless, so unguarded. The fight for control played out like a movie on his face, but he finally pushed down his frustration.

"I guess it started when I was fourteen," he said. "My friends and I invented a game called Breaking and Exiting. I don't know where we got the idea, probably from one of those cop TV shows. We'd wait for one of the neighbors to go on vacation."

"And then what? You robbed them?"

"No! We weren't bad kids, just a little wild. We'd go in and get out again without taking anything and without leaving any evidence that we'd been there."

"You never stole anything?"

"Well, one time Bob found a gold coin in Mr. Epistola's dresser drawer and we couldn't make him put it back, so we kicked him out of the game. We threatened to beat the living shit out of him if he told on us, and then rat on him about the gold coin, so he kept his mouth shut. But that was the only time."

"So you just broke in—and then left?"

"Not exactly," Derek said. "We'd look around first. You know, try to find the dirty magazines, check out the mom's underwear. If they had kids, we'd scope out their rooms to see what kind of toys they had, where they hid their comic books, that kind of stuff. We always raided the kitchen, too. If there were open bags of cookies or candy, we'd take half of what was left.

"We taught ourselves everything: surveillance, lock picking, tailing techniques. Some of it came from books, but a lot of it we just picked up in the field. We were pretty good, too. Nobody ever called the cops, and we must have done forty houses."

Derek smiled ruefully.

"I thought it was over when we graduated from high school," he said. "You know, kid's stuff. I went to U-Dub and worked for Boeing, then I heard about a hot new software company and switched jobs. When I started at Contrel, we were using mainframes and punch cards, but by the time I left we were writing PC apps, and along the way I worked on everything in between: DEC, Sun, Unix, MVS, you name it." He paused. "That's how I met Marjorie."

"Who's Marjorie?"

"She's... she was my wife. She was writing the manual for a project I was on, so we spent a lot of time together. She was so beautiful..." He looked at Carla with grief and guilt on his face.

"We got married in 1981," he said. "I'll never forget seeing her coming up the aisle in that white dress, with the sun shining through the stained glass onto her veil like... like a blessing."

He stopped. Carla said, "So what happened?"

Derek winced. "She caught me cheating. I don't know why I did it. God knows I love... loved her. I wasn't unhappy, I was just, I don't know... bored. No, not bored. Tired. I don't know. It was stupid."

"She divorced you?" Carla was curious. When she was a child, peoples' lives had held small tragedies like this, but for the last thirteen years she had been living in a more savage world, where gunshots followed harsh words, betrayals ended in death, and separations were never friendly.

"I begged her to give me another chance. Unfortunately, I'd admitted that it wasn't the first time—hell, it wasn't the tenth time. I was willing to go to marriage counseling, therapy, anything she wanted. But what she wanted was to leave. She moved out and filed for divorce. I got the house and some money."

"What did you do?"

"What do you think?" Derek said. "I fell apart. Lost my job, lost my appetite, didn't give a shit about anything. To tell you the truth, I have no idea what I did for that whole year—it's a complete blank. Then one day I woke up and realized that it was time to go back to work. I wanted to make it up to her, I guess I hoped that someday we'd get back together, but now...." He fell silent and Carla let him be.

"Then... let's see. A friend of a friend wanted the dope on some new system software at Microsoft. I knew some people there, I'd even been inside the buildings a few times, so I knew the layout. I broke in one night and got what this guy wanted. It was easy. Their security was a joke back then. All you had to do was wear jeans and a T-shirt and look like a geek who owns the planet. They all work weird hours anyway.

"That's how it started up again. Pretty soon I was making better money than I ever made at Contrel. Then the Gugliemos showed up. They knew what they wanted, they thought I could get it for them, and they would *not* take no for an answer.

"And that's how I met you," he said.

Carla wondered where his story would end. She felt some sympathy for him, felt a little bit guilty about yanking him out of his life, but she had her own problems at the moment.

"I need a shower," she said and walked out, leaving Derek sitting at the foot of the bed.

* * *

In order to catch her mother completely off guard, Carla told Derek to park the car down the street. They spent the afternoon loafing. Derek lay on the couch reading a book he'd found in her closet, chuckling to himself every now and then.

Carla sat in the easy chair, trying to recall growing up in this house, but recovered only a few fragments. She and her sister were forbidden to sit in her father's chair—the same one she sat in now—so they played in it every chance they got. Sometimes their mother would bustle in, wiping her hands on her apron, and shoo them out of the chair. As soon as she was back in the kitchen, they jumped right back in, giggling. Carla sniffed, but found no trace of the pipe tobacco aroma that had always followed her father.

Not much more would come back to her, so she got up to inspect the rest of the house. Paula's bedroom was surprising only because it was neat. Her sister had been a fourteen year-old slob when Carla left home. Carla sat on the bed, wondering what had become of the little pony-tailed girl she remembered. Paula had been a quiet child, unlike Carla, who was a noisy tomboy, the terror of the neighborhood. The music stand in the corner reminded her that Paula had started violin lessons when she was seven. Carla couldn't remember whether she'd been any good, she only remembered having to put up with the endless, mind-numbing practice noises coming from behind Paula's closed door.

There were no men's clothes in her mother's closet. She felt nothing but a brief pang when she wondered if her father were dead. On her fifteenth birthday, she had announced over dinner her intention to become a spy. Paula laughed and her parents smiled, but when it became clear that she was serious, and could not be persuaded to take up a more "feminine" pursuit such as nursing or teaching, her father had given up on her. He refused to say goodbye when she left for Israel and never wrote to her. In her mother's last letter, nine years ago, she'd announced that they were getting divorced.

There was nothing else to learn from her mother's bedroom. She recognized herself and Paula as children in some of the pictures on top of the dresser, but none of the other faces looked familiar. Carla went back to the living room and examined the photographs hanging on the walls. Most of them were of a slender, short-haired woman that she finally recognized as her sister. There was a wedding picture: Paula in a billowing white dress beside a tall, blond man wearing a tuxedo and a crooked smile.

She sat down in her father's chair, watching Derek read his book and trying to decide how long it was safe to stay here. Just after five-thirty, she heard a key turn in the front door lock. Derek rested the book on his chest and looked at her. She gestured to him to stay put.

The door opened and her mother walked in. *My God, she's gone gray*—but in fact most of her hair was still black. Her mother closed the door behind her and had one arm out of her long, tan-colored coat before she noticed Derek lying on the couch. She gasped and stepped back, the coat dangling from her shoulder.

Derek smiled reassuringly and turned his head to look at Carla. Her mother followed his gaze and cried out softly. She dropped her coat and ran across the room. Carla stood up and accepted a fierce hug without enthusiasm, wondering if her mother could feel the pistol at her chest.

"Hello, Mother," she said.

Her mother stepped back, holding Carla by the shoulders and looking her up and down. "Carla," she said, in the throaty voice that Carla had not heard in thirteen years, the voice she had followed in dreams and never thought to hear again in life—the voice that had defined her childhood. "I can't believe it. I feel like I'm dreaming."

Carla disengaged herself and gestured at Derek. "Mother, this is Derek Narr. Derek, my mother, Sarah Citrullo."

Derek stood up to shake hands, and she gave him the same appraising look she'd just used on her daughter.

"Carla, my dear," Sarah said, "is this handsome young man your husband?"

Chapter 14

St. Tropez, France
   Monday, February 27, 7:01 p.m. (11:01 a.m. MST)

The computer beeped only once, but that was enough to awaken Chen. It seemed to take forever to fall asleep these days, but even a mouse wrinkling its nose would startle him awake. So he'd taken to going to bed at dusk, but first Philippe's phone calls and now this...

He fell out of bed and walked barefoot to the desk in the corner of the one-room flat. He was a short man, thin to the point of emaciation, with coarse black hair. Above the indigo silk pajama bottoms, his sunken chest was bare, revealing protruding ribs. Had he shown up in an American hospital, the ER staff would have instantly suspected AIDS, but this was his normal appearance, the result of breeding, apathy toward food, and opium. Chen was thirty-three and he doubted, somewhat hopefully, that he would live to be thirty-four—but he'd expected to die before his next birthday every year since he was eight.

Chen reached for his glasses. When he set the thick, black plastic frames on his nose he looked like a very hungry, Chinese Buddy Holly. He peered at the computer screen, which showed that he had a new e-mail message.

The rickety wooden desk was bare except for a goose-neck lamp and the PC and printer that Philippe had given him. Chen owned few possessions; *things* did not interest him. He sat down in the rolling office chair, switched on the lamp, rubbed his eyes behind the glasses, and looked around for his cigarettes. Then he remembered that he had smoked the last one that morning, and cursed Philippe or whatever son of a mongrel whore bitch had wakened him by sending him e-mail. Chen grabbed the mouse and clicked on the flashing icon.

Carla. He hissed through his teeth as he read the message.

He considered deleting it, which might get the scheming, vicious slut in trouble with Philippe. Maybe Philippe would even kill her. After enjoying that fantasy for several minutes, Chen reluctantly concluded that he couldn't do it. For one thing, Carla could probably prove she'd sent the e-mail, and then Chen would be in serious trouble himself. More importantly, if Philippe didn't get this information, he'd never be able to sell the warheads and then Chen would not be paid.

Forced to do the right thing against his will, Chen printed the e-mail and spent several increasingly frustrating minutes trying to find his phone. In fury he kicked at a pile of clothes on the floor—and howled in rage, grabbing at his right foot and hopping on his left. The old-fashioned, bulky telephone had been hiding in the heap.

Chen dialed Philippe's number. When this job was over and he could afford a better place, he would burn down this vermin-ridden building—after first smashing the phone with a sledgehammer.

"Oui," Philippe said.

"I have e-mail from your favorite cunt." His toe still hurt.

"Is it the message we've been expecting?"

"No, you worm swimming in the sweat of a sick camel's balls, it's a fucking birthday card."

Philippe laughed. "I'll be right over."

I can't wait. Chen hung up and stared at the phone, trying to work up the courage to do what he had to do next. *I don't have to. But if I don't, she'll kill me. But if I do,* Philippe *will kill me.* He closed his eyes. *Better Philippe than her. But Philippe might kill her before she gets to me.* Sadly, he knew that was impossible. Philippe was smart and ruthless, but Carla was an entirely different circle of hell.

He reached for the receiver, pulled his hand back, glared at the damned thing for a moment, and tried again. This time he managed to pick it up, and dialed the number that Carla had made him memorize. Someone answered but didn't speak.

Chen said, "Center fire."

A man's voice spoke firmly: "Stay on the line." Chen heard several clicks but nothing else, not even breathing. After two minutes he was getting nervous. Philippe wasn't that far away. If he arrived and found Chen on the phone, or tried to call and found the line busy... *Hurry up!*

The man said, "Hang up and forget this number."

Chen followed the first instruction immediately and gratefully. For the second, he was going to need some help. Perhaps Philippe would loan him some money out of friendship—*that's a joke*—or to reward him for the e-mail. Chen tried to think. He would beg Philippe if he had to. He could tell him honestly that he'd never get back to sleep now without his opium. He started getting dressed in eager anticipation of going out. *And don't forget to buy cigarettes.*

* * *

Philippe read the e-mail for the tenth time in three hours. The paper was wrinkled: Chen's hands had been sweating and shaking as he handed it over and asked for a small loan. *Why would he be nervous?* Something to do with Carla, no doubt, but it was pointless trying to guess why she had done whatever she'd done to Chen: she'd been trained by the Mossad, and the Mossad weren't human.

He forgot about Chen for the moment, satisfied that Lanotte's plan rendered him harmless, and reread Carla's message. He'd known that if Hildreth were still alive, Carla could persuade him to cough up some names. Philippe doubted that Carla had left Hildreth still breathing, and that didn't bother him at all. He'd met Hildreth just once, at one of Pequinot's parties, and instantly hated the arrogant weasel. No, not a weasel... a wolverine: an ugly, vicious carnivore that would rather steal another hunter's kill than chase down its own prey.

One of the men on Hildreth's list was dead, a belated victim of the same operation that had eliminated Philippe's old boss, Pequinot. He'd heard of the other two, and thought they were both still alive. Two years away from this rapidly-changing business was enough time for Philippe to lose touch with the major players; all of the ones he'd known personally were now dead or retired. He hated having to use Carla to find buyers, but no one else he knew could have found Hildreth—or dealt with him once they'd found him.

And she had done it. Philippe set the paper aside and walked out onto his balcony. The stars shone brightly despite the lights of the town. He could hear the sea far below, a soft shush like the purr of a giant asthmatic cat.

Jensen had taken the videotapes to a courier service, which would deliver them to their destinations, Cairo and Beirut, within eight hours. It would take some time for the clients to contact him through the complex chain of cut-outs and drop boxes he'd constructed to ensure his safety, but he might hear from them as early as tomorrow evening. It was conceivable that a sale could be completed in less than a week.

I'm one step closer—and now Carla is expendable. She should show up at their rendezvous point in Cannes in a few days. He would have someone watching and waiting for her there, starting tomorrow.

Confidently at peace, Philippe looked up at the indifferent stars.

Chapter 15

Kalispell, Montana
Monday, February 27, 2:07 p.m.

At a knock on the doorframe, Chapa looked up gratefully from the report he was reading. He'd been fighting to stay awake. Forensics had written a small book to tell him what he already knew: Citrullo had shot Hildreth, his TV, and one of his German shepherds; the blood on the floor by the other dog wasn't Hildreth's; and Hildreth had died from a neatly grouped double tap between the eyes. The nine-millimeter slugs and casings had all been recovered, and all five had been fired from the same weapon.

Shaffer was standing in the open doorway of the office he was borrowing, looking unusually jumpy. Chapa gestured her to come in and happily set down the report and the pencil he'd been chewing.

"Uh, s-sir," she said, "I brought someone to see you."

An odd-looking man walked into the room. He was of average height, exceptionally lean, with a thick shock of white hair. Piercing gray eyes scowled out of an angular face. Although he wore a well-tailored dark suit, there was something ill-used about his appearance. *He looks like a spook.*

"Sir, this is Myron Walkenshaw, the CIA agent I've been liaising with. He's just arrived from D.C."

So this was the guy Shaffer used to live with. *It must be tough to have to ask an old boyfriend for help—no wonder she's nervous. But what's he doing here?*

Chapa stood up to shake hands and tried not to wince; Walkenshaw squeezed so hard that Chapa could feel his bones grind together. *Yeah, you're a tough guy, you jerk.*

"It's nice to meet you, Agent Chapa," Walkenshaw said in a deep voice that rumbled up improbably from his thin frame. "I've heard a lot about you."

"Good to meet you, too," Chapa lied. "I'm a little surprised to see you here, though. Have a seat."

Walkenshaw set down his briefcase and took the nearest chair. Shaffer settled into another, as far away from him as she could get. There was an awkward pause that Chapa used to study their body language. Walkenshaw sat comfortably in the uncomfortable fiberglass and steel chair, both feet on the floor and his hands resting in his lap, smiling pleasantly. Chapa guessed that, for Walkenshaw, his relationship with Shaffer was a thing of the far distant past, obscured by many subsequent women, dimly but fondly remembered.

Shaffer was something else entirely: hunched over slightly, clutching a sheaf of file folders tightly in both hands. She seemed ready to leap out the door at the slightest move by Walkenshaw. After a moment, she relaxed a little and shuffled through her files. "I have some news before we get to whatever it is Myron has for us."

"Okay," Chapa said.

"We finally found the border guard who was on duty yesterday morning. He left at noon and spent the day at his girlfriend's house."

"Did he see them?"

"He didn't remember the vehicle," Shaffer said, "but he positively identified Citrullo. He said she had a beautiful smile."

"I'll bet she did. Was Derek in the car?"

"He said there was a passenger, but he didn't get a good look at him."

So Derek and Citrullo were in Canada. Chapa realized that Shaffer had that look in her eyes: she was about to drop a bombshell.

"What?" he said.

"I've been thinking about Citrullo's tactics at the cabin." The analysis of the tracks left in the snow showed that Citrullo had spent some time reconnoitering alone while Derek waited in the woods, then they walked to the cabin together. Why hadn't he run away when she left him alone?

"She obviously has a lot of field experience," Shaffer said, "Now that we know she's Mossad, I've been reevaluating everything she's done so far, and I don't think Varnes's car crash was an accident."

"What do you mean?"

"Well..." Shaffer leaned back in the chair and crossed her legs. "If she's that good, she would have spotted Varnes following her and done something about it."

"What could she do?" Chapa said. "She didn't run them off the road."

"No, sir. She shot out their tire."

"*What?*"

"I called the state patrol and asked them to examine the car—what was left of it. There was a slug inside the left front tire. Ballistics confirms it was fired by the same weapon that killed Hildreth."

"That's not possible," Chapa said. "She was doing eighty on a winding, icy, mountain road. Varnes was at least a hundred feet behind her. Nobody could hit that target with a pistol, shooting backwards out the window while driving."

Walkenshaw stirred in his seat. "It's a difficult shot," he said, "but not impossible. Especially not for someone with her training."

Chapa frowned at him. "You know something."

Walkenshaw reached down for his briefcase, opened it on his lap, and passed a thick manila folder to Chapa.

"Your Agent Frieder contacted me yesterday morning," Walkenshaw said. "I called a friend in the Mossad and explained that we might have found their, um, missing agent. He was...," he paused, searching for the right word, "*uniquely* helpful. The Mossad will happily take whatever we give them gratis, and you can convince them to trade, but they *never* volunteer data. Never, until now." He gestured at the folder with a bony finger and Chapa opened it. "They faxed us this an hour later. It's Citrullo's complete history—I mean, *everything*. We've never had access to such detailed information on any Israeli operative before. After my section chief got a look at it, he assigned me to you full time, to use at your discretion for the duration of the investigation."

Thick sheaves of paper were attached to each side of the heavy folder. At the top right was a photograph, unmistakably the woman from Derek's house. He flipped through the dossier. Personal information, including performance reviews, was on the right. Summaries and evaluations of operations were on the left. Chapa flipped up the photograph and started reading.

Carla Citrullo, born February 28, 1964—her thirty-first birthday was tomorrow. Chapa would have guessed she was twenty-five. He skimmed rapidly: born in Canada, emigrated to Israel at eighteen, two years IDF (that was standard for women; men served three years), two years Aman, then transferred to Mossad. Three years of training, two years of field work, then back to school for—

"Jesus Christ," he said. "She's an assassin!"

After a year of kidon training, she'd gone back to the field and worked—killing people—for another year. Then, in September 1993, she'd vanished in the middle of a mission on the West Bank. At first the Mossad thought she'd been killed by the PLO, but before long there were rumors coming in from informants. She was still alive and working freelance. She'd been seen in the company of known arms smugglers.

That's the tie to Hildreth.

There was no clue as to why she'd gone AWOL. She'd graduated second in her class of Mossad trainees, and first in her class of assassins. She was apparently a successful and highly regarded agent. She'd been decorated twice, the first time for bravery while she was in Lebanon, for single-handedly saving a squad that was under heavy artillery attack. The second time had been for undercover work in Jordan during the Gulf War. There were numerous citations and her reviews were full of praise.

Chapa flipped back further in her file and found the psychological evaluations. Highly independent thinker, brave, resourceful, extremely intelligent. She had strong emotions but they were tightly controlled. He flipped to the next page. She was an expert in armed and unarmed combat, deadly with hands, pistols, rifles, knives, explosives... She was rated to fly helicopters and most small planes. She was an accomplished mountain climber and a part-time aikido instructor.

There was a contact report from an agent coded N23. Someone in France was bargaining to turn Citrullo over to the Mossad. Since the negotiations were proceeding through message drops and cut-outs, progress was slow.

So, she's gone renegade and the Mossad wants her back. If nothing else, they'd want to know why she left, but he could think of lots of other questions they might have, for instance who she'd been working with, where they were, what they were doing...

Why did the Mossad give us her file?

Maybe she'd learned something she wasn't supposed to know. Chapa recalled the saying that the Mossad had as many secrets as all the rest of the world combined—or was that the CIA? Maybe she'd tried to blackmail someone and the scheme fell apart. Or perhaps she'd been framed for something and run away to escape a rigged trial and execution. There had to be a lot missing from this dossier. He'd bet that the Mossad had a kidon team—assassins—out hunting her right now.

They want us to find her for them.

Chapa let the pages fall back into place. He flipped up the photograph and idly scanned the personal information again.

"Oh, my God," he said. He picked up the phone and called their pilot at the Kalispell airport, ordering the jet to be readied for immediate take-off.

"You must have seen this," he said, indicating the top sheet under the picture.

"Yes, sir," Walkenshaw said. "I thought you'd want a few minutes to look it over, at least once."

"What is it?" Shaffer said.

"She was born in Calgary," Chapa said. "Her mother still lives there. That's what... maybe a six hour drive from Hildreth's? So she could have got there yesterday afternoon. She may still be there."

"I've already talked to the Mounties," Walkenshaw said, "on my flight in from D.C. They're not only willing to cooperate, they'll back us up in force and let *us* bag her."

"Let's go, then," Chapa said. They all stood up and Chapa handed Shaffer the file on Citrullo.

"One more thing, sir," Walkenshaw said as they left the office.

"What?"

"I have a few, um, experts with me. They might come in handy when we find her."

Marksmen. He didn't want to shoot Citrullo if they could take her alive, but she was a professional killer. Sharpshooters just might be necessary.

"Okay," he said, "bring them along. And I want a helicopter ready when we get there."

"No problem," Walkenshaw said. He fell a step or two behind as he pulled out his cell phone and started punching numbers.

Chapa called out to four agents they'd worked with at the cabin. "Get your butts in gear, you're going to Canada."

"Sir," Shaffer said quietly as they found their coats by the door. "I'm not sure I'm comfortable with this. We'll be operating on Canadian soil—with the *CIA*."

"What do you think we should do," Chapa said, "stand down? Let the Mounties try to grab her?" She frowned but said nothing. They walked out into the bitter cold toward their car. "I'll make it clear to Myron that *I'm* in charge of this operation, not the CIA."

"Yes, sir," Shaffer said doubtfully.

Doubting what? That I'm in charge? Or that all of us together can take Citrullo down?

Chapter 16

Las Vegas, Nevada
Monday, February 27, 1:31 p.m.

Down on the floor, throngs of people fed coins into slot machines or surrendered chips to croupiers. The glitzy, artificial lighting was changeless, so Gugliemo wondered if these sheep even knew what time of day it was. The casino was only slightly less efficient at separating people from their money than if the marks had just dumped all their cash at the door and turned around to go home.

Some people called it entertainment. He watched a fat woman in a rose-colored polyester pant suit drop quarters into a slot one after another—yanking the handle, waiting, then feeding in the next coin—and wondered which was really the machine. At the blackjack tables, men and women hunched over the green felt, stiffening with each card, slumping when they went bust or puffing up when they beat the dealer.

What a sweet deal. You didn't even have to *ask* people for their money. They fell all over each other to *give* it to you.

He turned away from the window and looked around Maroni's office. If he could walk on clouds, this deep blue plush carpet was what it would feel like. He wanted to take off his shoes and socks and try it barefoot. The walls were papered in a classy, dark purple with a nubbly, raised gold paisley pattern. Gugliemo had been fighting an urge to run his hand over the wall to feel the texture.

The wooden furniture was dark, burnished cherry. Maroni, still on the phone with his FBI stooge, sat behind a desk that could have seated twelve for dining. A grandfather clock ticked softly in the corner across from a built-in bar that gleamed with brass trim. Wall sconces and a few well-placed lamps provided soft, indirect lighting.

Gugliemo sat down on the huge couch across from Maroni's desk. The black leather was supple; the couch was more comfortable than his bed. Some decorator had made—had spent—a fortune on this office.

132

Compared to this, Gugliemo's place was a sewer. He wondered if there were designers in Seattle who could do this kind of work. He thought of asking Maroni for the name of his decorator but decided that would be a very bad idea.

Maroni hung up the phone and swiveled his high-backed leather chair to look out on the floor. Cocktail waitresses, their trays held high, wove effortlessly though the crowds like porpoises through a school of tuna. Everywhere you looked money was falling like rain.

John Maroni was a portly man in his late forties, dressed in a suit of Italian linen, navy blue with a barely discernible pinstripe. The jacket hung on a coat tree by the office door, leaving him in a starched, brilliant white shirt with gold cufflinks, red suspenders, and a red-and-black tie. Thinning black hair, slicked back, exposed a widow's peak. Maroni reached behind him for his cigar, puffed a few times while continuing to watch the floor, then turned to face Gugliemo. Behind the round lenses of his glasses, fathomless green eyes focused on him. Gugliemo tried not to shiver under that stare.

"What's the word, Mr. Maroni?" he said.

Maroni took another puff of his fat Cuban cigar before answering. "What have you gotten yourself into, you fucking little weasel?"

Gugliemo fought down panic. He knew he was out of his depth here, but he had to pretend he could still swim.

"What do you mean?"

"Your tame geek has a new partner." Maroni blew smoke up at the ceiling. "A woman."

"Yeah, he's always got some new broad."

"Not like this. The woman he's with? She's a Mossad agent."

Gugliemo blinked and shook his head to clear his ears. Did he just say... *Mossad?*

"Muh... Mossad? Like the Israeli secret service?"

Maroni raised his eyebrows. "Two points. Maybe you're not as stupid as I thought. Now why would your guy hitch up with a spy?"

Gugliemo could think of nothing to say. *What the hell is going on?*

"Next thing," Maroni said. "The Feds think this broad whacked your tail. Shot the fuckers while they were following her at eighty miles an hour. That's some damned good shooting, huh?" He knocked ash into a gold-plated ashtray and leaned back in his chair.

"Then your lovebirds drove up to Montana, plugged some guy in a fucking log cabin, and split for Calgary."

Gugliemo's head was spinning. "Calgary? Like, where they crucified Jesus?"

"Jesus Christ on a donkey!" Maroni said. "That's *Calvary,* you imbecile. They're in Calgary, Alberta." Gugliemo put a finger in his mouth and tapped his upper teeth with the nail. He was drawing a blank. Maroni shook his head and went on with false patience, "Alberta, Canada? Right next to British Columbia, which—" his voice grew louder until he was screaming, "—is right on top of Seattle, you fucking *moron!*"

"Never been to Canada," Gugliemo apologized.

"Christ, it's no wonder you're in the crapper with the Feds. You're too goddamned stupid to live."

"Sorry, Mr. Maroni."

Maroni turned away in disgust. After a moment, he began talking again, his back still to Gugliemo.

"This is some weird shit. You hire a geek to toss the Feds. That was some pretty lame-ass thinking to start with. He probably pissed his pants and fell right into their lap. If this Mossad bitch hadn't come along, you'd be in jail right now, you stupid fucker. So where did she come from? How did they hook up?"

Gugliemo wanted to get up and run the hell home. This was too much for him. Having the Feds after him was bad enough; he hadn't slept in months. But now Narr was gone, not only gone, but working with a *spy?* What was that about? What the hell did he know about this crap—broads and blow, that's what he knew about. He ought to leave this to Maroni...

"Okay," Maroni said, turning back to face Gugliemo. "This is too interesting to let go. The Feds are headed up to Canada to grab them both, but it's going to take hours for them to get their shit together with the fucking Mounties. I'm going to lend you some of my best guys. You go up there with them, but they run the show, understand?"

"You... you want me to go to Canada?"

"Right. I'll send Pescado—he's a good friend; a real pro, and very tough. He'll bag the geek and the spy bitch and bring them back here."

"Uh..." Gugliemo swallowed hard. "You want me to go up there and snatch Narr and the broad?"

"What's the alternative, you dumb shit? If the Feds get there first, you can kiss your cheeks goodbye. Not that I really care, but I hate seeing family go to jail, just on principle. Like I told you, Pescado's good. He won't have any trouble with this Mossad broad, and I doubt if that computer nerd of yours would even strain his pinkie." He picked up the phone again and called Pescado, then dialed another number and told someone to fire up the plane.

Gugliemo watched Maroni at work. *Why do* I *have to go?* He knew better than to ask; things were bad enough already. Maroni's blood was up, there was no telling what he'd do if he really got pissed. He might demand that Gugliemo actually do the job himself, which would probably get him killed.

"Get going, Gugliemo," Maroni said as he hung up the phone. "The plane leaves in half an hour. I want you back here tonight with the spy and the geek. Something's going down, and I want a piece of it."

Gugliemo got up off the couch shakily and headed for the door.

"Hey, Gugliemo," Maroni said. He turned back with his hand on the doorknob. "After we're done with business, we can have a little fun, huh? I've never done a spy before. Could be interesting—for a while."

Maroni smiled a vicious, wicked smile that made Gugliemo shiver. He shut the door behind him without a word, wondering what sort of monster he'd apprenticed himself to.

Chapter 17

Calgary, Alberta
Monday, February 27, 7:16 p.m.

Shimon Eitan lowered his binoculars with satisfaction. David and Elias had taken up positions behind Sarah Citrullo's house, and it seemed this interminable mission might finally be over. For over a year he and his kidon team had chased Carla Citrullo across half of Europe, and now—on a hunch—he had finally caught up to her.

Eitan was a muscular, handsome man—short-cropped brown hair, a thin nose, and a cleft chin. Women occasionally mistook him for a movie star, and when he had the liberty, he took full advantage of this misconception. But not for a long time now.

Their first solid lead in months had come from a forger in Paris only ten days ago. Citrullo had hired the man to make her a Canadian passport, without knowing that he was a *sayan*, a Jewish volunteer agent. When the forger delivered copies of the week's work to his Mossad controller, Eitan had been notified immediately. They tracked her flight from Paris to Chicago to Vancouver, and Eitan's team was on the next plane to Canada.

In Vancouver, Citrullo's trail was already cold. Posing as policemen, they verified that she *was* on the flight from Chicago, but they could find no trace of her in the city: no hotel, no rental car, and no plane ticket out of town. After three days, Eitan was almost ready to give up and go back to Europe, perhaps even to fold the mission, when he'd had an inspiration.

It would be completely out of character, in fact it would violate Citrullo's psychological profile, for her to visit her family. She had no close ties to any of them. There had been no contact between them via post or phone during her last five years in the Mossad. Because it was so unlikely she would visit her mother, Eitan concluded that was exactly what she would do.

They watched the neighborhood for a day and observed that two houses were empty. One was too far down the street to be of any use as an observation post, but the other was nearly across the street from Sarah Citrullo's house. Elias, who could be charming when necessary, delivered a package for the absent couple to their neighbor and stayed for tea. The house would be vacant for several days as the woman's mother had just died unexpectedly. Eitan refused to attach any superstitious meaning to this stroke of luck. In another place, at another time, he might have contrived the mother's death himself in order to acquire such a perfect position—but in any case, it had not been necessary.

They moved into the empty house and began full-time surveillance. Now, only two days later, they'd struck gold: Citrullo had shown up at her mother's house just as he'd expected. She'd arrived with an unknown man, which was *not* expected, but that would pose no problem.

Eitan looked forward to finishing this assignment. Kidon missions were normally brief, often just a few days, a month or two at most. His team had been looking for Citrullo for fourteen months, ever since the Mossad learned she was still alive and working for arms dealers. The problem had been: *which* arms dealers? Months of field work convinced Eitan that she must be employed by someone new to the business, or perhaps coming out of retirement; they found no trace of her with any of the known, active dealers in Europe.

Now he lay the binoculars on the window sill of the darkened living room. From this vantage he could see right across the street and into Citrullo's living room. It was trivial to track the targets' positions. This could be the perfect hit: clean, swift, and no witnesses.

He walked down the hall into the only bedroom that faced the street, where the rest of his team waited. Yosef seemed to be asleep on the bed. Efraim was cleaning his weapons. Tamar was manning the listening device, a parabolic microphone aimed out the partially-opened window. Eitan had worried about leaving the window open in winter—it might arouse suspicions—but they'd had little choice, and no one seemed to notice.

Nothing interesting had happened until Carla arrived this morning and almost immediately leaped into bed. Listening in to the post-coital conversation, they learned a lot about Derek, but Carla's prodigious lies were even more fascinating.

This was the smallest force Eitan had ever led. A typical kidon team would number twelve, but because they'd anticipated a very long mission that might take them anywhere in the world, the office had allotted him only five men.

"What's going on?" he said.

Tamar held one hand to his earphones while he adjusted the volume and aim of the dish with the other hand. "Derek and Sarah in the kitchen—cooking, it sounds like." He swept the mike slowly across the length of the house. "I haven't heard anything from the client in a while," he said, meaning Carla. "She said she needed a nap."

"All right, carry on. Let me know when they start eating; I'll want to listen in again." He started to leave.

"Shimon," Efraim said. Eitan turned back. "Is it necessary? The mother?"

Oh Lord, spare me Efraim's scruples.

"We've been over this already," he said, "but I'll say it one more time." Yosef sat up in the bed, apparently not sleeping after all, and Tamar pulled his earphones down around his neck.

"Yes, we could have hit Citrullo the moment she showed up. But it's vital to listen to her interaction with her mother. She may say something the office will want to know."

Efraim looked pained but said nothing.

"We've all been trained to minimize collateral damage. We can't judge Derek's guilt or innocence, but we know for sure the mother is innocent. Nevertheless, you've all seen the order signed by the Prime Minister. Citrullo is condemned by the State and we are the arm of its justice. We've been chasing this traitor for over a year and this is the first time we've actually seen her face. We must learn everything we can, then we must punish her for her crimes, and we can't leave any witnesses behind.

"It's unfortunate, but sometimes it's necessary." He looked at each man in turn for a moment. "We're going in after they finish dinner. Set aside your pity: everyone in that house is already dead. Just do your jobs and we can go home again."

* * *

Before Sarah had a chance to settle herself and start in on the interrogation that everyone knew was coming, Carla went to her room to take a nap. Derek had seen Carla ruthless, even brave, but what she needed now was not a nap but a backbone. Left behind in his kidnapper's mother's kitchen, he did the only thing he could think of: he helped with dinner.

Sarah was in her mid-fifties and had the same green eyes and the same nose as Carla. Her hair must once have been the same dark black, but now much of it was gray. She was a few inches shorter than Carla, but like her daughter she was slender. While she defrosted some fish fillets and worked on a sauce, Derek prepared the salad, washing, spinning, and shredding lettuce and chopping vegetables—and answering questions. Sarah's frustrated inquisition was immediately redirected on him.

"Well, now, Derek, tell me something about yourself," she said as soon as Carla walked out. Derek gave her the highlights, omitting the nasty parts: his father's drinking, his own infidelities, his unusual vocation.

"What do your parents do?" she said.

"My dad worked for Boeing."

"Oh, he made airplanes."

"No, he was an accountant. He retired a few years ago."

"And what is he doing with all his free time?"

Drinking and watching TV. "Oh, puttering around the house, a little gardening... you know."

Sarah took the fish out of the microwave and blotted it dry with paper towels before slicing it into small, neat pieces. She set the fish aside and went back to her tomato sauce.

"What about your mother? Oh—am I being too nosy?"

Derek smiled and started peeling a carrot. "No, it's all right. Mom is a librarian."

"I see. So she's still working, even though your father's retired?"

Who'd want to hang around the house with a drunken bully? "I don't think she'll ever quit. If they want her to leave, they'll have to throw her out and lock the doors. She loves being around books and helping the school kids with their projects."

Sarah stirred her sauce and turned off the heat under the rice. "Do you have any brothers or sisters?"

"I had an older brother. He died in Viet Nam."

"Oh, I'm so sorry."

"It's okay. I don't really remember much about him, I was only fourteen when he joined the army. We got along okay, but he was five years older and he spent most of his time with his friends, not with me."

"It's so sad," Sarah said, with such intense feeling that Derek looked up, expecting to see her crying, but she was staring off into the distance. Had she lost someone in the war? She shook her head and smiled ruefully, a little embarrassed. "Now how did you and Carla meet?"

We collided trying to get into the same taxi. The hotel accidentally booked us into the same room, so we figured, what the hell? We sat next to each other on a plane coming back from a protest rally. I tripped over those gorgeous legs at a football game. I picked her up in a bar in Honolulu. She kidnapped me while we were both breaking into the FBI office in Seattle.

"I, uh... I helped her with a computer problem," Derek said.

"So you're in computers?"

Derek nodded glumly. *Here it comes. 'Oh, I don't know anything about computers.'*

He almost sliced his finger instead of the cucumber when she said, "That's interesting. We use Macintoshes at the realty and I just love them."

"That's nice," he croaked.

"We used to use PCs, but I hate Windows. Eight-dot-three, give me a break! I think Macs are a lot easier to use, don't you? But who knows what'll happen if Microsoft ever ships Windows 95?"

Now he knew where Carla got her knack for surprises.

"Are you almost finished there?" she said.

He nodded and pitched the last of the cucumber slices into the salad. Sarah glanced into the bowl, smiled in approval, and got a bottle of salad dressing from the refrigerator.

"If you'll toss this," she said, "I'll go get Carla."

* * *

Derek took some satisfaction from Carla's grumpy mood. It was *her* idea to visit her mother.

He tried the halibut hesitantly, but it was delicious. The tomato sauce was spicy, complemented perfectly by the herbed rice. Sarah poured a chilled Fume Blanc that Derek tasted and found to be quite nice, but Carla declined rudely, turning her wine glass upside down. They passed the salad around.

Carla tasted the fish and raised her eyebrows at Sarah. "When did you become a gourmet cook, Mother?"

"After your father left, dear," Sarah said. "I took some classes, just as a hobby at first, you know, a way to pass the time. But I suppose my palate got educated and I came to love it."

Carla tried the rice. "I don't think Father would've appreciated this."

"No," Sarah said without any trace of regret. "He was a meat and potatoes man, wasn't he?"

"How is Father?"

"Oh, I hardly see him any more these days. It's been nine years, you know. He married again, to a rather plump Italian lady." Carla and Sarah looked at each other and smiled. "She's quite a bit younger than he."

"How much younger?"

"Twenty-three years."

Carla did the arithmetic in her head. "That makes her two years older than me."

"Yes," Sarah said. "Would you say that was revolting—or pathetic?"

Derek choked on a forkful of rice. Carla slapped him on the back and handed him his glass of water.

"What happened between you two?" Carla said when he was breathing again. "You never said in your letters."

"I think he was waiting for Paula to graduate from high school. He moved out right after she left for university. But we'd been having problems for years, ever since..."

"What?"

"Ever since you left, dear." Sarah used her napkin and looked across the table at Carla. Mother and daughter stared at each other silently for a moment, expressionlessly, then Sarah resumed eating. "Well, that's enough of that. Derek and I had a nice chat while you were napping, and now it's your turn. I haven't heard from you in six years and then you pop up like a jack-in-the-box. I want to know everything that's happened since you left. You never did tell me one little thing about your life over there in Israel." She looked up from her plate expectantly.

"There's not much I can tell you," Carla said. "I was in the IDF—the army—for two years. I saw some action, but I don't have any war stories."

"Oh, my," Sarah said. "You were a soldier? Did you... did you have to shoot anyone?"

Derek choked on his food again, and Carla leaned over to whack him on the back—hard. He took a sip of water and apologized hoarsely. The coughing made it easier not to burst out laughing.

"Yes, Mother," Carla said. "I was a soldier. All young people in Israel serve in the IDF, and I joined right in the middle of that mess in Lebanon."

"I see." Sarah chased some rice onto her fork. "Well, what happened after the army?"

"I worked in Army Intelligence for a while, then I went to work for the government. That's what I've been doing ever since."

"That's nice," Sarah said. She waited for more. It didn't come. "Well, what kind of work do you do for them?"

"I can't tell you."

"What do you mean, dear? Why can't you tell me?"

"It's classified, Mother. I'm not allowed to discuss it."

"Not even with your mother?"

Carla was silent, so Derek said, "Oh, that's regulations. You have to sign an oath that you *especially* won't talk to your mom." Carla glared at him. Derek flung up his hands. "Sorry." *You're on your own, you big liar.*

Sarah was flustered, looking around the table as if searching for another topic.

"Well... What *can* you talk about? Where do you live? What do you do when you're not working? Do you have any friends? Is there... do you have a man?" She glanced at Derek briefly and blushed.

"My life is pretty boring, Mother." Derek decided to start counting lies: that was number three. "I'm busy with work. I don't have time for a boyfriend, let alone a husband."

Sarah looked at Derek again. Carla sighed.

"Derek and I aren't a couple, Mother," she said. "We met on a business trip and he's helping me with my work. That's all." *Is that two lies or three?* He bumped the count to six.

Sarah looked back and forth between Carla and Derek as if searching for the links that bound them. *Don't look too closely—you won't like what you see.*

"Sweetheart," Sarah said, "you've been gone for thirteen years. We got a few postcards, but never any details, and then even those stopped. Now we're together again after all these years, and you can't tell me *anything* about your life? You can't expect me not to be curious!"

"Believe me, Mother," Carla said, "I understand how you feel. But there really isn't much I can tell you. Look, maybe it would be better if we changed the subject. How's Paula?"

Sarah shook her head in disbelief, but finally she gave in and they stuck to family topics. Carla's sister was married, to a wonderful man even if he wasn't Jewish. No children yet, but Sarah was hopeful. Paula had recently been hired as third violinist in the Toronto symphony orchestra.

Aunt Jody, Sarah's older sister who lived two doors down, was having trouble with her hip again, but the medication was helping and her spirits were good. Sarah liked her job as a realtor, and she made a comfortable living despite the slow market.

Derek followed this trivia with interest. Once he might have found it boring, but after the last few days it was reassuring to hear that people still led lives that did not involve the FBI, guns, or chasing and killing each other. He helped Sarah clear the table while she continued a story about someone's dog chasing Jody's cats. Carla sat at the table, chin on fist, looking half asleep.

"What was Carla like as a little girl?" Derek asked Sarah as he carried two pieces of pie out to the dining room.

"Wait a minute," Carla said.

Sarah set down her own plate and smiled crookedly. "She was skinny."

"Mother."

"Oh, hush," Sarah said. She turned to Derek. "She was so serious all the time. Even at her eighth birthday party—" Sarah's eyes widened. "Oh my goodness, tomorrow's your birthday, isn't it?" Carla propped both elbows on the table and hid her face in her hands, shaking her head. "Well, I'll have to make your favorite cake for you, won't I?"

"What's her favorite cake?" Derek said.

"White cake," Sarah said, "with chocolate chips inside and strawberry frosting." Carla mumbled something. "I'm sorry, dear, what did you say?"

Carla lifted her head. "I said, if you make that, I'll throw up."

"What happened at her birthday party?" Derek said.

"It was a large party, perhaps twenty children. Everyone brought a gift, we had games, and a pony in the back yard. Carla scowled through the whole thing, even when she was opening presents. The boys teased her mercilessly, but she ignored them and refused to play the games. She never was interested in boys, not even in high school. She was a bit plain in grammar school, it's true, but my—how she blossomed in her teens. They used to buzz around her like flies, but she never took them seriously, I'm afraid."

"New subject," Carla said, disappointing Derek.

"I'll make coffee," Sarah said.

* * *

Derek took his previous seat on the couch and Carla sat in the easy chair again. When Sarah came in carrying coffee service on a silver tray, Derek moved aside the book he'd been reading.

"Oh my goodness, are you reading *Winnie-the-Pooh?*" Sarah said. She poured a cup and handed it to Derek. "Carla, do you remember when you got this?"

"No, Mother."

"You were seven. Your grandmother Citrullo came from Toronto for a visit. She stayed for a week, I think. She was already feeling ill, poor thing, she died the next month, do you remember?" Sarah handed a cup to Carla and poured one for herself, then sat down on the couch next to Derek.

"Anyway, she brought you this book as an Easter gift. She was so nice to you, but she never could remember that you weren't Catholic." Sarah smiled. "Well. Do you remember what she said when you opened it?"

Carla shook her head with an expression that might have been pain—or was she just trying to remember her grandmother?

Sarah said, "She told you, 'Once you let Mr. Pooh inside you, you can't ever get him out.' Then she kissed you and went off to bed. Poor old dear."

Derek looked at Carla's impassive face and wondered if she ever had let Pooh in. If so, he must have been erased by her training—he doubted very much that Carla had anything of Pooh left within her now. He took a sip of coffee. There was a moment of silence, then the doorbell rang, startling him.

"Now who could that be?" Sarah said. She set down her cup and stood up to answer the door. Carla flicked her eyes at Derek and glided out of the chair, reaching for her pistol. Derek had a horrible premonition. He felt his limbs grow heavy as Sarah opened the door.

Chapter 18

Calgary, Alberta
    Monday, February 27, 8:09 p.m.

Derek felt unnaturally alert in the seconds before the whirlwind hit. He noticed that the picture window curtains had been drawn. There were three bare spots on the wall of family photos where pictures had been removed. One of Carla's shoelaces was untied.

He was sitting on the end of the couch farthest away from the door. Carla, who had moved so quickly and quietly that Sarah hadn't noticed her, was now behind the door holding her gun in both hands, the muzzle pointed at the ceiling.

And then the door was fully open. Cold air wafted into the room.

Sarah said, "Can I help—"

"Just step back inside," a man's voice said. Sarah backed up, then the kitchen door crashed open—*we should have locked it*—and time slowed down.

Sarah turned to see what the noise in the kitchen was. Carla reached around the front door, grabbed her mother's arm, and spun her into the room. As her own body swiveled, Carla slammed her shoulder into the door. It must have caught the man outside right in the face: Derek heard a crack, a grunt, and a scream as the man stumbled backward off the porch and down the steps. Sarah was tripping over a footstool, her hands reaching out to catch herself.

Out of the corner of his eye, Derek saw someone rush in from the kitchen. Carla was down on one knee, facing the new threat with her gun raised and sighted, partially screened from him by the front door rebounding from the first man's face.

Three shots burst like thunder in the small room. Derek clapped his hands to his ears and finished turning toward the kitchen. A heavy-set man in a long dark coat was falling to the floor. The wall behind him was spattered with his blood. Derek got a brief glimpse of a ruddy face and thick glasses before the body collapsed in a heap with one hand stretched out, still holding a huge pistol.

Sarah's petite rump was up in the air as she tried to get off the footstool. Derek found himself standing in the hallway leading to the bedrooms, within arm's reach of her.

Someone wearing a black trench coat strode in the front door, his swarthy face convulsed in fear and rage, holding a pistol even more gigantic than the dead man's. This couldn't be the man Carla had hit with the door: there was no blood on his face.

The gunman hadn't noticed Carla behind the door. As he turned toward Derek and Sarah, Carla flowed like liquid, standing on her hands and flinging her legs in a smooth arc parallel to the floor. She caught him right behind the knees and swept his legs out from under him. Completing the 360-degree turn, ending up on her knees facing the downed man, she chopped her forearm onto his throat and knocked his gun out of reach.

He was gurgling, dying, as another intruder ran in from the kitchen, already shooting but aiming too high: Carla was still on her knees. She rolled over the choking man's body and fired twice. The shooter crumpled onto the floor.

Sarah scrabbled on her belly in the corner as if she wanted to crawl into the wall. Carla continued her roll and flowed up into a crouch in the corner diagonally opposite her mother, swiveling to cover the front door and then the kitchen.

Everything was quiet. The echoes of the gunshots faded away, but the acrid stench of gunpowder hung in the air, burning Derek's eyes. There was no visible smoke. A gun was lying on the frayed carpet a few feet away from him. As he stooped to pick it up, Carla's eyes flicked toward him and back to the front door. He pushed the door closed and leaned against the wall beside it.

"Now what?" he said. She grinned at him but said nothing.

Someone knocked politely on the door.

"Hey in there," a gruff voice said. "Don't shoot."

"Don't come in," Carla said.

"Yeah, okay. Let's just talk a minute, all right? We got off on the wrong foot here."

"No fucking kidding," Carla said.

"Hey, I'm sorry, we made a mistake. But you're some tough broad, huh?"

"If you open that door, you'll be dead before you can find out."

The man laughed. Derek heard the faint *snick* of a cheap cigarette lighter. "Hey, you got that guy Narr in there?"

"I'm here," Derek said, surprised that his voice was steady. He stepped away from the door.

"So, Narr, Mr. Gugliemo is very confused. What's the story, huh? He and you had a business arrangement. But you never showed up for the meeting, and now you got a new partner, huh? And two of our friends are smoked beef down at the bottom of a canyon somewhere. And now we have this little, uh, misunderstanding. So what gives, huh?"

Derek had no idea what to say. Even if he wanted to talk to this wiseguy, he wouldn't know where to start.

"You got a lot of Feds looking for you," the man continued. "I guess they're gonna be here soon." Derek frowned at Carla; she shrugged and kept her gun pointed at the door. "Narr? You still there?"

"I'm here," Derek said.

"You know, we didn't come here to hurt nobody. You guys started it. We just didn't know what to expect, because we heard about your partner's, uh... shady past. But I guess we scared you, huh?" Derek backed another step away from the door. "I got an idea. How about if you two come on out and we'll go talk to Mr. Gugliemo and his friend, Mr. Maroni. Just talk, I swear. We just want to straighten this whole thing out." *Right, you just want to straighten us out—on a slab.*

"We can hide you from the Feds. And, hey, I think they're bringing the CIA and the Mounties, and local cops, too. You ain't got a lot of time. So what do you say?"

Carla stood up and moved into the room, still aiming her gun at the doorway. She leaned against the wall beside the opening to the dining room and glanced at her mother, who was crouched on her hands and knees. Sarah's complexion had gone gray and her mouth was open and slack. She was shivering, looking from one dead body to the next, over and over.

"Get lost," Carla said.

"Okay, lady, I got another idea. How about if you give us Narr and you can go on your way? He's the one we came for, not you. Nothing's going to happen to him, I swear. Mr. Gugliemo just wants to talk to him."

Carla got down on one knee. She glanced back over her right shoulder into the kitchen. "No deal," she said.

The man laughed lightly. "Okay, I got another idea. Hey, Narr, how about sending the spy out and we'll call it quits? Lady, we could use a tough cookie like you, no kidding. Come on out—really. I think I'm in love here."

Carla grinned at Derek and raised one eyebrow.

The back door slammed open and Derek threw himself to his left, out of the line of fire from the kitchen. He heard someone roll into the mud room. Carla peeked into the kitchen again.

"I think you're out of options," the man said in a much less friendly voice.

Carla caught Derek's attention and jerked her head toward the kitchen. He nodded and moved back into the room, raising the dead man's chrome-plated pistol in both hands. His father had taught him to shoot, but not with cannons like this, just cheap .22 revolvers.

When he was ready, Carla emptied her pistol into the wall just to the left of the front door. The sound of five shots, incredibly loud, boomed off the walls and made Derek flinch. He almost missed seeing a very short man, gun in hand, running toward them from the kitchen.

Another shot rang out and the short man screamed and stumbled. He fell heavily and lay on the floor, moaning and twisting. Derek looked down at the gun in his hands and saw smoke coming from the muzzle.

Jesus Christ, I shot him! Now I'm a murderer, too. But he shoved that thought aside and tensed for someone else to come at him.

Carla already had a fresh clip in her pistol. She racked the slide to load a cartridge into the chamber.

"Who's next?" she shouted. "We've only got four dead scuzzbos in here. Give me more!" The short man moaned loudly from the floor. "Wait a minute," Carla said, and Derek jumped as she shot the injured man in the head. The body jerked and lay still. "Sorry, he was still alive. *Now* we've got four dead ones."

The man outside said nothing.

"I'm getting pretty fucking bored with this game," Carla said. "Come on in and let me finish it. Or you can wait until the cops get here. You want to tell them how *I* attacked *you?*"

There was a long silence. Then Derek heard a scrabbling sound in the kitchen and saw someone fling himself out the back door. He lowered the gun and discovered that he was breathing hard. Nothing happened for another long stretch of seconds.

Finally the man outside said, "Fuck you, bitch." His voice sounded different; Derek wondered if Carla had hit him. A few moments later he heard two car doors open and close, then tires screamed as a car peeled out.

Sarah was sitting on the floor, wedged into the corner, her mouth working slowly and silently. Carla holstered her pistol and squatted down in front of her.

"Mother," Carla said, but Sarah didn't seem to see her. Carla sighed and slapped her face. Sarah jerked and turned away from the bodies, looking at her daughter as if she were a monster. "Well, Mother, you wanted to know what I do for a living." She sighed. "It wasn't supposed to happen like this. I'm sorry. I'm really sorry."

As Carla lifted her to her feet, Sarah stared, dazed, at the four bodies and the spreading pools of blood. *Now she has an excuse to replace the carpeting.* Carla shook her head, took her mother's arm, and led her to the front door, stepping over the bodies.

"Derek," Carla said, "gather our stuff. I'll be back in a minute."

"Where are you going?"

"I'm taking Mother to Aunt Jody's. It's practically next door. Hurry up, the police are on their way right now." She led her mother out into the cold.

Derek looked at the pistol in his hand. He set the safety catch and tucked it into the small of his back.

As he packed, he felt confused because he didn't feel upset. *Maybe I'm in shock, too.* Yesterday he'd nearly had a breakdown when Carla shot Hildreth. Today he was a murderer, too, and taking it very calmly—repacking their bags while their victims' bodies cooled in the living room.

Wait a minute, I didn't kill him, Carla did. Right; tell that to the judge. *Anyway, it was self-defense. They were going to kill us, or take us back to Gugliemo so* he *could kill us.*

Still, now he was a man who had shot another one. Could you get used to this madness? *Sure, but can you do it without going mad yourself?*

When he came back into the living room, Carla was searching the corpses. He set the bags down and picked up *Winnie-the-Pooh*.

"Can you believe this?" Carla said. "All of these goons pack .38s. Is the U.S. *ever* going to go metric?" She pulled a couple of spare clips from a dead man's shoulder holster and handed them to Derek. "If you're going to play, you'll need these."

Derek stared at them for a long moment before accepting them. *I'm not just a bystander anymore.* He stuffed the clips and the book into his bag.

"What did your Aunt Jody say?"

"I didn't talk to her. I just leaned Mother up against the door and rang the doorbell."

"What?"

"We don't have time to play around, Derek. The cops'll be here in a couple of minutes. Do *you* want to try to explain this?" She grabbed her bag and opened the front door.

"Jesus," Derek said. "First you lie to your mother, you fill her living room with corpses, and *then* you lean her up against her sister's door like an ironing board."

"When did I lie to my mother?"

"You said you still work for the government."

Carla stared at him for a second before turning away and walking outside.

* * *

Tamar was panicking. "What should we do?"

"Calm down," Eitan said, "and shut up for a minute." *What a bloody mess.*

The two cars sped away, one of them peeling rubber. Eitan had been almost ready to go in—dinner was over and it was obvious Citrullo wasn't going to say anything useful—when the cars arrived. Six men went in, leaving the drivers behind, but only two came out, and one of those was severely wounded. Yosef had the license plate numbers, so eventually they should be able to identify the fools. Unless the cars were stolen.

For a moment, when the men emerged from the cars carrying guns, Eitan thought they were police and that his mission had failed. But when they barged into the house without showing their credentials, Eitan thought instead they might do his work for him. He should have known better. Citrullo alone could have taken out all six, especially if she wasn't worried about protecting her mother. Tamar had turned the mike on them and they'd listened to Citrullo's conversation with the men, who proved to be gangsters somehow connected with Derek. Now Eitan had two more names: Gugliemo and Maroni.

"Someone's coming out," Tamar said. Eitan picked up his binoculars. It was Citrullo and her mother. Tamar put his hand to his earphones and said, "Elias says he has a shot." Elias and David were still in position behind the house. "It's a little long, but he thinks he can do it. Should he take them out?"

Eitan thought fast. The police were only minutes away and he didn't have a clean exit for his team. *What if Elias misses?* He didn't have a rifle, just his sidearm. What if he just hit the mother? Citrullo was *dangerous*. Eitan was not supposed to sacrifice his team for this mission, and he had no intention of doing so.

"Negative," Eitan said. "Tell them to walk to the restaurant where we had breakfast two days ago and wait there. We'll pick them up later."

Tamar frowned but relayed the message. Eitan ordered his team to pack up, then watched Citrullo go back to her mother's house. A few moments later she and Narr walked away together down the street. *Why aren't they driving?* For the same reason he wasn't: there was only one way in and out of this accursed subdivision, and the police would be charging in before they could get all the way out.

Eitan watched the traitor walk away. He had names and license plate numbers. This was not the end of it.

* * *

The night was very cold, and once again Derek wasn't dressed for it. He was shivering before they reached the street, but he took a deep breath of the clean air and, for once, enjoyed the copper-flavored burn of the cold in his lungs. After the head-banging noise of the gunfight, the neighborhood seemed preternaturally quiet. The sky was clear, but the stars were faded by the streetlights and the haze of city light. Without hesitation, Carla walked off briskly to their left.

"Where are we going?" Derek said. "Why don't we just drive?"

"We're going there." She pointed ahead and to the right. "We're not driving because we'd never make it past the cops."

Derek couldn't make out what she was pointing to, but then he noticed that one driveway was still snow-covered. The small house was dark, evidently empty. They walked up the drive, leaving a trail of footprints on the virgin snow.

"I'd better shovel the drive," he said as Carla picked the lock on the back door. She popped the door open and nodded. This house had roughly the same floor plan as Sarah's, giving Derek an eerie feeling of déjà vu. He couldn't help looking into the living room to see if there were any bodies. In the tidy kitchen he found a garage door opener, which he used.

Carla found a stack of mail on the counter. "Your name is Leonard Starkey," she said. "Go."

A snow shovel was hanging just inside the garage. Derek ran back to the street and started shoveling rapidly, working as quickly as he could. He started by making tracks where car tires would run, switching from one side to the other every ten feet or so. The light outside the front door came on, followed by the living room and kitchen lights. No longer dark, the little house suddenly looked lived-in.

He had been outside for only a few minutes when two police cars screamed past him, sirens wailing and lights flashing, and stopped in front of Sarah's house. Derek worked faster. Carla came outside to give him a hat and gloves and immediately went back in. Derek gratefully put them on, smiling at the naïve idea that she cared whether he was cold: she just wanted him to look like an innocent citizen shoveling his drive. The hat was a bit too large and the gloves were tight, but he felt warmer already. Then the garage door began closing, hiding the fact that there was no car inside.

By the time Derek had shoveled tracks clear to the garage, three unmarked cars had sped past him toward Sarah's. He went back to the street and started clearing the full width of the driveway. An ambulance drove up and the crew hopped out and ran into Sarah's house, but after a moment they strolled back outside, leaned against their van, and lit cigarettes.

Before Derek had reached the house, two policemen walked out of Sarah's front door and looked both ways up the street. One of them pointed to Derek and the other started walking in his direction. Derek stopped working and took off Starkey's hat, running his fingers through his sweaty hair.

"Evening, officer," he said when the cop reached the drive. "What's going on?"

The policeman looked him up and down, frowning slightly. He was almost as tall as Derek, bundled up in a thick coat with a gun belt strapped over it.

"Good evening, sir," he said. "We had a domestic dispute over at Mrs. Citrullo's. I wonder if you might have seen anything?"

"Well, officer, I heard gunshots. To be honest, I wasn't too keen on coming out just then. I looked out the window and didn't see anything, then after it was quiet I stepped outside and heard a car peel out." The cop pulled a pad out of his coat pocket and started taking notes. "Hey—is Sarah okay? Was anyone shot?"

The policeman ignored his questions. "Did you get the license plate number?"

Derek scratched his head and put his hat back on. "Sorry, officer, I didn't. It was too far away."

"How about the make and model of the car?"

"Dark colored sedan, that's all I noticed. Sorry."

The cop nodded as if he hadn't expected more. "Did you notice how many people were in the vehicle?"

"Nope. I came outside just as they pulled out."

"And then... you decided to shovel your driveway."

Derek's blood froze, but he tried to look sheepish. "To tell you the truth, that was just an excuse to come out here and rubberneck. This is a quiet neighborhood, you know. Nothing like this has ever happened in the seventeen years I've lived here."

"Uh huh," the policeman said, frowning. "Did you try to call the police when you heard the shots?"

"Yeah, sure. But the line was busy. I figured all the neighbors were doing the same thing."

The cop looked Derek over again, looked around the yard, and concluded that Derek was harmless and useless.

"All right, sir, that's all the questions I have. We may want to contact you again, though. Can I have your name for the report?"

"Leonard Starkey," Derek said. His legs suddenly felt weak.

"Okay, Mr. Starkey, I'd appreciate it if you'd go back inside now. We have a lot of work to do here and it's a whole lot easier without crowds."

Derek looked around. He was the entire crowd.

"Okay, sure," he said, "no problem. Thanks, officer." He shouldered his shovel and walked back to the house. He could feel the policemen's eyes drilling holes in his back, but when he turned to stand the shovel up near the back door, the cop was gone.

Chapter 19

Calgary, Alberta
  Monday, February 27, 9:21 p.m.

Chapa slammed the car door and headed up toward the house. He was furious, but he couldn't decide whose ass to chew off: Walkenshaw for not having everything arranged, the Mounties for their goddamned bureaucratic crap—or maybe just the first nitwit who crossed his path.

An ambulance crew was smoking and laughing beneath the flashing yellow lights of their vehicle. Cars completely blocked the street, abandoned at all angles like jackstraws: Calgary cops, Mounties, CIA. The cop cars were parked in until everyone else left. The ambulance had to be the first to go.

Shaffer had snagged a ride with one of the Mounties and beaten him to the scene. She stood on the small porch watching a local cop take pictures of the wall.

"Is anyone still alive in there?" Chapa asked the cop.

"No, sir."

"Then get the fucking ambulance out of here, okay?"

"Yes, sir," the man said, running off without even asking Chapa who he was.

He started up the steps. Just to the right of the doorway at waist height, the wooden siding was splintered outward like bird bones. There was blood on the concrete. He tapped Shaffer on the shoulder and she followed him into the house.

The living room was a slaughterhouse. Four bodies lay on the floor, blood seeping into the carpet and more of it splashed on the wall. There were too many people in the room, but Chapa wasn't worried about forensic purity. He already knew the two most important facts: Citrullo had killed these people, and she had escaped again, for the third time.

"I don't believe this," Chapa said, surveying the carnage.

One of the Mounties he'd met earlier—the tall one, Jacquemart—stepped into the room, ducking his head to avoid the lintel.

"Three hours," Chapa accused him. "Three fucking hours you held us up, with procedures and forms and conferences and coordination and communication *bullshit*. Just long enough to let these guys get here first. And now she's gone."

The Mountie shifted his weight from one foot to the other. Chapa looked up at him expectantly, willing him to say something officious so he could eat him alive.

"Yes, sir," Jacquemart said without a trace of sarcasm. Chapa stared at him, deciding that the man probably agreed with him. His anger subsided a bit.

Shaffer was examining the bullet holes in the wall beside the front door. Chapa went over to get a closer look. *Tight grouping.* Citrullo was one hell of a shot: four holes formed a group about an inch in diameter. When Chapa leaned down, he could actually see through the wall. He stepped back, trying to figure the angle, over two bodies and around a pair of cops until his back was to the wall. Still wrong. He squatted down and everything lined up.

Shaffer crouched beside him. "She shot somebody right through the wall," she said. He nodded. "And she wasn't fishing. Look at the grouping. She must have known exactly where he was."

They turned their attention to the bodies. Two were lying face down in their own blood with their feet in the dining room. A third was face up, his head pointed toward the front door and his throat crushed. The last was in the center of the room, curled on his side; part of his head had been blown away.

"Does anyone know who these dumbshits are?" Chapa said.

"Vegas mob," Shaffer said. "We've got files on three of them."

"Derek's friends move fast. How did they know he was here?" She said nothing. He gestured at the bodies. "It's going to take forensics a week to reconstruct this."

"Yes, sir, but it's obvious." He shot her a questioning look and she waved her hand over the mess as if shooing flies. "These guys committed suicide."

Chapa threw back his head and guffawed. The police and Mounties stopped in their tracks, staring at him.

"You mean," he said, "we shouldn't underestimate her." Shaffer stood up, and so did he.

"These guys did."

The CIA spook, Walkenshaw, came out of the kitchen carrying a clipboard. "Hildreth's Blazer is parked down the street," he said. "It's got Alberta plates, but we matched the vehicle number. We think Citrullo and Narr may have been snatched."

"Are you kidding?" Chapa said. "Not a chance. At least half of their men were dead on the floor right here. They didn't have anybody left to bag them."

"One of the neighbors saw a car leaving shortly after the shootout," Walkenshaw said. "Maybe Citrullo stole their car."

Chapa thought of the blood on the porch. "No. The wiseguys would leave a driver behind with the engine running, and at least one man who didn't get dead was seriously injured. Where are they? Trust me, the goons drove away and our kids are on foot."

"We're checking that," Walkenshaw said. "Calgary PD is going door-to-door talking to the neighbors and looking for anything suspicious. The PD got here pretty quickly, so I don't think they could've gone very far on foot."

"Where's the helicopter?" Shaffer said.

"On the way."

"Find out who the witness is," Chapa said to Shaffer. "We should talk to him ourselves. There had to be *two* cars to hold all this beef." She nodded and went outside.

"Chapa," Walkenshaw said. "I want to apologize for the screwup. They told me everything would be ready when we ar—"

"Forget it," Chapa said, and turned away. He wasn't in the mood for apologies and he was too tired to beat the shit out of Walkenshaw right now.

Jacquemart came back inside, ducking again. "Agent Chapa," he said, "we've found Mrs. Citrullo." Chapa grunted in surprise, but then realized he meant Carla's mother. "She's two doors down, at her sister's house. I'd say she's still in shock, but she seems lucid."

Chapa went outside and shouted for Shaffer. She dodged through the cop cars and ran up to him.

"Got the eyewitness's name and address," she said, not even slightly out of breath. "What's up?"

"They found the mother. Let's go have a chat."

* * *

It was hard to believe that Jody Bittenfield and Sarah Citrullo were sisters: Jody looked old enough to be Sarah's mother. They were the same height, but Jody was obese, leaning on a cane that looked like a twig in her chubby hands. Her hair was white with an unpleasant yellowish tinge and her skin was wrinkled and dry.

Sarah sat in an overstuffed armchair in the nauseatingly cute living room. The furnishings were unrelenting schlock, lace doilies spread over every horizontal surface. Pastel porcelain cherubs covered the fireplace mantel. Chapa pulled up an ottoman and sat in front of Sarah, who watched him silently with haunted eyes. Shaffer settled on the edge of the sofa to his left.

Before he could open his mouth, Jody said from behind him, "Don't you harass her!" Chapa looked over his shoulder and saw her hovering in the center of the room like a hot air balloon. "She's been through hell tonight. That Carla, showing up with no warning after all these years and then killing people in Sarah's living room! What's gotten into her? That's not the sweet little girl I—"

Chapa nodded at Jacquemart, who led Jody into the kitchen, talking in a soothing tone over her uninterrupted monologue. A door closed and the reedy whine dropped to a whisper.

"Sarah," he said, "my name is Kevin Chapa. I work for the FBI."

Sarah's eyes twinkled. "Well, now, you must be lost," she said. "The United States is about a hundred fifty miles that way." She pointed at the wall.

Chapa smiled. "This is my associate, Agent Shaffer. We're working with the Mounties to try to find your daughter."

"You're not the only ones," Sarah said, shuddering. Shaffer grabbed a light blue afghan off the back of the couch and draped it around Sarah's shoulders. "Thank you, dear."

"What happened in your house tonight?" Chapa said.

Sarah's mouth opened but nothing came out. Finally, she said, "We... we were having coffee in the living room. Carla... she came back to visit after thirteen years. Can you believe it's been thirteen years? She had a very nice man with her, handsome man, good manners. I never did care for mustaches, though. She said they're not, well, *together,* but I thought they made such a cute couple." She pulled the afghan tighter around her shoulders. Chapa glanced at Shaffer, who grimaced and mouthed silently: *Cute?*

"Someone was at the door," Sarah said. "I got up to answer it. Who would be visiting so late? There was... tall man. Dark face. Big gun. He told me to get back, then I... I was falling down. Loud noise. And blood... blood all over the wall. Then I was standing by the wall. Carla was in the corner like a bad girl on a time-out. She had a gun in her hand. My little girl—where did she get that gun? Then..."

Sarah rubbed her face with one hand. She tucked her arm back under the afghan and settled herself deeper into the chair.

"What happened next?"

"She was kneeling down by the door to the kitchen. How did she get there? I was... I was sitting down, I think. Derek... he had a gun, too. There were... dead people on the floor. Carla was talking to somebody outside. He was laughing. Then Carla shot the wall. What did she do that for? And oh my lord, the noise! Another man ran into the room. I think Derek shot him... no, I saw Carla shoot him... right in the head. I saw... his head explode... Then..." She looked at him blankly. "Then I was sitting here."

Chapa sat back. Sarah's face was pale. He pitied her the nightmares she was in for.

"Can you remember anything else?" Chapa said.

Sarah thought for a minute. "Winnie-the-Pooh."

"Winnie-the-Pooh?" Sarah didn't respond. He looked at Shaffer. "Did you get all that?" She held up a small tape recorder. "Okay, Sarah, we're going to go now. Thank you for your help." Sarah's eyes followed his face as he stood up.

"Do you think you'll see Carla?" she said.

"I certainly hope so."

"Could you tell her something for me?"

Chapa nodded and Shaffer held the tape recorder out. "Sure, Sarah. What would you like me to tell her?"

"Could you tell her..." Sarah leaned forward conspiratorially. The afghan fell off her shoulders. "Tell her I think Derek is a very nice boy, and if she knows what's good for her she won't let him get away."

* * *

"That was right out of the Twilight Zone," Shaffer said as they walked back to the crime scene. The cold air felt good after the heat and chintz of Jody's house.

"Make sure the locals leave her alone until tomorrow, okay?" Chapa said. Shaffer nodded and hunched her shoulders against the cold. "Where's your buddy Myron?"

Shaffer shrugged.

"Walkenshaw!" Chapa bellowed into Sarah's house. The agent appeared and Chapa gestured for him to come outside. "Shaffer, why don't you talk to whoever about Sarah, and see what else they've got here? We'll go check out that eyewitness. You got the name?"

Shaffer handed him a slip of paper: Leonard Starkey, 17423 Hawkwood Place. Walkenshaw stepped outside, buttoning up his overcoat.

"What's up?" he said.

"This guy Starkey who saw the wiseguys leave. Let's go talk to him."

Walkenshaw nodded and they walked down the driveway. At the street Chapa looked both ways, checked the address again, and led Walkenshaw off to the left.

Chapter 20

Derek walked into the kitchen, shucking his coat and Starkey's hat and gloves. He looked for Carla in the brightly lit living and dining rooms, the open bathroom, and the dark bedrooms; she was nowhere to be found. He was heading back to the kitchen, confused, when he spotted her in the guest bedroom, kneeling in front of the window behind the single bed, looking outside. He knelt beside her and pulled back a corner of the paisley cotton curtains to look out.

"Where'd you get the binoculars?" he said.

"Found them in the closet. How'd it go out there?"

"Terrific! I buried him in bullshit and he went away!" Derek was still jazzed. *Maybe we'll even live through the night.*

"Great."

"Well, you could be a little grateful or something."

Carla looked at him briefly and put the glasses back to her eyes. "You did all right, Derek. You shot an assassin and you got rid of the cop. What do you want, a pat on the back? We're still alive. That's reward enough."

Derek watched the cops milling around and sulked.

"There goes your friend Chapa," Carla said.

"What?"

"Take a look."

She handed him the glasses. He swept the binoculars across the confusion and saw three people walking away from him. One was very tall, one was clearly a woman. The third might have been Chapa.

He handed the binoculars back. "I didn't see his face."

"I did. It's Chapa. The woman is his sidekick, Shaffer. The tall guy is a Mountie."

"How do you know?"

"Shoulder patch." She watched for a few seconds. "They're going into Aunt Jody's house. I guess they found my mother."

They watched people scurrying about like ants, streaming into and out of Sarah's house. The ambulance drove away, followed shortly by a police cruiser and two unmarked cars. A black coroner's van showed up. The driver got out and started talking to one of the cops. A bright light and a loud noise swept overhead.

"Police chopper," Carla said. "Looking for us." They watched in silence for a while. "I'm surprised none of the neighbors has given you up."

Derek watched her concentrate on the activity outside. He was changing his mind about her face, which was starkly lit by the street lamps. At first he'd thought she was merely pretty, but now she seemed beautiful.

"What do you mean?" he said.

"The cops are going door to door, talking to people."

"So?"

"Well, obviously no one's mentioned that a guy who looks nothing like Leonard Starkey was shoveling Starkey's driveway when they know he's not at home, right after a gunfight down the street."

"It's been a while since you lived here, right?" She nodded, still looking through the binoculars. "This is the 'burbs, dummy. No one's lying to protect us, they're just oblivious. I doubt if anyone even noticed me."

A gentle snow was starting to fall. In the light from the street lamps and the flashing police cars, it looked like glitter, floating down silently, turning and sparkling.

"Chapa's coming back," Carla said.

The woman and man they'd seen earlier walked up to Sarah's front door, then the woman wandered away. Chapa was joined by a man with white hair, and started walking their way. Derek felt a lump form in his throat.

"Do you think they're headed here?" he said.

Carla set down the binoculars and rubbed her eyes. "What did you tell the cop?"

"Uh... I said I didn't come outside until... um, after the car drove away. He asked if I got the plates, and how many people there were. I said I didn't see much of anything."

"Shit," she said, still rubbing her eyes. "You should've said you didn't see *anything,* period. You're the only eyewitness they've got." She stood up and started doing stretching exercises, twisting at the hips, flexing her legs. Derek watched in disbelief as she bent at the waist and put her palms on the floor. "So," she said with her head between her knees, "do you have any ideas?"

"Me?" He laughed wildly. "*You're* the mastermind. I could go find some strapping tape."

"That won't do it. That guy with the white hair? He's not Bureau."

"How do you know?"

"A hunch. He's dressed too well. He doesn't have the walk. He's probably CIA."

"Oh, Jesus." Carla finished her stretches and looked out the window again. The two men were almost to the driveway. She sighed and nodded, as if she'd reached a difficult decision, and walked out of the bedroom.

"What?" Derek said as he followed her.

She went into the kitchen and put her coat on. "I need your help to get them inside."

"Okay..."

"The CIA guy will hang back to one side."

"What for?"

"To offer covering fire if necessary."

"But he doesn't even know we're here."

"He'll do it anyway, out of habit. Now listen, I'm going outside to herd them in here. Chapa will ring the doorbell. Wait until the second time he rings, then answer the door with your gun in your hand, but with the safety *on.* Don't shoot anyone, and don't say a word. You got it?"

Derek nodded. She went out the back door without latching it behind her. He took the pistol out of his waistband and checked the safety. The doorbell rang, startling him. He longed to run out the back door and keep going; he wanted to say a prayer, but couldn't think of one. The chime rang a second time.

"Coming," he yelled. He took a deep breath, opened the door, and swung the pistol up.

Chapa was standing three feet away from him, his mouth gaping in surprise, his eyes falling to the pistol pointed at his chest. The other man was standing on the sidewalk below, a few feet from the steps. He was reaching inside his coat when Carla hissed, "Don't."

The agents froze. Carla walked around the side of the house with her pistol in her hand. If anyone were watching, her body would block their view of the weapon.

"Come on in," she said, "and I'll make some coffee." She nudged the CIA man with her gun. "Move!" He walked up the stairs ahead of her and they followed Chapa into the living room. Derek closed the door.

She waved her gun at a wall that was all bookshelves. "Move over there. Derek, hand me your pistol." She took it from him and flicked off the safety; Chapa's eyebrows lifted and she smiled at him. "He wouldn't have shot you, but I will. Derek, get their weapons." She pointed a gun at each agent's chest.

Chapa was closest, and raised his arms obligingly, so Derek started with him. He found a gun in a shoulder holster and tossed it back to Carla. It bounced on the carpet with a dull thud. After patting Chapa down, he reached toward the CIA agent—and the man whirled him around and put him in a headlock. Derek couldn't breathe, but worse than the pain was his surprise that this frail-looking, white-haired man could have incapacitated him so easily. Derek had thought he was strong, but he felt like a child in the man's grip: he couldn't budge the arm around his throat.

"Put the guns down, *now!*" the agent said in a basso rumble. Derek struggled against his grip, but he couldn't find any leverage. He was starting to feel faint.

"You know me," Carla said calmly. "I don't like to shoot Feds, but I have *no* compunctions against killing a spook. Absolutely none." Derek could feel the man's grip relax for just a second, as if she'd surprised him, but then the arm was tighter than ever around his throat. "Let him go, or I'll blow you out from under him, and you know I can do it."

"You'll kill him if you try."

Derek was having trouble seeing—something was wrong with the lights—but he thought he saw Carla shrug.

"Maybe. That would be too bad. But *you'll* be dead for sure. Let him go!"

"Go ahead, kill me—I don't give a shit. But before I stop breathing, this place will be swarming with cops, Mounties, CIA, and FBI. And then *you'll* be dead. So drop your weapons!"

"You're right," Carla said, and to Derek's amazement she dropped the guns.

He must have begun passing out, because Carla was suddenly nothing but a blur. He found himself on his hands and knees, breathing in deep, ragged gasps. The CIA man was unconscious on the floor and Chapa was just climbing to his feet. Derek tried several times before he managed to stand up. He staggered away from the body and fell onto a couch. His throat felt raw and he was still light-headed.

Carla covered Chapa with her gun while she searched the spook.

"Is he dead?" Derek said. Talking hurt. He swallowed, and that hurt too.

"No. Who is this guy?" she asked Chapa.

"Myron Walkenshaw. CIA." Chapa brushed off his coat, took it off, folded it neatly, and set it on the back of a chair. Then he sat in the chair.

"Don't know him. You okay?"

"Yeah, I'm okay. I've been hit harder." He looked at Walkenshaw lying on the floor. "I doubt if he has, though."

"How about you, Derek?" she said. He waved at her weakly. He didn't want to try talking again just yet.

Carla put Walkenshaw's two guns in her coat pockets and tossed a wicked-looking knife into the kitchen, where it clattered and slid across the floor. She stood up holding a radio transceiver.

"I feel like I'm getting to know you, Carla," Chapa said. "I should have expected this." He nudged Walkenshaw's body with his toe. "You're not going to make a habit of kidnapping me, are you?"

"I don't know, it's kind of fun." She leaned over to pick up Chapa's gun and slipped it into her pocket. She examined the radio.

"What happened at your mom's?" Chapa said.

"Some of Derek's pals wanted us to come out and play. I had to say 'no' four times."

"There's only one way this can end, Carla. Sooner or later, your luck is going to run out." Chapa settled back into the chair. "I've read your file, you know. I know how good you are, but do you really think you can stay one step ahead of us forever?"

"You think I should give myself up so I can spend the rest of my life in jail?"

"It's better than being dead."

She snorted and set the radio down on a small table out of Chapa's reach. Still covering him with her pistol, she loosened and removed Walkenshaw's tie.

"We're all going to die soon, anyway," she said. She fingered the tie and tsked. "Silk." Then she noticed Derek staring at her and Chapa tensing to jump. "Relax, I don't mean *today*. Geologically speaking."

Derek resumed breathing. He swallowed and it didn't hurt quite as much. He couldn't see where this parrying between Carla and Chapa was going. And how they were going to get away alive.

"Carla," Chapa said, "what's going on? Why did you kill Hildreth? Is it some kind of arms deal? Why go to your mom's house—you had to know we'd follow you here."

"I'll tell you someday over dinner. Your treat."

"You've got Derek into a lot of trouble."

Derek looked at him sharply. "How much worse can it get?"

Chapa looked back at him. "I thought you were a hostage acting under duress, but you pointed a gun at me, so now you're a player. That makes you accessory to murder, seven times."

Derek frowned and tried to count. "Wait a minute."

"You made me on the car at Snoqualmie," Carla said. "I'm impressed."

"You're in big—"

She cut him off. "Okay, that's enough. Derek, get our stuff. Chapa, can we talk to the helicopter on this radio?" He nodded. "Good. I want you to call the pilot and tell him to land in the cul-de-sac one block west of here, right now." She handed him the radio. "And don't presume on my goodwill. I'll kill you if I have to."

Chapa switched frequencies, relayed the order to the pilot, and handed the radio back to Carla.

"He says four minutes."

"Okay," Carla said. "We're not going to use tape this time." She bound Chapa's hands in front of him with Walkenshaw's tie. "There's a knife in the kitchen. It shouldn't take you long to get back to work. I'll leave your weapons on the street where the chopper picks us up." She checked the knot and stood up, holstering her gun. Derek handed her her bag.

"When what's-his-name wakes up," she told Chapa, "tell him he should've known better."

Derek picked up his gun, set the safety, and stuck it in the small of his back again. Carla led him to the back door, then motioned him to go ahead of her. She took a last look around and started through the door.

"Hey, Carla," Chapa said. She took a step back inside so she could see him. "Happy birthday."

* * *

They walked down the driveway and turned right, away from Sarah's house, hoping to stay inconspicuous, but then the helicopter zoomed overhead, its searchlight momentarily blinding them.

"Run," Carla shouted.

They ran full tilt toward the chopper's landing site. Derek's lungs ached immediately from the cold air, and his bags banged against his legs. He couldn't hear anything over the noise of the helicopter, but he imagined that every cop on the street had seen them lit up and was now chasing them. People were coming out of the houses they passed, some of them wearing pajamas.

They reached the cul-de-sac as the helicopter settled onto its skids. The engine whine lowered, but the blades still sent snow and dirt flying like invisible stinging insects. The pilot hadn't spotted them yet; his lips moved as he talked to someone over the radio. Carla ducked under the rotor wash and ran up to the pilot's door. He looked at her expectantly and she yanked open the door and stuck her pistol under his chin.

"Out!"

He fumbled with his seat belt and climbed down out of the chopper. Carla pulled a revolver out of his holster.

"Get lost!" she shouted. The pilot looked confused. She pointed his own gun at him. He threw his hands up and stepped back, but didn't turn and run away until she shot a round over his shoulder. She dropped the pilot's gun, holstered her own, then fumbled for a moment to pull the agents' pistols out of her coat pockets and dump them on the pavement too.

"Get in," she told Derek.

Derek ran around the front and opened the surprisingly light right-hand door. He'd never been in a helicopter before. After tossing his bags onto the bench seat in the back, he climbed in, shifting his feet to avoid the pedals on the floor. He closed the door and tried to latch it—you had to pull and turn the handle at the same time. Carla pointed to the shoulder harness and he fastened it gratefully. She handed him a headset with a small swivel microphone and he put it on.

"Do you know how to fly this thing?" he said. His voice sounded hollow in the earphones.

"No," she replied as she revved up the engine, gave it a little left pedal, and lifted up the collective with her left hand while she pushed the cyclic lever between her knees forward with her right. Derek screamed as they shot up into the sky.

* * *

"God cock sucking damn it!" John Maroni bellowed into the phone. Gugliemo held it away from his ear. He sat on the king size hotel bed and looked out the window at the lights of the city. *I want to go home.*

"Tell me again," Maroni said after a moment.

"We lost five guys," Gugliemo said. He tried to keep his voice from quavering. "Pescado went in first, with two guys behind him and three around back. It looked like the old lady was going to let him in, nice and quiet, but somebody slammed the door in his face. He fell backwards down the steps. Then that big guy, I forget his name, he charged in and went down. There was some shooting and Pescado sent the other guy around back, then he stood outside the door for a while, talking to Narr and the spy. Then Pescado got shot and the bitch was shouting that she wanted more. Christ, Mr. Maroni, it was the scariest thing I've ever seen."

"I'll bet," Maroni said coldly.

"Jinks came running from around back. He helped Pescado into the other car and we got the hell out of there. Jinks said all the rest were dead."

"How's my friend Pescado?"

Gugliemo swallowed. "He's dead, Mr. Maroni. He died five minutes after we left the house. We had to dump the body."

He could hear Maroni's phone hit the desk and then the sound of something breaking. The smashing and pounding went on for a long time. Then there was quiet, which was scarier.

"Okay," Maroni said, "I'm calm now. You probably didn't know that Pescado was my best friend. Now you tell me: how did she shoot him if he was standing outside the door?"

"Uh... she got him through the wall."

"She shot him through the fucking wall?"

"Yes, sir." Gugliemo wiped sweat off his forehead.

"I'm sending you more muscle," Maroni said. "I want you to find this bitch and blow her tits off. You hear me?"

"Uh..."

"No, wait." Maroni was silent for a moment. Gugliemo heard a lighter snap open. Maroni puffed on a cigar. *One of those good Cubans.* Would he be safe in Cuba? You could fly there from Canada. No—probably not, he decided sadly. Maroni would have contacts down there.

"It's stupid to kill the bitch out of revenge," Maroni said. "She's into something big, I can smell it, and I want it. So here's what you're going to do. When my guys get up there tomorrow, you find her. Snatch them both, and kill the geek right in front of her. Make it messy and take your time, you understand me? Soften her up and bring her back to me. When I've sucked her dry, *then* I'll kill her, nice and slow." Maroni exhaled loudly. "You understand, Gugliemo?"

"Yes, Mr. Maroni."

"Gugliemo?"

"Yes, sir?"

"Don't fuck up. Or you'll take her place."

Maroni hung up and Gugliemo sat staring at the phone in his hand until it began beeping. He set it down and went into the bathroom to throw up.

Chapter 21

Airborne over Montana
Monday, February 27, 11:28 p.m.

Carla couldn't remember the last time she'd been this happy. It was years since she'd had the opportunity to fly, and although she would have preferred a glider or a small plane, she loved choppers, too. The police helicopter she'd stolen was a Bell Jet Ranger in very good condition, steady and powerful under her hands, like an Arabian given free rein in a wide meadow.

She figured they'd just crossed the border into western Montana. She scanned her instruments again—airspeed, heading, fuel level—and wondered if there was enough fuel to get to their destination.

Too bad the bird didn't have radar. In the moonless night, their running lights illuminated the treetops whipping by a few meters beneath the skids. She was flying recklessly, staying low to avoid ground radar, and as fast as possible to reduce their time in the air. Cruising at two hundred kilometers per hour, she had to stay alert to miss tall trees, power lines—or a mountain.

She avoided towns as much as possible to reduce the chance that someone would spot her, but she couldn't help passing over the occasional ranch or backwoods cabin. Carla hoped she wasn't waking up any hermits, or if so that they wouldn't call the sheriff to complain about a chopper buzzing their house in the middle of the night. A trail of whining yokels could pinpoint her almost as well as radar. She wondered if the spook she'd knocked out would wake up and retarget one of their satellites to find her with infrared. Unlikely, but she needed to set down as soon as possible.

Derek had calmed down once he realized she knew what she was doing. Now he was watching the scenery flash by. Snow had been falling in Calgary, but here the clouds were patchy. Carla glanced out her side window. The tops of the tallest trees, dusted with snow, zipped by just below them. They were about forty meters off the ground, and it looked awfully cold out there.

"First time in a helicopter?" she said. The voice-activated microphone made her voice sound tinny.

"Yeah," he said without looking away from the window. "I've always wanted to ride in one. I just wish it were daytime so I could see."

"If it were daytime, we wouldn't be flying. We need to set down before dawn."

"Set down where?" He turned to look at her. Even in the dim light of the instruments, she could see he was exhausted.

"Idaho."

"Idaho? What's in Idaho?"

"Plastic explosives."

"Oh, yeah," Derek said as he turned back to the window. "I knew that. All my friends buy it there."

Carla chuckled. She asked him to look around for maps and was surprised when he found airspace maps for the U.S. as well as Canada.

"See if you can find Lister, Idaho." She probably could have found it faster herself, but she needed to keep her eyes up. She was getting tired, too.

When he located Lister, she explained how to identify airfields and calculate distances and headings. Lister did have an airport, he discovered, but Carla had no intention of using it. Derek guessed at the remaining distance and she did the calculations in her head. If she was right, they would arrive in Lister with about fifteen minutes of fuel left. She might actually be able to *land* the bird instead of crashing it in the woods somewhere.

When they'd been in the air about two hours, Carla spotted a glow on the horizon ahead, brighter to the south, that was probably Coeur D'Alene. Ten minutes later she pulled back on the cyclic and raised the collective to rise up and hover. The lights of the small town of Lister were visible ahead. Carla nudged Derek awake.

"Help me find a clearing," she said. "I need an open space at least ten meters in diameter, away from houses but not too far from the road." Derek rubbed his eyes and nodded, looking out his side window again.

The lights of Lister had grown much brighter and they'd passed over Lister Lake before she spotted what she was looking for: a pasture separated from a small road by a thick stand of trees with no buildings nearby. Snow had drifted up to make ridges at the post-and-wire fence. Carla set the Jet Ranger down slowly, using the rotor wash to blow away some of the snow, and touched down jarringly. Derek grinned at her clumsy landing.

"It's been a while," she said, "but we're still alive." She began the shutdown procedure.

They retrieved their bags, hopped out into the snow, and closed the helicopter's doors. Derek followed her toward the road through ankle-deep snow that gradually became deeper as they approached the fence. Carla held down the wire so he could climb over, then tossed him her bag and vaulted over using one of the posts as a balance point. They walked through the deeper night under the trees and had to wade through knee-high snow to get to the road.

"Next time I'll bring snow shoes," Derek said.

"Yeah, next time."

There was no traffic, so they walked on the hard-packed snow in the center of the road. Both sides of the roadway were walled by piles of plowed snow and gravel. Tall pines loomed in silhouette against the stars and the scudding clouds. Their breath was visible in puffs of fog. Derek muttered something.

"What?" Carla said.

"I said it's damned cold and we should have parked closer."

"Next time pack a warm coat with your snowshoes."

"Yeah, next time."

It took almost an hour to reach Lister. Gaps in the snow ramparts marked driveways, which were now coming more frequently. Isolated homesteads had been visible only by their security lights, but now the houses were close enough to the road to see that they were dark.

The country road dead-ended onto a highway and they soon came to a small motel. A tall hand-carved wooden sign announced the Lister Pines Motel, a one-story building with eight units. The shifting blue aura of a television shone through the windows of the office.

Carla opened a creaky screen door and a heavy wooden door peeling apple-green paint and stepped into the office. The only light came from the silent TV. On their side of the chest-high desk that bisected the room were a few rickety chairs and a tall rack of tourist brochures. On the other side, a woman in late middle age sat with her feet propped up, squinting at the TV.

"Excuse me," Carla said. The woman looked up slowly, revealing a thin, weathered face. She wore a bulky sweater, jeans, and cowgirl boots that were planted on the papers on the desk.

"Yeah?" she drawled.

"We'd like a room, please," Carla said. "With two beds, if possible."

The clerk looked from Carla to Derek. Her eyes narrowed.

"Sorry, honey, all our rooms are queens." She explained to Derek, "Saves on the laundry."

"That's fine," Carla said. "We'll take one."

The woman was silent for a long moment. "Didn't hear no car."

Derek rested his arms on the high counter and smiled sheepishly. "It broke down about a mile out of town," he said. "We had to hike the rest of the way in. I'll get someone to fix it tomorrow, but I'm too tired to deal with it now."

The clerk pursed her lips. "Nobody open at this hour, anyway. Try George's garage in the morning, just down the road. So... how many nights?"

Carla said, "I'm not sure how long we'll be around. Depends on the car."

"Okay. I need a credit card."

"I prefer to pay cash."

The woman blinked and sighed. She pulled her feet off the desk—they landed on the floor with a thunk—and stood up.

"Forty-nine dollars a night." Carla handed her a fifty and took her change and the keys. "Room three," the clerk said. She dropped back into her chair with a thud and a squeak and turned back to her silent TV.

Derek was grinning stupidly; Carla followed his gaze. The keys were hung from a board decorated with stickers of Pooh Bear, Piglet, and Eeyore.

The room was surprisingly nice, clean and freshly painted. The firm bed was covered with a faded quilt. On one wall hung a framed watercolor of a brook winding through pines with a snowy mountain in the background.

Derek rushed to the bathroom. He used the toilet, took a quick shower, and fell into bed. Carla took her turn, pulled on a T-shirt and panties, and climbed in beside him. Derek seemed to be asleep. When she rolled onto her side, he snuggled up, put an arm around her, cupping a breast, and sighed with contentment. Then she knew for sure that he was asleep.

* * *

Carla had been awake for some time, staring at the ceiling in the weak morning light. As the daylight brightened, she discovered her mother's face in the shadows on the textured plaster. Sarah stared back, expressionless, until the light grew strong enough to dispel the ghost. Carla blinked and a new illusion appeared: the flat light made the ceiling seem to be only inches above her nose. She blinked again and it retreated to its normal height.

Happy birthday to me.

Derek was still sleeping as deeply as a child, curled up on his side. He looked so much younger asleep, almost as young as she was—although she hadn't *felt* young since she joined the Mossad. Her profession fossilized people still in their thirties.

Carla slipped off her night clothes and began stroking Derek. When he was hard and starting to awaken, she rolled him onto his back and pulled off his shorts. She used her mouth to arouse him further, then mounted him and slowly rocked her hips. Not until the final moments did he awaken fully, then they both climaxed and she collapsed on top of him.

"Happy birthday," he whispered in her ear, but her mood had darkened further. She climbed off him without a word and went into the bathroom.

The motel's day clerk was a young man with close-cropped hair and a sharp-planed face, wearing a clean white T-shirt, faded jeans, and hiking boots that were propped up on the desk exactly as the night clerk's had been. He set down his magazine as they entered the office. Carla was surprised to see that he was reading *Scientific American*—she'd been expecting *Car and Driver* or *Field and Stream*.

She asked directions to a car rental agency and a good hardware store. He stood up and directed them to both, using as many gestures as words. Carla paid for another night.

"Where's a good place for breakfast?" Derek said, and the clerk suggested Ginnie's Cafe just down the road.

"I suppose you want to eat first?" she said.

"Yes, I do."

They had a quiet breakfast at Ginnie's, served by a plump, apparently mute waitress in a worn uniform. The coffee was good for a change.

The rental car office felt like a furnace after the biting chill outside. The blonde, ruddy-cheeked girl behind the counter smiled and apologized that all they had available with four-wheel drive was a Ford pickup, so Carla took it. The girl wanted a credit card impression, explaining cheerfully that they would not bill the card until the truck was returned. Carla looked at Derek, who gritted his teeth and handed over his Visa gold card.

"We're supposed to meet my brother for lunch," Carla said. "He works up at the Cutrock Munitions plant. Can you tell me how to get there?"

The girl tore a map off a pad, flung her long hair out of her eyes, and marked the route with a felt-tipped pen.

There was only one pickup on the tiny rental lot. Derek climbed in and fastened his seat belt.

"Cutrock Munitions plant?" he said as Carla pulled out

"I told you: we need some C-4."

"I thought you were joking."

"No, I'm not joking."

"What do we need explosives for?"

"I don't know yet."

She drove toward the hardware store, feeling cranky and not in the mood for one of his interrogations, but Derek persisted.

"So we're just going to waltz in and ask for some?"

"You can't buy C-4 at Wal-Mart," she said.

"How do you know? This is Idaho."

She pulled into a parking space near the hardware store.

"Maybe they'll have it here," he said. "That would save us a trip to the plant." Carla got out of the car. Derek followed and jogged a few steps to catch up. "You know, they *might* have it here. What do you think? Hell, I bet these people use C-4 to get their cars out of snow drifts. They probably use it to hunt moose. I bet they fish with it. Kids probably get it in their Easter baskets."

She ignored him and walked inside. For just a moment she was transported back to her childhood, before her father grew weary of his tomboy daughter, when their favorite thing to do on a Saturday afternoon was to browse the aisles at the old neighborhood hardware store together.

The floors were solid oak planks, at least fifteen centimeters wide. On the left as they entered was a room full of tack, farrier's tools, cowboy boots, and dusters. Gigantic bags of dog food were stacked beneath oxen yokes hanging on the wall. Straight ahead was the hardware. To the right were rifles, fishing supplies, climbing gear—and outdoor clothing. She led Derek in that direction.

"Find yourself a warm coat and some good boots," she said. Carla selected a Thermos, a plastic tarp, and a pair of lined boots. She was examining binoculars in a glass case when he came back with a red plaid woolen coat and some insulated boots.

"Lose the British army coat," she said. He returned with a gray one, some gloves, and a fleece cap with ear flaps.

A gray-haired man shuffled up and offered to help. Carla asked to see the Bausch and Lomb zoom binoculars. At the highest magnification, she could easily read the lips of a portly woman squeezing color onto a client's hair at the salon across the street.

"I'll take these," Carla said.

"Did you want the box?"

"No, thanks. We're going to use them right away."

A very short woman at the cash register smiled pleasantly and started punching in the prices. Carla looked around as the register chirped and noticed a display stand full of granola bars and jerky; she grabbed some of each and tossed them on the pile.

"Going birding?" the clerk said.

"Yep," Carla said, ending the conversation. The total came to over $400. Carla counted out $450. The woman made change without a blink and stuffed the supplies into two large shopping bags. Carla and Derek each grabbed one.

"How much money do you have left?" Derek said when they were outside again. "Your wad is getting pretty thin."

"I'm almost broke." She tossed her bag into the bed of the pickup. Derek did the same. "It's a good thing you brought a credit card." They climbed into the truck and Carla looked at the map they'd got at the rental agency.

"Won't they be able to trace us if I use my card?" he said.

"Yes."

She drove back to the cafe where they'd had breakfast. The same colorless waitress filled their new Thermos with hot water and let it stand for a minute, then filled it again with coffee. She took Carla's money without a word, pointing to the register to indicate the price.

Carla drove toward the south end of Lister Lake. Pine trees grew thickly on the right side of the road, thinning out on the left as they marched down to the deep blue of the water.

"I don't get it," Derek said. "Why don't you care if they trace my credit card?"

Carla ignored him and picked up the map, looking at the inked-in route leading to the explosives plant. It was just a few miles ahead.

"So you don't care if they know where we are?" Derek said. "Or do you think we'll be gone before they get here?" When she didn't answer he looked out the window and brooded. Suddenly he turned back to face her. "Like your mom's."

"What?"

"Right." He was excited—he'd finally figured something out. "Just like at Sarah's house. You *wanted* them to find us there. And at the FBI office, you didn't wear gloves. You were leaving your fingerprints on purpose, so they'd know you'd been there." She said nothing. "Come on, Carla, you're leaving a trail of bread crumbs, right? But why?" Carla glanced at him, then at the map again, still silent. "That was a nasty trick you played on your mom. Some bread crumb."

"I didn't expect them so soon," she said.

"What?"

Carla realized she'd whispered it. She cleared her throat.

"I didn't expect them so soon, and I didn't expect your scuzzbo friends at all. I thought we had another couple of hours before the FBI and the Mounties finished jerking each other off. We'd have been gone by then. And the Mob—I thought I'd shaken them off the trail." She looked at him again. "It was a mistake, okay? At worst I thought they'd question her for a few hours. I never thought she'd get caught in the middle of a gunfight. Do you think I'd do that to my own mother?"

Derek stared at her without answering. They passed a discreet sign for the Cutrock Munitions plant next to a two-lane drive that curved off into the woods. Farther on they came to a turn-out where the plows had pushed the snow from the road into a pile that towered above the car. Carla parked the truck there.

"Why?" Derek said.

"Why what?"

"Why are you leading them on? You could've disappeared without a trace, but you *want* the FBI on our tail. Why?"

"I'll explain everything," Carla said. "But not now. Let's focus on one thing at a time, okay?"

"You can't just keep blowing me off, Carla! If you want my help, you have to tell me what's going on."

"I will. Later."

Derek's hands balled into fists. He closed his eyes and breathed deeply. Carla waited for him to conquer his impatience. She didn't really want him to leave—she needed him for this phase of the op—but she didn't really think he would, either. In a moment he relaxed and opened his eyes again.

"Okay," he said, "but it better be soon." He looked around, at the packed snow looming over the car, at the woods, at the lake glimmering through the trees. "What are we doing here?"

"Bird watching. Put on your warm stuff."

* * *

The plant's driveway was plowed down to asphalt. Carla ignored it and looked into the woods.

"I remember this part," Derek said. He clambered over a ridge of plowed snow and led the way into the trees. She carried the tarp and the Thermos, the binoculars on a strap around her neck, and her pockets full of granola bars and jerky.

The dry, granular snow came just over the tops of her new boots, but they were laced tightly and her feet stayed warm and dry. She slogged through the drifts, wishing she'd thought to buy snowshoes. They stayed about twenty meters into the trees, following the drive as it curved to the right and then to the left. At its end, well into the woods, was a fenced enclosure.

The plant consisted of several drab brick and cinder block buildings. Looking through the trees from ground level, Carla couldn't determine their number or how they were organized; she needed to find an elevated position. She led Derek off to their left.

The compound was double-fenced: a short outer concrete wall supporting chain link topped by razor wire, and an inner fence of more chain link and razor wire. Both were four meters tall, with a gap between them where dogs would patrol, though they hadn't seen any yet. There was a guard house just outside the entry gate.

They followed the fence line at a respectful distance, wary of the possible dogs, to the northeast corner. Inside the compound the ground was flat, but here it sloped steeply, rising up into a hill that was cloaked with trees, some of which still had snow on their branches. All the trees within fifteen meters of the fence had been cleared, and no branches overhung the fence line, but Carla immediately noticed a geometry problem that their security had missed. She smiled and gestured for Derek to follow her up the hill.

Still safely under cover of the pines, Carla worked her way south until they found a good vantage point where they could see most of the plant between the thin boles of the trees. She refolded the tarp into a multi-layered square two meters on a side, set it on the snow, flopped on her belly, and raised the binoculars. Derek settled down beside her with a few soft grunts.

"What's the plan?" he said.

"That's why we're here, to make one. Be quiet and help me figure this place out."

They watched the plant for the rest of the day. There were four buildings and several parking areas inside the fencing. The largest structure, one story tall, ran the length of the fence, from the left of the front gate all the way to the back. They agreed this must be the factory where the explosives were manufactured.

The second largest, apparently a warehouse, was somewhat taller, perpendicular to the factory, and lay directly in front of their position. Shortly after they arrived, a forklift carrying a pallet of wooden crates rolled out of the factory and into the warehouse, returning empty. An hour later a heavy truck arrived at the front gate and backed up to the warehouse. They could hear clanking and banging, but couldn't see what was being loaded or unloaded.

When the whistle blew for lunch, a group of workers in clean coveralls under winter coats strolled from the factory to the third largest building, a two-story brick structure to the right of the gate. Obviously the cafeteria was there, and it became apparent that the administration offices were, too. Whenever they spotted a man in a suit, and the one time they saw a woman, they were either going into or coming out of that building.

No one entered or left the fourth and smallest building, between the administration building and the warehouse. Power house, Derek guessed: power lines on tall poles led to that building. It would have a backup generator and perhaps HVAC for the entire complex.

"Overhead power cables," she said. "Stupid."

After they finished the last of the coffee, they had to stand and stretch, stamp their feet, and run in place to stay warm. Late in the day, the forklift went back to the warehouse and carried a pallet of barrels to the factory. Carla wanted a second viewpoint, so she picked up the tarp and they hiked through the woods to the west side of the fence where they could see the front of the warehouse. The forklift came back about an hour later, and they watched the driver get out and do something at the door before going in.

"Card key?" she said. He took the binoculars, adjusted the focus, and stared at the big, open door. The forklift drove out again a few minutes later, and this time he could see the driver punch in a code.

"No, it's a keypad. There's probably another one at the loading dock." He searched the front of the building and found the gray metal box beside the dock entrance. He reduced the zoom and scanned the front of the building. "Three doors," he said, handing back the glasses. "The closest one's about twenty feet from the nearest wall. They've all got keypads."

"Okay. There's a loading dock and a drive-through for the forklift. What's the third one?"

"For the suits. They can't use the blue-collar doors."

Carla raised the binoculars again. "This is what you do, right?"

"Well, the payoff doesn't usually have quite the same bang." She glared at him. "Sorry. Yes, I do this kind of work all the time."

"Can you handle the keypads?"

"No problem, there aren't that many different types. I have the stuff I'd need in my computer case."

By the time the whistle blew at five-thirty, Carla had a good idea of how to break into the plant. They watched a score of workers file out of the factory, get into their cars, and drive away. A handful of people left the administration building half an hour later. Shortly after that, the second shift security guards arrived and stood around talking with the day shift for a while. When the first shift people left, the dogs finally made their appearance: two teams, one Doberman and one guard each, on constant roving patrols in the gap between the two fences. There were four guards beside the dog patrols.

Carla studied the security lights while the guards settled into their routines. The illumination barely extended outside the fence. Except for the sentries, the security people spent most of their time in the administration building, probably watching their surveillance TVs while they drank coffee and stayed warm. Occasionally one of them would walk the interior of the compound, checking door locks and chatting with the dog keepers.

"This is going to be easy," she said.

"Really? How're you going to get past the dogs? Or are you going in during the day?"

I'm not going in, my friend, you are. "Night is better. Fewer guards, and see how dark the northeast corner is? There's only one lamp nearby and the warehouse blocks the light."

"Great, but what about the dogs?"

"We'll throw them a bone," she said. "Let's go."

* * *

The hardware store looked almost romantic at night, lit by incandescent bulbs. The only person working there was a grizzled man whose name tag said Simon.

"Can I help you, ma'am?" he said, smiling. He looked relieved to have customers.

"I need some aircraft cable," Carla said. Simon led them toward the back of the store.

"Aircraft cable?" Derek whispered.

"Patience," she said, and he stomped noisily after her.

"How much do you need?" Simon said.

"How much is on the spool?" He measured the length against a yardstick screwed to the metal stand that held various spools of wire, cable, and rope. It came to almost one hundred fifty feet. "We'll take it all." As he began winding the cable back onto the spool, Carla said, "I need some way to fasten the ends to themselves."

"You mean a permanent loop?"

"No, I want to loop each end around a tree."

"That's a big dog run." He coiled the cable onto the spool so that both ends hung free, then took them down another aisle. With his tongue between his teeth, he ran a forefinger down a row of hooks and selected two shrink-wrapped snap connectors. Then he went to the end of the aisle and rummaged around in several drawers before he found two narrow, split cylinders. "If you'll follow me," he said, "I'll work this up for you."

At a workbench in the back room, Simon ran one loose end of the cable through a snap connector and crimped one of the fasteners shut to hold the loop closed. He repeated the procedure on the other end and handed Derek the coiled cable.

"Those snaps will hold the same load as the cable," Simon said. "About three hundred pounds."

Carla looked Derek up and down and smiled. He frowned back.

"Perfect," she said. "Thanks, Simon. I think we can find the rest ourselves." The old man smiled, nodded, and went back to his work.

"What the hell are you doing?" Derek said when they were alone.

"I'll explain when we get back to the motel."

She led Derek through the aisles, picking out a pair of elk hide gloves, four auto flares, a wide leather belt, a backpack, nylon rope, a pair of crampons, and more trail food. They carried the stuff up to the cash register, where Simon started ringing them up.

"Where's the best place to eat around here?" she said.

"Ginnie's Cafe. The rest aren't fit for a dog, if you had a dog."

Carla laughed. They drove back to the cafe and the same drab, silent waitress handed them stained paper menus.

"Long hours," Derek said as she walked away.

"She must love her work."

The place was empty except for one other couple sitting in the back booth with their heads together. Ginnie's was one of those artless small-town greasy spoons that somehow manage to limp along for generations. The walls were dark paneling; the blue Formica of the tables and the long countertop was worn through in spots, showing pale white bull's-eyes ringed in black; and the linoleum floor was decades past decrepit. Three things saved it: the service was swift, if surly, the food was plain but good, and the restaurant itself, though run-down, was antiseptically clean.

Derek was quiet all through dinner, but when they returned to the hotel and he dropped the cable onto the floor with an echoing thud, Carla decided she had better tell him her plan.

There was no writing paper in the room, but she found some almost blank pages at the back of the phone book and drew a map of the Cutrock Munitions compound, showing the fences, the buildings, and the hill behind the northeast corner of the fence. She marked the location of the three doors in the warehouse. Derek nodded as she added more and more detail.

"Okay," he said, "that looks good. But what's the plan?"

As she told him, his expression grew more incredulous. When she finished he was staring at her with his mouth open.

"Are you out of your fucking mind?" he said.

"It'll work."

"You're going to get me killed!"

"No, I'm not." She got up to use the bathroom. When she came back, he was still sitting on the edge of the bed, studying her map. She pushed him toward the bathroom. After he'd showered and climbed under the quilt, she sat up for a while longer, visualizing the plant and the security guards' routine.

This will work. She lay the map on the nightstand and turned off the light. *Some fucking birthday.* As she slid under the covers, she wondered if she'd live to see another.

Chapter 22

Kalispell, Montana
Tuesday, February 28, 5:41 p.m.

"We have a rough idea where they were headed," Shaffer said, standing in the doorway of Chapa's borrowed office. He barely registered her presence, watching the last sliver of sun vanish behind the Rockies, so different from the Cascades. The sky was deep blue.

Chapa had graduated from college, entered the FBI Academy, and married Jeanne within a single month. His first assignment was Phoenix, followed by Sacramento, New York, and Miami—where Jeanne had left him and still lived with their children. He'd requested a posting to Seattle after the divorce, wanting to get as far away from her as possible, but he hadn't counted the cost of being so distant from his kids. It also hadn't occurred to him that she could phone him night or day no matter where he lived—or that she *would,* almost daily, at every mini-crisis. Chasing after Carla the last few days was like a vacation from Jeanne's hysterical phone calls.

He realized that Shaffer had been standing quietly at the door for several minutes, waiting for him to notice her. He swiveled his chair to face her.

"Sorry," he said. "Are you hungry?"

She blinked. "Sir?"

"I'm hungry. That big guy with the fuzzy eyebrows told me about a good rib place. Let's try it." She hesitated and Chapa sighed. "You can bring your clipboard."

Chapa's mood improved the instant they walked into the dimly-lit restaurant: it smelled of roast meat. Shaffer managed not to fidget until after they ordered and the lanky waiter strolled away.

"Go ahead," he said. She lifted her clipboard with relief.

"A Lincoln county sheriff's deputy called this morning. Some Daniel Boone living in a cabin in the upper Flathead valley drove thirty miles into

187

town to complain about a helicopter buzzing his chimney last night. He said… wait a minute…" She checked her notes. "He said, 'The damned thing blew three shingles off the roof and scared the crap out of my wolf.'"

He laughed. "His wolf?" Shaffer didn't even smile.

"I called around. There were four other sightings, one in Canada and four in the States. She was headed southwest, flying low, but I checked with the FAA anyway. Nothing on radar. I'd guess she ended up in northwest Montana, or possibly northern Idaho."

Chapa took a pen out of his pocket and tapped the table with it, set it down, and twirled it a few times. "What's the range on that chopper?"

"About three hundred miles. I called all the airports in a four hundred-mile radius. None of them have seen her. We'll get a call when she tries to refuel."

The waiter brought their salads.

"I don't think she will," he said when his plate was half empty. "A helicopter's too conspicuous. She'll go back to driving."

"Any idea where she's headed?"

"Nope."

Shaffer toyed with the remains of her salad. "Sir, uh… did she say anything, um, helpful… when she…"

"When she tied me up again?"

"Yes." Shaffer looked relieved that she hadn't had to say it.

"No. She wouldn't talk about anything, but somehow she knew that Myron was CIA. And she handled us like children, just like at Derek's house."

She pushed her plate away. "What exactly did she do to Myron?"

"I have no idea," Chapa said. "I've never seen anyone move so fast. She was covering us and Myron had Derek by the throat. Then she dropped the guns. Next thing I knew I was on the floor. Myron didn't get back up."

The waiter brought their dinners and took away the salad plates. Chapa sliced a rib off the rack with his steak knife and chewed the tender meat off the bone. What's-his-name was right: the food was great.

"So, how is Myron?" he said.

"He's okay. His left wrist is broken, his right arm is broken in two places, she cracked three of his ribs, and he's got a concussion. The good news is that his jaw is only bruised."

"She said he should've known better."

"She's right," Shaffer said. "He saw what she did at her mother's house and he knew about her training. He didn't have sufficient force to pacify her, so he should've just played along—like you did."

"If she wanted me dead she'd have done it at Derek's house."

"Myron was an idiot."

"He was just being a spook." Her smile made him feel bold. "There's something I've always wanted to ask you. How did you two get together?"

Shaffer gnawed on a beef rib, eyeing him warily. She tossed the bone in the discard bowl and wiped her hands on a napkin.

"The University of Maryland asked me to come back and give a talk on preparing for a career in the Bureau. You know a lot of agents come from UM."

"Sure," Chapa said.

"Myron was in the audience. I'm not sure why, but I suspect he was trolling for potential spooks."

"That's pretty sleazy. You warm the kids up and he steals them."

"Yeah. Of course, *he* would say he was just dipping his net in the salmon stream, nothing wrong with that. Well, he introduced himself after. He was thirty-six then, and his hair was already white. He seemed so capable and... charming. I was pretty naïve, I'd only been in the Bureau a few years. We had dinner, he sent me roses, and a year later we moved in together."

"That was in D.C.?"

"Yes. When the Bureau moved me to Seattle, he got himself reassigned to the Pacific Rim so we could be together. He got what he wanted, but I discovered he wasn't what *I* wanted. He went away a lot, sometimes with only an hour's notice. When he'd show up again he couldn't talk about where he'd been or what he'd been doing. There were other women, which he denied, of course, but not all of his trips were Company business."

"How do you know?"

"Because I'm a Federal agent, sir." She smiled at him wickedly.

"So you kicked him out." He set down his last rib, unwrapped a Handi-Wipe, and washed the smeared sauce off his hands. "Have you, uh, gone out with anyone since?"

"This is getting a little personal, sir."

"Sorry. I didn't mean to pry."

She considered him as she wiped her own hands. "No," she said at last. "I put my love life on Pause for a while and just concentrated on work." Chapa understood that all too well. "I have my eye on someone, but there's nothing I can do about it right now."

They locked eyes. He looked down after a moment, but he felt hope—he thought it was hope—stirring in his chest.

"We've worked together for six years," Chapa said slowly. "We've built one hell of a case record together, but I've been thinking lately that you're overdue for promotion. Maybe it's time for you to be a lead agent, handle your own investigations."

Shaffer sat back in the booth and looked at him from hooded eyes. "I'm content with our professional relationship," she said. "It's been an honor working with you."

"Well, when this one's over, I'm going to have a chat with the SAC." Chapa's boss, the Special Agent in Charge of the Seattle field office, had to approve all promotions, but if Chapa recommended a promotion for Shaffer, his boss would okay it. Shaffer probably knew it, too.

"Thank you, sir." She picked up her clipboard and the waiter came to clear their table. They both asked for coffee. When he was gone, she said, "Sir, how do you think the wiseguys got to Citrullo's house before we did?"

"Good question. I've got a theory."

"Me, too."

"You first."

She hesitated. "The mob's got a stooge in the Bureau."

"Nauseating," Chapa said, "but logical. They say that shit didn't happen when J. Edgar was alive. No one had the guts to be dirty, because he'd personally eviscerate you if he found out, and he always found out." They contemplated the old days for a moment, although Hoover had died before either of them joined the Bureau. "Can you take it the rest of the way?"

"What do you mean?"

"Why did Carla go to her mom's house?"

"Doesn't make sense," Shaffer said.

"No, it doesn't. She got what she wanted from Hildreth, whatever that was. She could've vanished. What she *should've* done was ditch Derek—or kill him, too—hop across the border, and fly out of Canada on a fake passport. End of story, unsolved case. Instead, she hangs out at her mom's house all day. When she tied us up at Derek's house, she let us see her face and live, and she left fingerprints all over the place. What does that say to you?"

"She wanted us to find her."

"Not quite. She wanted us to *just miss her*—again."

Shaffer thought about that for several minutes. The coffee arrived with the check.

"If the wiseguys are watching us," she said, "maybe someone else is, too?"

"That's what I think. She's using us as a conduit to someone who has a man inside the Bureau. The shootout at Sarah's house—that was just bad luck, baggage that came with Derek. It wasn't part of the plan. She wants someone to know where she is, and she's using *us* to tell them."

"That's a stupid way to announce her twenty," Shaffer said. "Why not just... Oh."

"Yeah."

"Someone's chasing her. She doesn't know where they are."

"Maybe," Chapa said, "she doesn't even know *who* they are."

"Right. So when they come looking for her, they tap their Bureau source, find out that we're one step behind her, and join the chase."

"What do you think will happen then?" he said. She shrugged. "I'll tell you: they'll think she's cornered, but she'll twist around, and the chase will become a trap." He dropped a credit card on the bill and took a sip of coffee. "We don't need to work too hard to find Carla. Very soon, she's going to tell us where she is."

Chapter 23

Philippe paced the echoing warehouse like a caged tiger, turning away from the stacked crates and veering back. He felt the need to *do* something. Their first potential buyer, Yahya Khayrat, was flying in from Cairo in an hour. Philippe knew him by his filthy reputation, but they had never met.

Chen had called at noon the day before. "Philippe, you maggot-ridden dog fucker!" he'd screamed into the phone. "One of your mother-raping clients just woke me up to tell me he's coming tomorrow. Why can't you give them *your* fucking phone number?"

"Calm down, Chen," Philippe said. "Who called you?"

"Some kind of rat, how should I know? Gayrat, or something."

"Tell me you wrote it down," Philippe said threateningly.

"Of course I wrote it down, shit eater! But I'm not going to give it to you until tonight. I'm going back to sleep now, if I can, and I hope you piss yourself worrying about it all day." Chen slammed down his phone, but Philippe asked Lanotte to get the information from Chen immediately—without killing him.

Less than twelve hours after receiving their package, Khayrat had replied that he would be arriving in Marseille, the meeting place Philippe had specified, around thirteen hundred the next day, and he was eager to see the merchandise.

Philippe had to scramble to get everything ready in time, but now he had nothing to do until the Egyptian arrived. He sat down in one of Jensen's uncomfortable chairs, noticed that he was tapping his foot, and stood up in exasperation. He needed something to concentrate on. It occurred to him that he hadn't spoken to Felicia, his third wife, in several days. He took his phone out of his pocket and punched in her number.

"Alô?" Felicia purred.

"C'est moi," Philippe said.

"Ah, Philippe, is it? I was wondering just this morning if you were still alive, or if some tragic plane crash might have set me free to chase the boys I can see playing down the beach."

Philippe doubted very much if anyone was playing on the beach in Portugal on March first. At best it would be chilly, but Felicia had a rich fantasy life, which he did nothing to discourage—it added spice to their frenzied but sadly infrequent sexual encounters.

"I'm sorry, ma cher," he said. "Business has been very busy. But I'll be free in a few days, and then we'll spend much more time together."

"This is not the way I expected to spend my first years of marriage," she pouted. Philippe had married her just after he retired, almost two years ago. Like his other two wives, she thought it was simply business that kept him away so much of the year.

"Where are you now?" Philippe said.

"Well, since it is a beautiful, sunny day—" *in winter*, "—I am sitting on the verandah, quite nude, watching the boys play volleyball in the sand. The sun is hot on my body. I am dripping with sweat. The Baia de Setúbal is blue and a little choppy, but still there are some boys bathing. Wait— I think that one is nude. Perhaps he would like to help me with my suntan lotion?"

"That would be a very bad idea."

"Oh? You want me to be alone? Very well, I can play by myself. Since you can't be here, perhaps you should listen, neh?"

Philippe did listen, amused and a little aroused, as she moaned—softly at first, almost humming, but the moans grew louder until she gave a little shriek and was silent for several moments.

"That was very nice, mon cher," she said, "but now the boys are staring at me. Perhaps one of them could help me. What do you think?"

"I think that in a few days I'm going to come home and tie you up. When I get done with you, your voice will be hoarse from screaming and you won't be able to walk. You'll have so many orgasms your hair will melt. I'll poke my thing into every orifice until you beg for mercy, and then I'll fuck you one more time. I think you'll forget all about those silly boys on the beach and spend the rest of your life kissing my feet. That's what I think."

"It's not your feet I want to kiss."

"Tell me you love me," Philippe said.

"I love you beyond all sanity."

"Now tell me you'll forget about those boys and wait for me."

"I will love no one but my own hand until you return."

"Good. I have to work now. Go play with yourself again. I'll be home soon."

"Adeus," she said.

Philippe set the phone aside. When this deal was done, he would definitely visit Portugal first. After a week or two he would tire of Felicia and fly to Antwerp to see his favorite, his second wife, Yvette. He promised himself at least a month with Yvette before he went to Niterói and Camilla.

It was a mistake to retire so soon. He'd thought the small fortune he'd accumulated over the years with Pequinot would last him the rest of his life, but somehow it had run out after two years. Perhaps it was the four expensive houses, three of which were furnished with expensive wives. *This time, we'll be starting out with a* large *fortune. This time it will last.*

Of course, if he hadn't retired when he had, he'd have been killed like Pequinot. Philippe had tried to determine who had retired his old boss, but there were simply no leads. He suspected the RVS, the successor to the KGB, had settled their old grudge against Pequinot. The Russians were like a blind wild boar: they stumbled around helplessly, but if you got within reach of their tusks, they were deadly.

Pequinot had been careless. Philippe knew this, because Pequinot was dead.

Too bad, really. Jean's contacts would've been invaluable in this deal. Half of the brokers Philippe had known were dead, and he'd had no idea how to contact the others, so he'd been forced to rely on Carla and Olivier. Now Carla had succeeded. He wanted her dead, but only because she was exasperating and dangerous, not because she was less than frighteningly competent. Philippe checked his watch. Khayrat should be landing very soon.

It was a shame the man was Egyptian. Philippe had hated Egyptians on principle ever since Sadat made peace with Israel. The Mossad had been a constant danger to Pequinot's business, and Philippe had had close calls with them many times. He'd come to hate the Israelis, and because of Sadat the Egyptians as well—the only nation in the Middle East to normalize relations with Israel. Peace was so very bad for business.

He checked his watch and phoned Chen.

"I'm in position," Chen said before Philippe could utter a word. "The plane landed a few minutes ago. Suck your own cock and go to hell, will you please?"

"You should be more careful," Philippe said. "What if it hadn't been me?"

"No one calls me *but* you, you flea on the ass of a drowning, cancerous dog. Stop calling me every half hour."

Philippe smiled as he set the phone down. Chen had always been like that, even when they first met, years before Philippe worked for Pequinot, when Philippe was still trying to make a living brokering used parts for automobiles and airplanes. Lanotte had been his partner then, but the business had failed and a family friend had introduced him to Pequinot. Chen had been useful over the years, first as a source of stolen car parts, then as a source of information. Philippe still suspected that Carla had done something to Chen, but Lanotte had been unable to find any evidence and Carla really had nothing to gain from him. Just to be sure, Jensen and Lanotte would be following Chen, who would be following the Egyptian.

The phone rang. Philippe turned it on but said nothing.

"The pig has arrived," Chen said. He hung up.

The pig? That wasn't a code word. Philippe called the driver Lanotte had hired.

"Oui?" a rough voice answered.

"Thirty minutes," Philippe said.

"Oui."

The phone rang again. "Chen's following the limo," Jensen said. He hung up. In a while the phone rang once more.

"He's just left the hotel," Chen said. "He called me for instructions and he even got the silly code phrase right. I'm following him."

A moment later Jensen confirmed that Khayrat's limo was headed toward the rendezvous with the van.

Philippe stood up and looked over the setup. Jensen's arming boxes, those lethal but innocent-looking lunch pails, sat side by side on the makeshift bench. One of the warheads was visible in an open crate, the rest were scattered in among the tractor parts. Philippe rested his hand on the bomb, so perfect and so beautiful that he knew Khayrat would never be able to resist it.

He felt that he could see his future stretching out ahead of him, the bliss and comfort of his lovely wives, the thrill of other women when the charms of his wives grew stale. He thought he felt the warhead vibrate under his hand in perfect resonance with his future happiness.

* * *

Colonel Dan Tsidon sat at the little sidewalk cafe outside the hotel, taking early tea. The service was quite elegant: white linen tablecloth, crystal ashtrays, delicate silver, and an exquisite porcelain teapot with matching demitasse cups. It was a shame the weather was so chilly.

Tsidon was in his early fifties, dressed in a casual suit, open shirt collar, and no tie. He blended easily with the off-season tourists in Marseille, although he was somewhat thinner than the typical tourist. His face was unremarkable except for the white scar on the jaw below his left ear. On the table beside him lay a camera, a local guidebook, and a cell phone.

A black stretch limousine pulled up in front of the hotel. The fat Egyptian, Khayrat, and his two guards got out and walked into the hotel. The limo driver waited at attention by the vehicle for ten minutes until Khayrat and his entourage returned and the limo pulled away.

A rusty yellow Fiat drove past a few seconds later. *That'll be Chen.* Several other cars passed, then a dark blue Citroen filled with four of Tsidon's men, who ignored him. A moment later, a black Toyota 4Runner followed. *And the henchmen. Unusual thugs, those two.* He'd been watching them for several days and hadn't quite figured them out yet. He was looking forward to meeting them, and their elusive boss, too.

Another carful of his men drove by. Tsidon picked up the phone and called his lieutenant.

"Moshe? How's the traffic?"

"No problem, sir," Moshe Levy replied. "We're hanging back half a block from Chen."

"The goons are about five cars behind you."

"Yes, sir, we tagged them. I think we're going for a ride in the country now."

"Don't lose them. I want to wrap this up tonight."

"Yes, sir. I'll call you when something happens."

Tsidon poured himself some more tea and tried one of the lemon cakes: too sweet and not enough lemon. How French. He studied the visitor's guide to Marseille for a while. His phone rang and he flipped it open.

"Tsidon," he said.

"Sir," Levy said, "they've switched vehicles. They're in a white delivery van now. One of our men watched all three transfer from the limo to the van. The limo turned back and they're continuing east on the highway."

"Where are the goons?"

"Following the van, sir."

"And Chen?"

"He didn't stop for the switch. We let him go."

"Good. Stay with Khayrat."

Heading east, they could be going to Toulon, Cannes, or even Monte Carlo. Tsidon wouldn't follow just yet. If their final destination were far enough away, he'd hire a helicopter. Deciding to see some of the sights while he waited, he paid his bill and walked down La Canebière toward the Vieux-Port, threading his way through the crowds and glancing idly into the shops as he passed. He had thought to walk along the harbor and inspect the fish markets, but on impulse turned left at Rue de Breteuil and walked toward Notre-Dame de la Garde, sitting on its hill overlooking the harbor and the south city. Between the buildings he could occasionally catch glimpses of the nine-meter tall statue of the Virgin perched atop the sanctuary's steeple. But he never made it there; he had been strolling, happy to enjoy the sun and the cool sea air, and so was still several blocks from the cable railway leading up the hill when his phone rang.

"Tsidon."

"We're in St. Tropez, sir," Levy said. "The van pulled into a warehouse and the 4Runner followed it in."

Tsidon checked his watch: two and a half hours since Khayrat left the hotel. St. Tropez was close enough to drive.

"Begin surveillance," he said. "They won't transfer the warheads tonight. When the Egyptian leaves, one team stays on him and the other watches the warehouse. Give me the address." Levy read it off and Tsidon memorized it. "Find out who owns the place. I'm on my way."

He stepped into the street and hailed a taxi. On the ride back to the hotel to get his car, Tsidon reflected contentedly that his mission would most likely be over by midnight tonight. Then the Mossad would have possession of three working Soviet nukes, and, if he was lucky, of the men who had stolen them. A great prize for Israel!

Tsidon spent a moment wondering what had become of the katsa who'd made this possible: Carla Citrullo, his former student at the Mossad Academy. But then he pushed away idle speculation and concentrated on his plan to steal the Ukrainian warheads.

* * *

When the van turned into the alley leading to the warehouse, Jensen phoned ahead so the driver wouldn't have to honk his horn or idle in the street. Philippe stood by while a guard cranked open the heavy door and both vehicles drove inside. As the guard closed the door, Jensen and Lanotte got out of the car and slung their Uzis within easy reach.

"Everything went well?" Philippe asked the driver, an ugly man with a lumpy jaw and a crewcut.

"Yes," he replied. "The bodyguards have two sidearms apiece, but the fat one is unarmed. No bugs, transmitters, phones, or GPS devices. They're clean."

"Good. Lanotte, clear the room while we discuss business."

Lanotte whistled piercingly and jerked his thumb toward the nearest door. The ugly driver walked away and the men standing post stepped outside, shutting the doors behind them. When only Jensen and Lanotte remained, Philippe opened the back door of the van.

"Monsieur Khayrat," he said, trying to mask his instant disgust. "I apologize for the long drive. I trust it wasn't too unpleasant."

The Egyptian was incredibly obese. His bodyguards made no move to help as he struggled to rise from his seat, finally managing to hoist himself and waddle unsteadily toward the door. Philippe offered a hand but Khayrat ignored it, huffing and moaning quietly as he slowly took the two tall steps. Finally reaching the warehouse floor, he wiped the sweat from his face with a silk handkerchief. *Chen was right: he's a pig.*

"Monsieur Sottile, I believe," Khayrat said when he caught his breath. Philippe smiled coldly. It was no surprise to be recognized: he had been a major player, once. "A pleasure to meet you, sir, and long overdue. Jean Pequinot always spoke very highly of you."

Philippe nodded. "I know you by reputation, of course." Khayrat's hatred of Israel was common knowledge, as was his utter lack of scruples about what he sold to whom. "How gratifying to see that you're still in the business." And how surprising. If Philippe had been involved in the plot that had cleared the field two years ago, this slimy cut of meat would have been the first to go. The Egyptian's face was still red and sweaty. Philippe considered offering him the warheads for free if the swine could jog once around the warehouse without a heart attack.

Khayrat's bodyguards flanked their master, surveying the warehouse suspiciously.

"This way, if you please," Philippe said. He led the Egyptian toward the crates.

"I was most intrigued... by your presentation... Monsieur Sottile," Khayrat said between gasps. "I've been in the market... for this type of merchandise... for several years... but nothing has been available... until now. I have several... impatient buyers waiting."

Philippe smiled, consumed by contempt. He resolved to jack up his asking price.

They reached the stack of crates and Jensen's workbench. Philippe invited Khayrat to step in closer—as close as his vast stomach would allow—and get a better look.

Nestled inside the wooden crate, the warhead was a narrow, two meter-long cone of smooth, gray metal with a wide orange stripe around the base and an orange tip. Philippe rested a hand paternally on the nuke as he spoke.

"This is a MIRV from an SS19 mod-3 launcher," he said. "We are offering three of them for sale, individually or all together."

"Where did you get them?" Khayrat whispered. He reached out to touch the warhead, but jerked his hand back just short of it. His face was twisted up with greed.

"As you know, the Ukrainians are slowly decommissioning their missile bases in exchange for credits from the West. We, ah, liberated these from a certain emplacement shortly before they would have been removed and destroyed."

Khayrat smiled feebly.

"The nominal yield," Philippe said, "is five hundred fifty kilotons, over fifty times the Hiroshima bomb. Properly placed, just one of these would obliterate a small city. On a battlefield, the device could be even more effective."

Khayrat's hands were shaking.

"We will be accepting sealed bids for a short time. The opening bid is one hundred million dollars each." Jensen frowned at him, but Philippe shook his head subtly; they had been planning to ask seventy-five. "That price includes the mechanism for detonating the devices, but not delivery—land, sea, and air transport are available from the area. The winning bidder will also receive, as a free bonus, some very fine Ukrainian tractor engines." Philippe waved at the other crates and the Egyptian chuckled dutifully. "Now, my colleague will explain the arming boxes."

Jensen opened one of the lunch pails. Philippe's mind wandered as Jensen explained the device to Khayrat. He hoped they would hear from Carla's other contact soon. He really did not want to sell the warheads to this Egyptian hippo, but so far only Khayrat had responded. He had no doubt that Khayrat would pay what he asked: the man was drooling.

He couldn't wait much longer. Every day the chances improved that someone would discover the warheads and try to steal them. The Americans, the Russians, and the Israelis, as the three primary targets for such weapons, were desperate to keep them off the market. The Mossad would swarm over anyone suspected of offering nukes for sale. So the first trick was to sell them quickly and get out alive with the cash.

The second trick was to be on another continent when the damned things went off.

Jensen answered Khayrat's final questions and stepped back.

"Very impressive, Monsieur Sottile," Khayrat said. "Very impressive, and I want all three of them. I'll have a bid prepared for you tomorrow morning. Could you send someone by my hotel at eleven?"

"Of course," Philippe said. Should he be elated or depressed? This slug was going to be his only option.

After exchanging a few pleasantries, Philippe watched Khayrat climb laboriously back into the van. Lanotte went to get the driver. When the van had left and the big door was once more closed, Philippe collapsed into a chair.

"You raised the price," Jensen said.

"Did you see the man?" Philippe said. "I thought he would fuck the thing." Lanotte grunted assent and began closing up the crate. "I hate this damned business. The work itself is fine, but my God, the people you have to deal with! Did you see him sweating? There's a puddle on the floor!"

Jensen closed up the arming box and rearranged some tools.

"I need a woman," Philippe said after a moment. "I'm tired of this stupid warehouse." First the waiting, then his talk with Felicia, more waiting, and finally—Khayrat. It was too much. "Be sure there are extra guards tonight, Lanotte." The giant nodded and leaned back against the crate.

Chapter 24

Lister, Idaho
Wednesday, March 1, 10:23 a.m.

After breakfast Carla made a list of tasks to prepare for their expedition that afternoon, and they started working on them together. Derek carefully nursed his anger at what she wanted him to do, and at not being told *why*. He was sitting at the small, round table by the motel room window, tying knots in a nylon rope, when Carla broke the silence.

"You were talking in your sleep again last night," she said.

"I don't talk in my sleep."

"Sure you do. Every night."

"*If* I talk in my sleep, it must have started since you... since Friday." He tied the last knot and tossed the rope aside. "So, uh... what did I say?"

"I couldn't understand most of it, but you called out for Marjorie."

Derek felt the old bitterness welling up. He wished she would just shut up for a while.

"She was your wife, right?"

"Yeah."

"And you're divorced now?"

"Five years ago."

"That's a long time to be pining for an ex-wife."

"What the fuck do you know about it? Have you ever been married?"

"No." She gathered the supplies together and set them on the table. "You said you were sorry you cheated on her and wanted to get back together. So why don't you?"

"Because she's dead." That was the first time he'd ever said it out loud.

"I'm sorry." He looked up in surprise—she sounded sincere. "How did she die?"

"Breast cancer."

"Recently?"

"January third. She'd been sick for a year, but she never told me. Her mom called to tell me she was gone. I never got to say goodbye, I never... I never got to tell her how sorry I was."

He realized that some time had gone by and Carla was staring at him.

"You're not playing out some death wish, are you?" she said.

"What?"

"Did you stay with me because you figured you'd probably get killed, and that's what you really want—to be dead?"

"What?"

"Because if that's what you're thinking, tell me now. It'll be hard enough to live through the next few days without you *trying* to get us killed. I don't need you helping the bad guys."

Derek was confused. He'd seen her kill people ruthlessly, in cold blood. She'd broken into the FBI office and kidnapped one of their agents—twice. She'd taken out a CIA spook with her bare hands...

"I thought *you* were the bad guy," he said.

"Don't be a fucking idiot. I'm the hero. You haven't even *met* the bad guys yet." *Christ, if she's the good guy...* "Derek, look at me." He did. "Do you want to die?"

Under her glare, he felt himself shrink down until he was as small and tight as a baseball. His despair drained away and the truth bubbled up out of his mouth.

"No."

"Good." She turned away, apparently dismissing the topic.

"Wait a minute, now I have a question for you." Derek took a deep breath and gathered his determination. "If you're really the good guy, prove it. Why should I risk my life for you?"

He expected a flippant answer, or "shut up," or "be patient." But Carla sat down on the bed and looked at him seriously. He waited for over a minute while she thought.

"When we left my mother's house," she said, "you accused me of lying to her."

Derek thought back. It was hard to remember much about that night. It was still a jumble of rapid impressions waiting to be sorted out. "You said... you still worked for the government."

"Right. That wasn't a lie."

Derek could feel the ground shifting under him. "I thought you were retired."

"*That* was a lie. I still work for the Mossad."

"You're still a spy?"

Carla sighed and pulled her legs up under her. She planted her hands behind her on the bed and leaned back.

"My branch commander invited me to dinner a couple of years ago. I'd just got back from Syria and I was dog tired, but he's three levels above me, and when they ask, you say yes. He told me there was a special assignment they wanted me to volunteer for." She smiled grimly.

"What was it?"

"The fragments of the Soviet Union have been in chaos since '91," she said. "They're starved for cash, the armies are coming unglued, black markets are thriving, and people aren't getting paid. And some of these places have live nuclear weapons. It was just a matter of time before someone went after them.

"They wanted me to pose as a mercenary, an assassin for hire. Ex-Mossad are *very* rare. They hoped the smugglers would hire me."

"Did they?"

"Oh, yes," she said. "I'm not sure they could've got the warheads without me."

"But how could you pretend to be ex-Mossad? Why would they believe you?"

"No one would trust me unless they knew I was a rogue. I had to do things, vicious things, only a renegade would do. But the real proof wasn't what *I* did—it was what the *Mossad* did."

"Huh?"

"They spread a rumor that I walked away from an op in the West Bank because I would have been arrested when I came home. To make it believable, they made it true. My boss issued an order for my arrest, and when they found out I'd deserted, they got the Prime Minister to sign my death warrant."

"*What?*"

"They sent a team of assassins after me," she said.

"Are you telling me they're trying to kill you just so people will think you're for real?"

"Yes."

"But the assassins know you're still working for the Mossad, right?"

"No."

"And they're still trying to find you?"

"Probably."

"Do you know where they are?" he said.

"I have no idea. I'd guess they followed me here from Europe."

"So they could show up at any moment and gun you down?"

"They could try," she said, grinning.

Derek didn't think that was very funny. "Let me ask you something," he said. "Is there anyone who *isn't* chasing us?" She kept grinning at him. He put his head in his hands. The decision to come with her was looking more foolish by the minute. Then he realized he'd missed something. "Wait a minute, you said the scheme worked. You actually got some bombs?"

"Yes. We suborned the command of a Ukrainian missile silo and stole three warheads."

He thought for a moment. "I don't get it. You were supposed to *stop* these guys."

"That was the original plan," Carla said. "But my bosses decided they didn't mind if someone stole some nukes as long as Israel got them in the end. So they ordered me to help do the job and turn over both the warheads and the thieves to the Mossad."

"Then what the hell are you doing here?"

"Philippe sent me here to find Hildreth and get the names of buyers."

Derek shook his head in frustration. "Why didn't you just tell the Mossad when you had the bombs?"

"Because Philippe wouldn't tell me where he was moving them; they could be anywhere in Europe by now. I thought about tailing him, but if he'd caught me, he'd get away with the nukes. So instead I... enlisted one of his men. And when I e-mailed Philippe, I sent a copy to the Mossad, so they could watch the buyers, too. Starting from one end or the other, they'd locate the nukes."

"So it's over now—you can just go home, right?"

"No. If the Mossad captures Philippe, *then* it's over. I go back, they recall the kidon team, and I get a nice vacation. But if they don't get Philippe, he'll come after me. I'll never be safe until Philippe is captured or killed."

"Great! Someone else chasing us."

"That's what the C-4 is for. I'm not worried about the FBI, and your Mob buddies don't keep me awake at night either. But if the kidon team or Philippe gets near us, believe me, you're going to want something more than a sidearm."

Derek thought that over. "You'd kill a Mossad agent?"

"If I have to. I'm hoping they'll give me a chance to explain first. If they call for instructions, they'll be recalled and told to let me go. But kidon teams on assignment rarely call in. If they don't listen... I'll do what I have to do."

"How will you know if this guy—Philippe?—if he's been captured?"

"If I don't hear from him," she said, "I guess that means I can go home. If he contacts me and he's happy, that means three nuclear weapons are now in the hands of terrorists. If he's pissed, that means the Mossad got the nukes but not Philippe; he'll come looking for me, and he'll waste us both." She sat up. "It wasn't supposed to happen like this. I should've been there to help steal the weapons. Then I'd have looked Philippe in the eye and sent him straight to hell."

She began stuffing equipment into the backpack. Derek felt a little dizzy. With so many people after them, what were the odds that they'd live through this? And now he had no excuse not to go through with her crazy scheme at the munitions plant.

"Let's get some lunch," she said. "Then we'll go back to Cutrock so you can get set up."

"Carla." She stopped and looked at him. "You've told me everything, right? You don't have any more surprises?"

Carla closed the flap on the backpack and snapped the buckles.

"Partner," she said, extending her hand. He took it and she effortlessly pulled him onto his feet. "Now you know as much as I do."

Chapter 25

St. Tropez, France
    Wednesday, March 1, 6:57 p.m. (10:57 a.m. MST)

Guards were stationed at each of the warehouse's three entrances. There were no taller buildings nearby, so the back wall, without windows or doors, was Tsidon's only means of access to the roof, and it had no drainpipes, trellises, or fire ladders to make his job easier.

In a basement across the street, Tsidon waited patiently for the sentry to make his next pass. If he stood on tiptoe he could see out the high window, but he didn't bother. His men would tell him when the guard went by.

He'd broken every speed limit on the drive from Marseille. His men had done a good job in the meantime, but there hadn't been enough time for in-depth reconnaissance. They now knew the names and addresses of the four principals: Sottile, Jensen, Lanotte, and Chen. Levy discovered that the warehouse's owner lived right across the street in a tidy stucco townhouse. The old woman was a fount of information, most of it useless, but she had given them Sottile's name, which led them to his men.

Tsidon visited the woman as soon as he arrived, even though he knew Levy would have extracted everything useful from her. He had to steer her back onto the topic at hand a dozen times, but then he stayed long enough for a Tarot reading.

"Ah, you see here?" she cackled. "Your current endeavor will meet with great success." *Of course.* She laid another card in the pattern, and another. "And soon you will meet the woman of your dreams." *Nonsense.* He had no time for such things. Romance was impossible for someone in his line of work. He was lucky if he could find a woman to share his bed for a single night, let alone a week or the rest of his life.

He learned nothing new. The man who rented her late husband's warehouse was very nice—Belgian, but one couldn't be picky these days. His name was Philippe Sottile, and she didn't know his address. He'd paid two months' rent in cash, so she asked no questions. Yes, the warehouse was guarded day and night, but no, she didn't know why, or how many men, or anything about their comings and goings. That was their business and she had better things to do.

Tsidon kissed her forehead as he left. If he thought she might have alerted Sottile, he would've shot her between the eyes instead, but the woman was clearly addled and she never spoke to her renter. *The Mossad never kills innocent people.* Unless, of course, they had to.

Two of his men had followed Khayrat all the way back to the hotel in Marseille, passing Tsidon on the way. When it became clear that Khayrat was settled for the evening, Levy recalled the tail, but they wouldn't get back in time to help with the raid.

Sottile and his henchmen left shortly after Khayrat, but they'd lost the tail Levy sent after them in the warren of St. Tropez's streets. Four men watched the smugglers' homes, but so far none of them had shown up. That left Tsidon and five men to steal the warheads. It wasn't enough, but then again, he had yet to execute an op in which he felt he had enough men.

"Guard approaching your position," he heard in his earphone. He tapped the transmitter button on his collar to acknowledge.

Through the high window, Tsidon watched the heavy guard stroll by across the street. It was growing dark and there were no street lamps. When the man turned the corner, Tsidon went quickly up the stairs and out into the dusk. He stood in the doorway, listening to the receding footsteps.

"All clear," his earphone whispered.

Tsidon slung the sniper's rifle across his back. He was dressed entirely in black, with a climbing harness over his clothing and a gear pack slung across his shoulders. Standing at the base of the warehouse's blank wall, he pulled a thick tube out of his pack and aimed it at the roof. He pressed a button and a grappling hook shot out of the tube with a muffled pop, unfolding and trailing a thin climbing rope. Tsidon yanked hard and the rope went taut. It took only a moment to walk up the wall, roll over onto the roof, and pull the rope up after him.

Recent rains had left a few puddles in the low spots of the flat roof. There were several access hatches standing a few centimeters above the tarpaper. Tsidon ran lightly to the one closest to the center of the roof, flipped the simple latch and opened the door slowly, wary of rusty hinges, but there was no sound. Peering over the edge, he could see nothing: the interior was darker than the gathering night outside.

A ladder led down into the gloom. Tsidon gingerly climbed down a few steps and closed the hatch behind him.

He stood amid the trusses that supported the roof, crisscrossed like the steel web of a monstrous spider. As his eyes adjusted, he was able to make out a stack of wooden crates in the center of the otherwise empty warehouse. A board across two fuel drums made a crude table holding three metal lunch pails and several small bins.

A man sat at the table, smoking. Another leaned on the crates beside him, sharpening a knife on a whetstone. Tsidon could hear them talking, but the echoing space swallowed their words. One guard stood at each of the three entrances: the alley doorway, the garage door facing the old woman's house, and the loading dock. A sixth man walked the perimeter. Tsidon kept searching as his eyes adjusted further, but he spotted no one else.

He climbed slowly down to the bottom level of trusses, wrapped his legs around the junction of two metal struts, and let his torso fall so that he hung head down like a bat, suspended high above the concrete floor. His upper body was free; by bending at the waist, he could cover almost the entire floor of the warehouse. Very carefully, he pulled his rifle around, wound the strap around his left wrist, and released the safety.

Tsidon checked his watch and pressed the collar transmitter twice. In the two minutes he'd given himself, he tracked the roving sentry and rehearsed the firing order he would use. When his watch showed five seconds to go, Tsidon took a deep breath, let half of it out, and sighted on his first target, the guard at the alley door.

He fired twice, shifted to the garage door and shot two more rounds, bent to the right and fired twice more at the loading dock. He heard soft popping noises coming from outside. The sentry spotted him and got off one shot before Tsidon fired three times, dropping him. Before the third shot, the side door slammed open and two of his men dove through, rolled, and came up shooting at the idlers standing by the crates.

By then, Tsidon had taken aim in case his men missed, but the thugs were already dead. It was all over. The fire fight had lasted six seconds.

He safetied his weapon, slung it over his back, and pulled a rope bag out of his pack. After tying the rope to a truss, he threaded it through the figure-8 ring on his harness, dropped the bag, and rappelled down to the warehouse floor. His men dragged in the last body from outside as he unhooked the rope. Levy sent someone to get the lorry and Tsidon walked over to judge his marksmanship.

His first target had taken both rounds close together in the chest. At the garage door, the guard had one in the neck and one in the head. The third man was shot through the heart, but Tsidon couldn't find a second wound—he must have missed! The sentry, lying on the floor with his legs twisted under him, had taken one in the arm and two in the gut—he was still alive, though barely conscious. Tsidon drew his sidearm and shot him in the head.

He didn't bother checking the two who'd been together near the crates. They must have taken a dozen rounds each.

One of his men cranked open the garage door, the lorry drove in, and then the door was shut again. Tsidon joined the rest of his team at the crates. They spent some time looking for booby traps, but found none. One of the warheads was right out in the open, but it took some muscle to shift the crates around until they found the other two near the center of the stack. While Tsidon helped Levy drag the bodies into a heap, the other four men carried each crate on their shoulders like a coffin, to be strapped down in the back of the canvas-covered trailer.

When they were done, Tsidon picked up one of the lunch pails, lifted the lid carefully, and peeked inside. The beauty of the circuits, so elegant and simple, caught at his throat. He had extensive training in electronics, so he was able to trace the power source, the controls, the input jacks, and some of the other circuits. The circuit board itself was amazingly simple. There were three EPROM chips. Tsidon wished he could have a crack at figuring them out, but that job would be given to experts.

"Is that an arming box?" Levy said at his elbow. "It's so small."

"I want to meet the man who built this," Tsidon said. "It's a fucking work of art."

Levy hesitated, then said, "We're finished here, sir."

Tsidon closed the lunch pail and handed it to him, then carried the other two over to the lorry. They set them on the floor on the passenger side of the cab. The door was cranked open once more, the lorry drove out, and they closed the door. Tsidon touched the transmit button at his collar.

"Tsidon to eagles. Any sign of our friends?" Four negatives chorused in his earphone from the men watching for Sottile's crew.

"What should we do?" Levy said.

"Our orders are specific. Returning the warheads is our highest priority. Capturing the smugglers is secondary. We'll take the weapons to the ship. If we haven't spotted them by the time we're ready to leave, we cast off and let them go."

"Yes, sir." Levy was obviously disappointed.

"Leave one man here in case someone comes back. The rest of us will help stow the warheads. When we're done, we call in our surveillance teams and go home."

Levy walked off to give the orders, and the rest of his team cleared out. Tsidon checked the time: thirty-two minutes since his first shot. At the door he turned back for a last look around. A pool of blood was spreading across the concrete from the pile of dead guards and a work lamp shone on the empty bench. Tsidon smiled and softly closed the door.

Chapter 26

Carla's scheme was a stew of precision and vagueness. Derek had to memorize sequences, times, and Carla's hand-drawn map, but she hadn't been able to tell him any of the really important things, like *which* God-forsaken trees to use and how to avoid getting shot.

She dropped him off near the munitions plant driveway, and Derek trudged through the snow, while she drove away in her nice, warm truck, probably headed back to Ginnie's to have some pie and coffee while he froze his butt off out here in the woods. He'd spent the first half hour picking out a pair of trees, after which there was absolutely nothing to do but wait for nightfall and the shift change. One of the many things Derek didn't understand about this plan was why he had to sit out in the cold for five hours.

The flaw that Carla had identified in the plant's security was purely a matter of geometry. All the trees within forty feet of the fence had been cut down, but if you drew a line between any of several pairs of trees that stood outside adjacent edges of the fence, that line would cut across the corner. If you drew the line with, say, an aircraft cable, you should—theoretically—be able to pull yourself along the cable and drop down inside the compound.

And then get shot.

The afternoon dragged on. In grade school, every hour between lunch and freedom had lasted a week. For the first time in years, Derek felt the same way, except it was not freedom he was waiting for, but a chance to get killed. Carla had promised him a diversion, but it was hard to imagine what could prevent half a dozen security guards from noticing when he opened their front door.

The security lights blinked on at twilight, dazzling him, but the pools of illumination barely reached outside the fence. The corner behind the warehouse, where he was supposed to drop in, was in shadow. Derek looked at his watch. The whistle should blow in a few minutes, and shortly after that the second shift of security guards would come on duty.

He did some calisthenics to warm up. As he stretched he felt a few twinges and a slight stiffness that had not been there last year. *Getting old.* It occasionally amazed him that he was over forty. The knee that had retired him from college ball was aching with the cold. In a few more years that pain would be joined by a chorus of others.

When he started to work up a sweat, he quit—he didn't need pneumonia on top of everything else. Standing behind a tree, catching his breath, he watched the compound until the first shift security guards left. He had half an hour until Carla showed up. Time to get started.

He attached the crampons to his boots, then got out the lineman's belt and gloves. He drew a few feet of cable off the spool and let the end hang outside his pack, leaving the spool inside, then closed up the pack and put it on. He debated for a moment what to do with the tarp, Thermos, and plastic wrappers on the ground and finally decided to leave them there. He hated littering, but he couldn't carry the garbage out. Someone would find it, but by then they'd surely know he'd been here, anyway.

Under the pine he'd picked as the first anchor, Derek slung the lineman's belt around the trunk and buckled it around his waist. He pulled on the gloves, took a deep breath, and began climbing the tree.

It had been a long time since he'd been up a tree—literally, anyway—and it was a struggle to find the rhythm. He leaned back on the belt, lifted one clawed boot and dug it into the bark, then stepped up and slid the belt up at the same time. Several dead branches hung down, thin and bare of needles, and he snapped them off so they wouldn't snag the belt. As he got higher, the limbs became larger, and not all of them were dead and brittle. As he struggled to break them off, he wished that Carla had thought to buy him a hatchet.

About twenty-five feet up, Derek took off his gloves and reached behind him for the end of the cable. The tree was about a foot in diameter here. He looped the cable end around the trunk four times, just above a live branch, then snapped the connector to the cable. As he climbed back down, the cable paid out above him.

Twenty minutes left. He pulled the cable spool out, put the pack back on, and walked along the fence, letting out more cable as he went. At the fence corner, he checked for dogs, but the run was empty. When he stopped at the base of the second tree, there was plenty of cable left. He put the spool back in his pack, tightened the straps, and started climbing. There were fewer dead branches on this tree, so he climbed more quickly than before, looking over his shoulder occasionally to check his height, and stopped when he was level with the cable tied to the first tree.

Derek leaned back on the belt and pulled the cable spool out of his pack. After passing the spool around the tree once, he dropped it. The cable unwound almost to the ground, the spool rolled away and came to rest in the snow.

He couldn't believe how hard it was to take up the slack. The cable was only an eighth of an inch thick, but a hundred feet of it added up to a lot of weight. He leaned in and pulled back hard on the free end, again and again, ending each stroke bent back at the waist, angled out away from the tree. His arms were aching, but the cable had risen a few feet off the ground and had some tension.

He continued pulling until he thought he might almost be done, but the cable jerked and would go no farther. He looked around the tree trunk. The cable had snagged on the corner of the fence, where it couldn't rise past a fitting on top of the post.

"Shit," he said aloud.

He took a moment to rest and think. He needed four more feet of height to clear the razor wire. When his arms stopped burning, he pulled hard, but the cable wouldn't budge.

Seven minutes to go. If he couldn't be ready by the time Carla arrived with her mysterious diversion, they'd have to give up, and she might shoot him for screwing up. That didn't seem so bad considering what was probably waiting for him inside the fence.

He let out a few feet of slack, held the trailing end with one hand, grabbed the taut line with the other, and jerked the cable like a whip. A wave passed down the line until it reached the fence post. The cable snapped out horizontally and whacked back against the post with a heart-stopping clatter. It was still stuck. Derek swore under his breath and whipped the cable again, but it still wasn't enough to free it, and the cable clanged again.

"Goddamn it!"

He shook the cable viciously. This time the crest of the wave snapped the line out away from the post, then it jumped up and came to rest on a loop of razor wire. Derek started pulling as fast as he could, ignoring the growing burn in his back and arms, until he heard something and froze. A man was coming down the fence line with a flashlight and a Doberman on a leash.

Derek held his breath. The guard stopped at the corner, looking down the gap between the two fences, away from Derek. He was standing directly beneath the cable, but Derek's footprints and most of the line were in the warehouse's shadow. The dog snuffled at the ground and whined softly. Could it smell him? The sentry shone his light into the darkness but never looked in Derek's direction, and finally continued on. Derek let out his breath in relief.

It took a lot more pulling before he was satisfied with the cable's height and tension. The lowest point of its arc passed well above the razor wire, six feet in from the corner of the inner fence. He looped the extra cable around the tree, snapped the connector on, and looked at his watch.

He was late: Carla would be coming any minute. Derek took off his pack again, stuffed the knotted nylon rope inside his coat, then took out his pistol, checked the safety, and crammed it into his waistband. He put the pack back on, closed all the snaps, unsnapped the crampons from his boots and let them fall.

"I can't believe I'm doing this."

Grabbing the taut cable firmly with one hand, he unbuckled the lineman's belt with the other. Instantly he fell away from the tree, suspended by one hand and swaying like a pendulum. He flailed at the cable with his free hand and snagged it on the second try. His feet still swung wildly, almost hitting the tree. He stretched a leg so that his foot touched the trunk, which stopped the swinging, hoisted one leg up over the cable, then the other. He hung upside down from the line like a tree sloth.

Pulling himself toward the fence hand over hand, he chanted under his breath, "Fuck this, fuck this, fuck this..."

* * *

Hanging above the dark, narrow space between the back wall of the warehouse and the inner fence, Derek prayed the guard wouldn't come back. Carla was late.

He hooked his left elbow over the cable and let go with the other hand. Unzipping his jacket, he took out the knotted rope and tied it to the cable with a bowline knot. *Rabbit around and through—thank God for the Boy Scouts. Where the hell is Carla?*

He itched to check his watch but was afraid of losing his grip. After what seemed like an hour he heard a noise. At first he thought the guard and his dog were returning, but then it sounded like running water. In a moment the sound had grown in volume to the unmistakable whumping of a helicopter—*Carla's diversion.* He unhooked his ankles from the cable and his legs fell like dead weight, leaving him suspended from one elbow. After several tries he managed to wrap his legs around the knotted rope and climbed stiffly down to the frozen ground.

Derek ran along the back of the warehouse, turned right, and made his way along its short wall. He peeked around the front of the building; he was twenty or thirty feet from the nearest door.

The Calgary police helicopter was flying slowly toward the plant, following the driveway. Derek backed away from the corner and shrugged out of the pack. He pulled out his notebook computer, opened it up, hit the start key, and nothing happened. He started to panic. Was it frozen? He hit the key again and the machine chimed and booted up normally. After rummaging in the pack for a moment, he found a multi-bit screwdriver and the keypad probe, a small box like a voltage meter with three wires trailing from one side. He put the pack on.

Derek looked around the corner again. The helicopter's skids had caught in the power lines where they crossed over the fence, but the chopper flew on obliviously. The tension on the lines increased, until the wires gave way and snapped with a shower of sparks that faded with the security lights.

He stifled a laugh. Carla's instructions for him had been specific, but she'd refused to tell him the exact nature of the diversion that was supposed to save his life. *Not bad.*

The lights were out for about a minute before the backup generator fired up. Half of the security lights came back on, but the front of the warehouse was only dimly lit. The surveillance cameras would be online, though. It wasn't safe to move yet.

The helicopter was hovering forty feet over the parking lot. The guards ran toward it, converging on the far side of the chopper, so they were staring in Derek's direction. He counted them twice: all six were outside. The sentries still had their dogs, which were barking up at the noisy machine. Two others were aiming pistols at the helicopter and one was shouting into a hand-held radio.

When the helicopter slipped sideways and seemed about to land, the guards scurried aside, putting them between Derek and the chopper. Now they had their backs to him. Derek summoned his courage, picked up his computer, the probe, and the screwdriver, and walked around the corner of the building.

The keypad was a Westinghouse model that he knew. He glanced at the guards as he knelt down and carefully set his computer on the concrete. Carla was rising again, teasing the guards. The sentries were pulling their dogs, still barking and straining at their leashes, toward the administration building. The guns had been put away and now *two* men were shouting into their radios. One guard was waving Carla off, another was gesturing at her to land.

Derek swiftly unscrewed the keypad cover, plugged the probe into the modem port of the computer, and attached two alligator clips to terminals inside the keypad. He hit a function key to start the probe software, then hit another to select the keypad model. When he typed 1234 on the keypad, an oscilloscope simulation on the computer showed a sine wave that faltered and flipped abruptly into a square wave. In another window, key code possibilities scrolled by. Derek moved one of the leads and typed 2345. The sine wave was still flickering, so he moved the other lead. The wave became rock-steady and the correct key code, 7730, popped up on the display. He pressed a function key, the red light on the keypad turned to green, and the lock snapped open.

Derek stuck his foot in the door, disconnected the leads from the keypad, and hung the gray cover back in place. As he bent to pick up the computer, a bright light flared, briefly giving him a sharp shadow before the glare faded. Carla had dropped one of the flares, which now burned red on the asphalt of the parking lot, and was again settling toward a landing. The guards, still facing away from Derek, backed up. He stepped inside the warehouse.

* * *

As the door closed, he went blind. The building had no windows and the lights were off. He found a small flashlight in the backpack by feel. Its feeble light showed that the space was almost empty. Against the wall far to his left, barrels were stacked three high. Closer by, pallets were lined up in eight neat rows, but the rows were short and at most two pallets tall. *Peacetime must be bad for business.*

Derek shut down his computer and put everything away. If Carla stuck to her original schedule, he had four minutes left, but it could be less: she'd arrived late, maybe she'd leave early.

The rows of pallets, two to his right and six to his left, were well separated. He decided to work right to left, and got lucky. The nearest row was labeled Dynamite, and the end one C-4. Each pallet of C-4 held a waist-high stack of wooden boxes about a foot wide and two feet long. The boxes were strapped down with inch-wide metal bands. Derek found wire cutters in his pack. They were too small for the job, but he used them to gnaw through the strap on the nearest pallet and it parted with a zing. As he put the cutters back he realized he had no way to open the box.

I need a hatchet—again.

The flashlight's narrow beam showed a tall cabinet in the corner that might have tools. Derek flung open the doors. Small wooden boxes like cigar boxes lined the shelves: Fuses, Blasting Caps, Detonators. Detonators? Carla had told him to get some of those, so he took a box and set it near his pack. There were no tools. Maybe he could use blasting caps to blow open a box of C-4? *Stupid idea*—it would probably detonate the explosive... all of it.

He needed a crowbar or a hammer. It would take an hour to pry off the lid with his screwdriver, and he had one minute left on the original timetable. In desperation he shoved the top case of C-4 and it moved a little. He pushed harder. It weighed about a hundred pounds. He tugged at the box so it stuck out a little, then knelt down and bent his shoulder under the overhang, reached up to grab the edges of the box, and scooched forward. It slid onto his back. Balancing carefully, Derek stood up, grunting at the weight.

I hope this stuff is as stable as they say it is. He heaved the box into the air.

The crash echoed in the empty space. Derek gritted his teeth, certain that someone would come bolting through the door, but nothing happened. The box had landed on a corner, spilling several bricks of C-4, which were wrapped in oily-looking, olive drab paper. Derek pried away the broken slats, grabbed a brick that hadn't been crushed, and put it into his pack. He took three more and was about to stuff in the box of detonators when he remembered what he was holding—just one of them could blow off his hand. He eased the small box carefully into the pack, then closed it up and put it on.

As he cracked open the warehouse door, the sound of the helicopter blew in. So Carla hadn't abandoned him, even though he was behind schedule. Only five guards were visible, all staring at the chopper hovering about eight feet off the ground. She was still teasing them, bobbing up and down slowly. One of the men was shouting into his radio, and Derek saw her tap her headphones: *not receiving you.* She'd dropped the other three flares, too, reddish sparks sizzling on the ground, brighter than the emergency security lights.

Derek slipped out of the warehouse and ran back the way he'd come; twenty-five feet to the corner and he was out of sight of the guards, then along the length of the building to the rope. Climbing up was hard work. He had twenty pounds of explosive in his pack, and he was at least that much heavier than the last time he'd done this, in college gym class. He was sweating profusely by the time he swung his legs up onto the cable and headed back to the tree.

He lifted his butt when he went over the razor wire, even though the coils were a foot below him. As he passed the outer fence, the helicopter rose and flew swiftly away.

* * *

Headlights glimmered ahead of Derek as he trudged along Lister Lake Road. He stomped off into the snow and watched from behind a tree as two police cars sped past, sirens wailing. They turned into the munitions plant half a mile behind him and disappeared, but the sound lingered, quavering through the trees. He clambered back to the road and continued walking.

Another car, not yet visible, lit up the power and phone lines strung beside the road like the silhouettes of ocean waves. Derek climbed off the road and hid again. This time the car approached slowly, with no flashing lights. When it was a hundred feet away, Derek recognized the Ford pickup and stumbled out to the street, waving an arm.

Carla stopped the truck and leaned over to open the passenger door. Derek took off his pack and pushed it in ahead of him, then climbed up into the cab. She was grinning at him.

"How did it go?" she said.

"You were late."

"It took a long time to warm up the chopper. Did you get it?"

"Four bricks, a box of detonators, and frostbitten toes."

"Let's see." She wasn't talking about his toes. Derek opened his pack and let her look inside. She prodded one of the bricks of C-4, then took out the box of detonators and slid back the wooden lid. Pencil-shaped rods lay nestled in excelsior. She handed it back and put the truck into gear, did a three-point turn, and headed to town.

"I got your stuff from the motel," she said.

"We're leaving?"

"You want to run into Chapa again?" He snorted. She pulled the truck into a closed gas station and put it in park. "So, Derek—where do you want to go?"

"How should I know?" She waited, as if she really expected an answer. "Well, what are we doing next?"

"We're going to wait to hear from Philippe," she said. "Or wait until we don't. If he sends us a message, we'll trap him and kill him. Then I'm going home and you can do... well, whatever you're going to do with the rest of your life."

"Great." Derek settled in his seat. "Or this guy could kill *us*, right?"

"Maybe."

Derek thought about it. If someone was chasing them, he'd rather be chased in a place that he knew. Maybe then he'd have a chance...

"Let's go back to Seattle," he said.

"Good idea," she said. "No one will be looking for us there. Not yet, anyway." She put the truck in gear and drove south out of town, toward I-90. Derek closed his eyes when they reached the entrance ramp in Coeur d'Alene. He was asleep before they passed the city limits.

* * *

Chapa retraced Derek's route in the dark, from the blue tarp and its trash to the first suspension tree. He walked beneath the cable—his flashlight and the other two tracing out bouncing luminous patches like giant fireflies—and detoured around the fence corner, to the second tree. A lineman's belt and a pair of crampons lay on the ground. Chapa craned his neck back; the cable had to be thirty feet up.

"Find out where they got the hardware," he told Shaffer as they plodded through the snow back to the plant's entrance.

The local cop who was guiding them said, "Only one hardware store in town."

"Okay. Can your men interview the employees?"

"Sure. I'll take care of it." The cop ran back to the gate with long, loping strides through the six-inch-deep snow. After a moment all they could see of him was his flashlight beam jumping around, illuminating the trees.

"You just made him real happy," Shaffer said.

"I know." The cop thought he was helping the Feds, maybe storing up some credit that could help his career. All he was really doing was taking one more pointless, tedious inquiry off their hands. "I'm getting a little tired of cleaning up after Carla."

"Yes, sir."

They stamped their feet at the compound gate, but it was too late: Chapa already had snow in his shoes, and it was starting to melt. He entered it in his mental Carla ledger, one more item to pay back, and tried to ignore the discomfort.

He followed the footprints from the dangling rope around to the front of the warehouse. Chapa squatted down and shone his flashlight on them.

"He finally bought some boots," he said. Shaffer shuffled her feet. She was wearing tall, black leather boots herself. *Smarter than me.*

The flabby plant manager met them at the warehouse door, sweating despite the cold. Was he more upset about the break-in—which would require new security procedures, ATF re-certification, and a truckload of paperwork—or about being torn away from his TV?

"What's missing?" Chapa said, although he knew that Shaffer had already been through this. He examined the keypad's loose cover while the manager flipped nervously through pages on a clipboard. The plant was required to have accurate inventory records ready at a moment's notice for an ATF inspection. ATF agents were already on their way. Chapa wanted to be gone when they arrived, which would piss them off, but those guys made him nervous.

"Four bricks of C-4," the manager said, "and a box of eight detonators." He looked ready to faint.

Chapa walked past him into the building and shone his flashlight on the broken case and its spilled bricks of explosive. The doors of a nearby cabinet were open. He looked inside, then rejoined Shaffer on the stoop.

"Where's the helicopter?" he said.

"A few miles outside of town. She parked it right in the middle of a road."

"Calgary PD will be glad to get it back intact."

"Eventually," Shaffer said. For the moment, it was evidence.

"I guess they're driving again."

They watched the utility crew working in cherry-pickers to repair the power cables. The plant manager shifted from one foot to another behind them, but Chapa ignored him. He imagined Carla holding the guards' attention for ten minutes with her dancing helicopter, and Derek pulling himself hand-over-hand along the cable, dropping in, and simply walking out with enough explosive to destroy a building. He was having trouble picturing the tradecraft and the raw bravado of someone who could conceive of and execute that plan flawlessly in less than two days.

She's got more balls than Toys-R-Us.

"Did we leave any surveillance on Derek's place?" he asked Shaffer.

"We took it off after Hildreth."

"Start it up again."

"You think he'll go home?"

"No," he said. "Even if he wanted to, Carla wouldn't let him. But I have a hunch they're headed back to Seattle, so let's cover all the bases."

"Frieder and Holbrook?"

"Why not?"

As they walked back toward the plant entrance, the lights suddenly grew much brighter. Chapa stopped and looked up at the utility guys. He turned back to examine the face of the warehouse, now lit up almost as bright as day.

"Goddamn," he said, shaking his head. "You've got to love these kids."

Chapter 27

Ste. Maxime, France
Thursday, March 2, 8:01 a.m. (12:01 a.m. MST)

A gigantic nutcracker was squeezing Philippe's head. He groaned and rolled over, colliding with a warm body, and opened his eyes slowly. Daylight speared his brain. He gasped and leaned over to see what sort of girl he'd picked up last night. Sometimes, if he was drunk enough, he wasn't very choosy.

He'd done much worse. She was pretty, blonde, petite, and dead asleep on her back with her mouth open. Philippe pulled the sheet down and squinted at her tits approvingly. And she was a real blonde. The girl smacked her lips and rolled onto her side. She had a pert little ass and good legs.

"My sweet," he said, "I'd screw you again if it wasn't for this pounding in my head."

He showered quickly. The scalding water on his neck and shoulders made him feel a little better. He found aspirin in the medicine cabinet and took four of them with two glasses of water. Closing the cabinet door, he wiped away the condensed steam with his palm and stared at the bleary face glaring back at him. He leered at himself and padded back into the bedroom to find his clothes. As he was about to put on his trousers, he debated whether to wake her up and make her scream again like last night, but he doubted that his brain would survive her orgasm, so he finished dressing, left some money on the table by the door, and walked out into the hallway.

Ah merde. He couldn't remember which rooms Jensen and Lanotte were in. He lurched to the right and pounded on the nearest door. Jensen opened it immediately, as if he'd been waiting with his hand on the knob.

"Morning, boss," Jensen said, grinning. "Have fun?"

"I wish I could remember."

"She was a hot little number. I thought she was going to do you right there in the club."

"Shut up and help me find some coffee."

"Okay. Just a second."

Jensen grabbed his coat, then knocked on the next door. Lanotte came out and they walked down the stairs and out into the sunny morning. They took a table at the sidewalk cafe near the hotel. The air was cool but the sky was cloudless and cheerfully blue. *I hate days like this. When I have a hangover, the world should be gray.*

The waitress was a pretty thing, with chocolate skin, a thin nose, and big eyes. She was smart enough not to chatter at them, but simply took their order and left. All three of them watched her walk away.

"Nice ass," Jensen said.

"She's not your type," Lanotte replied.

"Bullshit. Great tits and a tight ass. A pretty face don't hurt one little bit, either."

"Shut the fuck up," Philippe groaned. It was blissfully quiet through the rest of breakfast, except for the traffic noise that made his brain jiggle around like aspic.

Lanotte drove the twenty kilometers back to St. Tropez. Jensen rode in the back and Philippe sat in the passenger seat with his eyes closed, ignoring the beautiful seascape, trying to tame his hangover. He'd almost managed to fall asleep when the car jerked to a stop, throwing him hard against his seat belt.

"Merde!" he said, holding his throbbing head in his hands. "Go easy, you oaf!"

Lanotte drew his pistol from his shoulder holster. "Where's the guard?"

Philippe instantly forgot his head. He unsnapped his seat belt and sprang out of the car, taking his own pistol from his jacket pocket. Jensen got out of the back with the Uzi he'd had stashed under the seat, scanning the roof lines and looking down the alley while Lanotte ran the other way.

"Loading dock's clear," Lanotte said. "No guard."

They walked quickly down the alley. A guard should be stationed outside every entrance, with another patrolling the building exterior, but so far they'd seen no one. They stopped beside the doorway, leaning on the stucco wall with their guns ready. Lanotte inclined his head at the door and Philippe nodded assent. Lanotte shoved the door and it swung open, unlocked. He stuck his head around the corner and immediately pulled it back, closed his eyes to study the fading image, then took another look.

"Oh, shit," Lanotte said.

Philippe swung around the corner, crouched and holding his pistol in both hands. There was nothing to shoot at. He squinted at a confusing pile of something near the tractor crates.

"What the hell?" He walked into the warehouse.

The guards' bodies were stacked in a rough heap. The stench of blood and feces was strong, but the sticky puddle spreading from the corpses was surprisingly small. Philippe's face felt tight, as if someone were pulling back on his scalp. The pounding in his head, which had retreated under the initial adrenaline rush, came back with the force of a tsunami. He staggered closer to the pile of bodies.

"Check the warheads," he said, his gun still searching for a target. It took only a moment to verify what he already knew.

"They're gone," Jensen said, grimacing in rage.

Philippe's fury overwhelmed him. His vision narrowed down to a pinpoint and his head was pounding so hard that he knew it would explode. With a howl he shot one of the dead guards in the head.

"You incompetent shit scum!" Philippe shot another one, then another. Suddenly he realized that the pistol was no longer firing—he had emptied the magazine. He threw the gun at the floor with such ferocity that the ivory grip shattered.

Lanotte was standing aside with a strange expression on his face. Philippe calmed down enough to recognize it—sadness. He couldn't understand that. He heard a loud noise and turned to see Jensen attacking the crates with a sledge hammer, shattering the wooden boxes. The sledge bounced off the engine blocks with a high ringing tone.

Jensen collapsed, sobbing, but Philippe realized that at least some of the pounding had been in his head, and was growing stronger. He spun on his heel, light-headed and so angry that his eyes felt ready to flame out of their sockets. If he'd had one of the warheads left, he would have detonated it without another thought.

Suddenly his rage acquired a focus. He knew without a doubt who had done this to him. Philippe fell to his knees, his hands spasmed into fists on his thighs, and he screamed into the echoing, empty warehouse, "Carla!"

* * *

"I don't have a lot of time," Philippe said.

He walked around Chen, inspecting him from every angle. Chen's face was a rictus of fear, beaded with sweat. He was tied securely to a rolling chair in the middle of his apartment, his feet fastened to the post and his arms jammed under the chair's arms and roped behind its back. *That has to hurt*. If they left him like that long enough, it would probably dislocate his shoulders—but they wouldn't.

Standing behind him, Philippe shoved the chair and Chen grunted in surprise and fear. The chair rolled half a meter and stopped.

"I have a plane to catch," Philippe said. "Otherwise, believe me, I'd make this last as long as possible. I know that you, for one, will be disappointed at this." He continued walking around his prisoner and leaned down to look him in the eye. "Tell me, right now, or I swear I'll leave Lanotte behind and he can take a week, or two weeks, making you die."

Chen was shaking and sweating, staring at him in terror, apparently incapable of speech. Philippe stood up and reached out his hand. Lanotte set a filleting knife in it. Without another word, Philippe slashed at Chen's face, cutting his cheek to the bone. Chen screamed in pain. Blood streamed down his face and into his open mouth. Something in his eyes changed when Chen tasted his own blood; he shivered violently and spat.

"*Tell me!*"

"It was Carla," Chen said. He closed his eyes and breathed shallowly, starting to hyperventilate. Philippe rested the point of the knife on Chen's right knee. It sank through the cloth and nicked the skin. Chen yelped and his eyes flew open.

"I want details."

Chen groaned. Philippe raised the knife and Chen's eyes grew wide. He quickly said, "We were in bed. Not my idea, no, the bitch seduced me. I was drunk. She's twisted, she made me lick her, then she wanted to tie me up. Oh gods, why did I let her?"

"Then what?"

"Just as I was, just as I was coming, she pulled a knife out of nowhere." His eyes strayed to the blade in Philippe's hand—still shiny and sharp as a razor—then snapped away. "She held it to my cock and she... she cut me. I was still coming, and I bled all over the bed, and it hurt, oh gods it hurt, but I couldn't stop coming. She laughed and said she had a deal for me. She wouldn't get off me, she sat on me while I bled like a pig and she held up the knife, right before my eyes."

"What was the deal?"

Chen spat again and winced, visibly trying to pull himself together. "When she sent me the contact names, I was to call a number. Wait for someone to pick up, and keep trying until they did. Then follow instructions."

"And you did it." Philippe said.

He didn't respond. Philippe lightly drew the knife along the backs of the fingers of Chen's left hand, leaving a thin trail of blood.

Chen yelped and started crying. "Yes, I did it."

"What instructions were you given?"

Chen looked up, confused, crying, pleading silently. Philippe raised the knife again and he sputtered, "Wait, wait! I can remember. Wait! It was a man... He said... He told me to stay on the line. I heard some clicks. Then he told me to forget the number and he hung up."

They traced the call. That would give them an address, then they'd tail him. *They were on us from the moment Khayrat contacted us.* He knew Chen would give him the number, but there was no point. Dead end, cold trail.

"What was your end of the deal?" Philippe said.

Chen snorted and tried to shake the tears out of his eyes, wincing with the pain. His cheek was still bleeding profusely.

"It was a typical Carla deal," he said. "I give her what she wants and I get to keep my cock. You know her, Philippe. She meant it."

"Chen," Philippe said gently. "She's in America. I'm here. You and I were never friends, but I've helped you dozens of times. I gave you work. I bailed you out of jail. I loaned you money for drugs. You'd have starved to death years ago if not for me. All you had to do was tell me. I would've handled Carla."

Chen spat blood. "*No one* can handle her. She's a demon from hell."

Philippe considered him, then squatted down so they were face to face. "Tell me what she did with my warheads."

"Philippe, I don't know." Chen looked scared again. "Maybe I can help you find out. Maybe if I contacted her, she'd slip up and tell me."

"*No one* can handle her," Philippe said, standing up. He walked behind Chen and leaned down to whisper in his ear. "I want you... to go get things ready for Carla."

"Philippe," Chen pleaded, but Philippe drew the knife deeply across Chen's throat, cutting from ear to ear and severing the windpipe. Chen's blood splashed across the room and hit the wall, pulsing weaker and weaker.

Philippe watched until it stopped and then looked up. Jensen and Lanotte stood well out of the way, their faces impassive.

"Let's go," he said. He found a rag on the floor and wiped a few drops of blood off his hands. "I'm going to make Carla give us back our warheads." He tossed the rag to the floor. "And then I'm going to take a month killing her. I'm going to make her the world expert on pain. She's going to wish the Mossad had gotten to her first."

Chapter 28

Seattle, Washington
    Thursday, March 2, 9:23 a.m.

Derek proposed a motel on the Eastside, where he lived, but Carla said no. If he'd suggested going back to his house, she'd have had to slap him around until he came to his senses. She wasn't leaving a trail any more, she just wanted to play it safe until Philippe contacted them, so she checked in at the Sheraton downtown. The room was a huge step up from the dives they'd slept in for the last week, but it was functionally identical: bathroom, bedroom, furniture.

After breakfast in the hotel's coffee shop, she went to the gift store and Derek attempted a joke about souvenirs, which she ignored. Back in their room, he stretched out on the bed, reading *Winnie-the-Pooh* and chuckling occasionally, while she sat at the desk, studying the street map she'd bought. She wasn't looking for anything in particular. Her training and her instincts gave her a deep need to know precisely where she was and how to get out.

Seattle's road system was complicated by Puget Sound and the long, narrow lakes that all ran north-south: there were limited routes across or around the water. Carla traced the major highways and the areas surrounding every exit, refreshing her memory. When she was done, she got up and walked to the window. From the seventeenth floor, the rush hour traffic on I-5 looked like matchbox cars. Seattle sprawled to the north, houses covering every hill, and Puget Sound sparkled on her left through the high-rises. She could see the Space Needle poised as if waiting for lift-off.

Philippe was her biggest problem. She could outfox the FBI, and the scuzzbos were fleas. The kidon assassins were a serious issue, but not if she got home before they found her. Her first concern was Philippe: was he dead, in a Mossad dungeon, or still alive and free and hunting her? He would know she was to blame for the loss of his nukes, and she had no doubt he would wring the truth out of Chen. So if he was alive, he would try to contact her, locate her, and kill her. But how?

Her gaze fell on Derek's computer case sitting on the floor, and it was suddenly obvious. Philippe's only contact with her since Poland was by e-mail.

"Derek?" He looked up over the top of the book. "Your e-mail address would be in the message I sent, right?"

"Of course," he said.

"Have you checked your messages in the last few days?"

"No. Why?"

"We might have got a response."

"I'll look," he said. He set up his computer, connected the modem to the phone's data jack, and started up the mail program. "Who are you expecting mail from?"

"Philippe."

He grimaced. "Terrific. I should have thought of this before. Now they know my e-mail address and they'll be coming for me, too."

"You're probably on the FBI's Most Wanted list by now," she said. "What's a few terrorists, assassins, and mobsters next to that?"

"Great. Maybe they'll put me on that TV show."

"Didn't you ever want to be famous?"

"Oh, sure." The phone dialed and hissed for a moment. "No new mail."

It was probably too early. She'd sent the e-mail to Chen only three days ago, and it might be a week before a customer met with Philippe. The Mossad couldn't move until then, because they had no idea where the warheads were hidden; they had to follow the buyers and Chen.

"It might take a few more days," she said. "We should check again later."

"I can have it check every hour if you want."

"Really?"

"No problem." He spent several minutes playing with the computer. "Okay, it's done. It'll beep when a message arrives."

"Good." Carla started pulling the clothes out of her duffel bag, stuffing them into the brown plastic laundry bag the hotel provided. It had been a week since she'd washed anything and she was long since out of clean underwear.

Derek followed her example. She called housekeeping and set the bags outside the door. Then she took the C-4, the detonators, and his screwdriver into the bathroom. Derek followed and watched her remove the panel that hid the plumbing under the sink. She tucked the explosives and the detonators up under the cabinet and replaced the panel.

"Come on," Carla said. She picked up the room key.

"Where are we going?"

"Shopping."

* * *

"Radio Shack?" Derek said, looking up at the red and white sign.

She locked the truck without answering and went into the shop. A bored middle-aged salesman stood behind the glass counter.

A younger man was adjusting packages of stereo cables on a wall rack. "Can I help you find anything?" he asked Derek. He was Japanese but tall, with short black hair and a piano player's hands.

"No, thanks," Carla said.

He looked startled: *she speaks*. "Okay, let me know."

Carla browsed the aisles. She picked out a soldering gun and solder and handed them to Derek. Pliers with a bent needle-nose. A voltage meter. Single-strand narrow gauge wire. Then two or more each of various capacitors, transistors, and other electronic components, all individually wrapped in small transparent plastic bags.

"What are we building," he said, "a radio-controlled airplane?"

"Close."

He was having trouble holding the pile of slippery widgets and dumped it on the counter with relief. The older salesman, whose name tag read 'Doug,' looked at Derek curiously.

"Can I see that Maxon CB walkie-talkie?" Carla said. Doug looked at her sharply, as if he hadn't seen her standing there. He wordlessly pulled a box down from the shelf just above his head. The hype on the back claimed that the range was two miles. "Can I look inside?"

"Go ahead," Doug said.

Carla opened the box, pulled out the cardboard packing and the plastic-wrapped radio, and unsnapped the battery compartment cover. It took AA batteries, but there were spacers in two slots: the case had been designed to hold more batteries than the circuits actually needed. Perfect.

"I'll take three of these," she said. "And batteries."

Doug reached for two more radios while Carla repacked the one she'd opened. He turned to the cash register and looked first at her, then at Derek, and finally concluded that she must be the customer.

"Can I have your phone number?" he said, waiting with hands poised above the keyboard.

Carla leaned over the glass case until only inches separated her face from Doug's. He nervously backed up half a step without moving his hands.

"No," she said firmly.

He seemed afraid to move. Carla restrained the smile that wanted to cross her lips. If she smiled, he'd probably wet his pants.

"No problem," he said at last in a shaky voice, and Carla drew back, feeling happy. During the several minutes it took to ring everything up and bag it, the other salesman watched anxiously without moving.

"Goodbye," she said pleasantly when it was done.

"How do you do that?" Derek said as they walked out of the store.

"Do what?"

"The snake and mouse trick. He wants to run, but he's hypnotized—he can't move. And then you eat him."

"It's like any other skill," she said, putting the truck in reverse. "Practice, practice, practice."

* * *

"No, it's like this," Carla said. She showed him the correct way to hook up the capacitors in series, then pointed to the schematic she'd drawn.

Derek could read electrical diagrams, which helped. When they'd returned she'd made a component list and drawn a picture. Now she was walking him step by step through the process of converting a hand-held CB into a radio-controlled bomb.

By removing the speaker and rearranging some of the parts inside, they were able to make enough space for a detonator and a small amount of explosive. The radio already had a circuit to detect an incoming signal: ordinarily it would light up the LED channel readout. They redirected that circuit and connected it to the one that Derek was building.

"When a signal comes in," she said, "the capacitors drain the batteries. Then they discharge into the detonator, which kicks the C-4."

"What happens if someone else is using the same channel?"

"If the radio is off, nothing. Otherwise, your worries are over."

"Great."

It took much less time for Derek to build the second bomb. They didn't install the detonators or explosive yet, for safety's sake, but that would take only a few minutes.

"How much C-4 would you use?" he said.

"One brick would be enough to level your house. So if you're trying to knock down a wall, or blow up a car, a piece about the size of a walnut would be enough. That's all that's going to fit inside this case, anyway."

"Is that what you're planning to use them for?"

"I told you," she said. "I don't know what we'll run into. I just want to be prepared."

"Be prepared?" Derek held up one of the radio bombs. "Like the Boy Scouts?"

Chapter 29

En route to Seattle, Washington
Thursday, March 2, 6:06 p.m.

Two hours out from Seattle, Lanotte was struggling to follow another of Jensen's attempts to explain particle physics.

"Cleveland?" Lanotte said.

"Yeah," Jensen said. "In a big salt mine. If the detectors are deep enough, cosmic rays can't get through. Only neutrinos can penetrate that far."

Lanotte closed his eyes and tried to concentrate. "Okay, there are massless or nearly massless particles called neutrinos."

"Right."

"They're produced in the guts of the sun."

"Right."

"So they put a neutrino detector in a salt mine in Cleveland to count how many are actually getting made."

"You've got it."

"Why?"

"What do you mean, why?" Jensen said. "They wanted to see if they were right, but they only found a third as many neutrinos as they expected. So either we don't really understand how solar fusion works, or the Standard Model is wrong about neutrinos."

Lanotte sighed and looked out the window. At least they were flying first class. He wouldn't have fit into a coach seat, but even so he felt claustrophobic. He turned back to Jensen.

"The more you tell me about this crap, the more certain I am you don't know what the hell you're talking about. Are you making this up as you go along?"

"No, listen," Jensen said, "it's not that complicated. You remember I told you there are three families of matter? Every family has two quarks, a charged lepton, and a neutrino. Plus the anti-particles and the carriers that mediate the four forces."

"I suppose," Lanotte said.

"Well, now we think neutrinos can mutate from one family into another. Since the detectors can only see neutrinos for the first family, and there are three families, that would explain why they only see one-third the neutrons they expect, *if* neutrinos are mutating all the time. But they have to have mass to mutate, and we know that if they have any mass at all, it can't be much. The upper limit is incredibly small, so maybe they don't have any mass, which leaves us with an unexplained shortfall of neutrinos from the sun. So maybe the sun doesn't work the way we thought it did."

Lanotte was staring at Jensen in disbelief. "This is total bullshit. It sounds like astrology. When something doesn't work, you just invent—"

Philippe raised his head over the back of the seat in front of them. "I hate to interrupt the lesson, but can we talk about work for a moment?"

"Thank God," Lanotte said. Jensen gave him a sour look.

"Jensen," Philippe said, "you copied all of Chen's computer files, yes?"

"Sure. I've got them on my notebook, right here. You want to check something?"

"Yes. I want you to look through his e-mail."

Jensen pulled his computer from under the seat and turned it on. After a moment, he said, "Got it."

"Good. Is the mail from Carla there?"

"Yeah, it's the only one."

"So. She wouldn't have her own e-mail account."

Jensen squinted at the screen. "No, she used someone else's. Uh... somebody named Derek Narr."

"Can we learn anything about this Narr?"

"Not from here. When we land I can log on and find out where he lives."

"Then that's where we'll start. Now, Lanotte, perhaps you should call your friends and have some... em, supplies waiting for us."

Lanotte nodded and grabbed the phone off the back of his seat. It was shame they couldn't bring their own weapons, but U.S. Customs was strangely rigid on certain issues. Philippe was not such a fool that he'd go searching for Carla without at least a pistol. A bazooka would have been better, but he'd settle for sidearms.

When Lanotte hung up and said it was arranged, Philippe turned around to resume his seat. They could just hear him say, "Go back to your silly physics."

* * *

By the time they'd gone through customs, taken the shuttle train to the main terminal, and collected their baggage, it was after nine p.m. It would be five in the morning in France. Philippe had slept on the international leg and spent most of the flight from D.C. to Seattle thinking. He wasn't tired, he wanted to go to work.

Carla had started from Seattle, so he would, too.

A light drizzle was falling as they piled their bags into the rental car's trunk. It took almost an hour to drive to their hotel in downtown Seattle.

The Westin's rooms were situated in twin, round towers that were encrusted with balconies, like a bad early sketch for the leaning tower of Pisa. The roof of each tower looked like a beret, flat and wider than the column itself. To Philippe's eye, the effect was gauche and ugly, exactly what he'd expected from America.

A porter took their bags as they finished checking in. The lobby was overdecorated and cluttered: low ceiling, columns, brass everywhere, plants, and semi-private sitting areas. Someone was murdering a Cole Porter song on the piano.

When they got off the elevator on their floor, Philippe was vaguely surprised that the hallways curved to follow the outside wall of the tower. After tipping the porter, Philippe went next door to Jensen's room.

The suites were not up to Philippe's old standards, but he was running out of money, and until he got his warheads back he would have to economize. At least this place was more tasteful than the American hotels he always saw in movies. The walls were pale yellow, with huge windows looking out over the wet, glittering city. The furniture was adequate: a large bed angling out from a corner, desk, dresser, couch and coffee table and, of course, a big television.

"I'm looking for Narr," Jensen said as he worked on his computer. Philippe sat down on the edge of the bed and watched. Nothing was happening. "I'm assuming she met him here."

"Likely," Philippe said. "She said she would begin with the FBI."

"Maybe we should just ask the Feds where she is."

Why did Americans have to be funny all the time? "There are better ways to find her." A list of names popped up on the display. Jensen highlighted one and Philippe read it aloud: "Derek Narr, Bellevue. What is *Wa?*"

"Washington. Let's look in the phone book." There were four phone books, as it turned out, and they found Narr's address in the Eastside directory.

"I'm hungry," Philippe said. "Let's eat, collect our weapons, and pay a call on Monsieur Narr."

* * *

Jensen drove, since this was his country. Philippe sat in the passenger seat while Lanotte navigated from the back. The concierge had given them a map that was worthless unless you wanted to walk to tourist sites or stay on the highways. They bought a better one in the hotel's gift shop.

Lanotte directed Jensen to a building on the south side of town, a few blocks away from the Kingdome. While the other two waited in the car, Lanotte knocked on the metal door of an abandoned factory. When it opened a crack, he spoke briefly to the person inside and was handed a cardboard box. The door clanged shut and he returned to the car.

They drove a few blocks away, parked on the street, and Lanotte handed out the goods. Each of them received a pistol with an extra magazine, and Lanotte kept the Uzi for himself. The last item was a long-barreled handgun that he examined and returned to the box.

"What's that?" Philippe said.

"Tranquilizer."

Philippe laughed and Jensen put the car in gear. Moments later they were driving north on the freeway.

They crossed a lake over a strange bridge that sat right down on the water. Despite the late hour, the traffic was heavy. Once Jensen left the highway, Philippe was assaulted by the alienness of this town, Bellevue. He'd been born in Brussels and spent most of his adult life in France, with frequent trips to many places in Europe and South America, but he'd never seen anything quite like this before.

The wide, straight street cut through a jungle of brightly-lit gas stations, shops, and parking areas. When the neon lights gave way to a residential area, brand-new mansions loomed beside run-down trailers and the skeletons of dead automobiles.

Jensen pulled off the boulevard into a maze of curving drives that were numbered instead of named. The houses were bizarre, architecturally null, too small to be estates, too large to be hovels, with enormous garages, crowded together like tenements—except they were opulent. Large lawns, deep but narrow, were decorated with artless shrubberies.

What kind of psychotics could live like this? It's appalling.

"Nice neighborhood," Jensen said.

Philippe turned to stare at him. Was that a joke? But he seemed to be serious.

Narr lived on a cul-de-sac. Philippe could think of no reasonable explanation for the gaping hole in the garage. Shards of wood and metal littered the driveway, so Jensen parked on the street and they climbed out of the car into the persistent drizzle. As they passed the garage, Philippe leaned down to peer into the hole, but it was totally black inside and he could see nothing.

"Bomb?" Lanotte said. Philippe shrugged.

The house was dark but the button for the doorbell was lit. Jensen pushed it, triggering an eight-tone melody that echoed inside the house, with no response. They stood for a moment in the dark, uncertain of what to do next.

"Easy to break in," Lanotte said.

"Wait," Philippe said.

He stood at the edge of the concrete porch and leaned over to look in the front window. No lights were visible inside, no movement. He turned and surveyed the street, empty of cars other than their own. The center of the cul-de-sac was a sort of garden, with a few bare trees and shrubs. Many of the neighboring houses were unlit and the rest appeared unoccupied—no, someone walked past a lighted upstairs window.

This doesn't feel right. Perhaps his instincts were confused by the weird sterility of this place, but perhaps not.

"Lanotte," he said, "do you suppose this house might be under surveillance?"

Lanotte stood beside him, looking over the neighborhood. "Perhaps."

"You could hide a thousand Feds in those bushes," Jensen said. "Or in the houses."

"There may be agents inside this house, too," Philippe said. "Waiting for us to break in."

"How would they know we were coming?" Lanotte said.

"Perhaps they aren't waiting for *us,*" Philippe said. "We don't know what happened here." They continued inspecting the still, dark street. "What could we gain by going inside? We should contact her the same way she contacted us—by the electronic mail."

"What if she's not with Narr any more?" Jensen said.

"Even if she's discarded the man, she might have his computer." Philippe stepped down off the porch and walked back to the car. The others followed. "Tomorrow morning, Jensen, you find us a base for operations. Someplace private, where we can lure her, and interrogate her, without attracting attention."

Philippe climbed back into the passenger seat, suddenly feeling weary. It would take a few days for the jet lag to wear off. He had best get some sleep now, while he could.

* * *

Special Agent Frieder sat back from the night scope as the car pulled away. He took off his glasses and scrubbed his face with both hands, then rubbed one hand over his shaved scalp. The raspy sound and feel of a day's growth was strangely satisfying.

"Got a smoke?" he asked Holbrook. His partner shook out a cigarette, offered his lighter, and lit one for himself. The family who owned the house didn't smoke, so Frieder took wry satisfaction in exhaling at the expensive draperies. He was using a crystal water glass as an ashtray—dropping coals on the wool carpeting might have been stretching it too far. The owners would probably call the office to complain about them smoking, but he didn't really give a shit.

Frieder stretched and yawned. They'd been watching Narr's house for almost twenty-four hours, and the three men who'd just left were the first interesting thing to happen.

"So they're gone?" Holbrook said.

"Yeah."

"Too bad they didn't try to break in. We could've bagged 'em and taken 'em downtown."

"Yeah," Frieder said. "That would've been the first real progress in this fucked-up case, and then Chapa would've had to kiss our butts."

Holbrook smoked for a minute. "We should run the plates."

"Don't need to."

"Huh?"

"It's a rental."

"How do you know?"

"Christ, Holbrook, where's your fucking brain?" Frieder took a deep drag and let it out. "The license plate prefix. Most of the rental agencies use the same prefix on all their cars. This one's a Hertz."

"Oh. Okay, I'll call Hertz."

Frieder stubbed out his cigarette and rewound the camera. He removed the film cartridge and stood up.

"Take this to the lab," he said, tossing it to Holbrook.

He reloaded the camera with another roll of high-speed film from the bag on the couch. Narr's visitors, whoever they'd been, had stayed in the shadows on the front porch, but it didn't matter. There was more than enough ambient light to get clear shots of their faces. Holbrook pulled on his coat and dropped the film in his pocket.

"Hey," Frieder said, "grab some coffee and something to eat on the way back, huh?"

"Sure," Holbrook said, and walked into the kitchen. Frieder heard the garage door open and a moment later Holbrook drove off. The garage door closed again, leaving the house in utter silence.

Frieder stared at Narr's house for a while. Then he got his jacket and patted the pockets until he found his own smokes, lit one, and settled back down to the hair-trigger boredom of the stakeout.

"Fuck," he said. "I wish they'd tried to break in."

* * *

The next afternoon, Philippe walked into the ugly building and surveyed the interior. It was a large room, though much smaller than the warehouse in St. Tropez. That thought made his fury unfurl and threaten to consume him, but he fought it silently and managed to bottle it up once more. There would be a time for anger and revenge when he had Carla naked and bleeding in chains before him.

"What is this place?"

"It used to be a foundry," Jensen said. "Bronzes, I think she said."

Most of the building was one empty space. The floor was poured concrete, the walls crumbling, sooty brick set in uneven courses with sloppy mortar. High above, the ceiling was supported by massive wooden beams, dark with grime. Stray shafts of sunlight shone through the clouds and the high, dirty windows.

From the center of the near wall, the old smelting furnace thrust into the interior of the building, made of newer bricks better laid than the walls. It was about two meters deep and three wide until shoulder height, where its size shrank to a chimney that ran all the way up to the roof. The waist-high furnace opening had been bricked in by another inept mason.

On the far side of the furnace, an office had been built from metal studs and glass panels, the lowest course of which was opaque green. Directly across from that was a corner room so small it must be a toilet.

Philippe spun on his heel and surveyed the foundry. The floors were bare and reasonably clean. Lanotte was inspecting the inside of the office, also empty. Jensen leaned against the furnace with his arms crossed.

"You love your filthy warehouses, don't you?" Philippe said.

"It was cheap, it was available, and it's private as hell. You could scream your head off and no one would hear it."

Philippe walked outside and looked up. The clouds were breaking up and it was cool, but at least it wasn't raining.

The street was Westlake Avenue, and Jensen had assured him that there was indeed a lake, just beyond the three gray office buildings across the way. Railroad tracks and a deep parking lot separated the buildings from the street; they were about seventy-five meters away from him. To their right was a restaurant, to the left a marine supply store.

On this side of Westlake were several one-story, decaying commercial buildings, apparently vacant. The surrounding yards and parking lots were overgrown with dead weeds and scattered with rusting shards of metal, bed springs, crumbling drywall, and automobile parts. The sidewalk was punctuated by straggly trees that also looked dead.

Ramshackle houses huddled close together atop the steep hill behind the foundry. Evergreen trees and dense undergrowth covered the hillside, which had been partially excavated and retained by a high wall of huge boulders to make room for the foundry.

It was perfect. In such a place, no one would know anyone else; businesses and people would both be transient. Anonymity would be effortless. He walked back inside the foundry and shut the door.

"This will do," he said. "Is there a phone?"

"In the office," Jensen said.

The only furnishing in the glass-enclosed room was a battered white phone sitting on the floor, attached to the wall by a very long cord.

"It's time to send e-mail to Carla," Philippe said.

Jensen sat down on the floor and leaned against the wall. He unplugged the phone, connected the computer in its place, and turned it on. After a few seconds he looked up expectantly.

Philippe began dictating. "My dear Carla, you exquisite bitch..."

* * *

The furniture arrived while Lanotte was on the phone. Still listening, he moved into the corner so the table and chairs could be put in place. As soon as the delivery men left, Philippe sat down and sipped from a large cup of coffee that Jensen had brought him. He shook out a cigarette and lit it, studying Lanotte's face, playing his old game of trying to read Lanotte's expression. After all these years, he still could not.

Lanotte said little during the long conversation, only asking an occasional question in his gravelly voice. He hung up at last and sat across from Philippe.

"I imagine," Philippe said, "she's left a trail of bodies."

"Yes. She broke into the FBI office here and hooked up with Narr somehow. She tied up a couple of agents—"

"Really? FBI agents?"

"Yes." Lanotte glanced up as Jensen came into the room, carrying his own coffee, and took another chair. "There was something about a shooting on the highway. She blew out the tires of a car, but I couldn't understand who got killed. Then in Montana—"

"Montana?" Jensen said. Lanotte stopped and waited patiently. "Sorry. I was born in Helena."

Philippe waved at Lanotte to continue.

"That's where Hildreth lived," Lanotte said. "She shot him—"

"Merde, she's been busy!"

"Then they went to Canada, where she put a CIA agent in the hospital."

"What was the CIA doing in Canada?" Philippe said.

"Probably trying to overthrow the government," Jensen said.

"*What* government?" Philippe said sarcastically.

"They were with the FBI," Lanotte said.

"What was the *FBI* doing in Canada?"

"Chasing Carla."

Philippe considered. This might be good or bad. If the FBI and the CIA were looking for her, she might lead them right to *him*—and the CIA would be very happy to get their hands on the sole survivor of Jean Pequinot's organization. On the other hand, she might be running scared; perhaps she would be more prone to mistakes.

"So, where is she now?"

"She flew a police helicopter to Idaho, where she and Narr stole explosives from a munitions plant."

There was a long pause.

"Helicopter?" Jensen said, just as Philippe said, "Explosives?"

Philippe felt a headache coming on, and he hadn't even been drinking. "Where is she now?"

"No one knows. She abandoned the helicopter in Idaho."

"When was the last time anyone saw her?"

"Two days ago," Lanotte said. "My friend promised to call back when he learns more."

"She could be anywhere," Jensen said.

"It doesn't matter," Philippe said. "When she gets my message, she'll come *here.*"

"How long should we wait?"

"A few days, at least. We'll find out when she surfaces again. Or she may walk through that door tomorrow. At worst we meet her in Cannes next week and take her there."

Philippe stood up. It was late afternoon and he was getting hungry. First he would find some food, then a woman. He was eager to try his luck with these loose American women he'd been hearing about for years.

"I'm going out for the night," he said. "You two stay here."

"What should we do if she shows up?" Lanotte said.

"We sent the message only a few hours ago, so I doubt she'll come tonight. But if she does, make her comfortable." He smiled wickedly. "Be careful not to hurt her, my friend. I have great plans for her future."

"I'll get the tranquilizer gun from the car," Lanotte said, and went out.

"Swift as a shadow, short as any dream," Jensen quoted. "If we can't trap her, you know we'll never be able to catch her."

"We'll trap her, Jensen, and this is no summer night's dream. We'll get her, and when we do, like the jaws of darkness, I'll devour her up."

Chapter 30

Seattle, Washington
Friday, March 3, 9:16 a.m.

Carla studied Derek's face over breakfast. She was growing fond of his great, bushy mustache, his hazel eyes, square jaw, and wrinkled forehead. A week ago today she had met him for the first time and almost immediately kidnapped him. She supposed that was as reasonable a way as any to begin a relationship. Certainly it was better than the flood of deranging hormones that had plunged her into several disastrous love affairs.

When Derek asked what she had planned for the day, she shocked him by saying, "Why don't you show me around Pike Place Market?"

"What?" He plucked his English muffin out of his coffee.

"I didn't have a chance to do any sightseeing last time I was here. I want to see the Space Needle."

Derek was too flustered to say anything for a moment, but then he started laughing. "You don't want to make bombs, or shoot someone, or study maps? You want to go sightseeing?"

"You've lived here all your life, right?"

"Yes," he said suspiciously.

"Perfect: a native. Show me the town."

It took a while to convince him she was serious, but finally he agreed. There was nothing else they could do until Philippe contacted her, or she gave up waiting for him, or the kidon team showed itself. It would do her good to take a day off.

Carla couldn't recall ever being a tourist before. Her parents had always spent their holidays in the mountains, usually in a small cabin with no electricity. She had visited some of the most interesting cities in Europe, but never for fun, and never the nice parts of town: always working, always probing the sludgy underside of society.

They took the monorail to the Space Needle. From the observation deck, Carla looked out over the patchy sunlight illuminating Elliott Bay and the grungy, charming city below. Back on the ground, they walked down a steep hill to the waterfront and the parks and shops on the piers. Derek introduced her to Starbucks and had black coffee; Carla took straight espresso, the closest she'd come in America to the thick, strong coffee she was used to.

At the Market they browsed the produce stalls, where tables bowed under the weight of a profusion of fruits and vegetables—yellow peppers that seemed to glow, perfect bright berries and translucent grapes, bunches of basil they could smell from meters away. The fish shop vendors cried out in sing-song, flirted with her shamelessly, and unerringly flung fish to the countermen without looking. Hundreds of artisans in their tiny cubicles sold toys, jewelry, photographs and paintings, wind socks and kites, clothing, and live parrots.

They boarded a boat for a tour of the harbor. From across the water, Seattle lost its grit and shimmered as if it were the pinnacle of civilization. Grand houses marched up from the waterfront like Rome in its glory days, green, peaceful, and scintillating in the occasional sunlight.

They walked six seedy blocks to Pioneer Square, where art galleries and parks filled with street people jumbled together in a confusing muddle that reminded her of Italy. They found a cab and rode it back to their hotel room, exhilarated, hungry, and lustful, and stumbled into their room to hear the steady beep that meant an e-mail message had arrived.

Derek opened the lid of his computer. "Uh oh," he said.

Carla pushed him out of the way and read the message.

My dear Carla, you exquisite bitch:

You've done it! Khayrat offered a price you wouldn't believe to forestall an auction. I hated to sell to the obese swine—you know as well as I do what he'll do with the merchandise—but he was drooling and insisted on raising the price. My condolences for your ex-countrymen, but this is business, no?

We will be in Seattle from 2 March to 5 March to settle some business of Jensen's. If you're still in the States, stop by at 2537 Westlake Avenue for your share—plus a bonus. Otherwise I'll meet you at the agreed place and time. Good work, you ruthless wench.

—Philippe

"I don't believe it," Carla said. She sat down on the bed and tried to collect her thoughts. There had always been a remote chance that Philippe would actually sell the warheads, but that had been the least likely outcome.

She was having trouble thinking around the mental image of a mushroom cloud over Jerusalem. No, wait—Arab terrorists would never bomb the Holy City, it was as sacred to Muslims as it was to Jews and Christians. But Tel Aviv was not. Half a million dead, the city wiped off the map, the land poisoned for thousands of years. The West Bank would certainly be hit by fallout, but that was a small price to pay for the eradication of the Jewish state. Where else? Haifa? Or perhaps the other two bombs would be reserved for America. Washington and New York?

Snap out of it. Think.

How could Philippe have eluded the Mossad? She'd thought she had everything covered. Chen was supposed to call Tsidon, and she'd mailed Tsidon the same information she sent Chen. They were supposed to track both the buyers and the sellers. For Philippe to sell the warheads, two unlikely things had to happen: Chen overcame his fear and didn't call the Mossad, and the Mossad didn't get her message.

"Is it possible," she said, "that one of my e-mails didn't reach its destination?"

"I doubt it. The Internet has a pretty robust routing architecture. If the message couldn't be delivered, it would've been returned."

"Could it take longer to reach one recipient than another?"

"Absolutely. It depends on the path the messages took and how many retries were necessary. Theoretically it could take up to a day longer."

Could that be it? Chen reneged and Tsidon's message took longer, allowing Philippe to sell the nukes?

No. Maybe Chen had disobeyed her, but one day's head start wasn't enough for Philippe to sell the warheads, even if Khayrat *had* been drooling.

Could he have fought off the bag team? But he hadn't mentioned any problems, and a gunfight with the Mossad would definitely count as a problem. But she didn't believe that Philippe could win a fight with the Mossad. Tsidon was absolutely the best. Philippe would've been dead before he even knew he was in trouble.

If Tsidon *had* acquired the warheads, why was Philippe free? That was easy. Tsidon's orders had been to grab the nukes and run. If they could snatch Philippe's team at the same time, so much the better, but he was not permitted to delay even one minute to do so. The Mossad wanted those warheads as soon as possible, with no complications and no mistakes. They could go back for the smugglers later if they wanted to. Philippe had probably been out whoring when Tsidon made his raid, and Chen unconscious in some opium den, so all of Philippe's team might have escaped.

Carla reread the message. There were two possibilities: Philippe had sold the missiles, or Tsidon had stolen them and Philippe was lying to trap her. He couldn't do that by threatening her, so he had to be nice.

She couldn't believe that Tsidon had failed. Therefore, Philippe was chasing her as she'd expected, and everything was fine, except she'd probably be dead tomorrow. Well, if she was wrong and terrorists had the warheads, there was one thing she could do immediately to try to stop them.

Carla created a new e-mail message, addressed to Tsidon. She repeated the contact information for Khayrat, just in case they hadn't received the first message, and typed a new message.

Sottile claims Khayrat has the merchandise. I can neither confirm nor deny. I will meet Sottile to learn the truth. If you didn't get the goods, go get Khayrat *now*.

Also, please recall the kidon team.

Sure thing. We'll reel them back in the next time they call us. Which would probably be right after they killed her. *Oh, lighten up: Philippe's going to kill you before the kidon even knows what country you're in.* She sent the message and looked up at Derek.

"What's going on?" he said. "Philippe sold the nukes?"

"No, I think he lost them, and he blames me. He's lying so I'll walk into his lair, expecting to be paid."

Derek closed his eyes for a moment. *He's not used to thinking like this.*

"I don't get it," he said. "If you stole the bombs, and he knows it, and he knows you know he knows, why would he expect you to put yourself at his mercy?"

"Because that's exactly what I'm going to do."

"What?"

"I have to know for sure. The only way to be sure is to go see him. After I'm certain, I might be able to take him out."

"So if he tries to kill you, you'll know the world is safe?"

"It's not that simple," Carla said. "Philippe was planning to double-cross me from the beginning. I'm too dangerous for him to let me live."

"Okay. If—just before he kills you—he tells you how *angry* he is because you stole his nukes, you'll know the world is safe."

"No. If he did lose the warheads, he'll torture me first to find out how to get them back. But I have the edge, Derek. I have a secret weapon."

"Oh, yeah? What's that?"

"You."

* * *

Carla followed the shore of Lake Union on Westlake Avenue, looking for 2537 and keeping track of side streets and possible escape routes. Philippe's building was a decrepit two-story brick bunker with small windows high up on the walls. Beneath a tall chimney, a faded sign painted on the bricks announced "F-rna- Foun-ry."

"This place is a dump," Carla said as they drove past.

"Yeah. Well, every place can't be Bellevue. Some parts of Bellevue can't be Bellevue."

"What's the next cross street?"

Derek checked the map. "Crockett."

Carla drove around, exploring the neighborhood, and parked on the first street uphill from Westlake. They could see the roof of Philippe's building between the houses and the bare-branched trees.

"Let's go get a closer look," she said.

"Are you sure that's a good idea?"

She paused with her door half-open. "What are you afraid of? Land mines? Sentries with machine guns? Tigers?"

Derek sighed and got out of the truck. He followed her down a dirt path that ran between two houses and into the woods, ending abruptly at a small cliff just above the foundry, where part of the hill had been excavated to make room for a corner of the building. The retaining wall of dry-set basalt boulders was slightly higher than the roof, only a few feet away. The space between was littered with dry leaves and fast-food trash.

"Look," Carla said. Beer cans and rubbish were scattered around the foundry's chimney.

"Looks like a party spot," he said. "It's an easy jump from here."

She walked along the rocks until she could see the other side of the building, then came back. "The door on Westlake is the only exit."

Derek clucked. "I don't think the fire marshal would approve."

Carla considered the building for a few moments. "Philippe's made a mistake," she said. "He's ambushed himself. If someone's covering the door, there's no way out."

"What're you thinking?"

"You haven't been listening, have you? You need to understand the tactical situation here."

"Why?"

"Because I'm going to be inside there and you're going to be out here alone. You may have to get me out."

"How am I going to do that?"

"By blowing up the building."

* * *

Back at the hotel, Carla showed him how to finish the bombs.

"C-4 is very stable," she said, "but you know that. You dropped a case of it on the floor."

"You should've bought me a hatchet."

"Uh huh. This is like modeling clay. Pull off a wad...," she demonstrated, "and mold it in here, where the speaker was. Now, be really careful with the detonator. If you drop it, it'll blow off your foot. It slides in here. Stick the end in the C-4 and connect these wires. Now you're ready to rock."

Derek closed the radio up and stared at it for a moment, then carefully set it down on the table before shuddering. After finishing the other one, he marked the transmitter—which looked identical to the bombs—with electrical tape so he wouldn't get them mixed up. He wrapped the radios in hotel towels, put them into his backpack, and they left again.

"I don't know exactly what'll happen," she said as she drove back to the foundry. "If Philippe did sell the nukes, which I doubt, he may let me leave, in which case I'll be inside for an hour or less. It's much more likely that they'll torture me for a day or two before killing me. That gives you plenty of time to get me out. But don't take *too* long, okay?"

"I can't believe you're going in there when you know they're planning to torture and kill you."

"I'm not thrilled about it, either," she said. "If you have a better idea, I'd love to hear it."

"Yeah, I've got a better idea. Let's get on a plane to Tahiti and disappear."

"You don't know Philippe. Sooner or later, he'd find us. Let's do this, then we can live happily ever after."

She smiled at him, but he turned away. It occurred to her for the first time that Derek might think the two of them were going to end up together; or maybe he thought *she* was implying that. She thought about it for a moment. The idea was so ludicrous it almost made her laugh.

Carla parked the truck a block away from the foundry and they walked the rest of the way. It was drizzling again, and dark except for the street lamps and the lights of the buildings on the lake. The gently settling mist gave each light a spherical halo. The traffic, which had been heavy this afternoon, was now almost nonexistent.

She stood across from the foundry with her fists on her hips, examining the place. Dim light filtered out through the small, dirty windows just under the roof.

"Are you up to this?" she said. He nodded glumly. "Okay, one more time. Wait for an hour. If I don't come out, use the bombs to block the doorway and blow a hole in the back corner of the building. I'll give you a hand signal when I go in. The number of fingers will tell you how many men are inside. If I waggle my hand, Philippe isn't there and you should wait until he arrives before blowing the place. Got it?"

"Yeah," Derek said unhappily. "Look, why don't we just wait until we know he's in there and blow up the building with him in it?"

"Because I need to know for sure where we stand. Get information. Kill bad guy. In that order, okay?" He nodded. "Derek." He looked at her. "Thanks." He nodded again and she slapped his cheek lightly. "Don't fuck up."

Carla crossed the street and walked up to the foundry door. When she looked back, Derek was gone; she hoped he was hiding and not really *gone*. She pounded on the heavy wooden door. Jensen opened it and smiled at her.

"Carla!" he said. "It's good to see you."

"Cut the shit, Jensen. Where's Philippe?"

Lanotte came into view and stood behind Jensen in his typical, hulking stance: feet spread slightly, hands clasped behind his back, and a scowl on his face.

"He's out right now," Jensen said, "but he should be back in an hour or so. Come on in." He opened the door wide and moved out of her way.

As she stepped forward, Carla swung her right hand behind her and made a V-sign with two fingers, wagging her hand. She walked into the large, bare space and turned to face Jensen and Lanotte, her back against a short brick wall that jutted out into the room. If the entrance had not been mostly in shadow, she might have seen what was happening in time to react.

She watched Jensen cross in front of Lanotte to close the door. As he passed him, the giant raised a gun from behind his back. She missed the first half of Lanotte's draw, so her pistol was out of its holster but not even aimed when the tranquilizer dart hit her in the neck. She instantly lost control of her body and felt herself falling.

From a mile away, she heard Jensen say, "Cunt," and then she blacked out.

* * *

"I do not fucking believe this," Frieder said. He took another look out the window of the office building and shook his head, smiling. They'd been watching all day, and now this.

"What?" Holbrook said.

"Put down that fucking sandwich and come look at this." He wrinkled his nose; he couldn't understand how Holbrook could eat that shit. Liverwurst was hog slop. "Citrullo and Narr just walked up."

Holbrook dropped his sandwich. "You're shitting me!"

Frieder phoned Chapa without taking his eyes off the subjects standing less than a hundred feet away.

"Frieder. You're not going to believe this. Citrullo and Narr just showed up at the Westlake stakeout."

"*What?*" Chapa said. "Hold on." Frieder could hear him shouting at someone. In a moment he came back on. "What're they doing?"

"They're just standing— Wait a minute. Citrullo's crossing the street. Narr's walking away."

"Shit! Uh... Okay, stay on Carla. She's the key to this thing. Finding Derek will be a cinch if we've got her."

"Are you sure, sir? I can send Holbrook after Narr while I watch the foundry."

"No," Chapa said. Frieder felt a surge of anger. He knew what Chapa thought of them: *Shaffer's a genius, we're just grunts.* "I want both of you to keep your eyes glued to that building. Do *not* let Carla get away. Call me if she comes out again, and if she does, you stick to her like Superglue. I'll have reinforcements there in twenty minutes."

Frieder watched the foundry door close behind Citrullo. What was she doing, waving her hand behind her back? Some kind of signal? Maybe Narr hadn't left, he was just hiding and watching.

"Hey, Holbrook," he said. Holbrook lowered the binoculars. "Chapa says to watch the foundry and forget about Narr, but maybe the geek's just hanging back. Take a stroll around and see if you can spot him out the windows—but *don't* go outside. And be back here in fifteen, or Chapa will chew you a new one."

He picked up the binoculars and studied the foundry. It was a stupid place for a clubhouse. Limited access and there was only one way out. He had these assholes trapped like a bee in a jar.

Holbrook had called Hertz last night and got the name of the guy who rented the car: Jensen. Hertz said he was staying at the Sheraton, but the Sheraton had no one registered by that name. After only ten minutes of calling, though, they'd found him at the Westin. The moron had used the same name for the car and the hotel. So Frieder and Holbrook had found the car in the valet parking lot and staked it out. This morning they followed Jensen to the foundry. After renting the place, Jensen had gone back to get the other two. The thin, faggoty-looking one had split a few hours ago, leaving the other two waiting, apparently, for Citrullo.

Holbrook came back and said he'd seen nothing out the windows. A few minutes later, three cars full of agents pulled up and parked in front of the office building where Frieder waited. Chapa led a dozen agents inside.

"What's happening?" he said.

"Nothing since I called you," Frieder said, irritated as always around his boss. Chapa was too Boy Scout for Frieder's tastes. "Jensen and one of his buddies is inside with Citrullo. Narr walked north on Westlake and we lost sight of him. Jensen's other pal drove off around four and hasn't come back yet."

"Okay." Chapa took out his phone and walked a few paces away, watching the foundry as he talked. Frieder overheard "helicopter" and "snipers," and smirked. *That's just like fucking Chapa: always over-reacting.*

Chapter 31

Seattle, Washington
Friday, March 3, 6:33 p.m.

It was more of a heavy fog than a rain, but still the droplets congealed, collected, and ran down Derek's neck. He shivered and tried to ignore it, watching in despair as another FBI car parked in front of the southernmost office building. Four men carrying sniper rifles jumped out and quickly ran inside.

Chapa had arrived ten minutes ago with a crowd of agents, leaving Derek scared and confused—his new, normal state of mind. Other, unseen agents must be reconnoitering the foundry just as he and Carla had done a few hours ago. Now he stood in the shadow of a stairway, a few hundred feet away from an office building full of Feds, all of them focused intently on the building from which he was supposed to free Carla.

Unless she just walked out, unsuspecting and free—free for the mere seconds it would take the agents to surround her and handcuff her. Derek was unsure of what he wanted and what he should do. If Carla did walk out, then terrorists were in control of three nuclear warheads, the world was in trouble, and she would spend a century or two in jail, but Derek was off the hook. If she stayed inside, either Philippe had sold the warheads and just wanted to keep her, or the warheads had been stolen and Philippe would torture her to find out where they were. Either way, Derek would have to execute another of Carla's insane plans.

Why should he bother? If he walked out to the street and cried "Uncle," it would all be over. The Feds would grab him, they'd storm the foundry and arrest everyone inside, and Derek's life would go back to normal.

Or maybe not. The FBI hadn't attacked yet, but they could have if they wanted to. They must be waiting for Philippe. When he returned, the FBI would go in, but Carla would be tied up, under the guns of ruthless arms dealers, and her chances of living through the raid were just about zero.

Although Derek wasn't feeling heroic, that pissed him off. Despite himself, he'd come to admire Carla and he was determined to free her, no matter what it cost him.

If only he could think how.

Derek studied the front of the foundry, the decrepit buildings beside it, the wooded hill rising above it, and the rickety houses clinging to the slope. He visualized the retaining wall behind the foundry, and the roof with its tall chimney and wind-blown trash. He tried to think like Chapa, who had twice been tied up by the woman he now had trapped. The FBI always attacked in force. They already had twenty agents in place.

Derek had a pistol and two radio-controlled bombs.

Then a plan popped into his head. It was an obvious way to remove the advantage of numbers that the FBI relied on, but it was nuts. He thought some more, but he couldn't come up with anything else. He needed three more bombs.

It was 7:20. He was going to have to hope that Philippe was gone for the night. With the FBI here, Carla's original idea just wasn't crazy enough.

Derek walked through the waterfront shadows, back toward the pickup. He needed to find another Radio Shack.

* * *

Gugliemo seethed as he packed. He had to call Mr. Maroni and straighten this out.

He'd been sitting in his hotel room, bored and flipping through the TV channels, when Broca barged in and told him to get packed. Broca seemed to think that *he* was in charge, but Maroni had ordered Gugliemo to take care of Narr and the spy himself—find them and bring them back.

Now the lovebirds were in Seattle again. Gugliemo stopped with a shirt half-folded. Maroni's men were taking him back to Seattle. He didn't have any contacts up here in fucking Canada, but he sure as hell knew who was who back home. He picked up the phone and dialed his security chief.

"Uh," Marty groaned.

"Wake up, you barrel of lard," Gugliemo said. "We're coming back."

"Mr. Gugliemo, is that you."

"Who the fuck do you think it is? Get up. I got a job for you."

"Yeah, okay, Mr. Gugliemo. I'm awake."

Bullshit. I've never seen you awake. "Listen. Narr's hooked up with a spy."

"What, you mean a real spy?"

"Yes, a real spy named Citrullo. The Feds have them surrounded somewhere in Seattle. I need you to find out what's going down. Call your snitches, street people, whatever—just find out where they are."

"Okay. I can do that."

"So do it. We'll be landing at Boeing field around three. Meet me there. And you'd better have something useful, or you'll be back on the street hustling phony Coach purses."

"Don't worry, Mr. Gugliemo, I'll take—"

Gugliemo hung up on him.

Broca said Citrullo was holed up somewhere, and the Feds would take her down as soon as somebody else showed up—Gugliemo hadn't got who. Broca thought it was a waste of time, but he was taking Gugliemo to Seattle because Maroni told him to.

"It's over," Broca had said. "In a couple hours she'll be dead, or else buried in the deepest hole the Feds can dig for her."

Bullshit. He'd seen this spy bitch in action. He zipped up his bag. The Feds let her slip out of their hands before, and Gugliemo knew they'd fuck up again.

Chapter 32

Derek waited in darkness beside a neatly trimmed, shoulder-high hedge. Looking down the hill between the houses and trees, he could see part of the foundry's roof, some of the buildings across the street, and glimmerings of Lake Union. Everything was quiet—no police cars and no TV cameras—so he knew the FBI was still hidden and watching. By now they must know that the door on Westlake was the only way in or out of the building, so they might have relaxed a little about the back of the building. Just to be sure, Derek continued to watch the street and what he could see of the foundry.

After half an hour without movement, he put on his backpack and walked down the steep driveway. A street lamp several houses away gave him a long shadow, which faded into the gloom as Derek left the street and found the path leading down the hill. He didn't dare use a flashlight, so he couldn't really see the trail, he had to feel it out from the bare dirt and lack of brush. Partway down, he stumbled over a root but recovered without falling, then immediately hit another bump and slammed down onto his hands and knees.

"Goddamn it!"

He stayed down for a moment, catching his breath, waiting for the pain to subside and trying to remember why the hell he was doing this. The night was cool but he was sweating. How much of a jolt would it take to set off the detonators on his back?

Derek resumed his blind trek and soon stood on the rock wall that held back the hill above the foundry. There was enough light for him to be sure no one was on the roof. The gap was about four feet and the roof was a foot or two lower than the rocks. He took a few steps back and contemplated the chasm.

"Goddamn it."

260

He ran toward the foundry, easily leaped the gap, and slowed to a stop. Somewhat surprised to be safely on the roof, he dropped to his stomach and waited.

Tiny cinders from the tarpaper roofing ground into the scrapes from his fall in the woods. He tried to ignore the pain and listen. He wasn't sure how much of a thump he'd made on landing. There were bad guys below him and FBI guys across the street, but when nothing happened Derek decided that no one had heard him. The night was silent except for the drone of traffic on I-5, far off across the lake. He started crawling toward the building's only door.

If the FBI were watching the roof with night scopes, they'd see him. But it was late, and Carla had gone inside over seven hours ago. He had to hope they only had a few men watching the building. If they were even a little bit lazy he should be okay.

He reached the front of the building and saw that he had another thing going for him. The foundry's brick façade came up almost a foot above the roof. If he stayed down, he'd be invisible to the agents across the street. He brushed cinders from his palms—*why were the damned things sharp?*—and unbuckled his backpack. He pulled out one of the towel-wrapped radios, unwrapped it, and stuffed the towel back in the pack.

It had taken him an hour apiece to make three new bombs. Using only Carla's schematic, without the benefit of her nerves, experience, or sarcastic advice, he'd been terrified of making a mistake, so he'd double-checked everything, testing each circuit, and taking special care when he molded the C-4 into the case and attached the detonator.

Now he reached to turn on the radio, but his hands were shaking. He set it down and wiped his sore, sweaty palms on the legs of his pants. He reached for the switch and again his hand stopped short.

Derek rolled onto his back. Low clouds sailed slowly by, a solid cover from horizon to horizon, but at least it wasn't drizzling any more. The belly of the cloud deck was a sickly yellowish gray, reflecting back the city's lights. *I wish it were clear. I'd like to see the stars again.* He didn't want to die under gloomy skies.

The FBI wouldn't be using CB channels, but the highway was only a few miles away; a trucker transmitting on the right channel would set the bomb off. It was possible it would go off as soon as he turned it on, especially if he'd screwed up the wiring.

He felt a sudden surge of confidence—*fuck it*—picked up the radio and switched it on.

The channel selector displayed a glowing numeral five, which faded quickly. Derek set the squawk and twisted the selector to channel two. The green digit faded again, conserving battery power. He set the radio in the corner, right up against the brick façade and directly above the doorway. He closed up his pack and pulled it on, then crawled back to the spot where he'd leaped to the roof.

The jump looked scarier from this side: the rock wall was a bit higher than the roof, and the gap looked wider somehow. He sighed and snapped the buckles on his pack, moved several steps back, took a deep breath and ran toward the edge of the building. He leaped across and landed safely on the slope above the foundry—but immediately lost his balance, fell onto his stomach, and began sliding back toward the edge.

Derek panicked, scrabbling for purchase, but when his shoes hit the rock wall, he simply stopped moving. He rested for a moment with his face on the damp ground, eyes closed, breathing hard.

"If I live through this, I'm going to become a monk. Raise goats, grow peas, and never take another risk in my life."

He got onto his hands and knees and looked down the face of the wall. It was constructed of dry-set basalt boulders, each two to three feet across, with big gaps between them. The climb down couldn't have been easier if there were a ladder. He eased himself over the edge and started working his way down, feeling for gaps with his feet and gripping the edges of the boulders. They were wet, but the stone was rough and he reached the ground safely.

The second radio was far easier than the first. Derek marveled at the idiocy of the human brain. Since the first one hadn't exploded, he somehow felt safe, even though he knew that the odds were as bad or worse this time. But the bomb didn't explode, so he set it to channel one and hid the radio in the leaves and litter right at the corner of the building's foundation.

Climbing *up* the wall was even easier, since he could see what he was doing. Derek walked back up the hill and set a third bomb at the base of a large cedar tree. The fourth went under a car parked on the street.

He leaned against the doomed car and reconsidered the fifth bomb. Maybe four would be enough. The fifth one was a big risk, and it might not be worth it. But he thought he knew how Chapa would react when they started going off, and reluctantly concluded that he needed the fifth bomb.

Walking north, Derek felt the shakes coming back. He was tired and scared, and very hungry. He hadn't eaten since the fish and chips on the waterfront over twelve hours ago.

He turned right at the next cross street and walked down the hill. The parking lot separating the waterfront buildings from Westlake Avenue had been full that afternoon, and there were still dozens of cars parked there. He didn't know why or care much, he was just grateful for the cover.

Ducking low, Derek ran from one car to the next, keeping the vehicles between him and the buildings where the FBI was staked out. It took over five minutes to reach a Cadillac Seville directly across from the foundry. The fifth bomb went underneath it, up against the right front tire so it couldn't be seen. Contemplating walking back up the hill made him feel like giving up, but after catching his breath he forced himself to start back.

Fifteen minutes later he was climbing into the pickup that he'd parked in a convenient driveway. He settled in for a long night's watch. When Philippe returned, Derek would be able to see him through gaps in the trees, and he'd blow the scumbag straight to hell.

He yawned and shook his head to clear away the drowsiness. He had to stay awake. If he waited too long after Philippe arrived, the FBI would storm the foundry and he'd lose his chance to rescue Carla. So he watched and waited, fighting to stay alert.

Through willpower and sheer determination, he managed to hold off sleep for a full fifteen minutes.

Chapter 33

Carla awoke lying on her side on a cold, hard floor, with a foul taste in her mouth and a desperate need for the bathroom. Trying to sit up, she discovered that her hands and feet were tied, but she managed to raise herself into a sitting position with her back against the brick wall.

Her hands were asleep, bound in front of her with a plastic cable tie that had chafed her wrists; her ankles were secured the same way. Her shirt had been ripped open but her bra and holster—empty of course—were still in place. Sleeping on concrete had left her chilled and aching, but she hadn't been beaten or raped.

Very gallant. They must be saving me for Philippe.

She looked around. The building was empty: brick walls, high ceiling, bare, oily floor. In one corner was a tiny room that she fervently hoped was a toilet. A brick enclosure jutting out into the room formed one wall of a glass-encased office to her right.

Carla could hear Jensen and Lanotte, but she couldn't see them. The only place they could be was in the glass box.

"Hey!" she said.

The voices stopped and their heads appeared over the smoked glass of the wall. Jensen walked out of the office and stood a few paces away with his arms crossed over his chest. From the look on his face, he might be torturing her himself right now if not for fear of Philippe.

"What do you want?" Jensen said.

"I need to use the bathroom. Help me up."

Lanotte appeared in the office doorway and leaned on the jamb, examining her as if she were a frog pinned down for dissection.

"Maybe later," Jensen said.

"It better be right now, or you're going to have a big mess on the floor."

He shrugged. "So what?"

"You don't have to untie me. Just carry me into the bathroom and dump me on the toilet."

Jensen grinned at Lanotte, but the giant stared back impassively. "No deal. You're going to have to hold it. Or piss your pants, I don't care."

Carla doubled over for a moment. Her bladder felt ready to explode. "Okay," she said, "when will Philippe get back?"

"Maybe an hour. Maybe three."

"Well, where the hell is he?"

Jensen smiled. "He went out shopping last night." *Meaning women.* "I think he was planning to get a few things for *you.*"

Terrific. Chocolates and roses would be sweet. And I could use a new shirt.

Jensen went back inside. Lanotte let him pass without taking his eyes off Carla. She met his gaze until he turned on his heel and followed his comrade. When she heard Jensen talking again, she scooched on her butt until she was sitting just outside the office door. Now she could hear them clearly, but the words didn't make any sense.

"—might be the source of mass for all other particles," Jensen was saying. "It's the last crucial missing piece."

"What do you mean, it's the source of mass?" Lanotte said.

"The joke is that other particles eat the Higgs boson to gain mass."

"But what the fuck does it mean?"

"It just means that all particles are massless unless they're bound to a Higgs boson."

There was a long pause before Lanotte said, "Did you ever find the thing?"

"The SSC *would* have found it. Or proved that it doesn't exist, or maybe that it's a composite particle, like baryons. Personally, I don't think it exists. It makes the Standard Model mathematically complete, but it raises so many other problems—"

"What the hell are you talking about?" Carla said.

Jensen stuck his head around the doorway, disappeared for a moment, and reappeared holding a pistol. "Back up." Carla scooted back a few feet. "More." She crabbed back until she reached the crumbling wall again.

"We were just discussing my old passion," Jensen said. "Particle physics. Pay attention, maybe you can improve your mind before Philippe splatters it all over that wall."

"Physics? I thought you were an engineer."

"No, I was a physicist."

"Why would a physicist work for a low-life arms dealer scumbag like Philippe?"

Lanotte pushed past Jensen and strode over to Carla, grabbing her throat in one huge hand, choking her.

"You shut up," Lanotte said. "You aren't worth Philippe's spit."

"Hey, Lanotte, calm down," Jensen said, putting his hand on his friend's arm. "You know the bitch is full of hot air. Philippe has plans for that body, so let's not bruise it, okay?"

Lanotte released her throat and Carla's rump bounced on the concrete. She hadn't realized he'd been holding her off the floor. It took a huge effort not to pee herself. Lanotte went back to the office door and Jensen squatted down, safely out of reach of a kick, so their faces were almost level.

"I'll tell you why I work for Philippe. I was one of the physicists who designed the Superconducting Super Collider. Ever hear of it?"

Carla shook her head and coughed discreetly. Her throat hurt.

"That figures. You're clever but ignorant, aren't you? The SSC would have been the biggest particle accelerator in the world, twenty times better than CERN. It was in fucking Texas, but hell, I would've moved to Siberia to work on it. The ring was *miles* in diameter—the biggest excavation since the pyramids." His eyes were focused on something in the distance. "It would've let us look at the rule book for the universe. Where does mass come from? How many families of matter are there? Are quarks fundamental particles?"

"So?" she said.

"So the sons of bitches canceled the project."

"Who?"

"Congress, you dimwit. In October of '93, they killed the most important research tool ever conceived and left us with nothing but the biggest man-made tunnel in the world—a fifth of it anyway."

"So you went to work for Philippe."

"No. I was on *wanderjahr*, surfing the tropics: Hawaii, Baja, Ecuador. I ended up in Niterói, in Brazil. I met Philippe in a bar, we got drunk together and picked up some women. The next day he took me to his house to meet Camilla and offered me a job."

"I don't get it," Carla said. "Why would a physicist become a stooge for an arms dealer?"

Jensen sighted his pistol on Carla's right eye. "*Unemployed* physicist. Times were tough, and there were a couple hundred of us thrown out of work at the same time. I didn't want to drive a cab, and this seemed like a good alternative." He closed his left eye and sighted down the barrel. "Besides, I love this job. I get to travel, the pay's great, and whenever somebody pisses me off, I shoot her." He lowered the gun. "Things were looking up—I figured someone would use one of the warheads to vaporize Congress, and then we'd be even. Until *you* stole them."

"Enough," Lanotte said. He pointed to Carla. "You: stay there. Be quiet and don't move or I'll find a way to hurt you that Philippe won't notice or care about."

They went back into the office. The lecture seemed to be over. She spent the next hour or so considering her options: there didn't seem to be many. Meanwhile, she flexed her hands to keep them from falling asleep again and did isometric exercises to loosen up her stiff limbs. Her wrists were bleeding from the cable ties, but the pain helped distract her from her bladder, which periodically threatened to burst before subsiding again.

I wonder what Derek's doing? She wished she had something to sit on. The concrete seemed to be getting harder, if that was possible, and colder. She tried to pull her torn shirt closed, but one side of it always wanted to flap open. She was hungry and thirsty. Why was it that a body could need to take in and expel liquid at the same time?

She was beginning not to care whether she peed herself or not when the door opened and Philippe stepped inside. Only after he'd closed and locked it did he look up and see her sitting against the wall.

Jensen walked out of the office. "Look what we found."

Philippe handed him a brown paper bag and walked slowly toward Carla. He crouched down, took her chin in one hand, and stared into her eyes. She could read what was coming in his eyes: soft questions, sharp pain, rape, and death. For just a moment she quailed and prayed that Derek would save her, but then she gathered her strength and hardened herself.

Philippe smiled when he saw her eyes change and stroked her cheek gently with the back of a knuckle. "My dear Carla," he said, "there are so many things I want to ask you."

* * *

Chapa lowered his binoculars. The third man had just arrived, parking his blue sedan half a block down the street and walking the rest of the way, carrying a brown and red Ace hardware bag. He picked up his radio.

"Snipers in position?" he said. The four shooters responded immediately. "Okay, everyone get ready."

He watched as forty agents swarmed out of the building, taking places behind parked cars or in the doorways of the neighboring buildings. One used a grappling hook to climb to the foundry's roof. There was no other way out of the building, not even a hatch on top, but he had two agents watching from the street above, just in case.

"Close the roads," he ordered.

Seattle PD started setting up barricades a block either way up and down Westlake.

Chapa and Shaffer walked out of the building where they'd waited all night. The clouds were breaking up, letting a few rays of sunshine through. He walked between the cars and stood in front of a Cadillac that was parked between the railroad tracks and the street, directly across from the foundry. Someone handed him a megaphone and he turned it on.

"Here we go," he said to Shaffer. After a week of chasing Carla, his curiosity was finally about to be satisfied.

Chapter 34

Seattle, Washington
Saturday, March 4, 8:34 a.m.

Philippe considered Carla's grimy face, ankles and bloody wrists bound with cable ties, and torn clothes.

"You've looked better, my dear," he said. "When we were lovers in Paris, for example."

"Jesus Christ!" Lanotte said. "Is there anyone you *haven't* screwed?"

Philippe turned to face his old friend. Lanotte was leaning on the office door frame, scowling. Philippe smiled despite himself; Lanotte didn't approve of his womanizing.

"Which one of us," Philippe said, "are you addressing?"

"Yeah," Carla said.

Lanotte shook his head in exasperation, causing his long blond hair to swing from side to side. Jensen was grinning. Philippe turned back to Carla.

"It would've been better if we'd stayed lovers," he said. "Then we wouldn't be in this unfortunate situation."

Carla laughed harshly. "The warheads were never yours, Philippe. I got them; they were mine. Do you think the Ukrainians risked their lives for the *money?*"

Philippe's smile faded. "Yes. Chen mentioned your unorthodox methods of persuasion."

"I did what was necessary. Who else could've done it? You? Jensen? Maybe one of your wives. Who do you think would've fucked the Ukrainians better: Camilla or Felicia? Or maybe—Yvette?"

Philippe controlled himself with a herculean effort. She was trying to goad him into losing his temper, and he mustn't give in. But the thought of one of his beautiful wives—especially Yvette—sleeping with that barbarian Gosanko nearly drove him mad. When he concluded his business with Carla, he would make her pay for that disgusting image.

He squatted down before her. "I didn't have time to reward Chen properly for his treachery. Perhaps you'd like to pay that account?"

"Tell you what, Philippe. Move a little closer so I can piss on your nice Italian shoes. These morons haven't let me use the bathroom."

Philippe studied her face for a moment. Actually it would be a good idea to let her relieve herself before they started, or he might indeed have to throw away these shoes, and he was quite fond of them. He stood up and hauled her to her feet.

"Lanotte," he said, "cover her. If she even twitches, shoot her in the leg."

Lanotte drew a pistol from his shoulder holster and smiled as he flicked off the safety.

"How about untying my hands?" Carla said.

"My, my, but you're bold," Philippe said. "No."

"At least undo my feet. How can I get in there like this?"

"Hop." He gestured at the tiny washroom. "There's the toilet."

He watched with amusement as she shuffled around and began hopping in small steps, swinging her bound arms for balance like a crippled rabbit. She reached the toilet, opened the door, hopped in, and closed it behind her. Philippe chuckled when he heard her lock it.

"If she's going to try anything," Jensen said, "it'll be the moment she comes out of there."

"Yes," Philippe said.

He walked into the office. Carla's Glock 17 and a spare clip sat on one corner of the table; the rest was littered with fast-food trash. He grabbed two of the wooden armchairs and carried them out, setting one with its back to the wall and the other facing it.

She'd been in there four minutes already. It was a good thing she had no makeup or it would take even longer. He wondered suddenly where her other things were.

"Jensen, what did she bring with her?"

"Not much. A pistol, an extra clip, a knife, and some money."

"That's odd."

Carla was *always* prepared. She must have suspected that something might go wrong. Where was her bag? What was her emergency escape route? Was he missing something? He walked over to the washroom and put his ear to the door, but heard nothing. He knocked.

"Carla," he said, "come out. Your time is up."

"Damn it, Philippe," she said, "I was lying on that cold fucking floor for fourteen hours. I'm constipated. Give me a minute, will you?"

Philippe grimaced. "Where's my bag?" he asked Jensen.

He emptied the paper sack onto the floor near the chairs: a propane torch, small spools of wire, pliers, a utility knife with various blades, a ball-peen hammer, and a small can of turpentine. Philippe sorted the things and checked the time. Another three minutes had passed.

"Carla!"

"All right."

The toilet flushed and he heard the water faucet. *Good God, was she washing her hands?* He stepped back from the chairs, out of Jensen's line of fire, in case she did try something.

Jensen was standing near the office wall, Lanotte stood near the chairs with his pistol aimed at the toilet. The door opened slowly. Carla shuffled around it and took a few hesitant hops out into the room. Philippe frowned. Something was wrong. She took another small hop and he saw that the cable tie around her ankles was gone.

"She's—" *free,* he wanted to say, but pandemonium burst out.

Carla fell, but the fall turned into a roll. Lanotte got off one shot, but where she'd been was nothing but air. From a crouch she whipped both hands—*free!*—at Jensen and Lanotte. As if by magic, a red blossom appeared on Lanotte's right wrist, with something dark sticking out of it. He howled and dropped his pistol. At the same instant, a knife sprouted out of Jensen's right biceps, jerking his arm away from his body. He fell to one knee with his mouth open in a silent scream.

Carla was running at Philippe. She was only a few paces away, with his death in her eyes, when he fired his gun at her feet. He hadn't realized he'd even drawn his pistol.

She skidded to a stop with his gun almost touching her chest. They stood motionless for a moment, eyes locked, until Philippe saw resolve in her eyes and knew that, despite the fact that he had a gun just centimeters from her breast, she was about to kill him—he had no idea how. But

Lanotte rose up behind her and punched her savagely in the kidney with his uninjured hand. Carla dropped to the floor.

The knife had passed completely through Lanotte's wrist; its point stuck two centimeters out from the flesh. It must have severed a tendon, because his hand was cocked back and he couldn't straighten it. Both men's wounds were bleeding profusely, but not spurting. Philippe found a first aid kit on the wall in the office, handed it to Jensen, and left them to nurse each other.

He dragged Carla's limp body over to the chair by the wall and dropped her into it. She was barely conscious, eyelids fluttering, moaning softly and drooling. Philippe grabbed a handful of cable ties from the office and used them to fasten each of Carla's ankles to the chair, making sure there was a rung below the loop. He fastened her arms together behind the chair, yanking viciously on the tie's free end, drawing fresh blood from her wrists.

In the trash on the office table he found a large soft drink cup. Philippe filled it with water from the washroom and sat down on the other chair, facing Carla. Her head lolled to the right.

"Carla," he said. "Wake up!" He threw the water in her face.

She groaned, opened her eyes, blinked them, and shook her head. Water dripped from her face and her chest was soaked.

"Almost," she said, grinning but obviously still in pain.

"Lanotte, you fool, didn't you search her?"

"Of course," Lanotte said. When Jensen finished taping his wrist, Lanotte walked unsteadily to stand beside Philippe. Philippe glanced up and saw that he was ready to pounce.

"Stop," he said. "We have to interrogate her first."

"No," Lanotte said, "first I have to disembowel her and strangle her with her own guts."

"No! We have to find out where the warheads are. Then—I swear it!—she's yours."

Lanotte took a step back, fighting down his rage. He walked shakily to the office and slid down to the floor with his back to its glass wall.

"That's no way to motivate the prisoner," Carla said hoarsely, and spat on the floor. She seemed to have nearly recovered from Lanotte's blow.

Jensen grabbed her arm. "Where was the knife? We searched you!" He turned to Philippe. "We even felt between her legs. She was unarmed!" He shook her arm. "Where did you hide it?"

Carla smiled up at him. "How's the arm, Mr. Super Collider?" She looked back at Philippe and shrugged. "They were inside my belt. You guys should be more careful."

Philippe nodded his head. Jensen unbuckled her belt and yanked it free. In the center were two loops that could have held small throwing knives.

Jensen threw the belt into the corner. "I think we should strip her and search her again," he said. "And this time, look everywhere."

"That won't be necessary," Philippe said. "We're going to start now." He leaned down and picked up the propane torch. "Do you know what these are for?" he asked her.

Carla glanced dully at the implements arrayed beside Philippe's chair. "Home improvements? Untie me and I'll help."

Philippe smiled at her. "My dear, you have no idea what's in store for you. The Mossad trained you in interrogation, but those are civilized techniques for squeamish fops. The people who taught *me* have no scruples at all. I'm sure you know who I mean. The pain won't stop when you talk—and you will talk. You see, inflicting pain can be an end in itself."

She looked almost disinterested, but that would change. Philippe picked up a spool of copper wire.

"You contacted someone," he said, "and that someone *stole my warheads.*" He waited for the echoes of his voice to die away. "First you're going to tell me how I can get my weapons back. Then you're going to tell me who took them, and how I can find these friends of yours. If you're very cooperative I'll kill you quickly, otherwise it may take a week or so. But you had better start talking *now!*"

Carla looked at him with a sleepy expression that, under other circumstances, he would have thought was boredom.

"Since you asked politely, I'll tell you. The Mossad has your warheads. As for how to get them back—you can't. They're gone, Philippe." She smiled at him. "If you want to play, go ahead, but that's all I can tell you.

I'm curious what the turpentine is for. But the Mossad has your bombs and *you can't get them back.*"

Philippe was stunned. The Mossad? It wasn't possible. She was being *hunted* by the Mossad! Why would she help them? He knew for a fact that a kidon team had been trying to find her for over a year. He'd verified it through three different sources before hiring her.

Then a truly nasty idea occurred to him. Was it possible that Carla was still working for the Mossad, that they put a contract out on her just to convince *him* that she was a renegade? The bastards were devious and ruthless enough to do that, but why would she agree to it? He searched her face, and the twinkle in her eye told him it was true—and she knew that he knew. She was insane. She'd allowed herself to be hunted by the most dangerous assassins in the world just so she could betray him—*use him.*

Philippe's mind went blank of everything but the desire to punish her. As he reached for the propane torch lighter, a voice boomed from outside.

"Carla Citrullo! Carla Citrullo and her associates! This is the FBI. You are all under arrest. The building is surrounded. There's no way out, Carla. Come out of the building with your hands up and no one will get hurt."

Philippe looked up at Jensen and Lanotte. "FBI? Which one of you fucked up?" He turned back to Carla. "Or did they follow you? Why do they want you? Are you working with them? Did you make some kind of deal?"

"Sorry, Philippe," Carla said. "I guess we'll just have to play later."

* * *

The amplified voice startled Derek awake. He jerked upright in the truck's cab. *Oh my God, I fell asleep!* It was a quarter to nine. Philippe must have returned and the FBI was about to raid the foundry.

"Carla Citrullo and her associates..." It was Chapa's voice. Derek tuned it out and tried to think. It might be too late for his plan to work... but maybe not.

He hopped out of the truck. Why hadn't the people who lived here awakened him so they could get out of their driveway and go shopping or something. *Goddamn it!*

A swarm of agents hunkered down around the front of the foundry. Westlake Avenue was blocked to the north, and although he couldn't see it there was probably a roadblock to the south as well. But Eighth was clear except for two agents wearing dark blue windbreakers with "FBI" emblazoned across the back in tall yellow letters. One carried a rifle on his shoulder, the other hefted a strange-looking weapon like a bloated Tommy gun. Both of them were staring at the foundry.

Derek moved so he could see the foundry's roof, and his heart sank. There was an agent there, pointing his rifle down at the doorway from behind the chimney. For a moment, Derek worried that they'd found the bomb. But the radio was black and hidden under the wind-blown trash in the corner.

"Carla Citrullo," Chapa said.

It was hard to focus over the megaphone. *They've covered the entrance in force. Only two agents out back, and one on the roof.* He decided to go ahead with his plan. The only change was that the FBI had had time to get into position—he'd known they would be here, but he'd hoped to surprise them while they were still moving in.

Derek ran back to the truck, grabbed the transmitter out of his pack, and turned it on.

* * *

"Look outside," Philippe said.

Jensen ran into the office, pushed the table up against the outside wall, set a chair on top of it, and climbed up. He could just see out the high windows facing Westlake.

"Feds everywhere," Jensen said. "I see a sniper—no, two of them." He craned to look down the street and almost tipped over the chair. "They have the street blocked off." He stepped down carefully and jumped back to the floor. "Now what?"

Philippe looked around the foundry. There was only one door; the windows were too small to climb through; the ceiling was unreachable, even with Jensen's makeshift pyramid, and anyway there was no visible access to the roof.

"Carla Citrullo," the voice boomed again. "This is the FBI. Come out of the building *now* with your hands up, or we will open fire."

The indignity offended Philippe more than the possibility that he was about to die. He was being told to surrender in *Carla's* name! They thought *he* was with *her!*

The foundry's floor was solid concrete. Philippe ran to the washroom and looked inside: sink, toilet, hand towel on a rack. His eyes strayed to the brick furnace that thrust out into the room. At waist height on the inside face, an area about a meter wide and half as high was constructed of a different brick. If this place was a foundry, and that was the furnace, then the discolored area was the furnace's mouth. Philippe picked up the ball-peen hammer.

"Do you see the old opening on the furnace?" he asked Lanotte. Lanotte looked and nodded. Philippe handed him the hammer. "Knock out the bricks!"

Lanotte took the hammer in his left hand, stood sideways to the furnace wall, and slammed it into the brick. It bounced back ringing, but brick chips flew. Lanotte braced his legs and began hammering regularly, *ping ping ping,* scattering shards of brick with each blow.

"Carla," the FBI man called again, "we know you have three accomplices in there. We have forty agents covering your only exit. There's no way you're going to get out alive unless you drop your weapons and come out with your hands raised, *now!*"

"Philippe," Carla said, "I think we're wanted outside."

"Accomplices," Philippe grumbled, ignoring her. He watched Lanotte hammering at the bricks. He had no idea what good it would do them if they *could* crawl inside the furnace, but it was better than doing nothing, and he would *not* surrender to the FBI.

"Hey," Jensen said. "She's the one they want. Let's just throw her out the door."

Philippe glanced at him and returned to watching Lanotte. The giant's left hand was oozing blood from a dozen places where brick fragments had sliced him.

"Come on," Jensen said. "They don't want us. Throw her outside, maybe they'll shoot her. At least it'll buy us some time."

"No," Philippe said. "We have to interrogate her."

"*What?* Didn't you hear what she said? The *Mossad* has the warheads, Philippe. They're gone forever, man. We're never going to see them again."

"Shut up," Lanotte said between swings.

Philippe turned to really look at Jensen. The man was sweating and panicky. His eyes were darting around, searching for escape. He was on the edge of a total breakdown.

"Okay," Jensen said, "then let's give ourselves up. *We* haven't done anything illegal. They'll question us, sure, but then they'll have to let us go. We can say she kidnapped us. Or we captured her and were just about to call the cops—"

"Shut *up!*" Philippe said. "You're babbling. Yes, they're after *her,* but once they find out who *I* am, they'll never let me go. The CIA will keep me in a cell for the rest of my life, and if they ever do decide to get rid of me, it'll be to hand me over to Interpol, or MI6, or the fucking Mossad. So just shut the fuck *up* and help me think of a way out of here!"

They only had a few more minutes before the FBI stormed the building. There had to be a way out. *Goddamn Jensen and his motherfucking warehouses!*

Lanotte broke through the wall. Two bricks fell away, chipped and shattered into small pieces. Philippe rushed over and helped Lanotte pull on the surrounding bricks.

"Carla Citrullo and her associates," the voice boomed again. "This is your last warning. Come out now!"

Lanotte slammed the hammer into the stubborn bricks and more of them fell out. The rest came away easily. The badly-mixed mortar had crumbled under Lanotte's hammering. When the last one had been removed, Philippe stuck his head inside. A chimney rose up above him, open to the sky. The furnace was about the size of a large closet, its floor level with the opening Lanotte had made, littered with leaves, loose mortar, and pieces of brick. Philippe jerked back as he heard something crash through a window. He saw something smash through another window and thick smoke began welling up: tear gas.

"Come on," Philippe shouted to Lanotte. He thrust his torso into the furnace opening and Lanotte boosted him inside. Something sharp cut his hand but he ignored the pain and turned around to help Lanotte. The shallow opening was too small for the giant's body; he was stuck.

Philippe pulled on his uninjured arm and Lanotte managed to get one shoulder inside. Then, with Lanotte pushing and Philippe pulling, he was able to squirm the rest of the way into the furnace, roll onto his side clumsily, and stand up. Now that the opening was unblocked, gas fumes wafted in, making Philippe's eyes water and burning his throat. He pulled a handkerchief from his pocket and held it over his nose and mouth, then squatted down to look back out into the room.

Through the thick fog, Philippe saw Jensen emerging from the washroom with a dripping towel held over his mouth. Carla was struggling against her bonds like a wolf in a leg-hold trap, coughing violently, her eyes shut tight and tears streaming down her face. Ordinarily, Philippe might have paused to enjoy the spectacle, but there wasn't time.

"Jensen," he shouted, "come on! Inside here."

Jensen turned toward Philippe's voice, spotted him, and took one step toward the furnace and safety.

Chapter 35

Seattle, Washington
   Saturday, March 4, 9:11 a.m.

"Carla Citrullo and her associates," Chapa's voice echoed. "This is your last warning." *Good,* Derek thought irritably.

A few people had come out of their houses to see what was going on. Derek hooked the CB radio to his belt and joined the small crowd gathering behind the two FBI agents. He was one of the few who were fully dressed. One gray-haired couple looked as if they were on their way to church, but several people were wearing nothing but robes over their pajamas.

"Folks, please," one FBI agent said. "Stay back. The situation could get dangerous."

"What *is* the situation?" a middle-aged woman said, clutching her robe at the throat.

"Yeah, we have a right to know," a teenage boy added. Despite the chill, he wore grunge skateboarder chic: low-riding shorts, a baggy green "Nuke Elvis" sweatshirt over a T-shirt, expensive running shoes, and a diamond earring in his ear.

The other agent held a hand to one ear and nodded. As he raised the strange gun to his shoulder, Derek realized what it was: a tear gas grenade launcher. The gun discharged with a strangely soft *chuff* and he heard glass breaking. Derek pushed forward to get a better look at the foundry, and the crowd flowed with him. Someone bumped one of the agents off balance; he cursed and screamed for everyone to get back.

The agents below were still in position on the opposite side of the street, waiting for the tear gas to work. The guy on the roof was standing on the far side of the chimney from the door and Derek's roof bomb. One of the men in front of Derek was talking into his radio, asking for Seattle PD to send a cruiser to Eighth Avenue for crowd control.

Derek couldn't be sure all the FBI agents were out of harm's way; he was going to have to risk it. He took a few steps back and the crowd flowed forward to fill the gap. Standing at the rear of the group, he took the radio off his belt and switched it to channel one.

"What the hell am I doing?" He pressed the transmit button and lifted it to his mouth. "Hello?"

Nothing happened. Derek checked the radio: it was on and set to channel one. *What the hell?* He pressed the button again.

"Hey!" he said.

A titanic roar erupted from the back of the foundry. A brief, brilliant flash of light was instantly consumed by a billowing, evil-looking cloud of smoke. The people around him screamed—half of them fought to break out of the crowd and run away while the other half pushed in for a closer look. Both agents held their hands to their ears, trying to hear their radios.

Derek stumbled as the church couple and a bathrobed woman pushed past him. He caught his balance, switched the radio to channel two, and pushed the button.

"What's—" he said.

A second explosion, louder than the first, erupted from the front of the foundry. This time there was no visible flame, just an instant, roiling cloud of thick, gray smoke.

"Jesus Christ," one of the agents said. "What the fuck is going on?"

"Get these people back," the other one shouted. That was hardly necessary. Only Derek, the skateboarder, and one middle-aged man were left of the crowd. Derek started backing away, holding the radio behind him. When the agents turned away, he set it to channel three and pressed the transmit button.

"Yo!" he said.

A rumbling boom exploded from the woods. A tall cedar tree wobbled, then toppled in slow motion toward them with a crashing noise that grew louder until it sounded as if the whole woods were coming down. The agents abandoned any semblance of discipline and ran with everyone else away from the falling tree. Hardly knowing what had come over him, Derek ran toward it.

As he reached the curb, the tree landed on the corner of a small two-story house, crushing it. Derek was pelted with fragrant cedar twigs, but he was already past the crunched house on his way to the dirt path. As he started down it, he heard more crashing sounds and looked up to see a second tree tilting away from him, then a third one falling toward the street.

As he ran past the raw, smoking crater that his bomb had excavated, Derek smelled a hint of sweetness under the dust and the cedar, like candy. He stopped to see what the agents on Westlake were doing. To his relief, they had all backed up and were now milling in a confused clump in the center of the parking lot. The agent on the roof was gone.

Derek set the radio for channel four.

"Abra cadabra," he said.

Another blast went off on the far side of the foundry. Derek saw a tire go spinning into the sky. He ran down the path, reached the rock wall, and stopped in amazement.

The entire corner of the building was gone. In its place a pile of rubble six feet high lay smoking, still settling. Water jetted up in a thin stream from the edge of the trash like a fountain. A wooden beam hanging into the rough opening creaked and groaned and settled a foot lower.

Derek left the radio on the rocks and climbed swiftly down the wall. At the foot of the debris pile, he drew his pistol from the small of his back and released the safety. After trying unsuccessfully to walk through the wreckage, he put the pistol back in his belt and made better progress scrambling over the shifting, unstable debris on hands and knees. Small fires dotted the pile, and he burned his hands several times before he reached its peak—where he found himself face to face with an unharmed toilet bowl, sitting like a crown atop the rubble.

Half stumbling, half sliding down the pile, he came to rest inside the foundry. Smoke obscured his view of the large open space, but he could see that his roof bomb had obliterated the doorway in the far corner, which was completely sealed by debris. The only way in or out was the hole he'd just crawled through.

A fallen ceiling beam abruptly settled further with a basso groan. Derek decided he'd better find Carla and get the hell out before the rest of the building caved in—but he could see no one. He looked into what had once been an office before all of the glass was blown out; only a few jagged shards hung from the metal studs. There were a table, a few chairs, and a lot of broken glass, but no people.

Derek turned back to the pile he'd climbed, wondering if Carla lay dead beneath it. The toilet bowl sparkled in the daylight. It would be just like Carla to be using the bathroom while the FBI demanded that she come out with her hands up. To Derek's left a small, dark heap of something lay on the floor. He stepped closer and saw that it was a body—but there were too many legs. He grabbed the corpse's arm and turned him over. The dead man was black, beefy, and Derek didn't know him.

But Carla had been lying beneath him. Her arms were tied behind her with... *a cable tie.* He safetied the pistol, jammed it into his pants, and felt for a pulse. He was surprised to find that she had one; she looked dead. The skin of her face was pale and dusty, smeared and streaked with filth. Derek used his pocket knife to cut the cord around her wrists and the ties that bound sticks to her legs—they were chair legs. She'd been tied to a chair when the bomb went off.

"Carla," he said, patting her face gently. "Wake up."

To his immense surprise, she did. She coughed and gagged, but her eyes fluttered open and stayed that way. She looked at him without comprehension. Derek performed the quick body scan he'd learned in first aid class. She was breathing, harshly but regularly, so the airway wasn't obstructed. Her pulse was rapid but strong. He felt her arms and then her legs, probed her ribs and her spine, felt her scalp. Nothing was broken, there was no gushing blood.

"I guess you're going to live," Derek said. Unless there were internal injuries. Or the FBI shot them when they walked out the door.

Carla groaned.

"Come on," he said. "We've got to go now."

He helped her to her feet. She shook her head, stumbled, and pulled away from his hand.

She coughed and whispered, "Where's Philippe?"

"Is that him?" Derek pointed to the dead black man.

"No, that's Jensen. Stupid son of a bitch saved my life." She straightened and coughed spasmodically.

"Carla, we've got to go. Right now!" He grabbed her arm and tried to lead her toward the junk pile, but she pulled away and stumbled into the office. "What are you doing?"

"Gun," she said.

She clumsily swept glass and trash off the table, found her gun and a clip and put them back in her holster. It wasn't until that moment that Derek realized her shirt was hanging open. But she wasn't ready to leave yet. While Derek fidgeted, Carla searched the dead man's body, finding a small wad of cash in one pocket and another, larger one in a gold money clip. She stood up too quickly and stumbled against the wall.

Derek helped her toward the rubble pile, and they scrambled slowly up it. Carla moved stiffly, but he didn't try to rush her. As slowly as they were moving, they were still making better progress than if he'd had to drag her up the mound. When they reached the summit of the pile, Carla noticed the toilet and laughed weakly, then they slid down the other side and stood at the base of the rock wall.

"Now what?" she said. She still looked dazed.

"We climb up."

"This is your plan? Blow me up and then make me climb a rock wall?"

"If you don't like it, we can start over. You want to go back?"

"Oh, piss off." Before he could react she started climbing.

Derek was amazed that no one shot at them, or even shouted at them, as they climbed the wall. Carla rolled over the edge at the top. When Derek reached her, he tried to stay low: he couldn't see what the agents were doing. No one was visible uphill and his view to Westlake was blocked. A sudden shift in the breeze shrouded them in smoke. Derek coughed and blinked his eyes at the acrid stench.

He picked up the radio he'd left there and tugged at Carla, and she obediently got to her feet. They clambered up the hill until he could see up and down Eighth Avenue. The agents had been joined by two cops who were turning people away from the crushed house. Unfortunately, they were between Derek and his truck, but he'd planned for something like this.

Halfway to the cops, a silver BMW was parked on the street. There was no one near it. Derek tuned the radio to channel five. He looked at Carla, crouched down beside him on the dirt path.

"What?" she said.

"Nothing," he said into the radio.

With a violent roar, the BMW lifted off the ground. It seemed to hover in the air for a moment, twisting and breaking up into pieces, before it fell back to the ground, shrieking like a demon. The fragments exploded in a fireball that settled down into an oily, smoking, crackling fire. Carla looked at the blaze with a slight smile on her lips.

"I never liked BMWs," Derek said.

They stood and walked the rest of the way uphill. The cops and agents had fallen back, and the citizens they'd been herding were running away, but in a few moments they would turn and be drawn back to the flames like moths. Derek led Carla toward the truck, staying as far as possible from the burning wreckage. No one bothered them as they walked up the driveway and climbed into the truck.

He drove into the street. A balding, barefoot man wearing only pajama bottoms was screaming in anger at the blazing car. As they drove slowly by, Derek noticed the man's tears, his hairy back, and his Tweety Bird pajamas.

Chapter 36

Seattle, Washington
    Saturday, March 4, 9:36 a.m.

"What's happening up there?" Chapa said into his radio.

"Nada," Frieder replied.

Chapa had sent a dozen agents up to Eighth Avenue after the second car blew up, but nothing else happened. It was ten minutes since the last bomb went off and he was getting itchy to go in.

"The bomb squad's here," Shaffer said.

"Great." He couldn't take his eyes off the smoldering hulk of the Cadillac. He'd been standing right beside a bomb the entire time he'd been telling Carla to give up. If the bomber had detonated them in a different order, Chapa would now be nothing but burnt shreds of meat in the road.

"Uh, sir," Frieder's voice came over the radio.

"Yeah?"

"One of the agents up here—Kantrowitz?"

"Yeah, I know him."

"He saw two people climbing up the hill just before the Beemer went boom."

"Get him down here, now!"

Chapa waited impatiently for them to drive the three blocks. The bomb squad was putting on their body armor. Shaffer was chatting with the captain in charge, who nodded a few times and reached into his truck for something. Chapa turned back to the smoking Cadillac.

A Bureau car roared down the street, turned into the parking lot without slowing down, and headed right toward him, screeching to a halt twenty feet away. Frieder and another man got out. Shaffer saw them and started over.

"Why didn't you report this immediately?" Chapa said before Kantrowitz could open his mouth.

"S-sorry, sir," the man said. He was in his late forties, with a rugged, weathered face. "We had a situation up there. Seattle PD was supposed to send a cruiser to help us out, but they didn't show up until after the bombs started. The residents were crowding up right behind us, they wouldn't stay back. One of the explosions knocked over some trees, crushed a house, and the owners were hysterical and blaming us. And the last bomb blew up some guy's BMW and *he* was screaming at us."

Kantrowitz's tortured face made Chapa decide not to reprimand him. But he was still angry.

"Tell me what you saw," he said.

"Yes, sir. Hopper and I were trying to keep people back from the smashed house. We finally got two cops helping us, and the crowd was starting to calm down. I turned to look down here at the, uh, the building, and I saw a man pulling a woman up the hill. They dropped to the ground, then the BMW exploded. The civilians all ran away, except for the car's owner, I guess, he ran toward the blast. When I, uh, when I stopped..."

"When you stopped running," Chapa said.

"Yes, sir."

"Go on."

"I saw the couple getting into a pickup truck. The man was driving. The truck was parked in one of the driveways—"

"Did you notice which one?" Chapa said.

"Yes, sir."

"Okay, you need to talk to the homeowners right away."

"Yes, sir."

"Did you get the truck's license?"

"No, sir, I was, uh, I was too far away. But it was a late model Ford F150 pickup. White."

"Did you recognize either of the people in the truck?"

"Uh..." The agent looked embarrassed.

"Did you review the briefing materials this morning?"

"Yes, sir."

"You memorized the photographs?"

Kantrowitz was in severe pain. Chapa changed his mind about a reprimand, but that could wait. He jerked his head at Kantrowitz. From an envelope under her clipboard, Shaffer took out the eight-by-ten photos that had been shown to every agent that morning: Carla, Derek, and the men that Frieder had photographed at Derek's house. The latter three were grainy but distinct. Kantrowitz pointed to the picture of Carla.

"That's the woman," he said. He leafed through the others and shook his head. "I'm really sorry, sir. The man was white, and kind of tall, but I don't recognize any of these pictures."

"What was his build?" Shaffer said. "What color hair?"

Kantrowitz thought for a moment, then shrugged. "Sorry, I don't know. I just didn't get a good look at him."

"What he was wearing?" Chapa said.

"I don't know, sir."

Chapa considered him. *How did this guy get through the Academy?* Finally he waved his hand in dismissal.

"Go check on the house where the truck was parked," he said, and Kantrowitz scurried off, relieved to still have his head. "He recognized Carla," Chapa said to Shaffer, and realized that Frieder was still standing there as well. "But not the man. What does that mean?"

"Either the guy with Carla is someone new," Shaffer said, "or Kantrowitz is just incompetent or blind."

"Cut the guy some slack," Frieder said. "He almost got whacked by a falling tree and blown up by a car, plus he had to corral a bunch of hysterical citizens."

"Agent Frieder," Chapa said, "are those sufficient reasons for an agent not to perform his duty?"

Frieder struggled silently for a moment to control his emotions, then shook his head. "No, sir."

"That had to be the truck they rented in Idaho," Shaffer said.

"Get Seattle PD to start looking for it. Okay, if Carla is gone, the fireworks are probably over. I want to go in. Ask your bomb squad buddies to clear the building."

Shaffer ran off to talk to them. Chapa turned to Frieder.

"You've seen these guys twice now—here and at Derek's house, right?"

"Yes, sir."

"Okay. I want you to go in with us." Chapa looked down the street to the blue sedan in which the third man had arrived. He pointed it out to Frieder. "While we're waiting, let's get that car impounded and searched."

"Yes, sir." Frieder walked away.

Chapa saw an agent who wasn't busy and called her over. He told the woman to organize a team to find the motel Carla and Derek were staying in.

"They have a pattern," he said. "Cheap but clean, with easy access to the highways. They were coming from Idaho, and Narr lives on the Eastside, so start there."

The woman ran off. Chapa paced up and down the parking lot. Every now and then his eyes strayed back to the wrecked Cadillac, but its fascination was waning. Eventually Shaffer returned.

"I sent one of our agents in with the squad," she said. "The dogs didn't find any more bombs. It looks like the building's clean, but it's still falling apart. And they found a body inside."

"Just one body?"

"Yes."

"Okay, let's go in. Frieder!"

Frieder finished talking to a local cop and headed toward them at a trot.

* * *

The foundry's entrance was gone, completely choked off with debris. They had to walk around to the back of the building and climb over a shifting pile of junk to get into the building. Chapa had just slid inside and was brushing the dust off his trousers when he heard Frieder laughing. He turned back just in time to see the agent push an intact toilet bowl off the top of the pile. It rolled down and out of view, followed a few seconds later by a resounding *clank*.

"Let's try to stay focused, all right?" Chapa said. The other two agents were careful not to look at Frieder, who sullenly ran down the hill of rubble.

Chapa stood in the center of the foundry with Shaffer, Frieder, and the agent who had gone in with the bomb squad. The smoking heap of junk that blocked the old entrance swept well into the room, fanning out in a jumbled pile of shattered wood, bricks, metal bars, and roofing that was chest high at the old brick furnace.

"The body's over here, sir," Tomlinson said. He was young, perhaps just a few years out of the Academy, and his blond hair and smooth, ruddy face made him look more like a surfer than an agent.

The dead man was lying on his back with his legs twisted under him. He was black, mid-thirties, with short hair and a beard. Chapa recognized him from the photographs.

"It's one of the guys from Narr's place," Frieder said. "The driver."

They found a wallet in his right back pocket.

"David Jensen," Chapa read as he held it up to the light. "Montana driver's license. Looks real."

"Montana?" Shaffer said. "Could this guy have something to do with Hildreth?"

Chapa shrugged and handed her the wallet. He walked into what had been an office. The room was strewn with glass fragments, except for one corner of the table that had been swept nearly clean. Another pointless mystery.

Five explosions. He had a pretty good idea who had set the charges.

"Were these guys with Derek or Carla?" he asked Shaffer.

She frowned and turned to Frieder. "What exactly did you see when Carla showed up?"

Frieder shrugged. "She knocked on the door. Somebody answered it—"

"You didn't see who?" Chapa said.

"No. She talked to whoever for a second, then she waved her hand like this." He demonstrated, holding the first two fingers out in a victory V and waggling his hand.

"Meaning two people inside?" Shaffer said.

"Maybe. Then she went in and the door shut."

"She wasn't coerced in any way?" Chapa said.

"Not that I could see."

"Is it possible they were holding a gun on her?"

"I couldn't see anything," Frieder said. "Citrullo was in the way."

Chapa thought it over as he looked around the room. There were two chairs and a table in the office, and two smashed chairs out here. The dead guy, Jensen, had been lying next to them. On the floor at his feet were pliers, wire, some cable ties. They'd seen the third man carrying a paper bag this morning when he'd arrived...

"I don't get it," Chapa said. "Three guys show up at Derek's house. You follow them here. One of them goes out for the night. Carla comes in voluntarily, but she signals to someone *outside* that there are two guys *inside.* She must have been signaling to Derek, right?"

Shaffer and Frieder nodded.

"The next morning, the third guy comes back, then the bombs go off. It had to be Derek who set off the bombs. Then we see one guy escaping up the hill with Carla, pulling her by the hand. One guy's left behind, dead. So where are Derek and the third guy?"

"I have an idea," Shaffer said.

"Let's hear it."

"We know Derek wasn't in here. Frieder saw him with Carla, but he walked away."

"Right."

"Derek set the bombs, but one of the other guys must have dragged Carla up the hill—Derek wasn't here, and that doesn't sound like him, anyway. Carla's been dragging *him* around all week."

"Okay."

"So either the third guy is buried under the rubble—"

"Excuse me," Tomlinson said. "The dogs are trained to find bodies as well as explosives. The only thing they reacted to was that." He pointed to the furnace, half-buried under rubble. "They sniffed around here for a while, and the squad probed at the base but didn't find anything. But the dogs ignored the piles of debris."

"Okay," Shaffer said. "Then my guess is that *two* guys went up the hill with Carla."

"Wait," Frieder said. "Kantrowitz said he saw Citrullo and one man. Two people."

"Yeah," Chapa said. "And he didn't recognize the man. He was a block away and obviously shaken up."

"It's the only thing that makes sense," Shaffer said. "There were three men in here with Carla. One is dead, two are missing. If only one of them went up the hill, where's the other guy?"

Chapa nodded.

"Let's clear some of this junk out of the way to be sure," he said. "But for now let's assume the other two guys survived and left with Carla." He looked around at the dusty, demolished building. "So where did they go? And what happened to Derek?"

Chapter 37

Seattle, Washington
Saturday, March 4, 9:45 a.m.

"Drive faster," Carla said.

Derek glanced at her. She seemed to be recovering: now she only looked half dead. Her pale, streaked face, the bruises already beginning on her cheeks and forehead, and the filthy, shredded clothes made her look like an earthquake refugee.

"I'm already going ten miles over the speed limit," he said, "and I can't go faster than this woman in front of me—at least, not for long."

"Pass the bitch and speed up."

"What're you going to say when we get pulled over?"

"We won't get pulled over." She leaned forward and squinted at the heavy traffic. "You drive like an old lady. Look at that—three cars just passed you."

"Are you sure you don't want to go to a hospital first?" He didn't speed up; he was already going too fast. "You could have internal bleeding or a concussion. You need to see a doctor."

"What'll I tell him, that I fell off a ladder?" She sat back and winced in pain. "He'd take one look at me and call the cops. Forget the doctor, I'll be fine. Just get me to the damned hotel."

They arrived at the Sheraton without being stopped by the police or having an accident. The valet parking attendant opened Carla's door and stepped back, eyes wide, as she struggled down out of the truck.

"Can you believe it?" she said. "I slammed my office door and the roof caved in."

The attendant closed her door and came around the car.

"It was an old building," Derek said. The kid nodded and drove off in their truck, shaking his head.

Derek handed her his coat and she put it on over her torn shirt. They hurried through the lobby and reached the elevators without attracting attention. Before they could push the up button, one of the cars arrived with a pleasant chime, disgorging a jabbering clot of men and women dressed for business, none of whom even glanced at them. It had been a while since Derek had worked in the corporate world. Today was Saturday; did they still have weekends?

In their room, Derek watched as Carla started stripping out of her clothes. She grunted softly as she pulled her bra over her head.

"Keep the holster and the shoes," she said on her way to the bathroom. "Toss the rest."

While she showered, Derek packed his things. He sat on the bed and waited for a long time. Had she fainted?

"Are you okay?" he said.

"Almost done."

Soon the water stopped and he heard her get out of the tub. She stepped out of the bathroom nude, still toweling her hair, and Derek gasped in shock. It was hard to believe she was the same woman who'd seduced him a week ago in Calgary, only hours after killing Hildreth; she'd been haughty and beautiful then. She dropped the towel and watched him watching her, then laughed.

"That bad, huh?"

Carla's wrists and ankles were bruised and abraded, but the bleeding had stopped. She was limping slightly, and no wonder: both knees would be purple soon. Her entire face and her left arm and ribs looked as if they'd been beaten with a baseball bat: they were puffy, bruised, and scraped. Derek tried to find a part of her body that had not been abused and gave up.

"You look as if you spent the night in a cement mixer."

"That's not far off, but it's nothing compared to what Philippe had planned for me." She took clean underwear out of her bag and started pulling it on.

After a moment of watching her struggle, Derek said, "Do you need help?"

"Thanks, but I've been dressing myself since I was four."

"Oh. Well, I bet you've never been blown up before."

"No. That was a first."

Standing by the small table in her white underwear—panties, bra, and socks—Carla's battered body looked even more vulnerable than it had naked. But she picked up her pistol, ejected the magazine, pulled back the slide to examine the chamber, and in a few swift movements disassembled the gun. Derek watched with a strange disorientation as this battered woman, bruised and sore, checked the action on her weapon and swiftly reassembled it. She thumbed the top bullet in the clip, slapped the magazine back into the grip, racked the slide, and reached for her holster.

"What?" she said as she noticed his expression.

He shook his head. There was no way to express the dissonance between what she was and what she appeared to be.

"What happened back there?" he said.

As she finished dressing, she recounted briefly and without emotion how she had been tranquilized, trussed up, and kept ready for Philippe. As she described how Philippe had been ready to torture her, she stopped abruptly, looking confused.

"How many bombs did you set off?" she said.

"Five. Four while you were still inside, one after we climbed the hill."

"Huh. I remember the last one, sort of. And the first one—that took out Jensen, blew him right across the room and slammed him into me. Knocked me over and crushed the chair. The blast would have shredded me if he hadn't blocked it."

"Sorry," Derek said. "I'll try to do better next time."

"No." Carla smiled at him weakly. "I'm alive and free, so it worked. You did great."

He shrugged. If Jensen hadn't been standing in exactly the right place, Derek would have climbed down into the foundry only to find Carla dead. As far as he was concerned, he'd failed. Finished dressing, she stood up and leaned down to kiss him on the forehead.

"Come on," she said.

She went back into the bathroom and returned with the rest of the explosives—the box of detonators and three bricks of C-4—and put them carefully into Derek's pack. He hoisted that and his bag, Carla picked up her duffel and his computer, and they went downstairs.

Derek looked up as they waited for the valet to fetch the truck. The sky was clearing, the clouds scudding away so quickly it looked like time-lapse photography. The same young man who had taken their truck returned it, apparently without recognizing them. Carla nudged Derek away from the driver's side as he tipped the valet.

"I'm driving," she said.

"You've got to be kidding."

"I'm driving."

"Okay, go ahead." He climbed into the cab and watched with less sympathy than satisfaction as she groaned her way up behind the wheel. "Where are we going?"

"Queen Anne, I think." She started the car and put it in gear. "We need to find a better base of operations. And a new car."

Derek looked out the side window as she drove north. Ivy hung down the retaining walls like verdant waterfalls. The walls receded and the view opened out, revealing a hill covered with houses on their right and Lake Union on their left. The blasted ruin of the foundry was over there somewhere, but he didn't even see a wisp of smoke to mark the site. Carla left the freeway and drove through the side streets confidently, as if she were a native. When they were deep in the maze of streets in the University District, Derek looked up and realized that she wasn't slowing down for the intersection ahead.

"Hey," he said, stomping for the brake pedal that wasn't there. "Stop sign."

Carla slammed on the brakes and they skidded to a halt in the middle of the intersection. A dark blue Infiniti sedan that had been crossing from their right swerved and jumped the curb, coming to rest on someone's lawn. The driver leaped out of his car and slammed the door, striding toward them. He was tall, overweight, with dark wavy hair and a well-cut business suit.

"Let me handle this," Carla said. She got out of the truck stiffly and closed the door.

The man screamed in her face, gesturing at his car, at the truck, at the stop sign. Derek couldn't make out what he was saying, but the message was clear. What really worried him was that Carla was taking it quietly, waiting for the screamer to run down.

Uh oh.

Without warning, Carla jabbed her left fist into the man's gut. He doubled over and slowly crumpled to the ground. She grinned at Derek and took a few steps back.

For a moment, Derek thought the loudmouth would be smart and stay down, but he regained both his breath and his anger without finding his wits. He surged back to his feet, face red and fists clenched, and jumped. Carla executed a perfect back spin kick, catching his jaw with the side of her shoe. He dropped like a sack of dog food.

It took him longer to get up this time, but eventually he did, still angry but perhaps a bit scared, finally. Carla waited calmly, relaxed, and the man rushed her. *Big mistake.* Derek remembered vividly what had happened when he tried the same thing. Carla stepped aside and hit him twice as he passed, her arms blurring. The third blow lofted him up and into the air. He flew clear out of the intersection, landing with a sickening thump on the grass. This time he didn't move, so Carla waved at Derek. He got out and looked at her over the hood.

"Nice car," she said. "I like the color."

Without a word, Derek reached back into the truck and grabbed his bags. Carla popped the trunk on the Infiniti and he piled his stuff inside. She dropped her bag in and closed the trunk.

"Hey," he said, grabbing her arm as she turned away, "do you think you might have over-reacted a little? You were the one who didn't stop."

"I was ready to apologize, but the son of a bitch spat in my face. He didn't need to do that. I've had a rough morning." She pulled her arm loose, but Derek grabbed it again.

"I'm driving," he said.

Carla shrugged and walked across the street to lean over the prone businessman. Derek couldn't tell if he was conscious or not.

"Sorry," she said. "Try being more polite next time."

They got in the car and Derek pulled off the curb and drove away. Carla played with the radio for a moment, then found the knob that reclined her seat. She settled in and sighed contentedly.

"Nice car," she said, closing her eyes.

"How can you fight like that when I just blew you up a few hours ago?"

"What do you mean? I should feel love and compassion for all living things because a building fell on me?"

"No... I mean, aren't you sore?"

"Yes." She shifted and grunted softly as if to prove it.

"But you tossed that guy like he was a bag of marshmallows."

"You know what you lack, Derek?" She looked at him seriously before closing her eyes again. "Focus."

Focus? How about psychosis? He drove for a moment in silence until he realized he had no idea where they were.

"Where are we going?"

"Find us a nice, quiet, secluded motel. I have to figure out how to get Philippe."

"Philippe? He's either dead or in federal prison by now."

"I doubt it," she said. "I don't remember what happened just before the first bomb went off, but he wasn't around when you showed up, was he?"

Derek shook his head, but she had her eyes closed. "No."

"He must've found someplace to hide. Now that he knows he can't ever get his bombs back, there's nothing left for him but revenge. He'll come looking for me, but I'm not going to wait for him this time."

"What do you mean?"

"We've been hunted long enough," Carla said. "It's time to become the hunters."

Chapter 38

Gugliemo watched the FBI agents from the seafood restaurant across the street from the ruined building. They're like ants, he thought: individually mindless, but collectively organized, purposeful, and dangerous. They'd been scurrying around as if someone had poked their colony with a stick, but now the snipers were gone and a lot of agents were leaving. The show was over.

He and Maroni's stooges had been watching from this booth all night. Gugliemo knew the restaurant's owner, Eric Sostanza. Sostanza had fawned all over them, but Broca, Maroni's man, had told Sostanza to get lost, and Gugliemo was once again surrounded by men who were, if not enemies, certainly not friends.

He'd napped as well as he could, crowded into a booth at the big round window with four of Maroni's goons. They'd been noisy all night, especially after helping themselves to a few bottles of wine—joking and smoking, jostling him occasionally and probably not by accident. When he'd suggested that he move to the next booth, they told him to shut up and do what he did best: sleep.

The booming, amplified voice had startled him awake, and when the explosions began, he and Maroni's men had laughed together, finally finding something in common. He loved watching the Feds get it up the ass, but when it was over he was still stuck with these morons who, for all he knew, had been ordered to hit *him* after they bagged Citrullo. He hadn't decided yet what to do about that.

Not that her capture was imminent. A little while ago, Citrullo had been surrounded by fifty Feds in a brick building with only one door—and she'd escaped. It was a drastic but brilliant solution to simply blow out a new exit. How had she managed to do it without shredding herself? He was dying to ask her, but not right away. The longer it took to nab her, the longer he could put off his own confrontation with Broca and his gang of idiots.

"Hey," Osoteo said. "They're taking down the roadblocks. Maybe we should go now."

Gugliemo looked at the bald, bullet-headed man with distaste. The oaf held a cigarette loosely in his huge hand, ignoring the fact that they were sitting in a non-smoking section.

"Good idea," Broca said. He took out a comb and slicked back his already slicked-back hair. "Hey, I'm getting hungry. You guys want to eat here?"

The restaurant had been open for lunch for half an hour, but no diners had been brave or stupid enough to get through the roadblock. The waiters in their prissy little black and red uniforms had been eying Gugliemo and the others uncomfortably for some time. Gugliemo had spotted one or two of the waitresses he'd like to get to know, but that was impossible with Broca and his crude peasants around. He'd have to come back when this was over.

"Fish?" one of the other men said. "You gotta be kidding me."

"I got an idea," Osoteo said. He pulled a book out of his jacket pocket. Gugliemo groaned when he saw it: *Seattle's Best Places. Tourists!* Osoteo flipped through pages with his spatulate fingers until he found what he was looking for. "There's a terrific Mexican place down near the Market." He scanned the short article, following along with a finger as he quoted. "Authentic Jalisco food. Homemade tortillas. Fantastic pork dishes. Quesadillas to die for. Best margaritas in Seattle."

"All *right,* Mexican!" the fish-hater said.

"Yeah, I could do Mexican," Broca said.

"I hate Mexican food," Gugliemo complained.

"Good," Broca said, clapping him congenially on the shoulder. "Let's go."

* * *

Shimon Eitan watched the mobsters leave the restaurant and pile into their big, black sedan. The car was a ridiculous stereotype: it screamed "Mafia."

These men were either stupid or ostentatious, which in their business was almost the same thing. From the front passenger seat of their Range Rover, parked in front of the next building, Eitan got a good look at them.

"Did you see him?" he asked Yosef, who was sitting behind the wheel. The other four members of the kidon team sat quietly in the back, restrained by professionalism from cursing their bad luck and the FBI's incompetence.

"Yes. He was one of the drivers in Calgary."

The thin, sickly-looking one had been manhandled into the sedan by four large, laughing men. The thin one wasn't a captive, precisely, but he wasn't an equal, either: an underling, a servant, or possibly a jester. In any case, his presence confirmed the link between these mobsters and the ones who had stormed Sarah Citrullo's house in Calgary. The Lincoln drove away.

"What should I do?" Yosef said.

"Follow them. It's all over here."

He didn't need to say what everyone was thinking.

They tailed the Lincoln at a discreet distance into the heart of Seattle. After driving through run-down, deserted neighborhoods where paper blew in the street and the few pedestrians scurried alone, hunched over as if afraid of the sky, they entered a clean, busy area where the buildings were all either new or recently refurbished. Crowds of well-dressed people walked by in pairs or larger groups. Yosef followed the black Lincoln into a parking lot and they watched the gangsters walk to a nearby Mexican restaurant and go inside.

Eitan led his men to a small bistro directly across the street from the Mexican place. The cafe was nearly deserted: a solitary man sat drinking a beer and reading a newspaper halfway down the bar that ran along the long wall. They sat at a large table by the window.

A thin woman, dressed in black leggings and a tight black sweater, came out of the back with menus and a tray of water glasses. She wasn't wearing a bra. Her breasts were not large, but they stretched the sweater in a provocative way, and she smiled at Eitan as she handed out the water. *I have to finish this job quickly and get back home.* Back to civilization, where the women had some sense of modesty.

When the waitress left, Eitan rapped the table and his men set down their menus and water.

"We must decide now," he said. "These men are an impediment to our mission. They got in our way before, and they may do so again."

"I agree," Yosef said. "If not for them, we would have eliminated Citrullo in Calgary and we'd be home by now."

Everyone but Efraim nodded. If things had gone as planned in Canada, the FBI would have arrived too late to interfere. They'd have found Citrullo's body, along with her mother's and Narr's, and been left with only questions. Instead they had witnessed one more instance of Citrullo's apparent invulnerability. Today's embarrassing lesson was still smoking down by Lake Union, and Citrullo was free once more. Eitan wanted to finish this *now*.

Efraim broke the silence. "This is wrong. Only one of these men was in Calgary, and he was just a driver. The guilty men are all dead, killed by the woman they were sent to kill or capture."

"What do you suggest?" Yosef said. "That we let them stumble about and thwart us again?"

"I believe it's wrong to kill the innocent," Efraim said. "It's true that these men belong to the same organization that hindered us in Calgary, but we have no quarrel with the Mafia. They're disgusting, but that's not sufficient reason to terminate them. We kill only those with blood on their hands."

"Or out of necessity," Eitan said. "Or to prevent bloodshed."

"We can't safely complete our mission with these gangsters blundering about," Yosef said. "They're a menace to our objective and to us. And despite what you say, Efraim, they're scum and they deserve to die."

No one spoke for a long moment. Eitan sipped from his water.

"Anyone else?"

The other three—David, Elias, and Tamar—shook their heads. Efraim looked miserable, Yosef determined. Eitan was proud of these men that he had come to know well over the span of a dozen missions. What he admired most after their austere professionalism was that they spoke if they had something to say, and otherwise kept their mouths shut. He regretted that they were only six against the five mobsters. Like the FBI, the Mossad preferred to engage the enemy only on its own terms, and with overwhelming force. Nevertheless...

"Yosef is right," Eitan said. "We'll hit them as soon as they leave the restaurant. In the meantime, have something to eat." He turned to look back at the kitchen. "Where is that whore waitress?"

* * *

Gugliemo took another bite of enchilada and gagged. He dropped his fork, wiped his mouth, and took a drink of water. *How can anyone eat this shit?* He'd ordered the crab enchiladas just to irritate the young punk who hated fish—he could never remember his name. They'd sounded good on the menu, but this soggy mess was inedible.

The ambiance didn't help. Piñatas and straw sombreros hung from the rafters, and huge clusters of hot peppers dangled in the corners of the room. The blaring, insistent music and whining singers were giving him a headache. But Broca's men were having the time of their lives, laughing and guzzling Coronas and wolfing down the gooey, over-spiced food. He hoped they all got the runs.

"Hey, I heard a great joke the other day," Osoteo said.

"Let's hear it," Fish-hater said.

"Okay. Let's see... okay, I got it. Why do Italians hate Jehovah's Witnesses?"

"I dunno."

"Italians hate *any* witnesses."

The other men choked, recovered, and pounded on the table, laughing. Gugliemo wished he still had the gun that Broca had taken away from him in Calgary. He'd shoot every one of these stupid, mother-humping, steroid-pumped, cockroach-brained peasants right between the eyes, and let their bloody faces fall into their bean burritos and *carnitas de casa*. Then he'd go get some real food, at his favorite Italian restaurant, where they made the pasta fresh every day, in small quantities. They had a lasagna that was heaven on earth, so light it almost floated off the plate—

"Hey, stupid," Broca said. "What's the matter, you don't like the food?"

"He ordered fish," Fish-hater said. "The guy's a dope. He coulda got fish back at the other place."

Crab is not a fish, asshole.

"Hey, Gugliemo," Broca said, standing up. "Here comes the check. Your turn to pay."

He walked off toward the restrooms, laughing. Gugliemo sullenly dropped some bills on the check and put his wallet away.

"What's the matter with you?" Osoteo said, chucking him on the shoulder. "That's only three percent tip."

"The service sucked," Gugliemo said, "and the food was dog shit."

"You're mistaken," Osoteo said, leaning toward him menacingly. "The service was flawless and the food was ambrosia. Leave twenty percent."

Gugliemo tossed more money on the table. Osoteo leaned back and grinned at him. Broca returned and the rest of them stood up.

The morning clouds were almost gone, leaving behind a washed-out winter sky. The alley outside the restaurant was in deep shadow, which seemed appropriate to Gugliemo, considering how shitty his life was going. He was sick of winter, sick of the rain, and he wanted summer. He thought of his favorite summer pastime, boating on Puget Sound. He would anchor way out in the Sound, far away from the ferry and shipping routes, with no one else in sight and the city just a glimmer on the distant shore. His boat would rock on the gentle waves, while a willing, stacked blonde slowly untied her bikini...

Gugliemo looked up as a movement caught his eye. Six men were crossing the street toward him. They all had short, dark hair, all wore similar casual clothing. He wondered if they were a post-grunge rock band, or perhaps software engineers. There was something unusual about the way they walked...

Osoteo, leading them back to the car, slowed down to let the group walk in front of them, but one of the men veered straight at him. Broca and his thugs were reaching to draw as they went down. The shots were strangely quiet. Were these guys Feds? They wouldn't just shoot, would they?

He found himself standing alone. Maroni's men lay dead on the sidewalk around him. Five of the executioners were already walking calmly away with their guns holstered. The last one, a startlingly handsome man with a cleft chin, faced Gugliemo with a grim smile on his lips and a pistol trained rock-steady on Gugliemo's chest.

Gugliemo saw in his eyes something he'd never seen before; he wasn't quite sure what it was. He'd known psychopaths, vicious killers, and twisted, demented men who enjoyed giving and taking pain as if it were sex, but he'd never seen anything like this, not even in the eyes of John Maroni. His blood ran cold and he held out a shaking hand.

"Who—" he said, but the bullets slammed into his chest with a searing pain.

He was lying on the ground. It was impossible to breathe, and he couldn't feel his arms or his legs. His vision fuzzed over, and narrowed down until the only thing he could see was his murderer raising the gun for the final shot. For a brief moment, Gugliemo realized that what he'd seen in the man's eyes was his own death.

Chapter 39

Seattle, Washington
Saturday, March 4, 4:14 p.m.

Carla opened her eyes to another cheap motel room. She must have fallen asleep. The afternoon light was fading. The room was quiet, only the ever-present traffic noise in the background. Derek was sleeping in a low-backed chair by the doorway, slumped down so his head was supported by the back. It was amazing that he hadn't been crippled by his bad posture.

As she sat up on the bed, Carla felt a pang of homesickness. She missed the sunshine and Mediterranean climate of Tel Aviv. The dreary winter days and constant *weather* here were so depressing.

Snap out of it.

She got up, saw herself in the bathroom mirror, and froze in dismay. Large bruises were forming on her right cheekbone and left temple, and her right eye was swollen partially shut. A series of very fine, parallel scratches on her forehead pointed like the feathers of an arrow to a serious abrasion at the scalp line. She really didn't want to know what the rest of her body looked like.

She felt old. Her back was stiff and every breath hurt her ribs. All of her limbs felt creaky and her head was starting to pound. She found a bottle of aspirin in her duffel and washed down four pills with a glass of water. She almost laughed and nearly choked when she discovered that it hurt to swallow. *Well, when you hurt, there's only one thing to do.*

Her groans woke Derek. He stirred and sat up, rubbed his face with both hands, and watched her quietly. Carla continued her stretching exercises, though each motion sent spears of agony shooting up her back. She tried unsuccessfully to touch her toes, grunting with pain at each attempt. Derek stood up and announced that he was going out for a paper.

By the time he returned, she was warmed up and ready to stop. He plopped down in the chair by the door and started studying the front page. Carla did a last few slow crunches and climbed to her feet. She was breathing hard, but she felt much better. She grabbed a towel from the bathroom and stood behind Derek, looking down at the paper and wiping the sweat off her face and neck.

"We made the front page," Derek said. "With pictures."

A large color photograph of the foundry dominated the page, capped by the headline: "Terrorist bombs destroy building." Smoke rose from the collapsed building, fire trucks and police cars filled the foreground, and dozens of serious-looking officials stood by. By the time this picture had been taken, of course, the story was already over. Carla leaned in closer to read the text, but Derek jerked the paper up to stare at the bottom of the page.

"What?" she said.

"Look." He pointed to a smaller story in the bottom right corner: "Five shot near Pike Place Market."

William Gugliemo, head of a Seattle family that owned many of the local strip clubs, had been found shot dead outside a popular Mexican restaurant near the Market. Four other men, all from Las Vegas, had been killed as well. Employees of the restaurant stated that the men had just finished eating lunch. "They left a great tip," their server reported sadly. "At least they didn't die hungry." The police suspected that the execution-style shootings were mob-related.

Carla skimmed the rest: conflicting reports from eyewitnesses, suspected turf wars, drugs, FBI investigation. Derek turned to page nine to finish the story.

"My friends did us a favor," she said when he was done.

"What friends?"

"The kidon team."

"The Mossad assassins?"

"They must have got tired of tripping over your scuzzbos and decided to take them out."

"It says here that the mob did it."

"They're guessing," Carla said. "It's a classic Mossad hit. Broad daylight, a crowded city street, no coherent witnesses. Two taps to the chest, one to the head. Very fast, very clean."

"Well, that makes our life easier, right?"

"Maybe. But I'm a little worried. If they were irritated enough by Gugliemo to terminate him, they must have run into him before."

Derek didn't make the connection. Carla wondered what might have happened in Calgary if the mob hadn't tried to force their way into Sarah's house. Maybe she owed the dead scuzzbos an apology.

"Well," Derek said, "that's one group down. Now we've only got the FBI, the CIA, your assassins, and Philippe after us."

Carla shook her head again. "You've got it all wrong. Philippe's not after us any more. We're after him."

* * *

As dusk fell, Carla left the motel alone. Derek had had enough excitement for a while and was content to watch TV in their room while she went scouting. She would have talked him out of it if he'd wanted to come with her: she had to move quickly and silently, and even bruised as she was, he would have slowed her down.

A mile from the motel, Carla stopped at a shuttered-up gas station with half a dozen cars parked on the cracked asphalt lot, all with For Sale signs in their windows. The nicest one was a fairly new Ford Taurus sedan. She walked around it once, peeked in the windows, and kicked the tires, meanwhile checking out the neighborhood. Only one car went by while she examined the Taurus. No one seemed to be watching her, and the closest street lamp was burned out. This had been a commercial area once, but all of the low, brick buildings were vacant, their windows boarded up and their walls tagged with flowing, incomprehensible graffiti. She took the screwdriver out of her back pocket and swiftly removed the Taurus's plates.

A few blocks away, she pulled into the crowded parking lot of a church. A service was in progress: Carla could hear the wheezing of an organ swelling and dying on the breeze. She glanced around and, seeing no one, swapped the stolen plates.

Ten minutes later, she drove slowly by the remains of Philippe's foundry. A Seattle cop car was parked out front, keeping guard over the small piles of rubble that had spilled into the street. Wide yellow "POLICE

LINE DO NOT CROSS" tape roped off the building. Carla passed it, pulled over, and parked on the street.

The night was dark and cloudy, but she couldn't risk just going up and poking around. Bureau agents might still be watching the building and Seattle PD probably had another cruiser on Eighth. Even if the cop on Westlake was half-asleep, she didn't think she could sneak by him. So she walked behind the office buildings on the lake shore and stood in the shadows across the street from the demolished foundry.

She leaned against the damp siding and waited.

Chapter 40

Seattle, Washington
Saturday, March 4, 7:31 p.m.

The interminable day passed slowly. The small patch of sky visible through the chimney opening went gray as clouds gathered, and was now black with night. Philippe decided there was no point in waiting any longer: it had been hours since he'd heard a sound. He needed a bathroom and Lanotte needed a doctor.

The problem was how to get out. The entrance that Lanotte had hammered open was once more closed by bricks—as well as boards, chunks of concrete, metal bars, and other rubbish. The explosions had choked off their escape route but also saved them from being discovered. Throughout the day, Philippe had listened to the voices of firemen, policemen, and FBI agents, resigned to the idea that eventually someone would unblock the furnace mouth, discover them hiding within, and haul them away. Although the debris that blocked their escape had shifted a few times, and Philippe had heard someone moving the rubble around—probably searching for his body—no one had discovered their hiding place.

Lanotte was sleeping against the back wall of the furnace. Philippe shook his shoulder.

"Wake up, old friend," he said. "It's time to go."

Lanotte awoke reluctantly. He tried to raise his right hand to his face, but groaned in pain and set it back in his lap. Philippe saw him look upward.

"I don't think we can climb the chimney," Philippe said. Lanotte grunted in pain or amusement. "We must clear away the debris."

Philippe began exploring the small avalanche of junk that had fallen into the furnace. Most of it was small and rough, and he shoveled it aside, almost immediately cutting his hand on something. He sat down and tried kicking the blockage. Unseen objects clunked down outside, but there was no other effect. He reached behind him, trying to brace himself on the wall, but it was too far away.

Lanotte stirred at last, gently urging Philippe out of the way. He sat down as Philippe had, with his feet resting on the stuff blocking their escape.

"Sit with your back against mine," Lanotte said. "Brace your feet against the wall."

Philippe did this and grunted assent when Lanotte asked if he was ready. But he was not ready for the savage force of Lanotte's back slamming against his as Lanotte kicked at the rubble. The debris shifted a bit and Philippe tried to catch his breath. Lanotte kicked again, knocking the wind out of Philippe, then a third time. More debris fell into the furnace, and he was choking on the dust.

"Once more," Lanotte said.

Philippe tried to prepare himself, but Lanotte's kick threatened to snap his legs and collapse his lungs. He looked over his shoulder, but couldn't see anything. Lanotte shoved with his foot and debris rattled away. Philippe crawled around and saw dim light coming through the opening.

"Let me see if I can widen it," he said. Lanotte moved out of his way.

The hole was just large enough to put his arm through. By pushing around its edges, Philippe was able to enlarge it until he had cleared most of the opening. But the upper left corner was still blocked by what felt like a huge piece of wood. Shoving it had no effect.

"There's something big in the way," he said. "I'll crawl out and look at it from the other side."

It took over a minute for Philippe to twist his body through the blocked mouth of the furnace. He got one arm and shoulder out first, then contorted his body to free the other arm. He pulled himself down the meter-high slope of rubble until his feet were free, rolled the rest of the way down, and stood up.

Several of the ceiling beams had fallen, and one of them was blocking the furnace mouth. Strangely, opposite corners of the foundry were destroyed, but the rest of the building was intact. Philippe spent a few seconds trying to figure that out before giving it up and concentrating on the task at hand.

Lanotte could not get past the fallen beam; he'd barely squeezed through when the opening was unobstructed. Philippe knew he couldn't move the beam on his own, and Lanotte wouldn't be any use from inside with only one good arm. He looked around for a pry bar, but found nothing.

Perhaps he should leave Lanotte behind. Even if they managed to move the beam, it might make a lot of noise, and who knew what was waiting for them outside? Better to guarantee his own escape—find Carla and make her pay, in blood and pain, for what she'd done to him. He would add Lanotte's life to the debt she owed him for the warheads, for Chen, and for Jensen.

But Lanotte was his oldest friend; in fact, his last remaining friend. Philippe wanted to exact revenge on that Mossad bitch, but he couldn't imagine what he would do afterward if he left Lanotte behind to die or be captured. And even injured, Lanotte was an asset against Carla.

Philippe walked across the wreckage to the end of the beam. It rested on the floor near the edge of the furnace, buried in junk. He braced his feet, wrapped his arms around the beam, and tried to shift it, but it wouldn't budge.

"Lanotte." His friend stuck his head out of the furnace mouth. "This beam is blocking the hole. I can't move it by myself, but perhaps if you shove while I lift, we can slide it over."

Lanotte pushed his head out farther and looked up and down the length of the fallen beam.

"Yes," he said.

Lanotte's head disappeared. As Philippe prepared himself, he realized that he had a more urgent problem: if he tried anything strenuous, he would piss himself.

"Lanotte," Philippe said. The man's head reappeared. "Wait a moment. My bladder's about to burst."

Philippe ran into the ruins of the office and relieved himself in a corner. He sighed in relief, zipped himself up, and went back.

"Are you ready?" he said.

"Yes." Lanotte's voice was muffled.

Philippe bent down and wrapped his arms around the beam.

"Push," he said, and he pulled on the beam as hard as he could.

Nothing moved at first, but Philippe continued to pull until his back was a searing sheet of fire. Suddenly the beam shifted toward him. Philippe panicked, thinking the whole thing would crash to the floor, crushing him. He released it and stepped back, but his right foot caught in a hole in the debris and he fell over backward, twisting his ankle. He cried out in pain and terror, expecting the beam to fall on him—but it had stopped moving.

The wooden beam had shifted half a meter away from the furnace. Afraid of injuring his ankle further, Philippe didn't move as he watched Lanotte squirm out. Lanotte took his time, moving slowly, but finally his legs were free and he rolled to the bottom of the waist-high pile. They both lay still, breathing heavily.

Lanotte got up first, climbing slowly to his feet and shuffling over to where Philippe lay on his back with his foot still twisted beneath him. Very gently, Lanotte freed Philippe's foot and carefully probed his ankle with his hands.

"It doesn't feel broken," he said. "Try to stand on it."

He helped Philippe up. Gingerly, Philippe tried to put weight on the injured ankle and was rewarded with a vicious stabbing pain, as if someone had thrust a red-hot spike up his leg.

"Son of a bitch." He leaned on Lanotte and suddenly thought what a funny, hopeless pair they made. He was crippled and Lanotte had only one hand. *Come on, let's go get Carla.* He giggled but quickly regained self-control.

"Let me try again," he said. He set his right foot down softly, then slowly increased the pressure. The pain was less intense this time, and then he was standing unsteadily on his own. "It's not broken, but it hurts like the devil. Let's get out of here."

The only way out was over a pile of debris where the washroom had been. Philippe limped over to it and didn't even try to walk up, he simply fell to his hands and knees and crawled. Lanotte climbed slowly beside him, holding his right hand up out of harm's way. When they stood outside beneath the leaden sky, Philippe looked up at the rock wall rising beside them—it was out of the question for either of them to climb it—then along the back of the building.

"What do you suppose happened to Jensen?" Lanotte said.

"He's dead. He was standing right next to the wall that blew up."

"What about Carla?"

"I don't know. I'm too tired to think, and this ankle hurts like hell. Let's worry about her tomorrow, all right?"

"It's fine with me if we never worry about her again."

Philippe didn't know what that meant, and he hurt too much to care. He led the way toward the street, leaning on the foundry's brick wall in lieu of a crutch. His ankle was on fire.

At the front corner of the building, Philippe looked both ways. A police car was parked to their left, facing in their direction. To the right it was clear.

"Police car," he said, pointing in its direction. "One man. He'll see us if we walk out."

"Then we have to go the other way."

"I suppose." That meant they had to walk around three sides of the foundry. "Perhaps it's just as well. I parked the car that way."

They hobbled back the way they'd come, passed the debris pile, then continued down the long wall of the building. It seemed to take all night, but finally they reached the other front corner of the foundry. The cop was now to their right. Despite the cool air, Philippe was sweating. His ankle was throbbing malignantly.

"What should we do?" Lanotte said.

"What choices do we have? Did you bring your rocket launcher? Let's just walk away. Perhaps he won't see us, or if he does he may not realize where we came from."

So they stepped out into the open and walked as best they could away from the police car and the foundry. Philippe half-expected to hear a siren or the hammer being cocked on a revolver, but nothing happened. Shortly they came to the place where he'd parked the car, but the space was empty. He was so far from surprise that he realized he would have been astounded if it had actually been there. He patted his pockets, found the car keys, and tossed them into the street.

"What's wrong?" Lanotte said.

"They took the rental car. Come along, let's find a telephone."

They continued down the street. Philippe grimaced at every step; the throbbing in his ankle was getting worse. In a few blocks they found a phone booth in the parking lot of a convenience store, and the taxi arrived fifteen minutes later.

"Where to?" the driver said.

"Westin Hotel," Philippe said.

"Are you sure that's a good idea?" Lanotte said as the cab pulled away.

"I don't care any more." Philippe looked out the window at the brightly-lit houses drifting by. He wanted to blow up every one of these complacent, happy, ignorant Americans. "All I want is to lie down and sleep for two days, and I don't really care if it's in a hotel or a jail." *And then, when I'm rested, I want to skin Carla alive.*

They were downtown. The brilliant lights of a shopping center dazzled Philippe's eyes; in the afterglow he saw a rapid succession of vivid interior images. The red-haired slut from last night getting out of bed, shaking her long hair as she walked toward the bathroom; for just an instant she was haloed in the dark room by the bathroom light, and a tiny shaft of light had speared Philippe from between her thighs. Carla skidding to a stop with Philippe's gun pointed at her heart, a tiny *moue* of surprise on her lips; he should have shot her right then and to hell with the warheads. Jensen looking up from a half-crouch with a dripping towel held over his face, while tear gas fogged the room; taking a half-step toward Philippe before disappearing in a fury of sound and light.

Philippe was flooded with a resurgence of hate and resolve. *I swear to God, I'm not done yet. That bitch is dead.*

Chapter 41

Seattle, Washington
Saturday, March 4, 8:09 p.m.

A furtive movement caught Carla's eye. Philippe stuck his head out from around a corner of the foundry and she smiled. The paper had mentioned one dead man—obviously Jensen—but said nothing about prisoners. If the Bureau didn't have Philippe, he must be hiding inside the building somewhere, and she'd guessed that he'd wait until dark before coming out.

She had no idea where he'd hidden; the foundry had seemed barren and open, but then again, he'd had at least a day to get to know the place. Carla still couldn't remember exactly what had happened: her last clear memory was Philippe reaching for the blowtorch. Then Derek had pulled Jensen's body off her and they'd crawled out of the building. Ten minutes or more could have passed while she was unconscious, plenty of time for Philippe to hide himself.

He wouldn't step out from that corner, he'd be walking right in front of the cruiser. Would he try to climb the hill, as she and Derek had? There were police up there, too. In the hours she'd waited here, she'd seen the cop on duty up there get out of his car twice for a smoke.

Long minutes passed before Philippe appeared on the other side of the building. She didn't think he'd try to shoot his way out—he had no idea what the situation was and no transportation; he'd probably just try to walk away. He might get away with it, but probably not. If the cop glanced in his rear-view mirror he'd see Philippe, and after a few questions Philippe would be in custody and Carla would have lost her last chance at closure.

She didn't really have a choice, so she walked out into the open, heading straight for the police car.

When she'd covered half the distance, she could see that the cop was watching her. Out of the corner of her eye she saw Philippe and Lanotte come around the corner of the building and walk north on Westlake. They were facing away from her, intent on hobbling away. She continued walking through the parking lot toward the policeman. As she got closer to the street he stepped out of his car and hitched up his belt.

"This is a restricted area, miss," he said.

Carla stopped with the full width of the street between them.

"Oh, sorry, officer," she said. "I was just on my way home—working late again. What happened? Was it really terrorists?"

"I can't say. The FBI is still investigating."

"Oh. Okay. Well, I don't want to bother you. Thanks."

"No bother. Good night."

"Good night."

She headed toward her car. She was dying to look back and see where Philippe had gone, but she walked at a normal pace until she reached the Infiniti. She was astonished that she'd been allowed to walk away; she'd been expecting a fight, or at least to have to run for it. Was it possible the Bureau was *not* still watching the foundry? The cop hadn't recognized her—hadn't he been briefed? Were they sloppy or were they letting her go so they could follow her?

A moment later, she waved as she drove by the cop, and he waved back. She passed Philippe and Lanotte walking north on Westlake. Philippe was limping and Lanotte cradled his right arm in his left. Carla smiled as she drove past: they were both injured. That would help.

She watched from a nearby parking lot as they waited for the taxi, then she followed it downtown.

* * *

"I don't believe it," Yosef said as they watched Citrullo walk out into the open.

"You lack faith," Tamar said from the back of the Land Rover, and David and Elias chuckled.

"It was a good bet that she would come back," Eitan said. "It smelled like unfinished business."

Eitan watched two men sneak out from behind the building and hobble away. Citrullo talked to the police officer for a moment and then walked in the opposite direction.

"What should I do?" Yosef said.

"Those men are the reason she came back," Eitan said. "But she's the client, so we stay with her. No—" He reached out as Yosef was about to start the vehicle. "Wait a moment. Hand me the binoculars."

Eitan watched Citrullo walk away. He was about to tell Yosef to drive after her when she got into a car and drove past them. He nodded and they followed her at a safe distance.

* * *

The taxi stopped in front of the Westin Hotel, paused for a moment, then continued without letting any passengers out. Carla pulled over and watched it turn right at the next street, then followed it around the corner. The cab turned right again and stopped at the hotel's lounge entrance. As Carla drove past, Philippe and Lanotte climbed out stiffly and went into the building.

Carla parked her car and walked back to the hotel. Her body ached and the stiffness was coming back, but she ignored it and strode briskly, heading to the main entrance instead of following them into the lounge. By the time she got to the revolving door, she was breathing heavily. *Next time,* I'll *set the bombs and* Derek *can get blown up.*

She took an escalator up to the lobby and stepped aside to survey the place. Chandeliers and sconces filled the large space with a golden light that glittered off bronze fixtures and marble. On her left, couples and groups of men in suits lounged in an open area, drinking and laughing while a stout young man in a tuxedo botched a Fats Waller song on a baby grand piano. To her right was the reception desk, and straight ahead, far down a long hall, were the elevators to the north tower. The south tower was behind her.

She wanted Philippe's room number, but they wouldn't just give it to her, even if she knew what name he'd used to register. As she pondered, an elderly man in a business suit came up the escalator and strode off toward the north elevators.

What was it Philippe said in his e-mail? They were settling some business of Jensen's?

She walked up to reception, where a young blonde woman stood behind the counter's gleaming brass and dark wood. She was a mannequin: perfect skin, black suit, stiff white shirt. She looked up from shuffling index cards and involuntarily grimaced at Carla's appearance, but recovered gracefully and asked if she could help.

"Car accident," Carla said, gesturing at her face.

"Of course, ma'am." The clerk smiled sympathetically. "What can I do for you?"

"I'm looking for a friend of mine, David Jensen? I think he checked in a few days ago."

"Just a moment, please." The clerk stepped over to a computer terminal and typed. "Yes, ma'am, here he is. I can ring him for you if you like."

Idiot... Oh, give him a break, he's dead.

"Can you give me his room number? I'm early, I can just go on up."

"Sorry, ma'am, we're not permitted to do that, but I can call him for you."

Carla nodded and the clerk dialed the number and handed her the phone. Of course, no one answered it, so she handed it back.

"No answer."

"You can leave a message if you like."

Carla pretended to think about it. "No, thanks, I'll just wait for him down here as we originally planned."

"You're welcome, ma'am."

Carla turned away from the desk. *Now what?* Directly ahead of her was an overstuffed sofa and a small table with a hotel phone. She laughed to herself and sat down beside the phone, sinking deeply into the cushions. Around the buttons were dialing instructions for various hotel services. Carla picked up the receiver and punched in a number.

"Room service, may I help you?" a woman's voice said.

"Yes," Carla said. "This is Mrs. David Jensen. My husband asked me to order dinner for him before I went out, and I almost forgot. I'm in the lobby and I'd really rather not go all the way back up..."

"Of course, ma'am. Room number, please?"

"Um..." Carla let the silence drag out for a moment.

"Just a moment, Mrs. Jensen, I can find the number here... 1436, is that right?"

"Yes, of course, that's it."

"And what would you like to order?"

"Mr. Jensen would like your best steak, rare, French fries, a salad with Thousand Island dressing, and... Oh my. I forgot to ask him what he wants for dessert. May I call you back?"

"Of course, Mrs. Jensen. We'll hold the order."

"Thank you, I'll just be a minute."

Carla hung up and walked back to the escalators. Riding down to the street, she smiled to herself. If Philippe was going to be that stupid, he didn't deserve to live.

* * *

Philippe was feeling reckless, but not stupid. If the FBI had Jensen's body they knew his identity. They probably knew where he was staying, and they'd be watching the hotel lobby. He and Lanotte waited just inside the doorway that led from the bar to the lobby. The north tower elevators were only a few steps away. When the bell rang they hurried out, catching the elevator door just as it was closing.

Lanotte followed him into his room. Philippe called the concierge and asked for a first aid kit, a good one. The woman asked if anything was wrong and offered to call for medical assistance. Philippe demurred, saying that he needed it for the next day but would like to have it as soon as possible as they would be going out quite early. While they waited, he took a quick, scalding shower. His hands were raw and covered with small cuts, but there was nothing seriously wrong with him other than the sprained ankle. Someone knocked at the door half an hour later, and Philippe answered in his robe. A smiling, curious bellboy handed him the first aid kit, but Philippe gave him nothing but a big tip.

They went into the bathroom. Sometime during the long day, Lanotte had tied a strip of cloth around his wrist, and Philippe soaked it in warm water until the blood-soaked rag could be peeled away. The wound was puffy and red, probably already infected. Philippe poured hydrogen peroxide over it and Lanotte flinched without moving or making a sound.

"Can you straighten your hand?" Philippe said.

It was cocked back as if he were waving. He tried moving it and said no.

"You need a doctor. I think a tendon will have to be reattached."

"They'll call the police."

"Perhaps. But your hand is worthless like this. You can't shoot left-handed, can you?" Lanotte grunted a negative. "How will you wring Carla's neck if you can't make a fist?"

"I'll use my legs," Lanotte said, so seriously that Philippe burst out laughing.

He smeared some antiseptic cream on both sides of the wound and bound it with gauze.

"I'm going to get some ice."

He limped down the curving hall to the machine and filled his ice bucket. Lanotte watched glumly from a chair as Philippe filled a towel with ice and took the other chair, holding the cold pack against his throbbing ankle. After several minutes, Lanotte cleared his throat.

"Perhaps..." he said, but ran down and had to start again a moment later. "Perhaps we should admit that we've failed." Philippe frowned but said nothing. "The warheads are gone, Philippe. We'll never get them back. We tried to take revenge on Carla, and look at us."

Philippe sighed and shifted the ice. The cold hurt, but he knew he should hold it there as long as he could.

"What do you suggest we do? Start over?"

"I don't think I can do that. I'm tired, Philippe."

"What are you saying?" He was getting angry now. "You just want to give up? Let the bitch go? Let her keep our warheads, let Jensen's murder go unavenged, forget everything? Two years of work, you just want to throw that away?"

Lanotte looked up at the ceiling. He settled his bandaged arm more comfortably and looked back at Philippe.

"Yes," he said.

"You've—"

"Let me speak, Philippe. Forget Carla. If we find her again, she'll kill you. She almost killed you this time, and she was tied hand and foot! And forget your wives, too—just ditch them. What are they good for but to spend your money? Clean out their accounts and sell the house in France. I have a little money my parents left me, and together it should be enough to disappear. Let's find a quiet, cheap place in Tahiti where you can drink and screw in peace for the rest of your life."

Philippe was astonished. He and Lanotte had been friends since grammar school, and that was by far the longest speech he'd ever heard the man utter.

"I can't believe what I'm hearing," Philippe said. "You want me to admit defeat and slink off the battlefield?"

"What is there left to win?"

"Honor. Revenge. Blood." Philippe threw the ice pack in the direction of the bathroom. "I don't know. What do you want?"

"I want to go home," Lanotte said. "I want to get out of this filthy business. I want to stop thinking about weapons and killing and fighting." Philippe stared at him in amazement. "I don't care about the money, Philippe! I never did. Let's cut our losses and get out of here."

"What about Jensen? Don't you want to avenge his death?"

"What are you talking about?" Lanotte said. "She was tied up when the explosion happened."

"You know what I mean. She arranged it. It was her idea."

"For all I know, the FBI bombed the building and Carla died in the explosion."

"Bullshit! She's alive. And the FBI didn't blow us up, she did I'm going to find her, I'm going to skin her alive, and I'm going to make a shirt out of her skin."

Lanotte sighed and settled down into his chair, closing his eyes.

"Are you going to sleep?"

"Yes."

"Don't you want the bed? Don't you want to sleep in your own room?"

"No," Lanotte said. In a moment, he was snoring.

My God, he's acting strangely. It must be the stress. Not every day did a building crash down around one's ears. Philippe lay down on the bed in his robe, wondering if he'd be able to sleep at all. The moment he closed his eyes, he was gone.

* * *

Driving back to get Derek, Carla listened to a soft jazz station on the radio and daydreamed about going home again after all these years. It was because she was *not* paying attention that she detected a pattern in the traffic behind her. Half a dozen pairs of headlights were visible in the rear view mirror. None of the cars was doing anything unusual, but she was convinced that one of them was following her.

The next red light was a small side street. When the light turned green, Carla drove into the intersection and without warning turned right. The car behind her honked twice and gunned its engine, speeding away. She kept her speed down, watching the mirror. Three more cars went through the intersection, then one turned after her and followed slowly, maintaining its distance.

Carla turned left onto the next street, a narrow two-lane of boarded up brick buildings and vacant, weedy lots. She drove slowly until the car passed by behind her. Then she stopped in the middle of a block and waited.

Mossad agents were trained in operational security. Standard procedure when you were being followed was not to try to lose the tail—if you could no longer see them, it might simply mean that the second team was better than the first. The correct thing was to stop doing whatever you were doing and let them follow you to the laundromat or the grocery store. Better to postpone the mission than risk being tailed to it.

Fuck standard procedure. She would never have a better chance at Philippe, and she couldn't afford to have these guys, whoever they were, follow her back to the motel. And if it *was* the kidon following her, they intended to kill her.

A few blocks ahead, a sport utility vehicle crossed into the intersection. It drove slowly until its driver could see her, then it suddenly sped up. Carla smiled: he'd panicked.

She made a quick U-turn that took her up onto the sidewalk. At the next alley she turned left and sped up, swerving around parked and derelict cars and Dumpsters, then turned left again onto another minor street. She had no idea where she was going, but this maze of closed businesses and lonely, broken-down houses was perfect for getting lost. She turned into another alley at random and parked up close to a garage that looked ready to cave in, turned off the headlights, and waited.

She pondered whether it was the kidon or the FBI who had found her. They must have picked her up at the foundry and followed her to the Westin. If it was the kidon, their only hope now was to go back to Philippe's hotel and wait for her to show up. *That might not be a bad thing.* It was risky to go home without neutralizing the assassins: they might kill her right on her own doorstep. For the first time she had a chance to predict their next move.

While she waited to be sure she'd lost them, a plan pieced itself together in her mind. It amused her to think that the best punishment for Philippe might be to leave him alive, but defanged.

Three pedestrians turned the corner ahead and started toward her. Carla drew her pistol and prepared to peel out if necessary, but as they came closer she saw that it was neither FBI nor kidon—just three young black men. She'd heard stories about the inner cities in America, so she kept her gun out, but the teenagers merely glanced at her curiously as they passed, hands in pockets, talking earnestly among themselves.

Fifteen minutes later, Carla put her gun away and pulled out, turning her lights back on. It took several minutes of hunting to find a street she knew from her maps, but soon she was roaring up an entrance ramp to I-5. As she merged into traffic, she kept one eye on her rear view mirror until the ramp disappeared into the darkness and headlights behind her. No one had followed her onto the freeway, so she slowed down and headed back to the motel.

* * *

"That was unfortunate," Eitan said. Yosef gripped the Range Rover's steering wheel as if he would tear it off, knuckles white and face stiff with embarrassment. Eitan reached up and turned on the reading lamp, studying a map of Seattle. The others sat in the rear, glumly silent.

"Sorry, sir," Yosef said finally.

Eitan approved of the fact that Yosef had waited to get his voice under control before speaking. His clumsy mistake would have flunked him out of the Academy.

"Does anyone have a suggestion?" Eitan said.

"Perhaps," Tamar said, "we should go back to the hotel and wait for her there. She may return."

"I don't see any alternative," Eitan said. Yosef still stared straight ahead, afraid to look at his superior. "Take us back to the Westin Hotel."

"Yes, sir," Yosef said. He relaxed his death grip on the wheel and pulled back into traffic.

"We will attempt to discover what she was doing there. And perhaps she'll return. If not, tomorrow we start searching again."

They still had other leads, among them the name Derek Narr. But Eitan was betting that Citrullo would come back to the Westin and finish her business there; she hadn't been inside for more than ten minutes. He still reviled her as a traitor, but he was coming to remember how much he admired her tradecraft and her *chutzpa*. He hoped they'd have a few moments to speak before he had to kill her.

Chapter 42

Seattle, Washington
Saturday, March 4, 9:52 p.m.

It took all of Chapa's self-control not to stare or crack a smile. He'd called a status meeting to review the investigation into the foundry bombing, and Walkenshaw had unexpectedly walked into his office and sat down stiffly. Chapa remembered thinking, when they first met last Monday, that the CIA agent looked ill-used. Now he looked like the loser in a championship fight. The left side of his jaw was purple with a hint of yellow, his left wrist was in a brace, and his right arm was in a cast from fingers to shoulder.

"How're you feeling?" Chapa said.

"Just fine, thanks," Walkenshaw replied. He was studying a folder on his lap, turning the pages awkwardly with his left hand, avoiding eye contact.

"When did you get out of the hospital?"

"This morning."

He obviously didn't want to talk about it, so Chapa let it go. Shaffer scurried in late, as usual, and took the chair beside Chapa's desk. After a moment she looked up from sorting the papers on her clipboard to examine Walkenshaw.

"You've looked worse," she said. He glared at her.

"Let's get started," Chapa said. "Where are Frieder and Holbrook?"

"They're back at the foundry," Shaffer said.

"What... Why?"

"They went back to check out an idea Frieder had, and... it panned out."

"Cut the dramatic buildup, Shaffer, and tell me what they found."

"Yes, sir. Okay, Kantrowitz said he saw Carla and a man coming up the hill. We assumed that since four people went in, and there was only one body in the building, three must've left. I suggested that there were really two men with Carla, and Kantrowitz just didn't see the second one."

"Right."

"Frieder didn't buy that. He went back to the foundry and talked to the cop stationed outside on Westlake, who reported that nothing had happened all evening—except that a woman stopped on her way home from work and talked to him briefly."

Chapa planted his elbows on his desk and dropped his head into his hands in despair.

"Yes, sir," Shaffer said. "He showed him Carla's picture and the cop said it was her."

"I don't fucking believe this," Chapa said.

"You pulled all your agents out?" Walkenshaw said, looking up for the first time.

"Yes, *Myron,* I did." Chapa raised his head. "The forensics and bomb teams stayed most of the day, and we had a crew looking for bodies under the rubble. After all the evidence was collected, we left."

"You should've left someone to watch the building."

"That's easy to say now, but there was no reason to think she'd come back, and I had to assign some agents to the Gugliemo assassination."

"They used unmarked cartridges—it was a Mossad hit."

"*No fucking kidding!*" He stood up abruptly, knocking his chair over, and turned to stare out the window. It was drizzling again. After a minute he calmed down, picked up his chair, and dropped back down in it.

"Sorry," he said. "Myron, give me a break. Tomorrow morning the SAC will rip off my head and hang it on his wall, but until then let's just skip the critiques, okay?"

"There's more," Shaffer said. Chapa sighed and gestured at her to bring it on. "Frieder went inside. He thought Carla might have been distracting the cop from something..."

"Just spit it out."

"You remember the furnace thing that stuck out into the room? It has an opening that was obscured by debris from the explosions. Someone was hiding inside and escaped after the search teams left."

"How could they have missed that?"

"The roof was unstable there," Shaffer said. "The teams were just looking for bodies under the rubble. They didn't want to shift anything more than necessary, especially the ceiling beams. The bolt-hole was half-hidden behind one of those."

Chapa rubbed his eyes and leaned back in his chair. "So now you think Kantrowitz was right: there was only one man with Carla, and it was Derek?"

"Yes, sir."

"Derek set the bombs, detonated them, went down into the collapsed building, grabbed his kidnapper, dragged her to safety, and blew up the Beemer to cover his escape."

Shaffer hesitated. "Correct."

"Well," Chapa said, "Derek has got to be the worst case of Stockholm Syndrome since Patty Hearst."

"I knew this guy once—" Walkenshaw said, but Chapa glared at him and he shut up.

"Anything else from Frieder?"

"No, sir. He's got a team checking out the furnace."

"All right, Carla and Derek are together again, and two of Frieder's bad guys are loose. What about the dead one?"

Shaffer passed him a sheet of paper.

"He had a Montana driver's license for David Jensen," she said. "That's his real name. We have his fingerprints on file, and they match the corpse."

"Why?" Chapa said. *Why did they have Jensen's prints?*

"Handgun permit. He's a U.S. citizen, but he's been missing for a couple of years. The IRS has a tick on his name: no returns filed since 1992."

"Who was he?"

"A physicist, sir."

Walkenshaw looked up at that.

"A physicist?" Chapa said, looking down at the sheet she'd given him.

"We know quite a lot about him, except where he's been for the last three years. He was born in 1960 in Helena, went to college at Cal Tech on a full scholarship, Ph.D. at Stanford, and worked on the SSC until it was canceled."

"SSC?"

"Superconducting Super Collider," Walkenshaw said. "A particle accelerator in Texas. Congress pulled the plug in '93."

"He was one of the first scientists fired," Shaffer said. "He must've found a new line of work."

"So we don't know who his associates are?"

"No, sir. The car we impounded was rented in his name at the airport on Thursday. He checked into the Westin downtown that same day."

"We have someone watching the hotel?"

"Yes, sir."

"Okay. I doubt they'd go back there, but look at the registrations, see who else checked in at the same time."

"Right." She made a note on her pad. "We're still investigating the Gugliemo hit. Carla didn't do it. The witnesses' accounts conflict, of course, but everyone says the hitters were men. Between two and eight guys, all tall, all short, wearing suits, wearing casual clothes; the usual. I think everyone hit the dirt at the first shot."

"Keep working it. Walkenshaw, you can help us out there, if you feel up to it."

"Sure."

"Next," Shaffer said, "we have a positive ID on Carla this morning shortly after she escaped." Chapa nodded; he'd heard some of this earlier. "Seattle PD investigated a car jacking in the U district. A local resident was almost hit by a pickup truck that didn't stop at a stop sign. When he got out to complain, the driver decked him and stole his car. He was taken to the hospital but released immediately." She smiled, but glanced at Walkenshaw's injuries and her smile vanished. "It took a while to get him to admit he was knocked out by a woman, but he picked Carla out of a sheaf of mug shots. The pickup was the one Derek rented in Idaho."

"When did the APB go out?"

"About eleven."

"She'll have changed the plates by now, but we should keep looking. What kind of car was it?"

"Infiniti Q45, dark blue."

"She's trading up," Chapa said. "How's the motel search going?"

"We're nearly done with the Eastside. Should we start on this side of the lake next?"

Chapa swiveled in his chair for a moment, trying to think if there was some obvious place he should be looking for her. The Eastside had seemed like a good bet.

"Yes," he said.

"I've got some interesting tidbits from the bomb guys," Shaffer said.

"Really."

He'd noticed her chumming up to the bomb squad all day. Was she interested in the subject or the crew?

"Bill Jacobson was in charge," Shaffer said. "He says they must have used over half a brick of C-4 in the five explosions."

"So they still have at least three bricks left."

"And some of the mechanisms survived. Bill said he's never seen anything quite like it." *So, we're on a first-name basis with the bomb squad.* "The detonators were wired into walkie-talkies. No exotic materials—you can pick them up at any Radio Shack."

"Well, let's talk to some Radio Shack people, then," Chapa said.

She made another note on her clipboard. "That's it."

Walkenshaw was still studying his folder, as if he hadn't been paying attention to their conversation.

"Walkenshaw?" Chapa said. The CIA agent raised his head and Chapa was startled again by the man's disconcerting gray eyes. "Any idea what's going on?"

"The physicist is... interesting. If you add him up with the guy Citrullo shot in Montana, it starts to make sense."

"What kind of sense?"

"An arms deal. A big one. My guess is something went wrong, and we're chasing after three groups of scumbags playing out a vendetta."

"I'm lost," Chapa said. "Where are you getting this shit?"

Walkenshaw held up one of the grainy photos from Derek's house; it was one of the two men who were now missing again.

"When I got these pictures this morning, I ran them through our ID system. At first I drew a blank, but then I overrode the filter that keeps dead guys from popping up. I know who this is. His name is Philippe Sottile, and he used to work for Jean Pequinot. Ever hear of him?"

Shaffer shook her head, but Chapa nodded. "Big arms dealer, right?"

"Right. He smuggled a lot of munitions into Afghanistan. Also Iraq, Pakistan, Bangladesh, Sri Lanka, Nicaragua, Peru, you name it. His entire organization, along with quite a few other bad guys, was wiped out in an international rat hunt a few years ago. Off the record, I can tell you that the Agency was involved, but most of the work was done by Interpol and the Mossad. The tips that started the raid came from..."

"John Hildreth," Shaffer said.

"Right. We thought Sottile had been killed along with the rest of Pequinot's men, but apparently not. It looks like he's coming out of retirement and Citrullo got involved somehow. She's ex-Mossad, I guess she'd fit right into his new organization."

"Okay, but what's with the physicist?"

Walkenshaw put the photo back into his folder. "If you're just moving rifles or surface-to-air missiles, you probably don't need a physicist. But what if you're selling something... bigger?"

"Bigger. Like what?"

"Nuclear weapons."

"Oh, Jesus," Chapa said.

"Don't worry," Walkenshaw said. "If something had reached the black market, we'd know about it. I think the deal fell through, and Sottile is going after Citrullo. Could be revenge, could be money, who knows? And the Mossad is probably chasing them both."

Chapa closed his eyes for a moment. It wasn't often that he felt out of his league. When he opened them again, Walkenshaw was grinning at him.

"Could get interesting, huh?" He looked at the clock on Chapa's desk. With both arms in casts, he couldn't have worn a watch unless he strapped it to his ankle. "I've got to run, got a meeting at eleven. I'll get started on the Gugliemo hit in the morning."

After he left, Chapa looked at Shaffer for a moment. It was late, and the later in the day it got, the more of her long, blonde hair had escaped from her ponytail. It was like an hourglass. Shaffer's round face was drawn and her eyelids drooped. None of them were getting much sleep, but they weren't making much progress, either.

"Want to get something to eat?" he said.

Neither of them had eaten since a takeout lunch from the deli near the foundry. Shaffer looked down at her clipboard and shook her head.

"Still a lot to do, sir," she said. She stood up and looked at him for a moment. "Maybe some other time."

Some other time. Chapa watched her leave. *After life gets back to normal.* Yeah, right. He was beginning to think that Carla would elude them forever.

Chapter 43

The elevator door opened on the fourteenth floor. Derek followed Carla out into King Midas's foyer. The golden colors of the lobby were echoed here: brass fittings, sconces throwing a romantic glow over the filigreed wallpaper, a small wooden table with a vase of daisies.

The core of the Westin's towers held the elevators and service areas, so the guest rooms, about a dozen per floor, were situated around the perimeter like wedges of pie with their points cut off. Carla walked to the second room on their left and put her ear to the door.

"This was Jensen's room," she said. "I doubt they're sharing, so Philippe will be in one of the adjacent ones."

"How do you know?"

"They always do that."

She led him to the next door. This room was also quiet, and no light shone through the peephole.

"Can you handle the lock?" she said.

The stainless steel box was smooth except for the key card slot and two tiny status lights. It wasn't one of the cheap ones with accessible screws, or he could've simply opened the cover and shorted the mechanism.

"I can open it," he said, "but it'll take a minute."

"Okay, I'll be guarding the elevator."

Derek watched her vanish around the curve of the hall. He unzipped his computer case and booted his PowerBook. While it started, he rummaged in the case and found a skeleton key card on a wide ribbon cable, plugged the cable into an adapter and attached that to the computer. When the machine was ready, he started the decoder program and inserted the card into the door lock. The lock clicked almost immediately. Derek opened the door an inch and hissed at Carla.

She came down the hallway with her pistol drawn. Derek moved out of the way as she swung the door open and slid into the dark room.

A moment later, she came back and gestured him inside. Derek picked up the open case and computer and went in. She flicked on the light, illuminating a king size bed jutting out from a corner toward the wall-to-wall windows. Carla flipped open the lid of a small suitcase on the bed and nudged the contents with the muzzle of her gun.

"This is Lanotte's," she said. "Philippe will either be next door or on the other side of Jensen's room."

"How do we know which?"

"Look at both." Derek was still holding his stuff. "Leave the case here," she said. "Just bring the computer."

Carla wedged a wooden hanger under the door and they went to the next room. She listened at the door, looked through the dark peephole, and gestured at him to get to work. The lock opened as easily as the last one. She disappeared into the room and returned a few moments later.

"It's a young couple, asleep," she said. "He's got to be in the other one."

The peephole for 1437 showed a light on, but the room was quiet. When the lock clicked open, Carla nudged the door open a crack.

"Draw your weapon," she said, "and come in behind me."

Derek set down the computer, pulled the gun out of his waistband, and followed her into the well-lit room.

* * *

Philippe heard a sound and came half awake. He listened for the noise to repeat, but when it didn't he rolled onto his side and drifted off again. Seconds later, he heard the door closing softly and jerked upright to see Carla and a strange man standing near the bathroom, covering him with drawn pistols.

He blinked back tears of rage and frustration. The indignity was too much, but he forced himself to calm down and relax his clenched fists. *At least she isn't smiling.* He might have lost all self-control if she were gloating, and she'd have shot him before he took two steps. *Be calm.* If she'd wanted him dead, he'd have died in his sleep.

He sat up against the headboard and adjusted his robe.

"What time is it?" he said.

"Almost twelve-thirty."

Philippe examined her face appreciatively: it was scratched and bruised even worse than his. He hoped it hurt.

Lanotte stirred in his chair, rubbing his neck with his left hand and yawning. He opened his eyes and took in the situation without surprise or anger; indeed, he looked almost grateful.

Philippe tried to think how to gain control of the situation. His sidearm was with his clothes in the bathroom, and he wasn't sure where Lanotte's pistol had gone. Well, then, first he had to discover what she wanted.

"I presume you're not going to shoot us," he said.

"Not unless you force me to," Carla said.

She jerked her head and her companion disappeared into the bathroom, returning in a minute with Philippe's gun. He showed it to Carla and put it in his coat pocket.

"Perhaps you had something more elaborate in mind," Philippe said. "One last fling, with a surprise ending?"

"Oh, there'll be a surprise," she said, smiling viciously. "But not the one you're afraid of. Derek, toss him his clothes."

The stranger went back into the bathroom.

"Derek? So this is the elusive Mr. Narr."

"This," Carla said, "is the guy who blew up your grubby little building."

Philippe caught his clothes without taking his eyes off Derek. The man was about Jensen's height but somewhat beefier, with a thick mustache over a square face. This was the tool Carla had used to kill Jensen and escape Philippe's justice. He filed that tidbit away for later.

"Get dressed, Philippe," Carla said.

He swung his legs off the bed, slipped on his briefs and his trousers, dropped the robe and finished dressing. When he was done he stood waiting for further orders, still trying to think of a way to turn the situation.

"Lanotte," Carla said, "I don't like you very much, but my business is with Philippe, not with you. So you're free to leave after we're gone. Go back to Brussels and meet a better class of people."

Lanotte stirred in his chair, cradling his right hand on his lap. "You know I can't let you have him."

"You have two choices. You can go home and live a happy life, or you can die in that chair."

"Lanotte, my friend," Philippe said, "do what she says. You can't help me any longer." Lanotte shook his head sharply, sending his long, dirty hair flying. Philippe sighed. "The demon is right. Go home and live a quiet life."

Lanotte looked resigned, which gave Philippe hope. The worst case was that he'd do what she said: go home and forget about him. But perhaps he'd come after them and manage to free him. At least he didn't look as if he would try anything foolish.

"Just one second," Carla said, "then we can go."

She nodded to Derek, who moved away from her to cover them. After shifting her gun to her left hand, she pulled a marking pen out of her hip pocket and swiftly wrote something on the wall. Philippe couldn't see it, and it took a moment before he realized that she was writing right to left. *Hebrew? What the devil is she doing?* She finished quickly, dropped the pen to the floor, and shifted her gun back to her right hand.

"Time to go," Carla said.

Philippe took a step toward the door, but Lanotte shoved him back with his injured forearm and surged up out of the chair. His enormous hand dwarfed the gun that was rising toward Carla, but before he could reach his feet or fully raise his weapon, her pistol fired. A small red spot appeared in the center of Lanotte's dirty shirt. The giant dropped back into the chair, his hands falling to the floor. Lanotte looked down at the blood on his shirt, looked up at Carla—bewildered—and peacefully closed his eyes. His chin sank to his chest.

"*Lanotte!*" Philippe said. "Jacques!"

He fell to his knees and felt his friend's neck. No pulse; he must be doing it wrong. Philippe hauled Lanotte's injured right arm up onto the chair, but the wrist was still.

This isn't possible. My only friend in the world, dead?

Before he knew it, Philippe was on his feet, rushing toward Carla, his vision narrowed down to the neck he was going to snap with his bare hands... Then he saw the gun pointing right between his eyes, and knew that if he took another step she'd kill him.

"We can end it right here," she said, "if that's what you want."

"I'm going to kill you," Philippe said.

"No," she said, "you're not."

She grabbed his arm and shoved him into the hall.

* * *

When the argument started behind the Westin's reception desk, Eitan set down the *New York Times* and strolled over. He interrupted a heated exchange between a young blonde woman and an equally young Oriental man.

"Excuse me," he said, pulling out his fake police badge and flashing it quickly. "Carl Rasonabe, FBI. What's the problem?"

"There's been a—" the young man said, but the woman interrupted him.

"Frank, let me tell it. I'm in charge." She turned to Eitan. "We've had reports of gunfire on fourteen. I think we should call the police, but Frank wants to check it out first." She was beginning to sound hysterical. "I've never had to deal with anything like this before, I'm just the assistant manager."

"What's your name?"

"Maria."

"Okay, Maria," Eitan said. "Frank is right. It's probably nothing, so let's hold off on calling the police until we know what happened. Now, where's the night manager?"

"He's, uh, he's out right now, at dinner." She stood a notch straighter and said, "He left me in charge."

"Good. Maria, let's go up and have a look around. Frank, you stay here and hold the fort, okay?"

The young man nodded, relieved to be left behind. Maria came around the desk and Eitan took her arm gently, gesturing for Yosef, who had also been waiting in the lounge, to come along. They all walked to the elevator together.

"What room was the disturbance in?" he said as they rode up.

"I'm not sure. The man in 1438 said it was in the next room, but I forgot to ask which side. So it's either 1437 or 1439."

Eitan stepped out of the elevator alone; Yosef kept her from following. The tightly curved hallway was empty, and 1438 was directly ahead. He gestured and Yosef urged Maria out into the hall.

"Ask him which room," Eitan said. "And please do it quietly."

Maria knocked softly at 1438. Eitan and Yosef stood to the sides with their pistols drawn. As they waited, Eitan noticed the curve of Maria's calf below her black pleated skirt. *Concentrate.* The door opened a hand's-breadth, to the extent of the chain. Eitan saw one eye and rumpled gray hair.

"Yes?" the man said.

"Sir," Maria whispered, "I'm the assistant manager. Which room was it?"

A finger poked around the corner of the door, pointing to their left. Then the hand withdrew and the door slammed shut.

Eitan led them to 1437. There was a light on inside, but the room was silent.

"Passkey?" he said, holding out his hand.

Maria set a plastic key card on his palm. Eitan pushed her back gently, inserted the card and, moving swiftly, opened the door and stepped inside with his pistol raised.

He was astonished to see a message written on the wall in Hebrew, but he ignored it for now and moved into the room. The first line had jumped out at him, though: "To complete your mission..."

Yosef followed him, moving wide to cover his right. Eitan glanced into the bathroom, but it was empty. Whatever had happened here was over. In a chair by the window, a huge dead man slumped, a small red blotch staining the center of his filthy shirt. *Right through the heart.* Clean—when the heart stopped beating, the bleeding would halt as well—but not very professional. It might have taken him up to a minute to die, plenty of time to shoot back. But this man had not fought back, he'd simply sat back and died. His gun lay on the floor near his left hand.

"This is one of the men who escaped the foundry," Yosef said.

They searched the room quickly, but found nothing of interest. Eitan was about to turn to the scrawled message when he heard a gasp. Maria had followed them in and was now standing by the foot of the bed, wide-eyed and even paler than before, staring at the corpse. Eitan nodded at Yosef, who ushered her outside, closing the door behind him.

Here is the handwriting on the wall.

> To complete your mission, meet me at 23:00 Sunday at the east end of Ship Canal Park. I have a gift for you, an enemy of Israel, whom I was sent undercover to ensnare. Your mission was part of my cover, Eitan. Let us talk before you shoot.

Eitan was startled and immensely puzzled. *How can she know my name?* He read the message again, then used his field knife to slit the wallpaper around it, peeled the message off the wall and put it into his coat pocket.

She must have guessed he'd be the first to arrive. Even if she were wrong, she could just cancel the meeting. *But how does she know my name?* Kidon team members never knew each other's real identities. Everyone on his team knew him only as Chaim, and Yosef, David, Tamar and the rest were all pseudonyms; he'd never met any of them socially.

For a moment, Eitan's determination wavered. If she knew his name, she might be telling the truth about his mission. Was it possible he'd been sent to kill her just to provide a convincing cover story?

Then he regained his composure. *Think of the people she's been consorting with.* She had access to every piece of filth in Europe. It was hard to believe, but she must've stumbled across someone who knew he was after her. Perhaps one of the Mossad's native agents had been bribed or tortured. Who knew? And she was very good: if anyone could compromise his identity, she could.

He refused to believe that fourteen months of hunting her had had no other purpose than to make the world believe she was a rogue. *His* mission was not meaningless!

This is irrelevant. His orders were to terminate her, and in the absence of countermanding orders, that was what he would do.

He left the room and, on the elevator back down to the lobby, calmly explained to Maria that she need not call the police.

"Our men will be here soon," he said, patting her arm.

He would deploy his men outside to watch all the exits. Citrullo must still be in the building, and he couldn't entrust the success of his mission to the ambush she had planned for him at Ship Canal Park.

Chapter 44

Seattle, Washington
  Sunday, March 5, 12:42 a.m.

If Carla had killed Philippe along with the big guy, the whole thing would be over. Derek was disappointed but he knew better than to ask what she needed him for.

Philippe didn't seem dangerous—he was battered, bruised, and limping badly. But Carla wasn't taking any chances: she covered him carefully while Derek packed up his computer. They got his computer case from Lanotte's room and she told him to head for the stairs.

Derek was surprised the hallway was empty. Running *toward* gunfire wasn't a survival trait, but that's what the people outside the foundry had done, and he'd expected a screaming mob when they left Philippe's room. *Why couldn't she use a silencer like in the movies?*

The metal stairway and unpainted sheetrock walls were lit by a single bare fluorescent bulb. He held the door open and Carla urged Philippe out onto the concrete landing. Derek was about to head down when she stopped him with a hand on his shoulder.

"Up," she said.

"What?"

"They'll expect us to go down. Go up."

"How far?"

She just pointed up the stairs with her pistol. Derek started climbing. Maybe she'd planned a clever and daring escape from the roof—it was only thirty-three floors up.

Philippe had a difficult time with the stairs, gripping the railing with both hands as he hopped up one step at a time on his left foot, keeping his weight off his right. Derek usually took them two at a time, but he didn't want to get too far ahead, so he was forced to trudge at a funereal pace.

"You'll just have to be patient," Philippe said, breathing heavily. Carla followed vigilantly, indifferent to their rate of progress.

Eventually they reached the landing at fifteen. Derek paused, hoping they were done, but she gestured at him to keep going. After what seemed an hour, she told him to stop at the seventeenth floor. Philippe leaned against the wall, gasping and sweating. Carla put her pistol under his chin.

"Listen to me, Philippe," she said. He nodded breathlessly. "The moment you're dead, I'm free. We're going to put our guns away and you're not going to try to escape. You can't run, but if you even twitch, I'll snap your neck like a wishbone. And if I can't reach you, I'll just shoot you—or Derek will." Philippe glanced at Derek, who smiled in agreement. "I don't care if we're surrounded by police or FBI or God's own angels—I'll kill you first and deal with the consequences later. Do you understand me?"

"Oh, yes," Philippe said. "I understand you perfectly."

"Good." Carla holstered her weapon and Derek pulled his coat aside to replace his gun in the small of his back. Philippe took out a handkerchief and wiped the sweat off his face. "Let's go," she said.

Derek opened the door to a hallway identical to the one they'd just left. Immediately to their right was a doorway into the core of the building with a sign that said "Not an exit."

"That must be the exit," Carla said. Derek grinned at her. "There should be a service elevator. Check it out."

The room was bigger than the guest rooms, full of shelving, work tables, cabinets, and cleaning equipment hanging on hooks. It was unoccupied. Derek spotted the service elevator and went back to get Carla and Philippe.

The elevator required a key. Carla handed Derek her picks and he quickly unlocked it, pressed the down button, and they waited.

In the silence, he suddenly remembered picking the lock on the FBI's service elevator, just a few blocks from here. He counted back and was startled to realize that was only nine days ago. It seemed like a lifetime, and the person he'd been before—the Derek who had never built a bomb, never killed a man, never seen a dead body outside a coffin—seemed impossibly remote. Beside those nine days, the first forty-two years of his life were indistinct and wispy, nothing but a dream.

Nothing was happening. He pushed the down button again. Philippe had caught his breath and Carla was looking twitchy.

"Shit," she said, "it must be locked down." She glanced around the room and found nothing to help. "We'll have to use the regular elevators."

They went back into the hallway and halfway around the tower to the elevator. The moment he pushed the button they could hear the cables hum. The car arrived, empty, and they stepped inside.

"Where to?" Derek said.

This elevator didn't go to the parking garage; to get there they'd have to transfer to another elevator in the lobby, which seemed like a bad idea. He noticed there was a thirteenth floor, but no buttons for six through nine.

"Push ten," she said.

"Service floors?"

"Maybe."

Philippe, leaning against the wall of the elevator car, cleared his throat. "I hope we're almost done walking. My ankle hurts."

"You can stop breathing any time you want to," Carla said. "Until then, shut up."

When the elevator stopped, they walked as quickly as Philippe could move to the stairwell at the end of the hall and down one flight. A sign on the door read, "Hotel staff only." It was locked, but Carla handed Derek the picks again and in a moment they were inside.

It looked like a small restaurant kitchen. Shining stainless steel tables were surrounded by floor-to-ceiling racks of pots, pans, tableware, and large cans of food. A pair of commercial refrigerators stood against one wall. As they went farther into the room, Derek spotted a black woman wearing a phone headset sitting at a computer station, filing her nails as she read from a thick book on the desk. She wore a light blue smock and her short hair was trapped in a hair net.

A young man in a white waiter's outfit bustled into view, stopping in mid-stride when he saw them. He frowned and was about to say something, but Carla drew her pistol, and instead he stepped back clumsily, raising his hands.

"Don't be alarmed," Carla said. The woman at the computer looked up and squealed, raising her hands, too. She looked *quite* alarmed. "My name is Susan Wertheimer. I'm an undercover cop. This—" she nodded her head at

Derek, "—is my partner. We caught this man breaking into a room upstairs and we're taking him in."

The woman with the headset was squeaking in fear.

"Stop that noise," Derek said briskly in his best cop's voice. "And put your damned hands down. Both of you. You're not in trouble."

They dropped their hands reluctantly.

"We need to get down to the parking garage," Carla said. "Can we use the service elevator?"

The waiter nodded. His hands fluttered at his sides, as if he would raise them again at the slightest excuse.

"We tried it but nothing happened," Carla said.

"Oh, oh..." the woman said shakily.

Her face was sweating. Derek remembered when Carla had had the same effect on him, but he was having trouble sympathizing with the woman. He was about to get shot, while she went back to taking room service orders.

"Yes?" Carla said.

"We lock the elevator down at night." She shrank back as she spoke, terrified of calling attention to herself. "I can call it for you."

"Would you, please?"

The woman turned to her computer and Derek stepped forward to watch her work. With a few clicks of the mouse, she activated the elevator and called it to the ninth floor. Derek glanced at the book she was reading: Business Accounting. *Good for you.*

The waiter had drifted over to the operator's other side, as if to protect her. *Bad move. I could shoot you both with barely a twitch between shots.*

Jesus, I'm starting to think like Carla!

"The elevator's this way," the waiter said.

He led them to an area where room service carts were crammed together, took a key on a loop of coiled yellow wire from his pocket, and unlocked the elevator. The door opened immediately.

"Thanks for your help," Carla said as they entered. "I'll be back in a little while to get your names for my report."

The young man's eyes went wide as the door closed. Derek looked at Philippe, who was just lowering his hand.

"What?" Philippe said. "I was just thanking him as well. Here's one for you, too."

And he gave Derek the finger.

* * *

Derek was relieved that the parking garage was deserted. He'd been afraid they'd have to shoot their way out. Carla pointed at a distant exit, and they walked as fast as Philippe could manage. The low concrete ceiling and tightly-packed cars gave the garage a claustrophobic feeling, and the old, stale smell of spilled oil and gasoline nearly made Derek gag.

As they stepped outside, Derek saw something out of the corner of his eye: a man had been waiting at the exit. Carla kicked a gun out of the lurker's hand. He spun and lashed out at Carla's head with his foot, but she ducked under and her arms blurred as she punched him in the groin, the stomach, and, as he jerked forward, the throat. The attacker flopped onto his back as if poleaxed.

There was a second man behind the first. Derek turned and tackled Philippe, who had taken one step away. He heard a gunshot and a ricochet close by his ear, and looked up. Carla snapped out of a roll and shot the gunman twice in the chest. He fell to the ground, his pistol clattering into the street.

"Let's go!" Carla said.

Derek yanked Philippe to his feet and dragged him to their car, which was parked on the street nearby. A moment later she was driving and Derek was in the back seat guarding Philippe.

"What the fuck was that?" Derek said.

"Kidon," Carla said, keeping her eyes on the road.

"Well, you solved that problem, didn't you?"

"That's not the whole team, Derek. There'll be at least four more. The rest were probably watching the other exits. These men were careless—they weren't really expecting us or they'd have taken up better positions and we might be dead."

"Well, that's close enough to dead for me."

"Me as well," Philippe said. "By the way, nice tackle, Mr. Narr."

"Shut up," Derek said, and they rode in silence back to the motel.

* * *

Philippe sat on the twin bed farthest from the motel room door. While Derek covered him, Carla opened a bag of cable ties that she'd bought on her earlier outing.

"I thought you might like to know how this feels," she said. Philippe glared at her. "You're right handed, aren't you, Philippe?"

She pulled his right wrist down to his right ankle, looped the plastic strap around them both, threaded it, and yanked hard. Philippe grunted in pain and Carla yanked again.

"You can use the bathroom if you want," she said. "Hop in there, use the toilet, and sleep on this bed. That's more than Jensen and Lanotte did for me."

Philippe rolled off the bed onto his feet. The binding allowed him to walk like a chimp, back bent and hand strapped to ankle. He slammed the bathroom door behind him and locked it.

What did she have in mind for their sleeping arrangements? It was bad enough to sleep in the same room as Carla's nemesis, but there was no way he would sleep *with* Carla with this guy here. She answered his unspoken question by pulling a chair in front of the door and sinking into it. She looked exhausted, and Derek felt like he could sleep for a month.

The toilet flushed and Philippe knuckle-walked back to the bed. He kicked off his shoes and slid under the blankets fully clothed, facing the wall. After some thrashing, he managed to get himself completely covered, ending up in a fetal crouch.

"Good night, Philippe," Carla said.

"Choke on your own vomit." His voice was muffled by the blankets.

Carla laughed softly. Derek was about to suggest that they sleep in shifts, but she waved at the bed.

"Go to sleep, Derek," she said. "By this time tomorrow, it'll all be over."

* * *

Eitan's men regrouped at the Range Rover. Yosef and Elias were missing.

"What happened?" Efraim said.

He'd been with Eitan covering the front of the hotel.

"I heard three shots," Tamar said, "a single and a pair." He and David had been watching the lounge entrance. "When I turned the corner, the police were already there. I saw our men lying on the ground, but it was too late to help."

"They weren't moving," David said. "I think they're dead."

"She came out through the garage," Eitan said.

He was furious: his orders had been explicit. *Do not engage Citrullo. Notify the rest of the team if you spot her and we'll follow her together.* Yosef must have been eager to compensate for his earlier clumsiness. Now the fool was dead.

"What do we do now?" Efraim said.

Eitan stared at him, his face hot with anger.

"We have no choice. We have to meet her on her own ground. Tonight, at eleven."

* * *

Chapa wearily sat down on the bed, pulled his feet up, and leaned back against the pillows. The corpse had already been removed, and they'd cleared the Seattle PD out of the room so their own forensics people could look it over. Jensen had paid for this room and two others. If Chapa's team had jumped on his instructions to check out the hotel, they might have got here in time to catch Carla. He was getting thoroughly sick of thinking "if only" and "just missed her." *Goddamn it right to fucking hell.*

"What've we got so far?" he asked Shaffer.

"No forced entry. One nine-millimeter shell casing over here by the bathroom. It's a Luger, so we know it wasn't the Mossad; they'd be using unmarked shells." Chapa tried to keep his eyes open. "A piece of wallpaper cut off by the door. That's kind of weird."

Shaffer had been leaning against the wall, reading from her ever-present clipboard, but now she came into the room and sat down on the sofa. She pulled out her ponytail's elastic band and shook her head. Her blonde hair was shoulder length, slightly wavy but kinked from being in the ponytail all day—or, for all Chapa knew, for the last week. He liked blondes. His ex-wife was a blonde.

"The stiff was in that chair," Shaffer said, "shot once through the heart. Belgian passport, name of Jacques Lanotte. He's on his way to the morgue now."

Chapa felt his eyelids drooping and shook his head. Maybe sitting on this nice, comfortable bed wasn't such a great idea. He needed some coffee. Shaffer was looking at him blankly; she had to be as tired as he was. He'd almost fallen asleep in his own bed when she called to tell him there'd been a shooting at the Westin.

"Is Lanotte one of our guys?" he said, meaning the foundry escapees.

"Yes. There's one left."

"Sottile." Shaffer nodded. "No one saw them leave?"

"We're checking. The man next door heard the shot and called the front desk, but he didn't see anything."

"Why did they wait so long to call the police?"

"The assistant manager said someone claiming to be FBI came up here with her and inspected the room. He said more agents would show up soon. But then he vanished and nothing happened for a while. She was freaked out—she saw the body—so she called the cops anyway. They got here just in time to miss the shootout down by the parking garage."

"Who's following up with the assistant manager?"

"Walkenshaw. He's got an artist with her trying to get an ID on the phony Bureau agent."

"Okay. What happened outside?"

"About half an hour after Lanotte bought it, shots were fired near the Virginia Street entrance to the garage. No eyewitnesses. Two bodies found, both male, no ID. Both of them were carrying nine millimeter automatics with unmarked shell casings."

"Great," Chapa said.

"So that's two assassins down. One of them got off a single shot and we recovered the cartridge. There were also two Luger cartridges in the street, and those slugs killed the shooter. The other guy just had his throat crushed."

Just?

"I know we're going to be here all night," Chapa said, scrubbing his face with his hands. "But I already know what happened. Carla came up here to bag the bad guy that bagged her. The big guy objected, so she plugged him. They got outside somehow, two of the assassins jumped her, and she dusted *them*. Then she vanished into the night. We showed up late, as always, and we still have no fucking idea where to find her. Right?"

Shaffer nodded and ran her fingers through her hair.

"I need some coffee." He swung his legs off the bed. "Get Seattle PD back in here. I want them to interview every single hotel employee. Someone had to see Carla leave. And I want to talk to the assistant manager myself. And get Walkenshaw to check out the two dead Mossad guys. Maybe he has a file on them, too."

He waited for Shaffer to finish scribbling.

"This is in no way intended as harassment," he said, "but I like your hair that way."

"Thank you," she said, without smiling.

He walked past her with a conscious effort not to touch her. She followed him into the hallway.

Chapter 45

Seattle, Washington
   Sunday, March 5, 8:37 a.m.

Derek woke up exhausted. All night he'd had nightmares of bombs, guns, and helicopters mixed in with a candy store he'd loved as a child and the park where he'd played on the swings when he was five. He rolled over to find Carla still sitting in the same chair, watching him like a cat, motionless except for half-open eyes that tracked him as he got up to go to the bathroom. Philippe was still asleep when he came out, one thin, tanned leg thrust out from beneath the blanket. Derek dressed quickly.

"I'll go get some breakfast," he said. Carla nodded wordlessly.

The Texaco station nearby had a convenience store. He grabbed a box of assorted doughnuts, poured three cups of coffee, and loaded them into a cardboard carrier. The rumpled clerk stopped reading her People magazine just long enough to take his money.

It started drizzling as he walked back, but it stopped a minute later. He took up Carla's station for a moment so she could use the bathroom, then they sat quietly side by side, chewing tasteless doughnuts and drinking bitter coffee, watching Philippe sleep. Derek ate the powdered sugar ones, Carla stuck to the cinnamon, and neither of them touched the waxy chocolate ones.

"I have to go out," she said when they were done. "I'll be gone for a few hours. Don't let Philippe off that bed except to go to the bathroom, understand?" Derek nodded. "If he gives you any trouble at all, shoot him. I mean it. Make absolutely sure he's dead, and get out. If there are police here when I get back, I'll meet you at the video store down the street. Okay?"

"Okay."

Derek got his gun from the nightstand and sat down near the door. He was determined not to fall asleep on duty as he had yesterday, but watching a stranger sleep had to be the most boring thing in the world. Every so often he stood up and paced or stretched to stay alert. He considered drinking Philippe's coffee, which was probably cold by now, but resisted the idea. Any more coffee would make him need the bathroom in a hurry. He couldn't risk leaving Philippe unguarded while he went to pee.

Nearly an hour after Carla left, Philippe rolled onto his back and groaned. He struggled to sit up.

"Where's the bitch?" he said, rubbing his eyes with his free hand.

"Out."

Philippe grunted, got off the bed, and chimp-walked into the bathroom. Derek moved the box of doughnuts and the cold coffee onto the nightstand next to the bed, and resumed his post. Philippe took his time, but eventually the toilet flushed, the sink ran, and he came back out. As he climbed onto the bed, he noticed the food, scowled and muttered something, but he ate four chocolate doughnuts and drank all the coffee.

"I wish I had a toothbrush," Philippe said. They glared at each other for a while. "So, Mr. Narr, tell me about yourself."

"Why?"

"Because I'm in pain, I'm wide awake, and I'm bored."

"The story of my life is not going to relieve your boredom."

"I'm sure you're right, but it would help pass the time." Derek said nothing. "Well then, tell me how you and Carla became... partners."

Derek had no intention of telling this terrorist anything, least of all that Carla had kidnapped him.

"You are lovers, no?" Philippe said. He nodded as if Derek had responded. "I thought so. Carla and I were lovers once, in Paris. Last year. It was nice, but we both became distracted by business. She's quite accomplished in bed, isn't she? Voracious, you might say. Predatory, even."

"Shut up," Derek said.

"Sorry. I didn't think. You're probably in love with her. I imagine it would be painful to hear about her past, em, liaisons."

"No, I'm not in love with her."

"But you're helping her willingly. I hope she didn't promise you any money. Did she? There won't be any money, I assure you. We *could* have made a fortune, but you and Carla ruined the chances of that."

"Good."

"Ah, I see. You're doing this for your country. A patriot. Very commendable."

That wasn't it, but Derek realized that he couldn't have explained why he was helping her. He knew he didn't love her; he could no more love an eagle.

"Not a patriot?" Philippe said. "For all mankind then: because it's the *right* thing to do?" He searched Derek's face. "Ah, I understand. You don't know why you're helping her."

"Shut up."

"But *I* know. I do. How long have you known Carla? A week? I've known her for over a year, my friend, and I can tell you exactly why you're helping her. Would you like to hear?"

"No."

"Well, I'll tell you anyway: she's bewitched you." Derek snorted. "You don't believe in witches? How is that possible? You've been screwing one! Don't you recognize her for what she is? She's mesmerized you, Mr. Narr, and you'll never be free again. Even after she throws you away like a soiled napkin, you'll still be her slave."

"Do you think you can talk me into letting you go?" Derek said.

"Of course not. How could I break the spell of the great Jewish Witch? I'm just whiling away the time in pleasant conversation."

"You want to talk? Okay, I have a question for you. How could you sell nuclear weapons to terrorists when you know they'll use them to murder millions of innocent people?"

"Innocent?" Philippe looked confused. "What do you mean?"

"You know what I mean. People who are not soldiers, who're just trying to live their lives and raise their kids in peace. You'd give their enemies the means to incinerate them—and for no reason."

"But there was a reason, my friend. Money."

"What?"

"I had merchandise to sell, I needed the money, I found someone who was willing to pay my price. That's all."

"But you knew how that *merchandise* would be used."

"Not at all. I could speculate, but even if you're correct, what is that to me?"

"So you don't care if innocent people are killed?"

"There's that word again," Philippe said. "Who do you suppose is innocent?"

"What do you mean?"

"Let me ask it another way. Who is *not* innocent? Who deserves to be blown into dust by a nuclear inferno?"

Derek was speechless.

"Exactly," Philippe said. "No one. No one at all. But if no one is guilty, then no one is innocent. Yet the bombs exist. And which government is the only one in the history of the world to use these terrible weapons—not just to build them but to actually drop them on people who are, as you say, just trying to live their lives? As a citizen of a nation that has committed mass murder in the past and whose official policy is to be prepared to do so again, what moral position is it, precisely, that you're trying to take?"

"Oh, no, you don't—"

Philippe's voice went hard. "Why should I care what happens to strangers? Just like you, I care what happens to me and the people I love. If a city full of Israeli reservists and their families is destroyed, or if every politician in Washington D.C. is vaporized, what do I care? As long as my family and I are happy and wealthy, that's enough."

Derek was so outraged that he couldn't think of a rational response. His first impulse was simply to shoot the son of a bitch.

"Did Carla tell you," Philippe said, "that I could never have stolen the warheads without her? It's true. She convinced the soldiers at a Ukrainian missile base to hand over three MIRVs. Of course, it was an understaffed missile base, and quite a bit of money was involved, but we never would've reached financial negotiations if not for Carla. Did she tell you how she did it?"

Derek shook his head numbly.

"Sexual blackmail. She seduces a victim, usually a lonely, confused man, and gets him to trust her. Then, one day, they are making love. At the climax of the act, she threatens his life, and more to the point his manhood, if he won't do as she says. I'm told it works very well. This, I'm afraid, is what she has planned for you."

"Bullshit," Derek said.

"Of course you think so. Who would wish to believe such a thing? Yet it's true. This is not something she would advertise about—"

The door opened and Carla walked in carrying a large, brown paper bag. She looked at Philippe, then at Derek. Derek found it impossible to meet her eyes. *Could it be true?*

"Telling tales, Philippe?" she said

"Not at all. Just idle conversation."

She spilled the contents of the bag onto the table, and Derek knew what was coming next.

"I need two more bombs," she said. "Just like before, only this time the explosive will be outside the radio, so run leads through the case."

"Okay," Derek said.

He moved his chair over to the table and started sorting parts. Carla brought him the schematic, the soldering iron, and other tools from her bag. She leaned down and put her lips to his ear.

"Philippe's lies would make Beelzebub blush," she said.

She sat by the door, watching Philippe, and Derek began constructing the bombs with an inexplicable feeling of relief.

* * *

Just before noon, Eitan and his three remaining men drove to Ship Canal Park to evaluate the tactical situation. The morning drizzle had ended and the sun was trying to shine through thin clouds. The shortest path from their hotel room to the park led them directly past the foundry, still taped off and guarded by a police car. Eitan was surprised they hadn't begun demolition of the building. The ruins must be dangerously unstable.

The park was a thin strip of greenery along the north edge of the canal that connected Lake Union to Puget Sound. Tamar parked the Range Rover in the long, narrow parking lot and all four of them got out and looked around. Trees and shrubs along the curving entry drive blocked the view to certain parts of the parking lot until one was well within the lot.

They spent over an hour discussing the best way to ambush Citrullo before Eitan was satisfied. On the drive back to their hotel, he sat lost in thought, and his men respected his concentration by remaining silent themselves. When they passed the foundry again, it barely registered that the cop on duty was talking to a tall black man.

* * *

Walkenshaw and Shaffer burst into Chapa's office, startling him—he'd been falling asleep at his desk.

"We've got a break," Walkenshaw said.

"A big one," Shaffer said.

Chapa rolled his chair back and poured himself a cup from the coffee maker on the low bookshelf. He took a sip and waved at them to sit down.

"Okay, what is it?"

"I couldn't sleep after the Westin thing last night," Walkenshaw said. "I was reading witness statements from the Westin and the Gugliemo hit, and I thought... maybe the phony FBI agent was a Mossad hitter. So I spent some time with Maria—uh, the assistant manager—and a police artist."

He handed Chapa the sketch of a handsome man: short hair, cleft chin, Roman nose.

"Two witnesses confirmed that this man was one of Gugliemo's killers. I ran his picture through our computer and got a match."

He handed Chapa another sheet of paper.

"His name is Shimon Eitan, a war hero and a Mossad assassin. This is a very dangerous guy, maybe even more dangerous than Citrullo. He's a natural leader, highly trained, and very, very good at his job."

"Okay," Chapa said, "that's nice to know, but so what? We don't have a clue where he is."

"Yes, we do," Shaffer said.

"Huh?"

"Your guy Frieder's been helping me out," Walkenshaw said. "Driving me around and whatever. After we IDed Eitan, he drove back to the foundry on his lunch break. I don't know, I guess he wanted to bask in glory or something. He figured out Sottile was hiding inside, right?"

Chapa nodded warily.

"Guess who he sees drive by?" Walkenshaw said.

"Oh, come on."

"No shit. He's just standing there, chatting up the baby-sitter, and he looks up as Eitan drives by in a Range Rover. Frieder got a good look at him. So he jumped in his car and tailed him to a small hotel on First Hill. He called it in, and now we've got three units watching the place. They can't scratch their butts without us knowing it."

Chapa was wide awake now. This was the first solid lead they'd had since Derek had vanished from his office over a week ago. For the first time, they knew where one of the dancers was *before* the music started.

"Good work," Chapa said. "We should get over there, too." He grabbed his coat and started out the door. "Is Frieder still there?"

"Yes," Shaffer said. "He wouldn't leave."

"Good." Chapa pulled on his coat and started walking toward the elevator. "I owe him an apology."

* * *

When Derek awoke from a nap after finishing the bombs, Carla asked him to go get some lunch. He found a Mexican restaurant that did carryout. When he handed Philippe his food, Philippe stared at the plastic fork speculatively, as if wondering how to use it as a weapon, but then he began eating with it. When they finished, Carla took a nap while Derek watched their prisoner do nothing.

She awoke around dusk and went into the bathroom, returning with the remaining C-4 and the wooden box of detonators. Philippe closed his eyes in pain as he realized that the means of escape had been within his reach all day. Carla packed the explosives and the bombs Derek had made into his backpack.

"I'm going out," she said. "Keep a close eye on our friend here. Same rules as before. If he even smiles funny, kill him and meet me at the video store."

"Happy to," Derek said.

Philippe waited a while before starting in on him again. "Who will she be blowing up tonight?"

"I don't know."

"Hmm. You know, you killed my friend Jensen when you demolished the foundry."

"Too bad," Derek said.

"He was a smart man. Arrogant, like all Americans, and black, but I liked him. He was a physicist, you know."

"No, I didn't know."

"He built arming boxes for the warheads that could fit into a lunch pail. Amazing piece of work. Not like those crude little bombs Carla taught you to make. Those are child's play."

"Maybe children make bombs where you come from," Derek said, "but not here."

"Have you considered that you might be killed with your own bombs? Carla hates loose ends."

"What are you babbling about now?"

"You. What do you think she plans to do with you when she's done?"

"She'll let me go. She was willing to let me go in Montana a week ago."

"Perhaps," Philippe said. "But she's very thorough. Why do you think I'm still alive?"

"If you ask me, that was a mistake."

"I think it's obvious. She wants to wrap up all her problems at once. Me, the kidon, the FBI—and you. One boom and all her worries are over. She returns home a heroine, all ends neatly tied in a bow and no dissenting voices."

"Shut up," Derek said.

"It's ironic, don't you think? You nearly killed Carla with your last bomb, and now *she* will use your final bomb to kill *you*."

Derek glared at him, but then his sense of humor took over and he laughed. Philippe looked startled.

"She's right," Derek said. "You could talk the devil into selling you hell. Do you think there's any chance I'd let you go?"

Philippe tried to say something but Derek cut him off.

"No fucking way. Not even if she were planning to kill me. You—you'd nuke a city just to support your *lifestyle* and say it wasn't your fault because you didn't push the button. So shut the fuck up or I swear I'll shoot you just to shut your lying mouth."

Philippe stared at him for a moment, lips drawn tight. Then he rolled onto his side, facing away from Derek, and pretended to sleep. Derek was trembling with anger and the horrifying itch to shoot this motherfucker in the head. He couldn't wait for Carla to get back so they could put an end to this whole sick, twisted affair.

So when Carla returned well after dark and said they couldn't leave until one o'clock, Derek almost screamed with frustration.

Chapter 46

Seattle, Washington
   Sunday, March 5, 8:56 p.m.

"It's time," Eitan said.

Citrullo had set the meeting for eleven, but he wanted to get there early enough to command the good ground. She would arrive early as well, but two hours would be enough to get them there first.

They did a final weapons check, then left the hotel. Eitan felt a growing warmth in his belly as Tamar drove them to the park. Their ordeal was nearly over, and he was looking forward to avenging the deaths of Yosef and Elias.

* * *

The FBI triple-teamed the Mossad agents: one car driving ahead of them and two behind. When the Range Rover made a turn, one of the following cars pulled ahead while the old leader fell in behind. The trailing cars took turns at close and far surveillance. It was impossible for the Range Rover to escape them, and almost as difficult for them to realize they were being followed.

Chapa drove with Shaffer, a few minutes behind the tails and in constant communication with them, and they were followed by two more cars. In all, they had seventeen agents in six cars, with another dozen agents standing by and a helicopter warming up.

Would it be enough? He pushed that thought aside. This time they weren't mopping up after Carla, they'd be there in force when the drama began. But a tiny voice in his head reminded him that he'd thought the same thing outside the foundry just before Derek blew it up.

A voice on the radio said, "They're crossing the Fremont Bridge."

Then the Mossad agents pulled into Ship Canal Park. Chapa wished he could've known they were headed there; he'd have had a car in place ahead of time. The park was too small for him to follow them in surreptitiously, so he'd have to settle for surrounding the place.

He held out his hand and Shaffer handed him the radio.

"I want police boats at both ends of the canal," he said. "And get more agents down here. I want to be ready to block all roads into and out of the park area on a moment's notice. Get the snipers into position and put that bird in the air."

The confirmations came quickly. Chapa parked his car down the street from the park and settled in to wait for Carla.

* * *

It was so easy to fool people who assume you think the same way they do. Carla checked her watch: one o'clock, time to go.

"Take everything," she said. "We aren't coming back."

Derek had packed earlier, and now was looking with a strange expression at his computer case lying on the bed.

"What?" she said.

"I was wondering whether to bring the computer. Something tells me that part of my life is over."

"Bring it." She moved it to the chair by the door. "I'll tell you why. You're going to live through this tonight. I know it's hard to believe right now, but tomorrow you're going to begin living your life again, and you'd regret it if you'd left this behind." He looked doubtful. "Besides, you never know. We might need it tonight."

"Uh huh. Maybe it'll stop the bullet with my name on it."

"Ha," Philippe said from the other bed. "Maybe it will stop one bullet. What if there are fifty?"

Derek looked ready to kill him. Carla picked up a cable tie and the wire cutters and walked toward Philippe.

"Shut up and put your other hand down here," she said.

Philippe complied, putting his free wrist near the one bound to his ankle. Carla wrapped the tie around his wrists and fastened it with a yank. Philippe grunted softly and Carla pulled on it again.

"You're cutting off the circulation," he said.

She cut the strap that fastened his wrist to his ankle. His back popped as he straightened it for the first time in twenty-four hours.

"Get up," she said, "and behave yourself, or you won't live to see the surprise I've got planned for you."

Philippe got off the bed clumsily. She shoved him toward the door and handed Derek the transmitter radio. They grabbed their bags and herded Philippe out to the car.

As she drove toward the Fremont Bridge, with Derek covering Philippe in the back seat, Carla thought of the kidon team waiting for them. They'd expected her two hours ago, and had certainly arrived an hour early, or perhaps two. By now they'd be edgy and nervous, wondering if they'd lost her again. They couldn't leave for fear of missing her, but they'd be wondering if this was a hoax. The strain would've worn them down, dulling their edge.

She knew they'd have set an ambush, but she also knew their style—she'd been taught by the same instructors at the same academy. They wouldn't spray her car with bullets on sight: they'd block her in, perhaps disable her car, verify her identity, and calmly execute everyone in the car. Mission accomplished, time to go home.

The streets were nearly empty. As they turned onto Fremont Avenue, Carla stopped the car and looked over her shoulder at Derek.

"Have you ever been here before?" she said.

"The Fremont Bridge? Sure, lots of times."

"What does that mean?"

She pointed to a sign, illuminated by a nearby street light, that read, "Welcome to Fremont, Center of the Universe. Turn your watch back five minutes."

Derek leaned forward so he could see it and barked a laugh. "I have no idea. I've never noticed it before."

"Oh." She hated life's tiny, unsolvable mysteries.

"But I think we can safely say that Fremont is not a drug-free zone."

The bridge spanned the ship canal. Lake Union was just a little way off to their right. The draw span at the center of the bridge was a grated metal deck about sixty meters long, flanked on both sides by a pair of three-story towers, one on each side of the road, at each end of the span.

The top of each tower was capped like a mushroom with an observation or control booth. This afternoon Carla had twice watched the bridge being raised, and both times the bridge operator had been in the southeast tower. All four towers were dark now, although the neon was lit: another irritating mystery. One neon sign showed Rapunzel letting down her hair, the other depicted the Crocodile pulling on the Elephant Child's new trunk.

The bridge had two lanes in each direction and was much longer than the draw span, at least a kilometer all together. Most of it was concrete, elevated well above grade with warehouses and industrial shops flanking or nestled beneath it.

"Is your seat belt on?" she asked Derek as they left the bridge behind.

"Yes. Should I do Philippe's?"

Of course Philippe couldn't fasten his own belt. But she didn't want Derek leaning over him; he might try something tricky and she was about to have her hands full.

"No, he'll just have to hang on."

Trees around the curving park entrance screened much of the parking lot from view. The assassins would be waiting out of sight near the entrance. They'd let her in, block her retreat or possibly ram her—and it would all be over.

Unless she changed the rules. As soon as she turned into the entrance, Carla punched the accelerator. The Infiniti was moving at almost a hundred kilometers per hour when she shot past the Range Rover hiding behind the trees. She rocketed halfway across the lot, let up on the gas, and spun the wheel without touching the brakes. The tires squealed and the car threatened to tip over, but then the rubber found purchase and she spun the wheel back and floored it—and they were speeding back toward the entrance after a shrieking, high speed 180-degree turn.

The Range Rover was moving in slow motion to block their exit. Carla drove straight at it, still accelerating, vaguely aware that someone in the back seat was screaming. At the last instant before impact, she nudged the wheel to the left and swerved onto the grass. The sudden change in surface—from damp asphalt to wet lawn—sent them into a spin that she controlled by tapping the brakes and savagely yanking the wheel. For just a moment, the car balanced on its two left tires, still moving at more than eighty kilometers per hour, but then the right side thumped back into contact with the earth, sending huge divots of sod flying through the air. Carla jerked the car back onto the driveway, peeling rubber, and floored it again as she turned out of the park.

She noticed an unusual number of occupied cars parked on the road but didn't have time to figure out what it meant. It was only two blocks to Fremont and she had to get the timing exactly right. The assassins had to be behind her, but not too close. She prayed there'd be no other traffic on the bridge.

"Derek," she said, "do you have the radio?"

They were speeding parallel to the ship canal, coming up on Fremont. Carla kept one eye on her rear view mirror. Halfway to the turn, she saw the Range Rover scream around the corner. She'd been letting up on the gas, but now she floored it again—and they were at the turn. She tapped the brakes and took the turn on two wheels, swerving into the oncoming lanes—which luckily were empty. Once more she punched the accelerator, and now they were on the concrete part of the bridge, heading toward the draw span towers.

"Derek!" she said. "The radio?"

"I've got it," he said. They were on a straightaway, so she risked a glance at the back seat. Derek held the radio in one hand and his gun in the other, pressed against Philippe's ribs. Philippe was cradling his head in his bound hands.

What the hell happened back there?

She had no time to think about it. They were coming up to the draw span, and the Range Rover was taking the turn onto Fremont even more sloppily than she had, sending up sparks as they grazed the guard rail on the wrong side of the street. Carla kept her foot on the gas until they cleared the grating, then she slammed on the brakes.

The anti-skid brakes worked perfectly. The brake pedal vibrated under her foot and they screeched to a stop without skidding, about thirty meters past the end of the grated deck.

Carla yanked the radio out of Derek's hand, popped her seat belt, and flung herself out of the car. The Rover had almost reached the draw span, headed straight toward her and coming on fast. Carla was barely aware of

Derek getting out of the car as she ran back toward the bridge, turned on the radio, and set it to channel one.

"Hey!" she said, and the bridge erupted.

She'd set the charge right at the north edge of the draw span, just behind where the Rover was now. An enormous sheet of flame gouted up, followed immediately by roiling black smoke. Below the painful roar Carla could hear a deep basso rumble and then a shriek as the drawbridge mechanism fell into the canal.

They were still driving toward her, trying to escape the blast. Carla drew her gun, aimed quickly, and put a shot right in the center of the windshield. She was prepared to shoot the driver next, but the Rover squealed to a halt, two-thirds of the way across the draw span grating, about thirty meters away. Four men tumbled out of the car, drawing their pistols. They wouldn't be able to hear her over the continuing rumble as the north end of the bridge collapsed, so she shot out the driver's-side headlight.

The pistol shot was inaudible over the uproar, but it got their attention. Carla waved the radio at them and mimed pushing the transmit button. One of the men started to charge her, but the rest held him back. She glanced back. Derek was huddled behind the car, apparently expecting falling debris, but she had shaped the charge carefully and there was no shrapnel. In fact, the collapse of the drawbridge mechanism was just about over, and the noise was diminishing.

The cacophony stopped. The silence, punctuated by occasional chunks of concrete falling into the canal, was eerie. The draw span stood intact, resting on its own, stable foundations, but its north end gaped out over a chasm—ten meters of the concrete road that had abutted it was gone.

"Eitan!" Carla shouted at the top of her lungs. One of the men at the Range Rover looked up. "Where do you think I put the second bomb?"

* * *

"Jesus Christ!" Chapa said. The bridge half a mile ahead of them exploded in a fireball that roared up into the sky. Billows of ominous black smoke erupted behind the Mossad's vehicle. "She blew them up!"

They'd been waiting for over four hours, and Chapa cursed himself for carelessness. Most of his men had been deployed on the ground around the park, with quite a few others placed at strategic points so they could close off the streets if necessary. They'd seen Carla speeding into the park, but they were completely unprepared for her to zoom back out again only seconds later. He was still in the middle of shouting orders to close in when they lost her.

Now this! She'd blown up the Fremont Bridge just to kill the assassins.

"Jesus Christ! Give me the damned radio!"

Shaffer handed it over without a word, her mouth gaping in astonishment.

"We're all on the wrong side of the bridge," Chapa said. He visualized a map of the area. The Aurora bridge was nearby to the east, but it was elevated and there was limited access on both sides of the canal. There was a bridge at 15th to the west, but that was twenty blocks away. They were stuck here—no way to get to the other side before it was all over. He felt like screaming. He felt like shooting somebody. She was going to get away again!

"Where's the fucking helicopter?" he shouted into the radio.

"Refueling," someone answered.

He could barely hear the response over the thunder of the collapsing bridge. Chapa seethed with helpless fury. The helicopter had been hovering uselessly for four hours, and now when he actually needed it, it was on the ground.

"Get it back here right fucking now! Get the Seattle PD to close off the south end of the bridge. There should be a patrol car parked right outside the foundry, it's only a mile away. Don't let her get away or someone's ass will be hanging on my wall tomorrow. Units three and four, take the Aurora bridge over to the south side *now!* Burn rubber, goddammit, I mean *now!*"

Chapa threw down the radio and got out of the car. Shaffer followed him. He watched the smoke billow up.

"Binoculars?" he said. She ducked back into the car and came out with a pair. He put them to his eyes. "I can't see a fucking thing."

* * *

Carla switched the radio to channel two and held it ready in her left hand, her pistol in her right. Eitan's team had their weapons drawn but were neither shooting, running toward her, nor getting back in their car. Carla called Derek and he came out from behind the car.

"You missed!" he said. "You missed them. What the hell are we going to do now?"

"Calm down. I meant to miss them."

"You *planned* it this way?" He sounded hysterical.

"Yes."

"Well, Jesus, I'm glad there's a plan. What a great fucking idea, a plan. Why didn't *I* think of having a plan?" Was he cracking up? "Jesus Christ," he said, "you blew up the Fremont Bridge!"

"Shut up. I don't have time for this. What happened back there?"

"What? Oh, in the car?" He turned back for a second. "You took a turn on two wheels and Philippe tried to take my gun away. I talked him out of it."

"Good. Go get him. And grab one of the cable ties out of my bag."

Derek half dragged Philippe out of the car. Carla kept one eye on the kidon team. They were watching attentively but not moving. Philippe came up to her, looking at the Mossad agents and the gaping, smoking abyss behind them. His forehead was bleeding from a fresh cut where Derek must have pistol-whipped him.

"Well, Carla," Philippe said, "you're on center stage again. We're all dying to see what you'll do next."

Eitan and his men were standing their ground for the moment, but that wouldn't last long.

"Philippe," she said, "if I gave one little mouse shit about you, I'd call up all three of your wives and tell them what a corrupt, rancid piece of carrion you are. But you know what? I don't care. You mean nothing to me, and you never did. You were just part of the job. If it'd been up to me, I'd have killed you before we ever saw Derazhnya. But it's over now, Philippe. Your life is over."

She turned to Derek. "March this dreck over there." She pointed to the west edge of the bridge. "Tie his ankles with the cable tie and wait for me."

"What are you doing, Carla?" Philippe said. "Carla!"

She ignored him and Derek nudged him with his pistol. When they were out of the way, she turned back to the assassins.

"Eitan!" she shouted. "I have something to tell you."

One of the men stepped forward and holstered his weapon. Carla kept hers out.

"So talk, Citrullo," he said.

"Your mission was a cover. Disinformation. I still work for the Mossad. That's how I knew who they'd send after me—that's how I knew your name."

One of Eitan's men shouted something and started forward, but Eitan turned and ordered his men to stand fast.

"That means nothing," he shouted back. "You have contacts all over Europe—"

"No! I was sent undercover to find smugglers, and I found them. This man was plotting to steal nuclear weapons and sell them to terrorists. I helped him do it, under orders, and then I betrayed him. The missiles are safe in Israel. You were ordered to try to kill me so I'd have a convincing background. I was successful because everyone believed I was a renegade, a rogue—a mercenary. You made that possible."

Eitan was shaking his head. Several of his men were shouting among themselves, but she couldn't make out the words and Eitan ignored them.

"You don't have to believe me," she said. "Call the office and ask them. They'll give you the recall code."

"No. My orders are to execute you, and I have no reason to disobey them."

"Yes, you do." She held up the radio. "There's another bomb. If you move, I'll detonate it."

Eitan's men stood perfectly still, their argument suspended in mid-sentence.

"Get back in your car," Carla said. "I'm leaving this man for you. The police and FBI will be here in a few minutes. You might want to hand Philippe over as a gesture of good faith. I don't think they're going to appreciate the fact that you've been operating illegally on U.S. soil."

Eitan stood defiantly as his men hesitated, then they climbed back into the Range Rover. He looked at her speculatively, perhaps wondering if he could hit her at this distance, but she'd already proved she could hit *him,* and his gun was in its holster while hers was drawn. After a moment he turned on his heel and got back in the car.

Carla called Derek over. He left Philippe standing at the bridge railing, bound wrist and ankle. She handed him the radio.

"Go back to the car. If they shoot, if they move, if anything goes wrong, blow the second charge."

"Where *is* the second charge?" he said, but she spun him around and shoved him back toward the car.

She ran ahead of him and opened the Infiniti's trunk. Coiled within was the pre-cut cord she'd bought that morning from a bungee-jumping place. She'd had to offer them a ridiculous amount of money before they'd agree to part with it. She carried it over to where Philippe leaned on the bridge's sidewalk railing. Twenty meters below them, the ship canal ran straight as a sword to the sea. She gauged their distance from the edges of the draw span. This looked safe enough.

Working swiftly, she tied the cord securely to a stanchion, then turned Philippe so he faced the water and tied the other end to his feet. Philippe twisted to look down at her working and moaned.

"What the hell are you doing?" he said. "Carla, you can't...Wait, wait a minute, you filthy hag, what are you... Stop! *Oh merde!*"

Carla gripped Philippe just above the knees and heaved him over the side of the bridge. For a long, timeless moment, she saw the entire scene frozen, like a photograph. The Mossad men were plastered to their car windows, their mouths puckered in Os of surprise. Philippe hung suspended in mid-air, a rictus of fear on his face, the bungee cord still loose and coiled like a snake. Smoke and dust from the demolished end of the draw span hung in soft cumulus shapes in the air. Derek stood off-balance by the car, his mouth gaping and his eyes wide. The water in the ship canal flowed like a silver ribbon in the dim light, straight and true to the sea. On its banks, poplar, willow, and oak trees stood in woody dignity, serene and haunting.

Then time rushed in on her again. Philippe's scream echoed as she ran toward the car. She could hear the Range Rover starting up, its tires beginning to hum on the deck. The instant she cleared the grating, she shouted at Derek.

"Blow it!"

The blast knocked her off her feet, but she rolled and came up running again, safe. She whirled around and saw that the charge had been perfectly shaped: there was no shrapnel and no damage to the draw span. But through the boiling, surging smoke, she could see that the concrete approach to the draw span was completely gone.

Philippe's head lifted out of the water as the bungee cord snapped back. His mouth was open in a terrified scream that she couldn't hear. She *had* measured the cord correctly: he would stop bouncing with his head just above the water, but not before being dunked a few more times. Only a few meters away from him, the bridge was gone, but he hung safely from the draw span, which still stood solidly on its undamaged supports.

The Range Rover skidded to a stop and the assassins tumbled out. They were stunned but powerless, trapped on an island of steel and concrete that had once been a bridge.

Carla looked past them and was filled with unexpected delight as she recognized Chapa standing at the edge of the far gap, as close to the splintered end of the bridge as he dared, a radio forgotten in his hand—staring at her. She smiled and waved, and laughed as he screamed at her, his voice lost in the groans and rumbling of the explosion's aftermath.

She spun and ran back to the car. When Derek was inside, she drove away toward freedom, moments before a wailing police car turned onto Fremont.

Chapter 47

Seattle, Washington
  Monday, March 6, 1:08 p.m.

Chapa and Shaffer watched from behind a two-way mirror as an FBI interrogator wrapped up his first session. Sottile was bruised and exhausted, and since he was cooperating they were taking it easy on the poor guy. The sorry son of a bitch had thought he could beat Carla.

The interrogation had begun at three in the morning, but Sottile held out for a lawyer for the first two hours, refusing even to admit his name. But then he snapped and agreed to cooperate if they would just let him get some sleep.

"No problem," the interrogator said. "We just have one question before you go to bed. Where is Carla Citrullo?"

Sottile stared at the man in disbelief, then he burst out laughing, and the laughter turned to tears and wracking sobs. Chapa let him sleep for four hours, and after a good meal, Sottile told them everything they wanted to know: how he'd stolen the missiles; sent Carla out to find Hildreth; come after her when she betrayed him; found her, trapped her, lost her, and lost to her. They'd go over it again and again to get all the details—Chapa was particularly interested in the name of Sottile's contact inside the FBI—but for now he was content.

The interrogator opened the door to leave, and Walkenshaw brushed in past him. Sottile looked up at him numbly. Walkenshaw seemed older: the lines in his face had deepened, his gray eyes were bloodshot, and his asymmetrical casts looked ridiculous.

"What happened to you?" Sottile said.

"The same thing that happened to you," Walkenshaw replied as he sat down across the table from him.

Sottile laughed and leaned forward, looking into the CIA agent's eyes. They both nodded slightly. Whatever relationship they might come to have, they both knew they had at least one thing in common.

"Carla," Sottile said with a sad smile.

* * *

Walkenshaw talked to Sottile for only an hour, and most of his questions seemed off the subject to Chapa. He was obsessed with Hildreth, Pequinot, and Khayrat. When he finished, he joined Chapa and Shaffer and they watched a guard escort Sottile out of the room.

"Are you satisfied?" Walkenshaw asked Chapa.

"What do you mean?"

"I mean, is your curiosity satisfied?"

Chapa considered that. He'd still give a lot to talk to Carla face to face, but that would never happen. Now that her business here was finished, she'd vanish like the morning fog. But now he knew *why* she'd kidnapped Derek, and perhaps why Derek had helped her despite that.

"Yeah," he said. "I'm happy."

"Good," Walkenshaw said. "Because the Agency has a request. No paperwork, just, uh..." He paused and looked from Chapa to Shaffer. "Off the record."

* * *

Chapa couldn't decide if he was upset. "Do you believe that guy?"

"I used to live with him, remember?" Shaffer said.

It was only two-thirty in the afternoon, way too early—but what the hell.

"Want to get some dinner?"

Shaffer was studying her clipboard. "What about Myron's request?"

"I don't know. At the moment I don't care. Don't change the subject."

Shaffer searched his face, then took his arm. "I have a better idea, Kevin. Why don't you come over to my place and let me cook you dinner?"

"You can cook?"

"Oh, yes," Emily said. "I can cook."

Chapter 48

Carla parked the car at the curb in front of her mother's house. Sarah wouldn't be home for a while, but that was fine. She had a few things to work out with Derek first.

Going through Canadian customs had been tense. The border was only a few hours north of Seattle—not enough time for things to settle down, and the FBI might still be hot for her blood. Derek had been sleeping, but he woke up and blinked at the checkpoint guard, a middle-aged woman with a severe face and a big gun. Although she looked at them suspiciously and asked several questions as she peered into the back of the car, they were allowed to leave the U.S. Carla pulled over on the Canadian side and asked Derek to drive. She was asleep before he put it in gear.

That was long hours ago. Now Derek was asleep in the passenger seat, looking like an untroubled boy in his thirties instead of a screwed-up man in his forties. She watched him dream for a few minutes.

Her mother's house looked perfectly normal. Carla couldn't tell if the siding she'd shot out had been replaced, but from the street everything looked fine. It must have got warmer in the past week: most of the snow was gone.

She looked at Derek again, trying to imagine what it had been like for him, but she couldn't do it. Kidnapped and thrown into one gunfight after another with no training and no experience. She was amazed that he'd come through it intact—more or less sane, no major injuries. He'd even saved her life once or twice. She was very glad she hadn't just shot him in the FBI office the night they'd met.

"Derek," she said. He stirred but didn't awaken. "*Derek!*"

He snapped upright in his seat. "What? What's wrong?"

Carla laughed. "Nothing. We're here."

"Do you have to keep doing that?"

"Yes. Listen, we have to talk before I go."

"What do you mean, before *you* go?"

"I'm leaving. I don't think Mother would be happy to see me, anyway. Now, listen to me. Are you listening?"

He yawned and rubbed his eyes. "Okay."

"I'm leaving you with Sarah. You'll be safe here for a while."

"What do you mean, for a while? How long do you think it'll take the FBI to figure out where we are?"

"It won't be *us*, just you. And don't worry about the FBI, they're going to let us go."

"What?" He frowned. "Why would they do that?"

"Because the CIA will understand the value of what I left them on that bridge. They've got a man everyone thought was dead, who has first-hand knowledge of decades of international arms smuggling, and the only man to successfully steal nuclear weapons from a former Soviet nation. The CIA will keep him for a few years, then they'll hand him off to Interpol, or MI6, or the Mossad."

"So what? The FBI still wants *you*. And me, I guess."

"No, they don't. The CIA will ask them to let us go."

"Huh?"

"That's the way the game is played, Derek. We've given the CIA something they've never dreamed of: four Mossad assassins who were operating inside the U.S. That's a *big* no-no. Do you have any idea how much leverage this will give the CIA with Israel? We're Santa Claus to the spooks, and they always repay a favor. That's how their twisted sense of honor works."

"So we're off the hook? The killers will let us go, too?"

"Yes. The CIA will hand them back directly to Tel Aviv, and they'll learn the truth the moment they get off the plane. I might even be there to tell them myself."

She smiled at the idea. She hoped Eitan would understand that she'd done what she had to do to survive.

Derek blinked in wonder. "So it's over."

"It's over for me," she said. "You still have a problem."

"What're you talking about?"

"You're guilty of serious federal crimes, Derek. Assaulting a federal officer; kidnapping a federal officer; murder; breaking and entering; illegal theft, possession, and use of controlled explosives; reckless endangerment; grand theft; destruction of public property. And accomplice to all of that."

"Oh, shit." Derek leaned his head against the side window. "But you said the CIA would make them leave us alone."

"If it weren't for them, we'd be in jail already. The Bureau won't chase you, but that doesn't mean they'll ignore you. If you show up and thumb your nose at them, they'll have to arrest you, and you'll spend the rest of your life in jail. They're sworn to uphold the law."

"So I'm screwed."

"Maybe. Maybe not. I have an idea."

He opened his eyes and looked at her hopelessly. "What?"

She hesitated. She really didn't know how he'd take this.

"We both know I couldn't have finished my mission and come out alive without your help, and when I get home, the office will know it, too. They have a slush fund for things like this."

"A slush fund."

"Yes. So here's my suggestion. Stay at Sarah's house for a while. Get some rest. Let her cook for you. Swap computer stories. Tell her anything she wants to know about me. Sometime in the near future a courier will show up with a new identity for you—a Canadian identity—and enough money to get started again. Find a nice town, set up a little computer consulting business, and have a good life."

He stared at her with his mouth open. After a moment, she reached over and put a finger under his chin to close it.

"Anyway," she said, "that's my recommendation."

It was amusing to see him utterly speechless, so she leaned over and kissed him. She took her time, then she reached across him and opened his door.

"I have to go," she said. "Sarah should be home in an hour or so."

Derek climbed out of the car and opened the back door to get his bags. He set them on the curb and shut the doors, then came around to the driver's side. Carla powered down the window.

"How will Sarah take this?" he said. "I mean, she didn't have much fun when I came to visit her last time."

Carla laughed.

"Well, I won't be here this time, so things will go more smoothly. And I saw the way she looked at you, she liked you a lot. Believe me, I know my mother. She'll have convinced herself by now that you were a victim just like her. She'll welcome you with open arms."

Derek looked at the house doubtfully. "How will you... I mean..." He shook his head. "Will you be okay?"

"I'll be fine."

After a long moment, he said, "I'm not going to thank you."

"Well, I am going to thank you. I know I screwed up your life, but you saved mine, and I'll never forget it."

"But I'll never see you again, will I?"

She looked away for a moment, then looked back, smiling softly. "No," she said. He nodded and turned to go. "Derek?"

"What?"

"Give me your gun."

"Oh, yeah." He pulled the dead mobster's pistol out of his coat pocket. "I guess I won't be needing this any more." He handed it to her and she tossed it on the passenger seat. "Oh, wait a minute. I have something else to give you."

She assumed he meant the spare clips, but he ran around the car and dug into his suitcase. He came back and handed her a book: *Winnie-the-Pooh.* She laughed, but she took it.

"Are you sure you don't want to say hi to your mom?"

"I'm sure." She started the car and he took a step back. "And anyway, you know what I told you about the FBI not showing up?"

"Yeah?"

She smiled up at him. "I could be wrong," she said, and she drove away, laughing.

— The End —

www.ingramcontent.com/pod-product-compliance
Lightning Source LLC
Chambersburg PA
CBHW051444260626
47162CB00001B/241